THE GOLDEN SHEEP

(3)

Kaori Ozaki

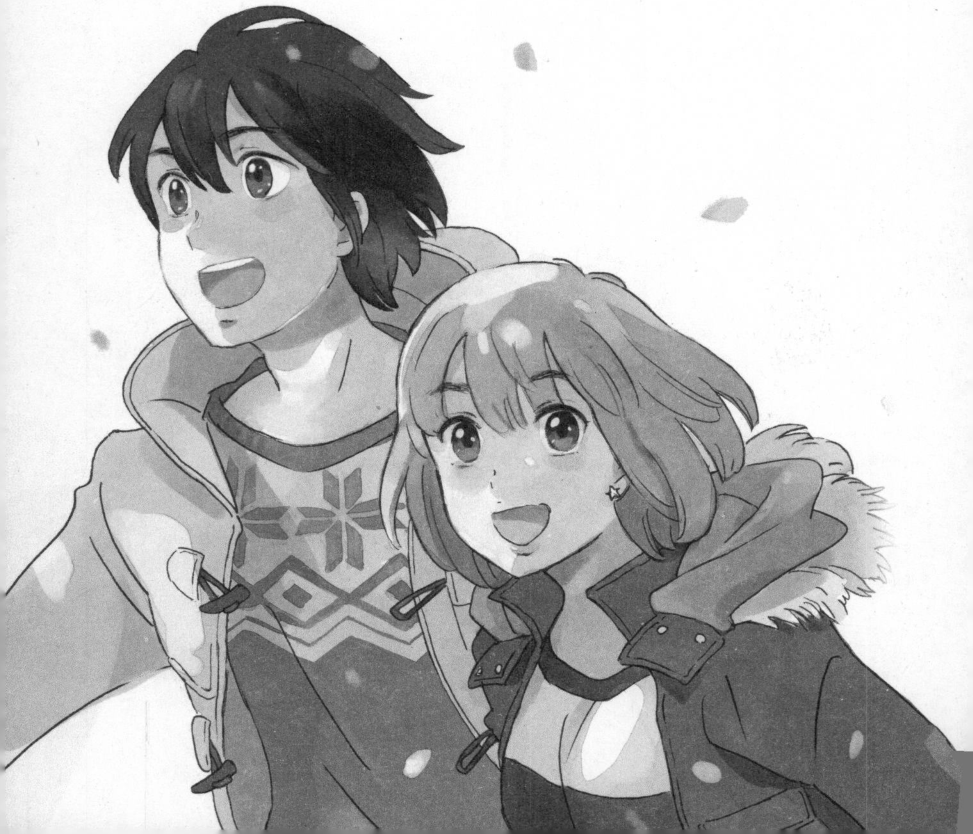

contents

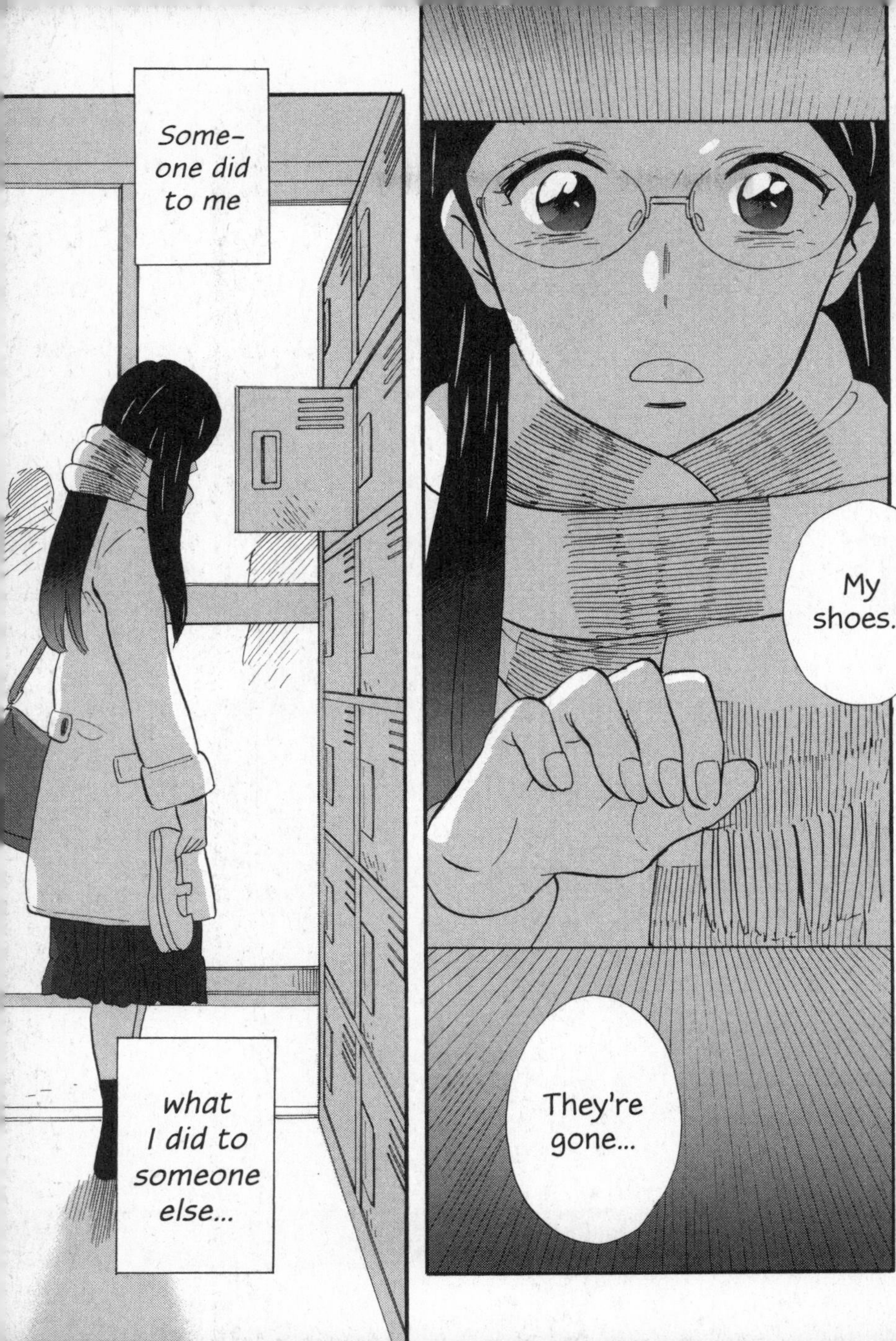
My shoes...
They're gone...
Some-one did to me
what I did to someone else...

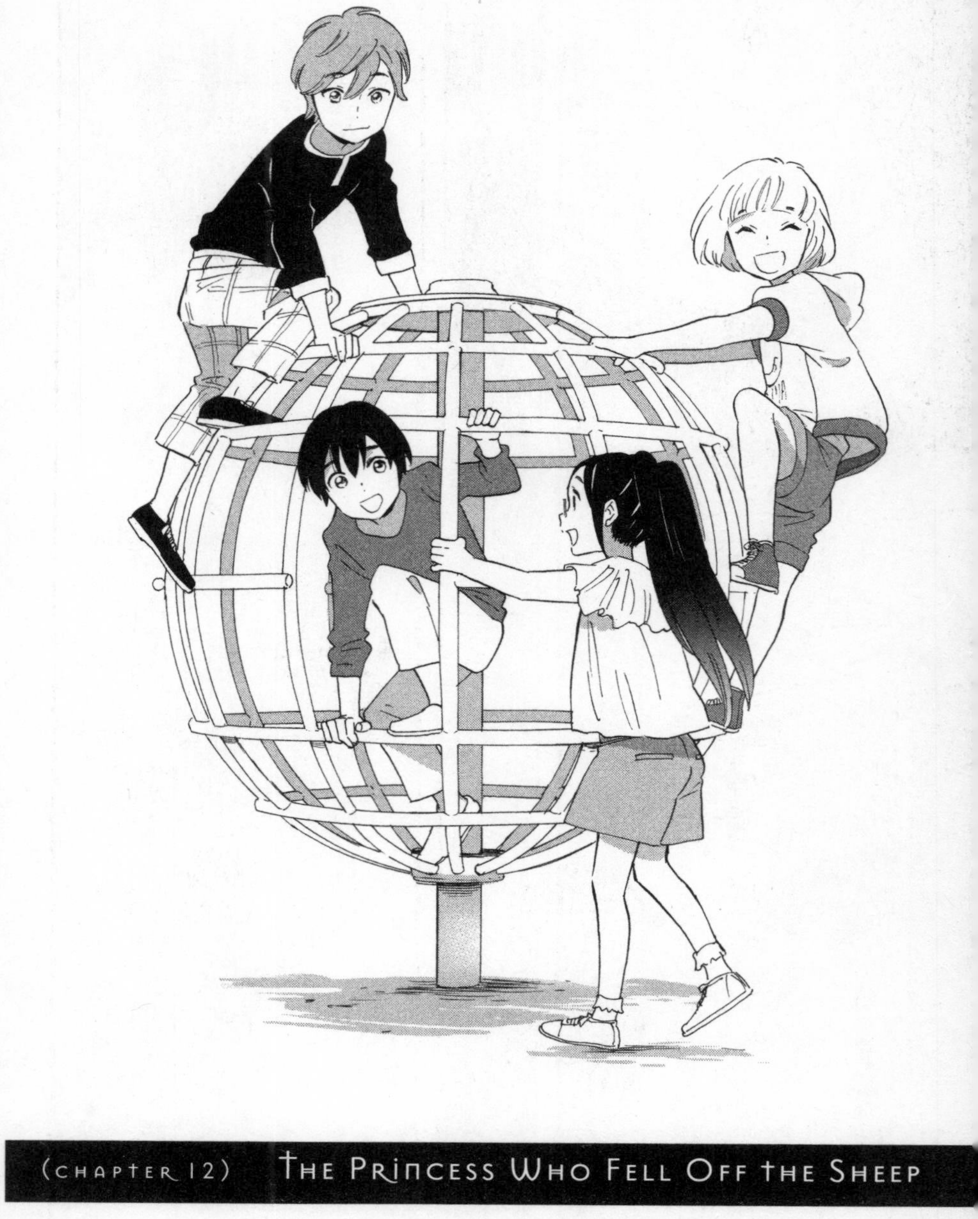

(CHAPTER 12) THE PRINCESS WHO FELL OFF THE SHEEP

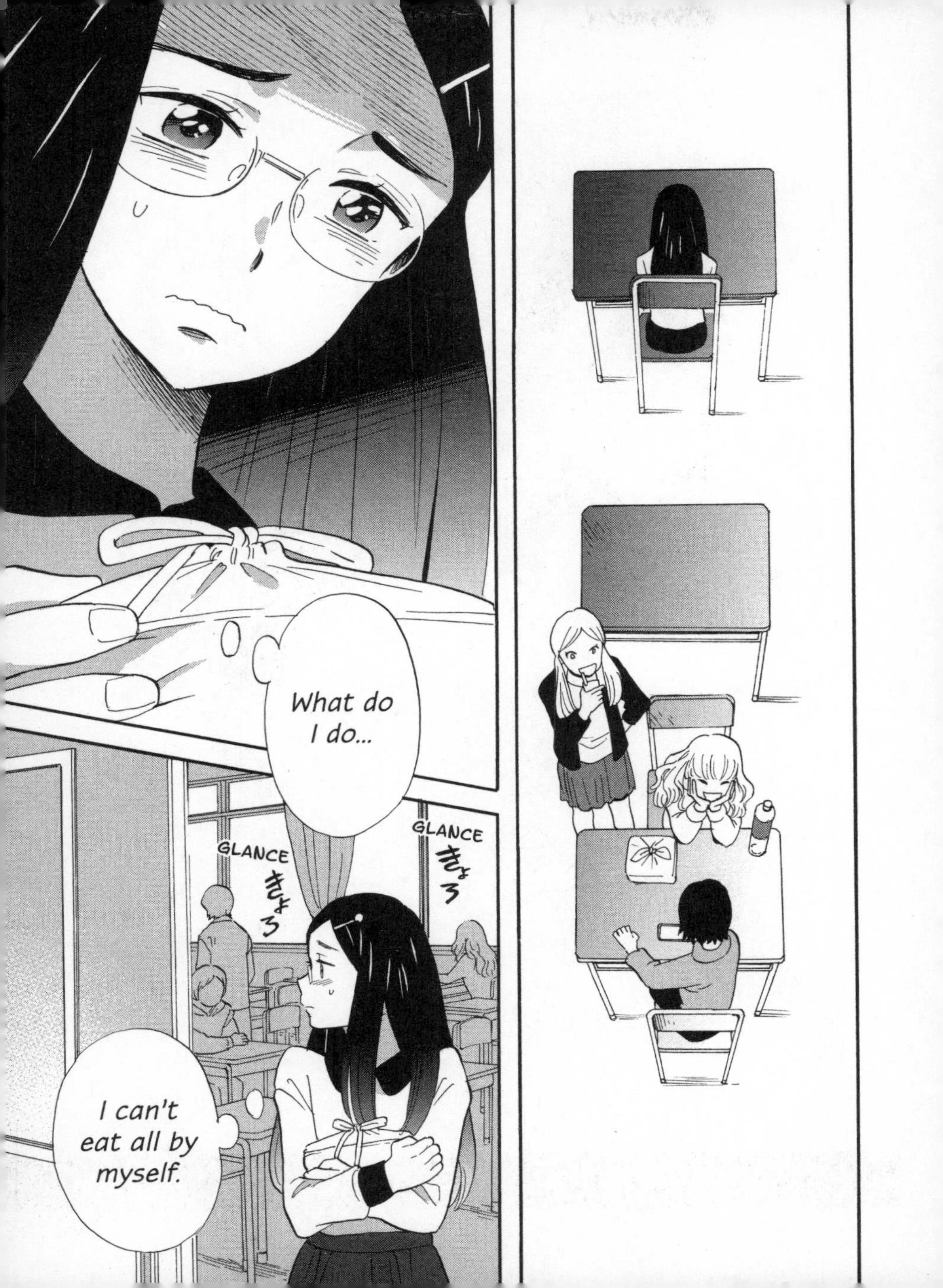
What do I do...
GLANCE きょろ
GLANCE きょろ
I can't eat all by myself.

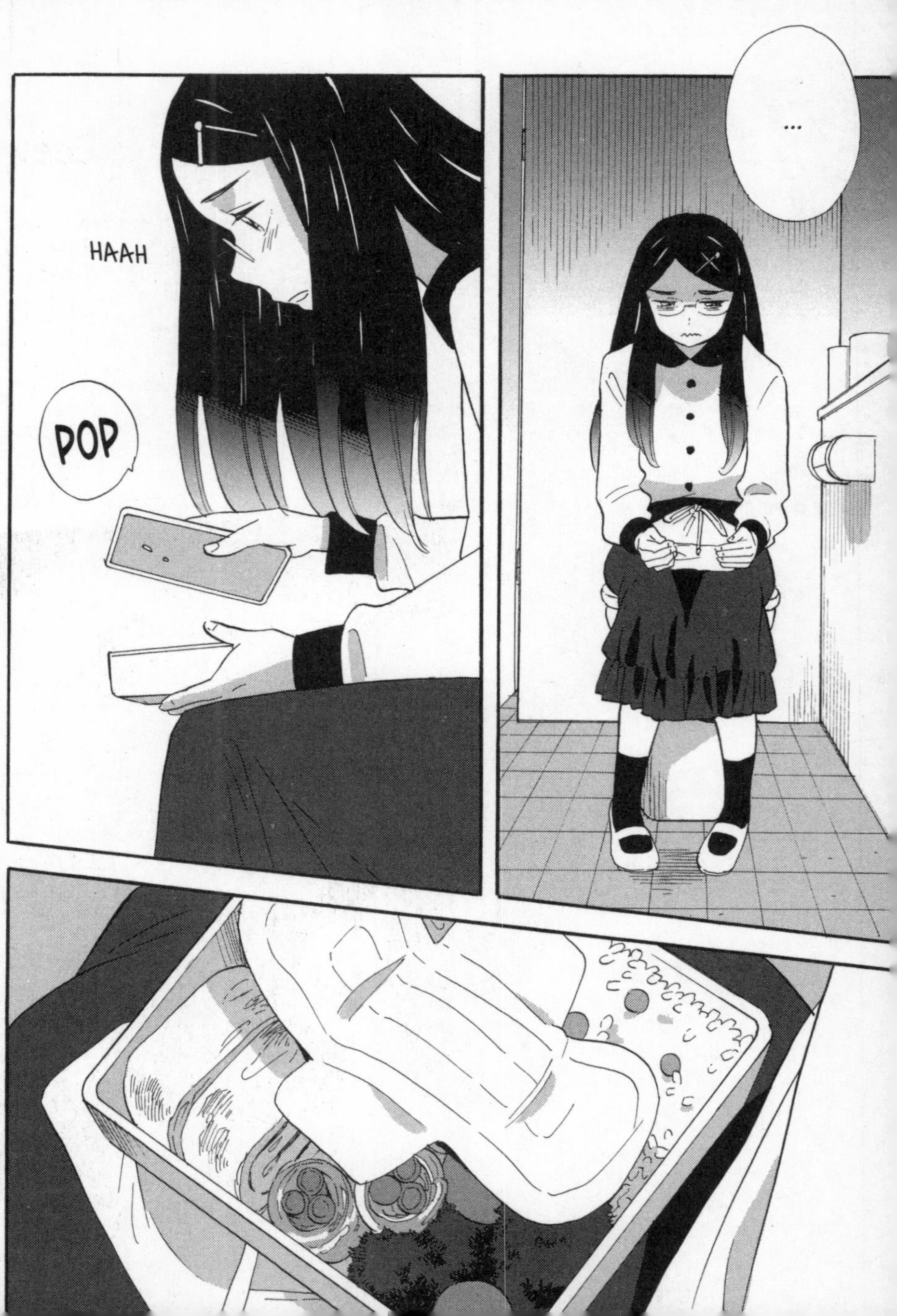
...
HAAH
POP

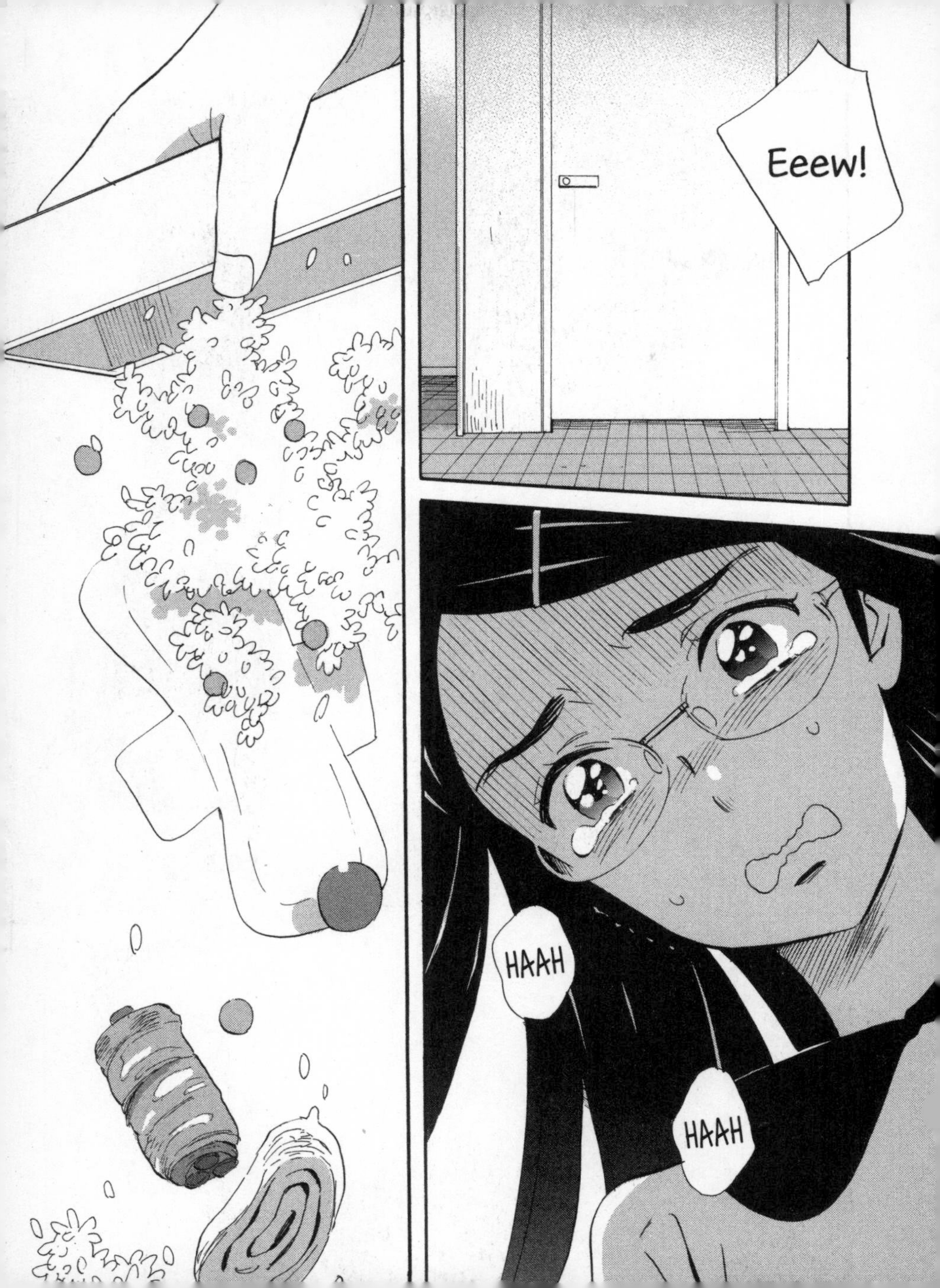
Eeew!
HAAH
HAAH

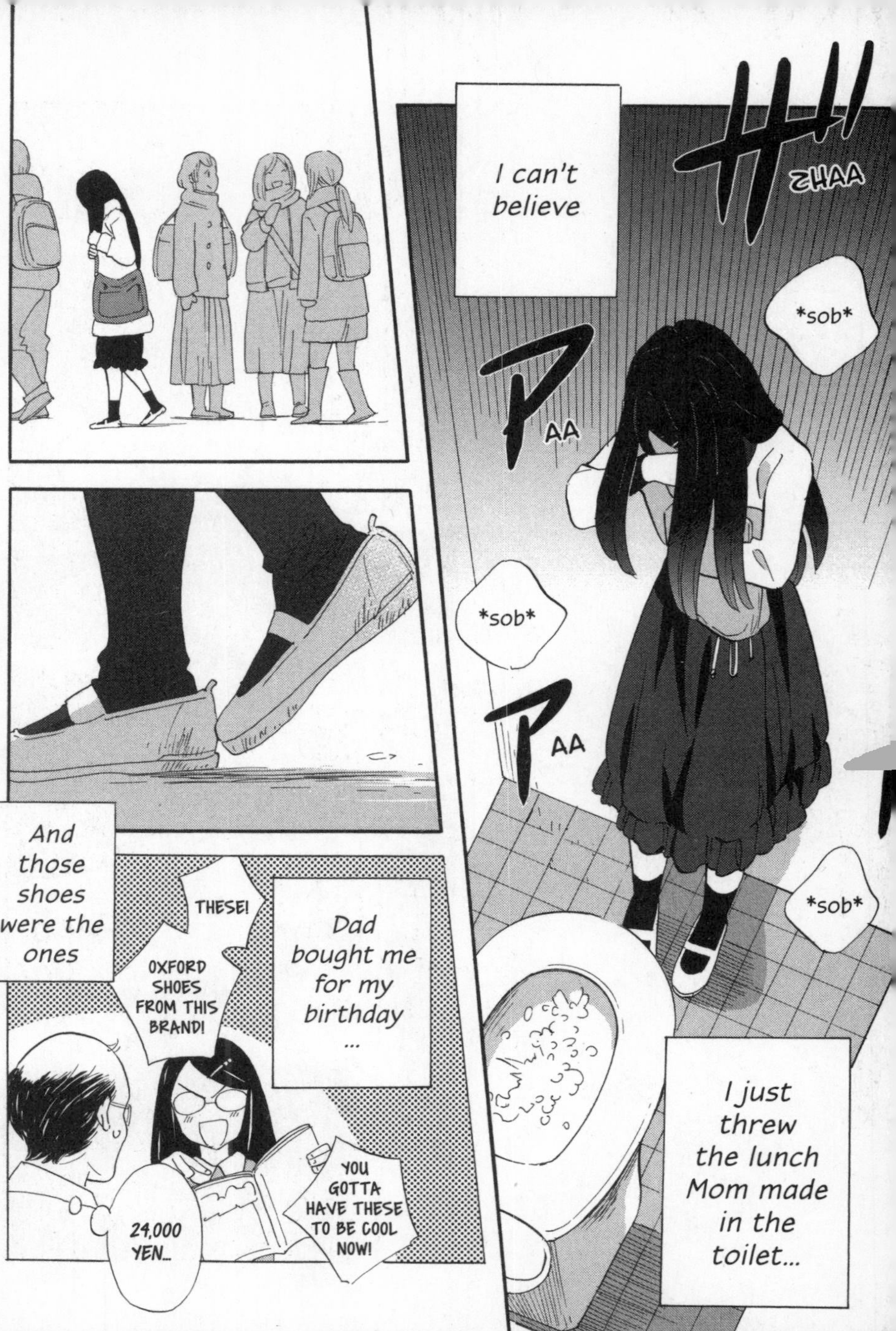
I can't believe
ZHAA
sob
PAA
sob
PAA
sob
I just threw the lunch Mom made in the toilet...
And those shoes were the ones
Dad bought me for my birthday ...
THESE!
OXFORD SHOES FROM THIS BRAND!
YOU GOTTA HAVE THESE TO BE COOL NOW!
24,000 YEN...

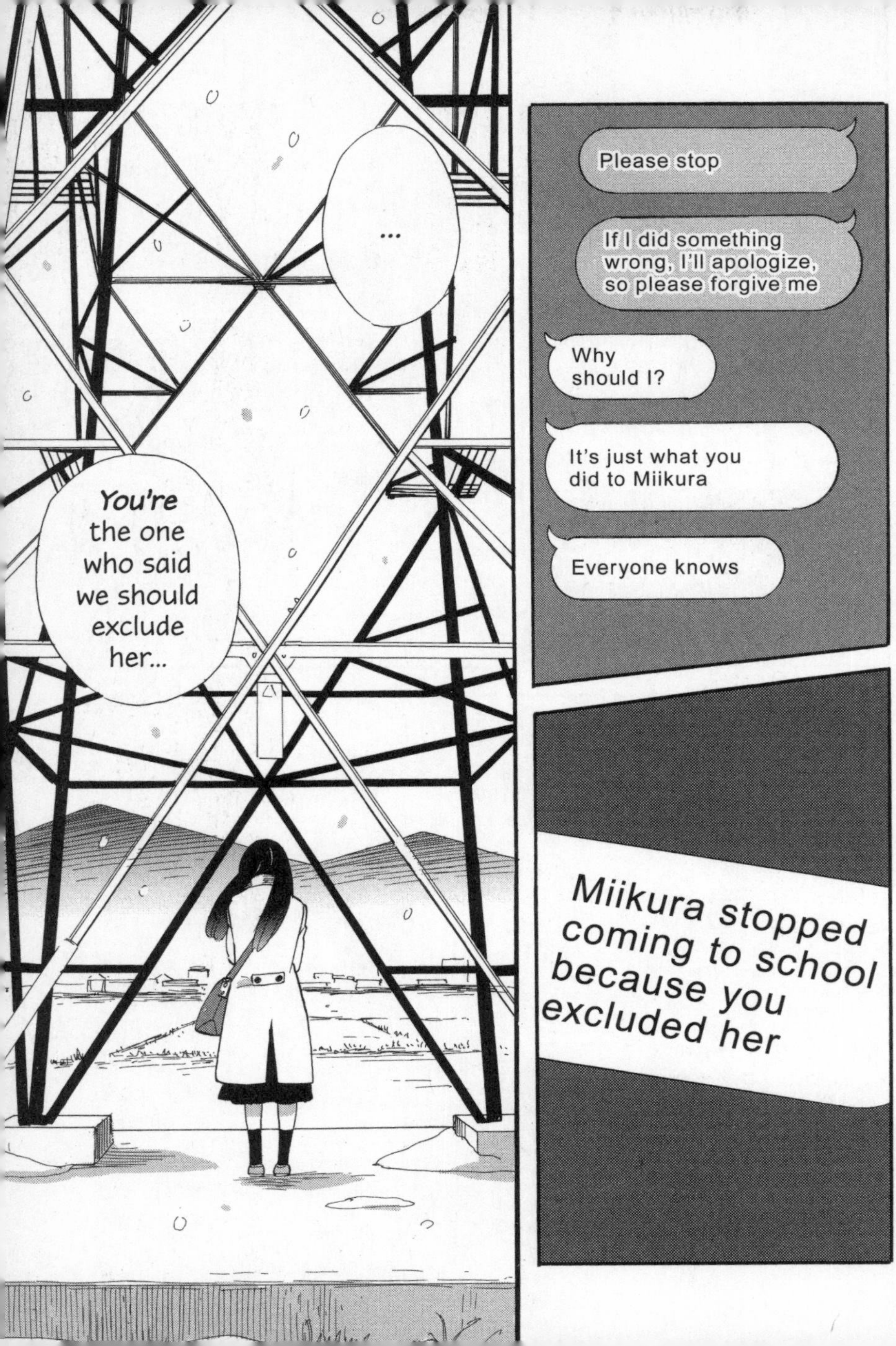
Please stop
If I did something wrong, I'll apologize, so please forgive me
Why should I?
It's just what you did to Miikura
Everyone knows
Miikura stopped coming to school because you excluded her
...
You're the one who said we should exclude her...

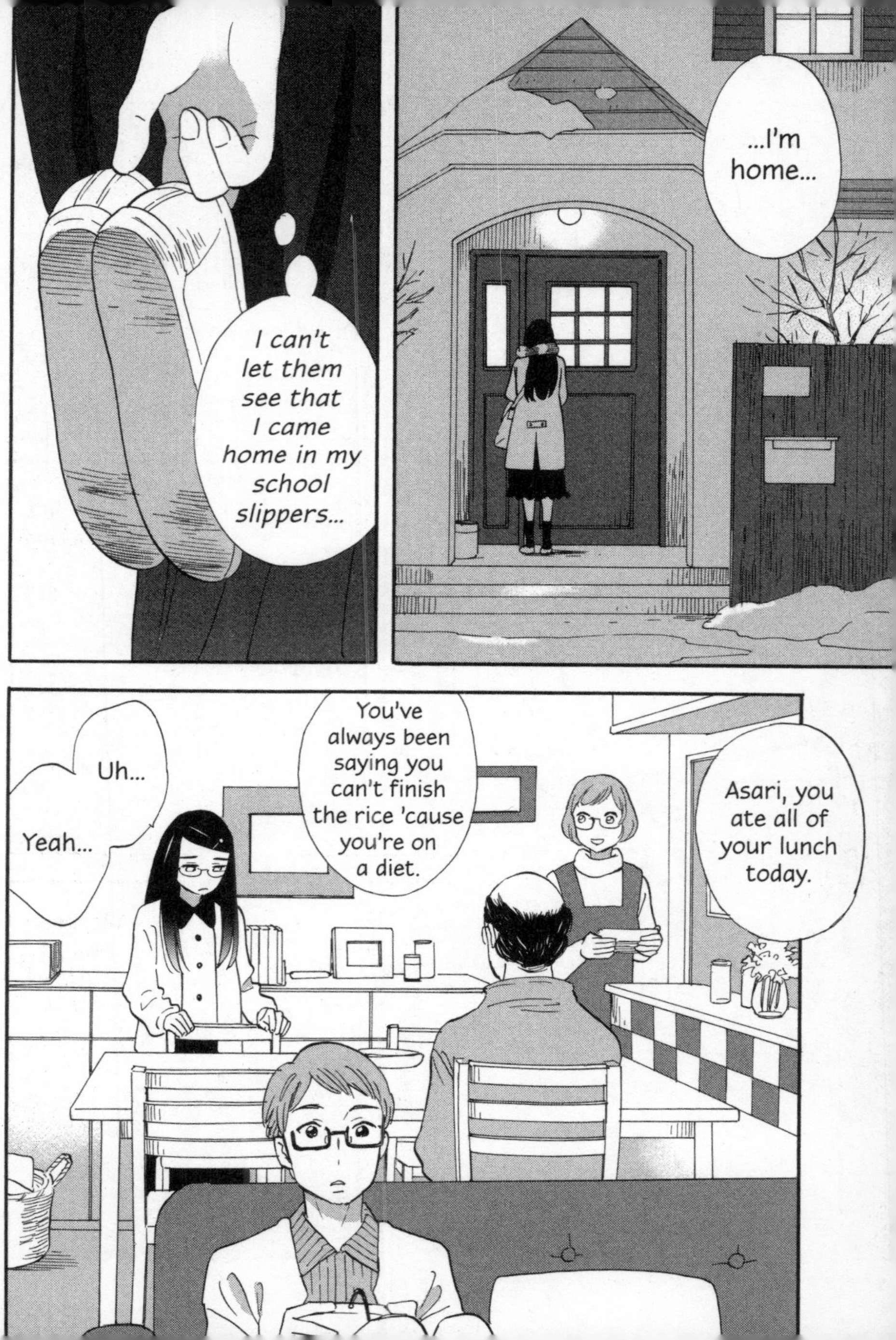
...I'm home...
I can't let them see that I came home in my school slippers...
Asari, you ate all of your lunch today.
You've always been saying you can't finish the rice 'cause you're on a diet.
Uh...
Yeah...

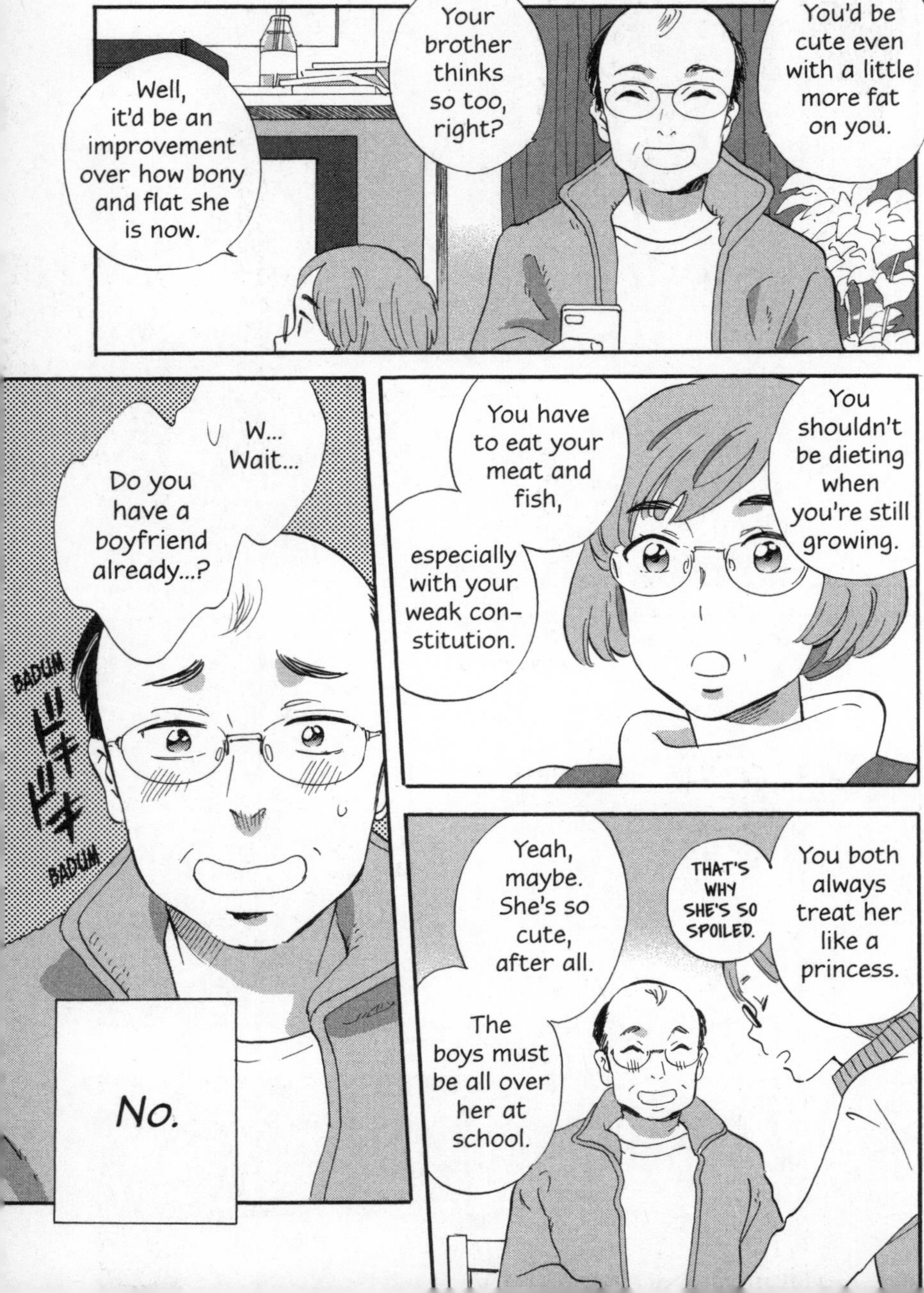
You'd be cute even with a little more fat on you.
Your brother thinks so too, right?
Well, it'd be an improvement over how bony and flat she is now.
You shouldn't be dieting when you're still growing.
You have to eat your meat and fish,
especially with your weak constitution.
You both always treat her like a princess.
THAT'S WHY SHE'S SO SPOILED.
Yeah, maybe. She's so cute, after all.
The boys must be all over her at school.
W... Wait...
Do you have a boyfriend already...?
BADUM
BADUM
No.

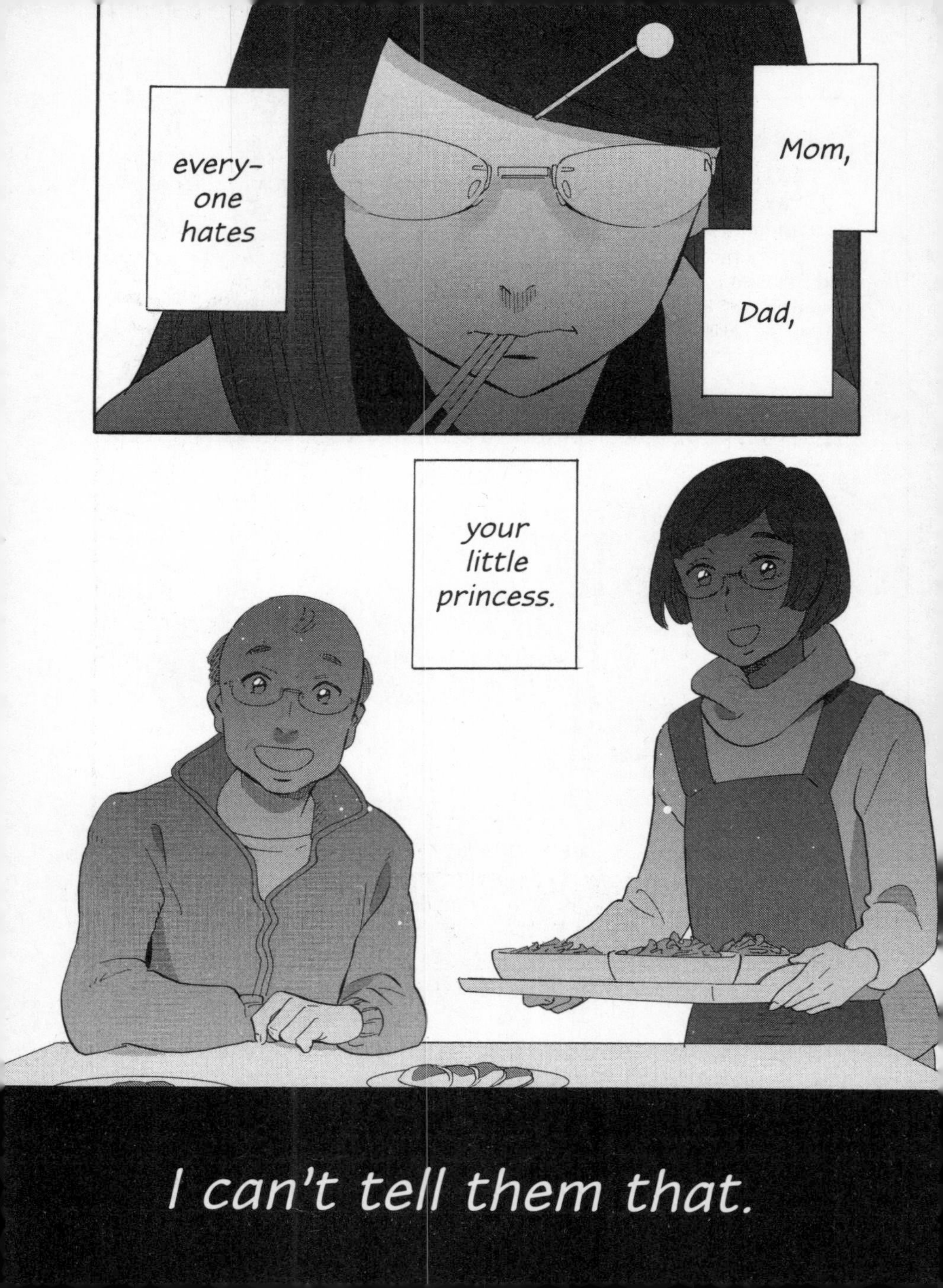
Mom,
Dad,
every-one hates
your little princess.
I can't tell them that.

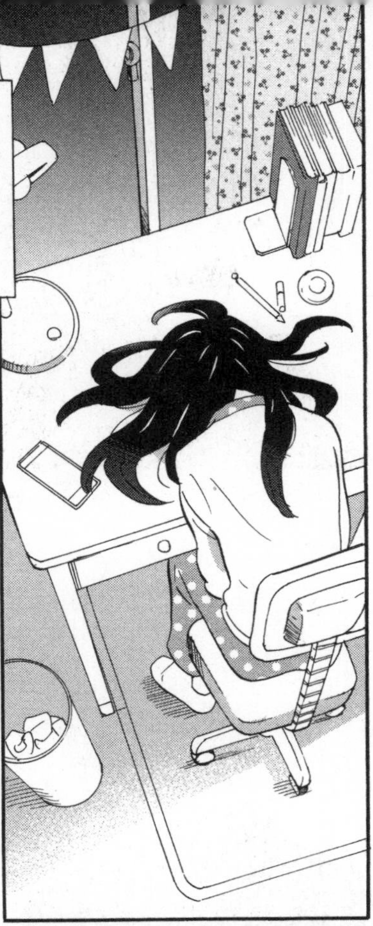
As long as we're trapped in the institution of school,

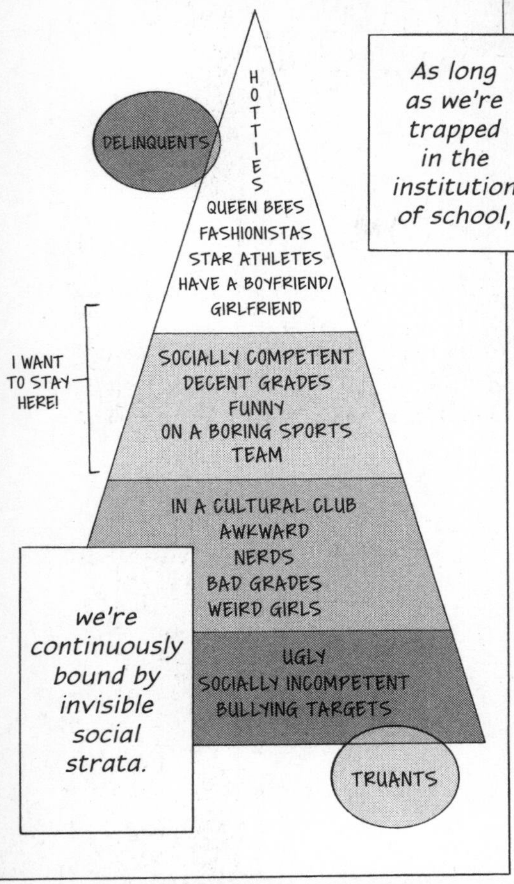
HOTTIES
DELINQUENTS
QUEEN BEES
FASHIONISTAS
STAR ATHLETES
HAVE A BOYFRIEND/ GIRLFRIEND
I WANT TO STAY HERE!
SOCIALLY COMPETENT
DECENT GRADES
FUNNY
ON A BORING SPORTS TEAM
IN A CULTURAL CLUB
AWKWARD
NERDS
BAD GRADES
WEIRD GIRLS
UGLY
SOCIALLY INCOMPETENT
BULLYING TARGETS
TRUANTS
we're continuously bound by invisible social strata.

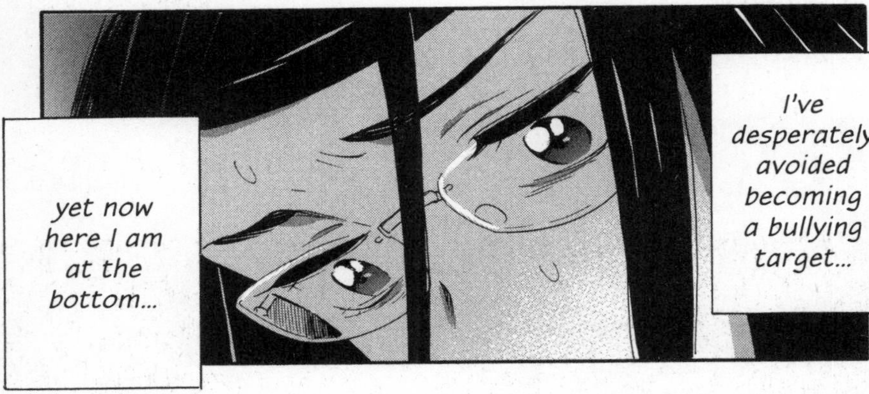
I've desperately avoided becoming a bullying target...
yet now here I am at the bottom...

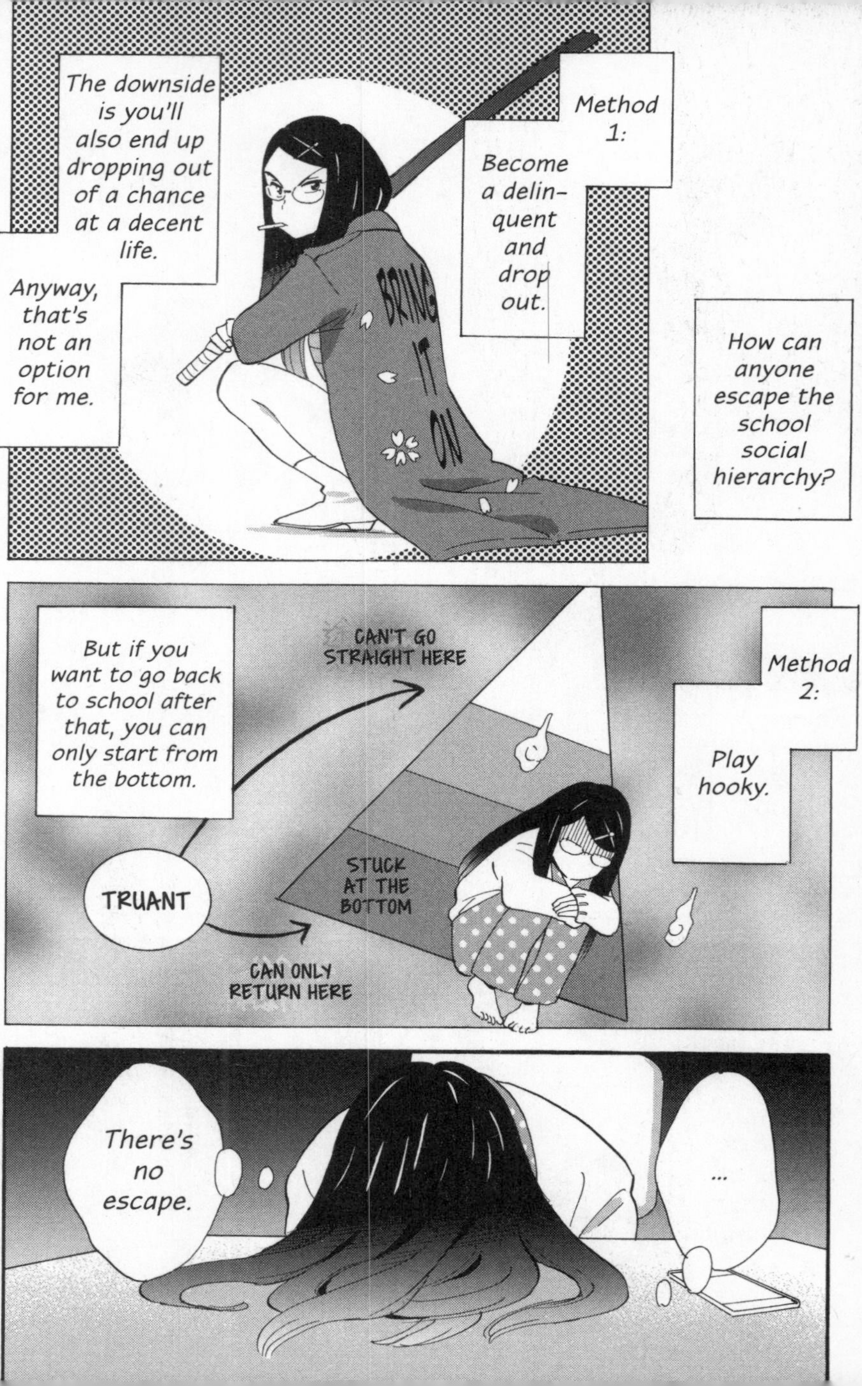
How can anyone escape the school social hierarchy?
Method 1:
Become a delin- quent and drop out.
The downside is you'll also end up dropping out of a chance at a decent life.
Anyway, that's not an option for me.
BRING IT ON
Method 2:
Play hooky.
But if you want to go back to school after that, you can only start from the bottom.
CAN'T GO STRAIGHT HERE
TRUANT
STUCK AT THE BOTTOM
CAN ONLY RETURN HERE
...
There's no escape.

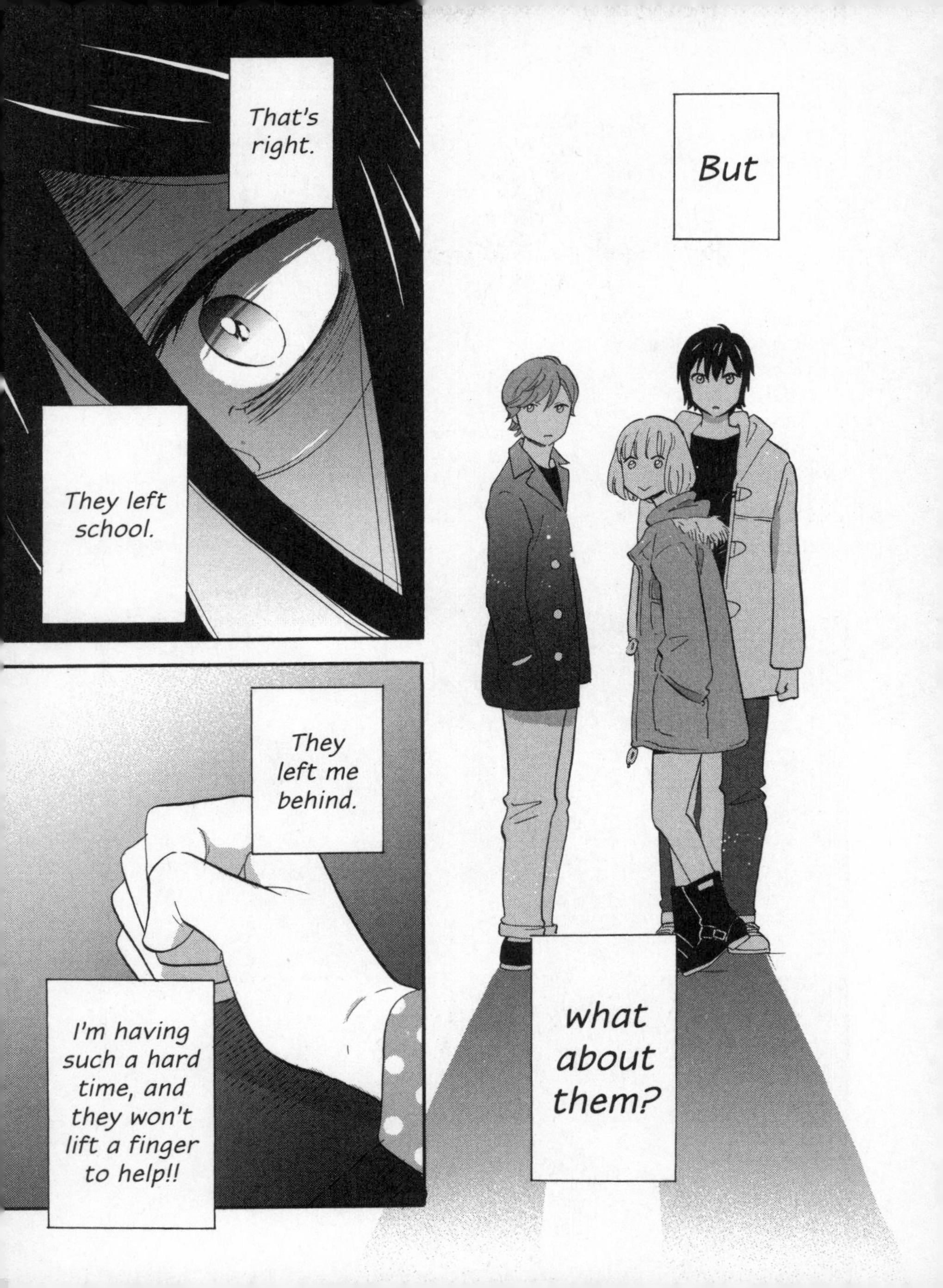
But
what about them?
That's right.
They left school.
They left me behind.
I'm having such a hard time, and they won't lift a finger to help!!

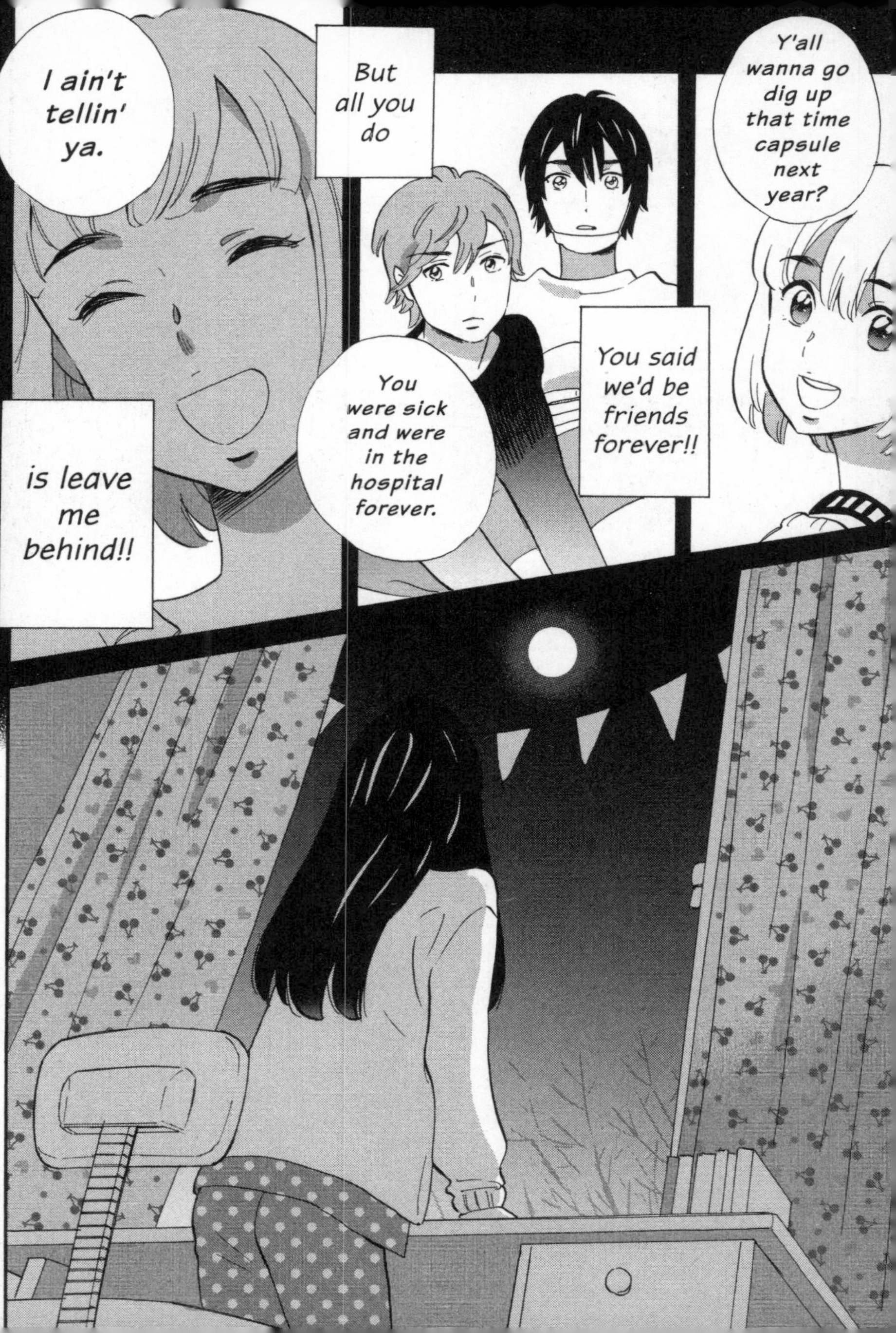

Y'all wanna go dig up that time capsule next year?
You said we'd be friends forever!!
You were sick and were in the hospital forever.
But all you do
I ain't tellin' ya.
is leave me behind!!

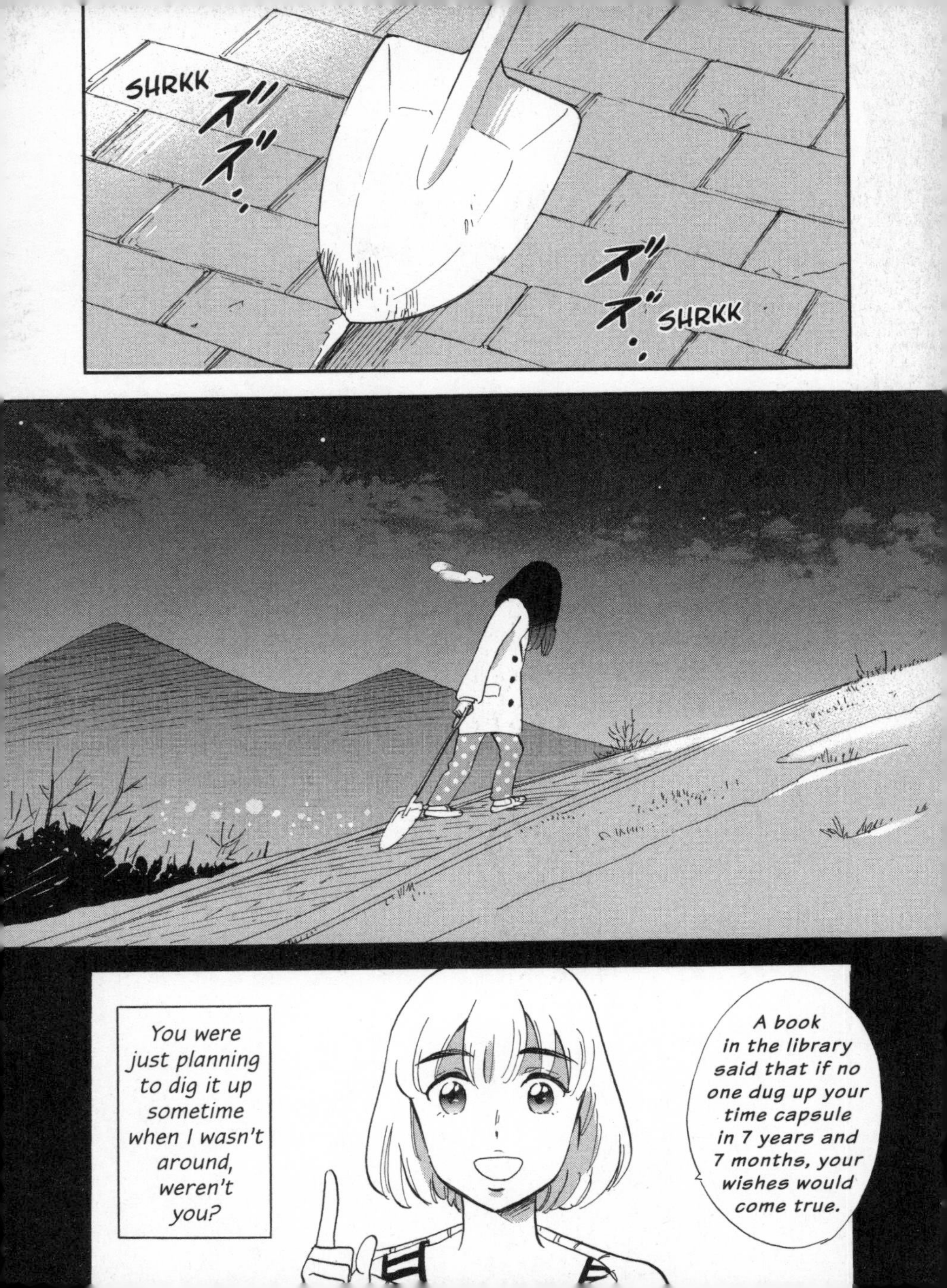
ズズ‥
SHRKK
ズズ‥
SHRKK
A book in the library said that if no one dug up your time capsule in 7 years and 7 months, your wishes would come true.
You were just planning to dig it up sometime when I wasn't around, weren't you?

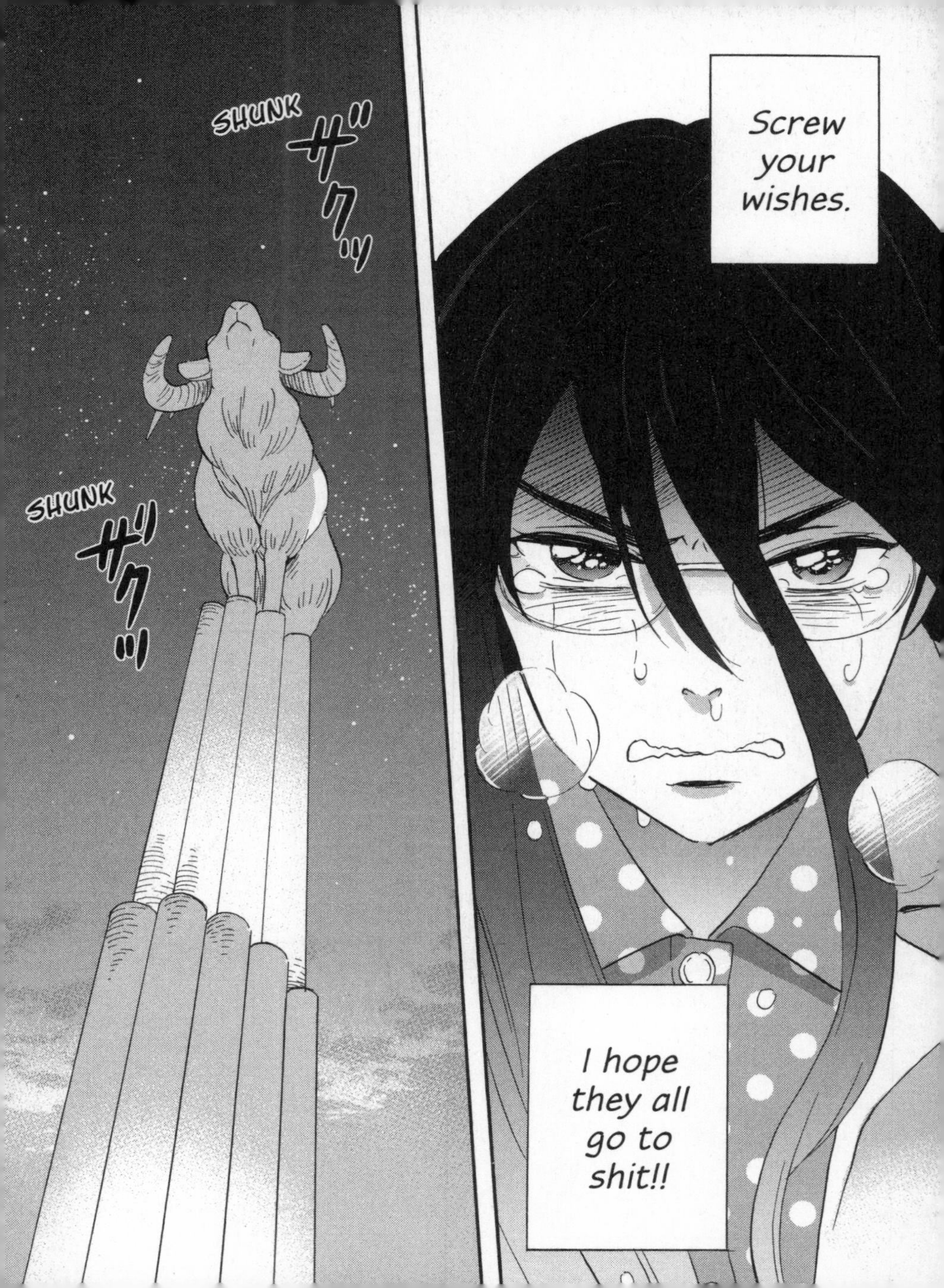
Screw your wishes.
I hope they all go to shit!!
SHUNK
ザクッ
SHUNK
ザクッ

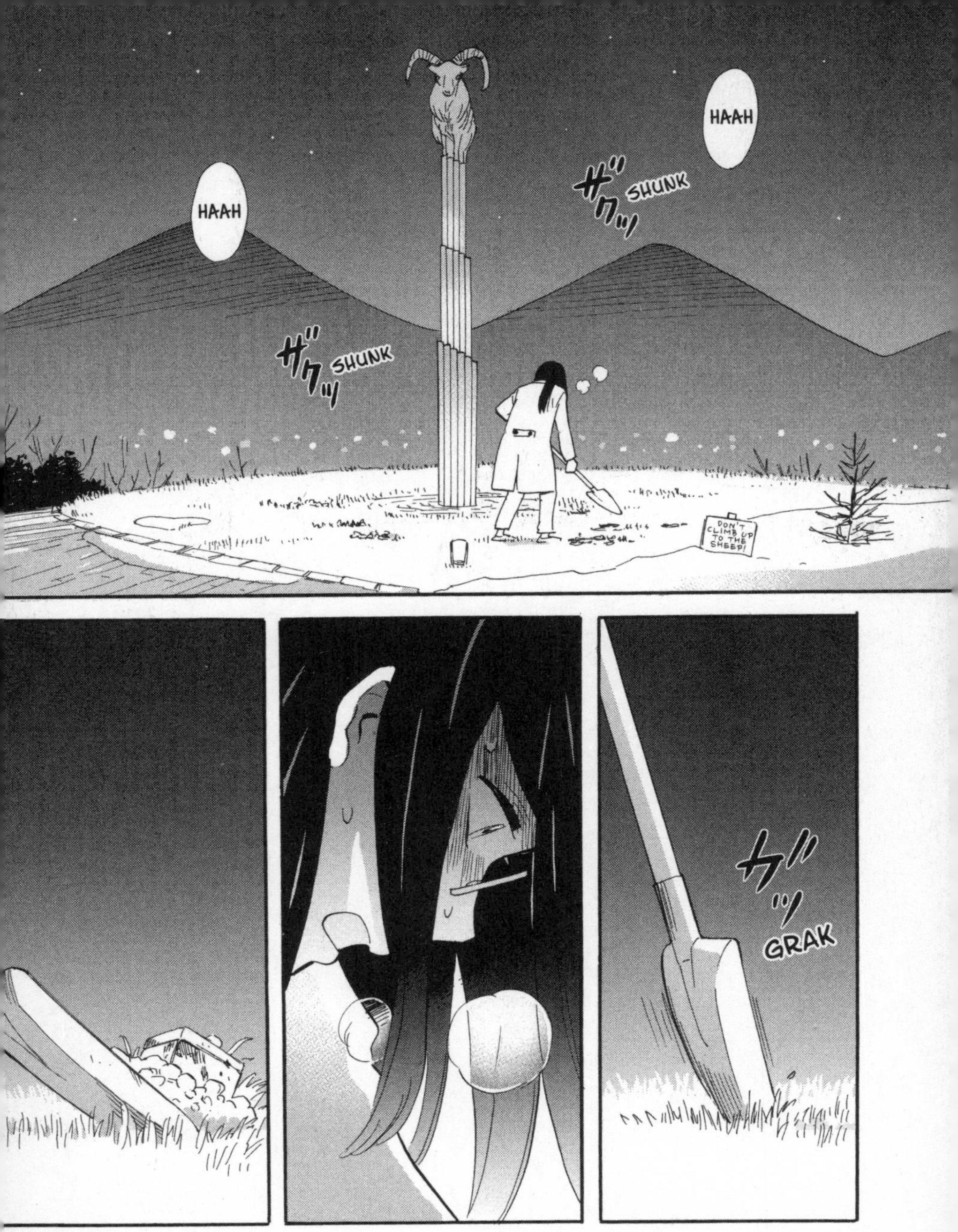
HAAH
ザクッ SHUNK
HAAH
ザクッ SHUNK
DON'T CLIMB UP TO THE SHEEP!
ガッ GRAK

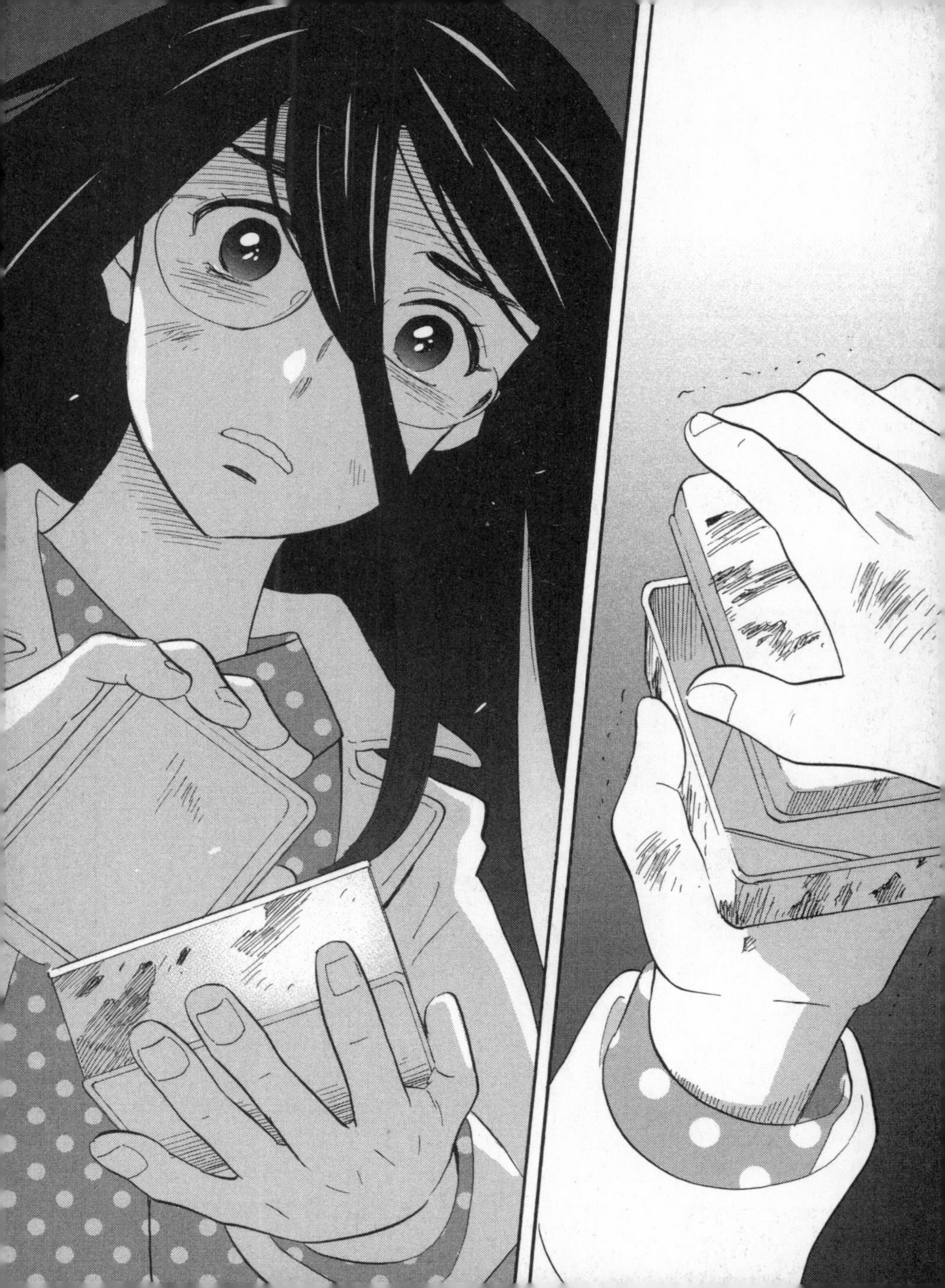

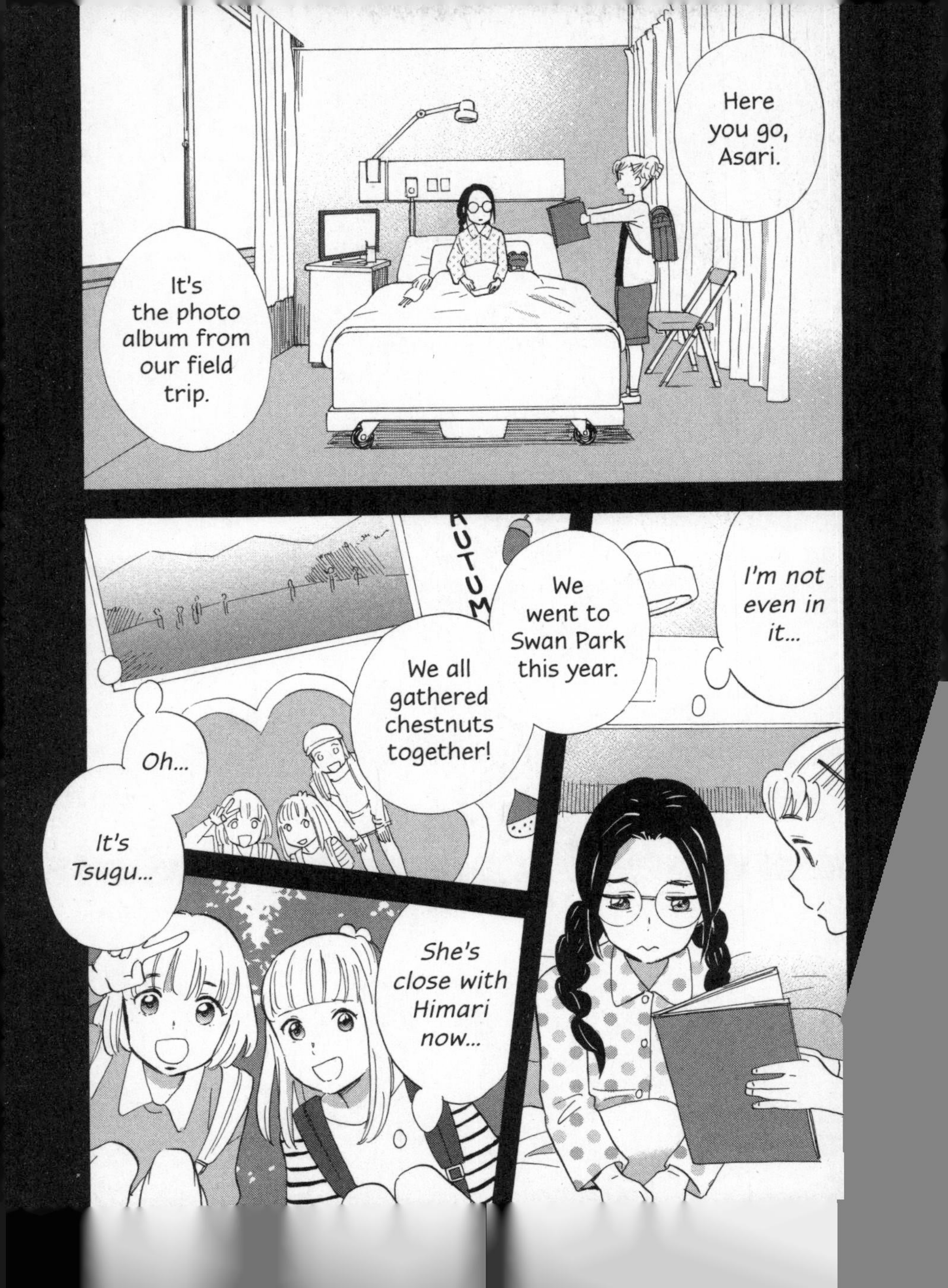
Here you go, Asari.
It's the photo album from our field trip.
I'm not even in it...
We went to Swan Park this year.
We all gathered chestnuts together!
Oh...
It's Tsugu...
She's close with Himari now...

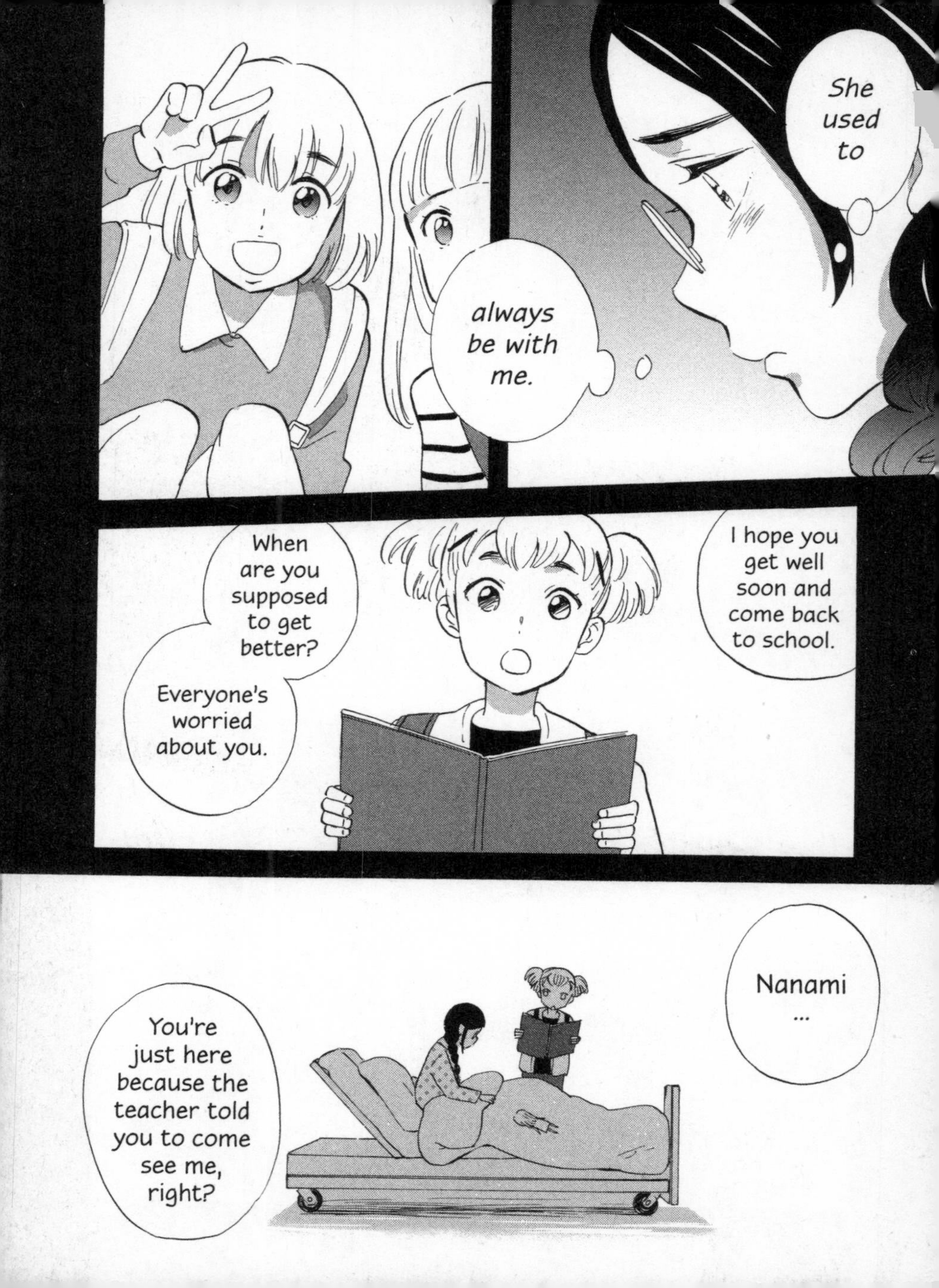
She used to
always be with me.
I hope you get well soon and come back to school.
When are you supposed to get better?
Everyone's worried about you.
Nanami ...
You're just here because the teacher told you to come see me, right?

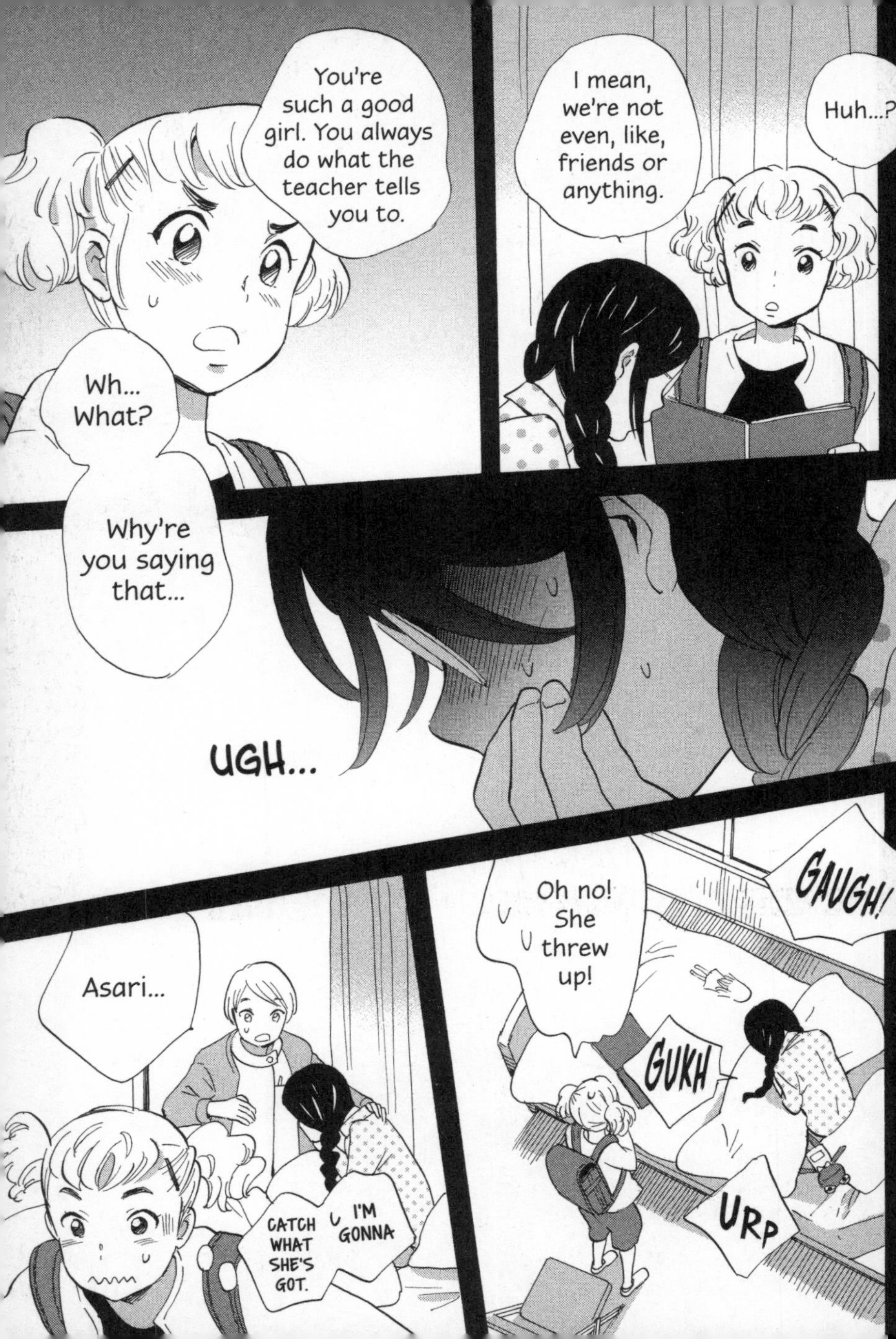
Huh...?
I mean, we're not even, like, friends or anything.
You're such a good girl. You always do what the teacher tells you to.
Wh... What?
Why're you saying that...
UGH...
GAUGH!
Oh no! She threw up!
GUKH
URP
Asari...
I'M GONNA CATCH WHAT SHE'S GOT.

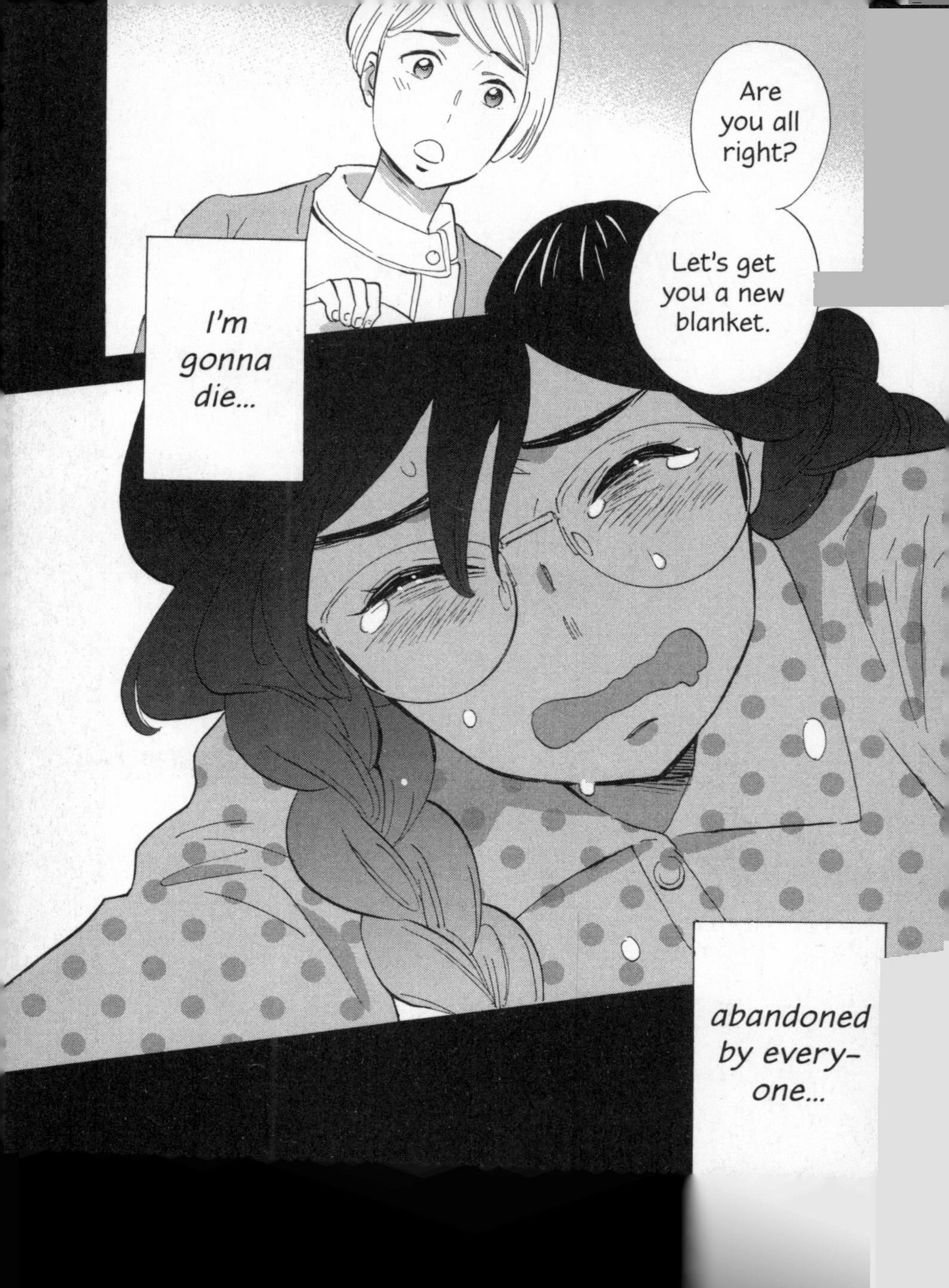
Are you all right?
Let's get you a new blanket.
I'm gonna die...
abandoned by every-one...

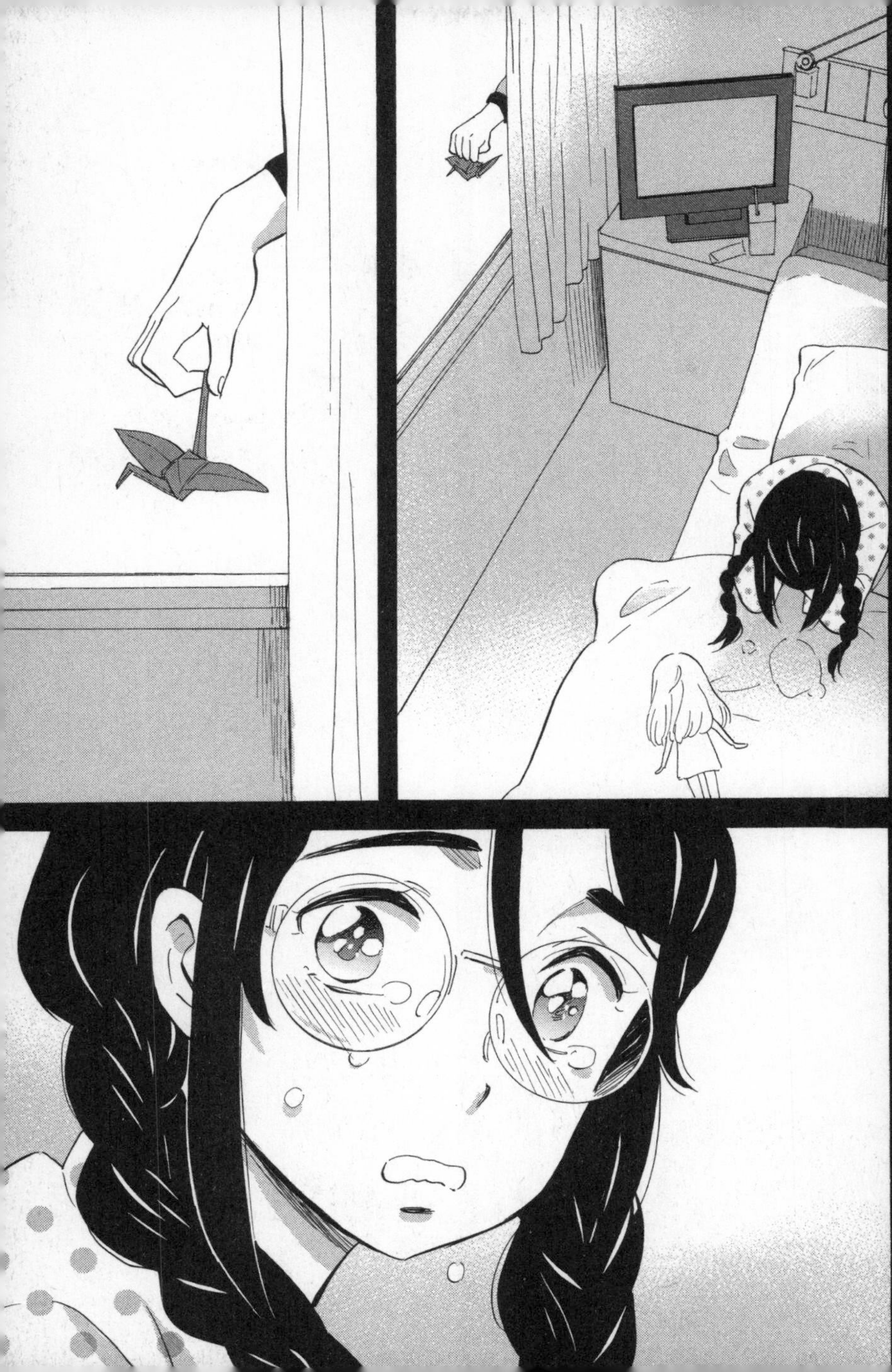

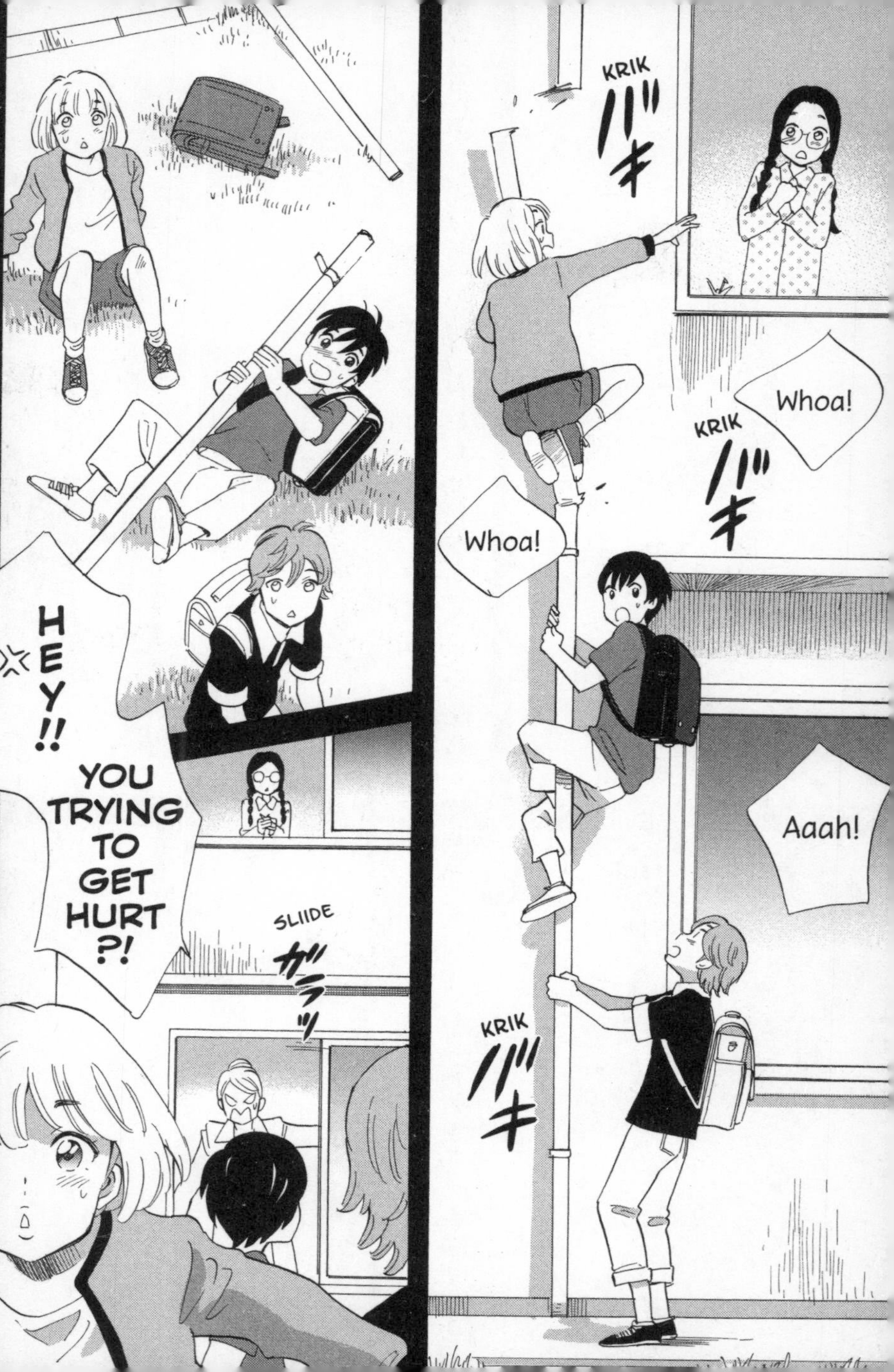
KRIK
Whoa!
KRIK
Whoa!
Aaah!
KRIK
HEY!!
YOU TRYING TO GET HURT?!
SLIIDE

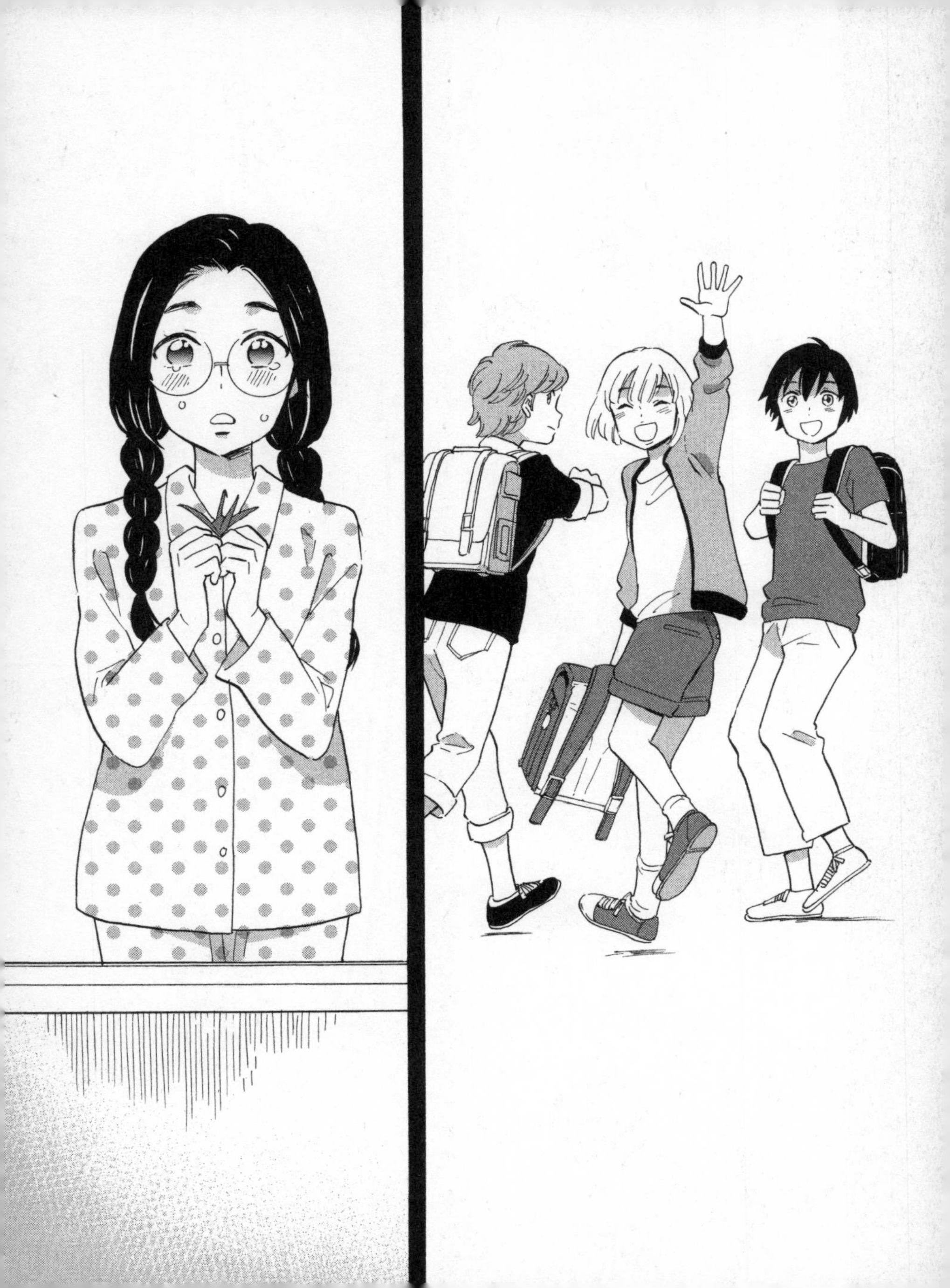

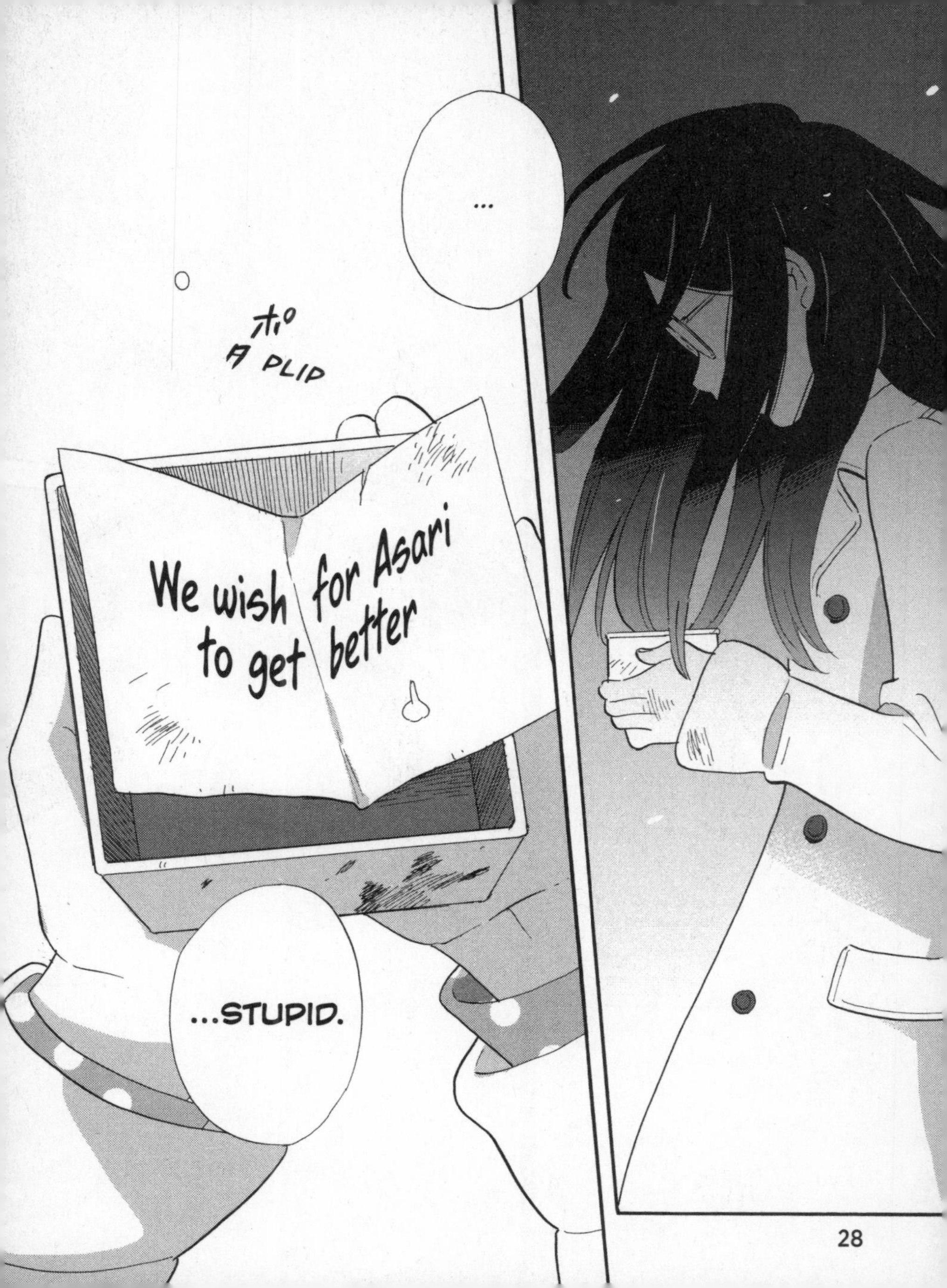
...
ポタ PLIP
We wish for Asari to get better
...STUPID.

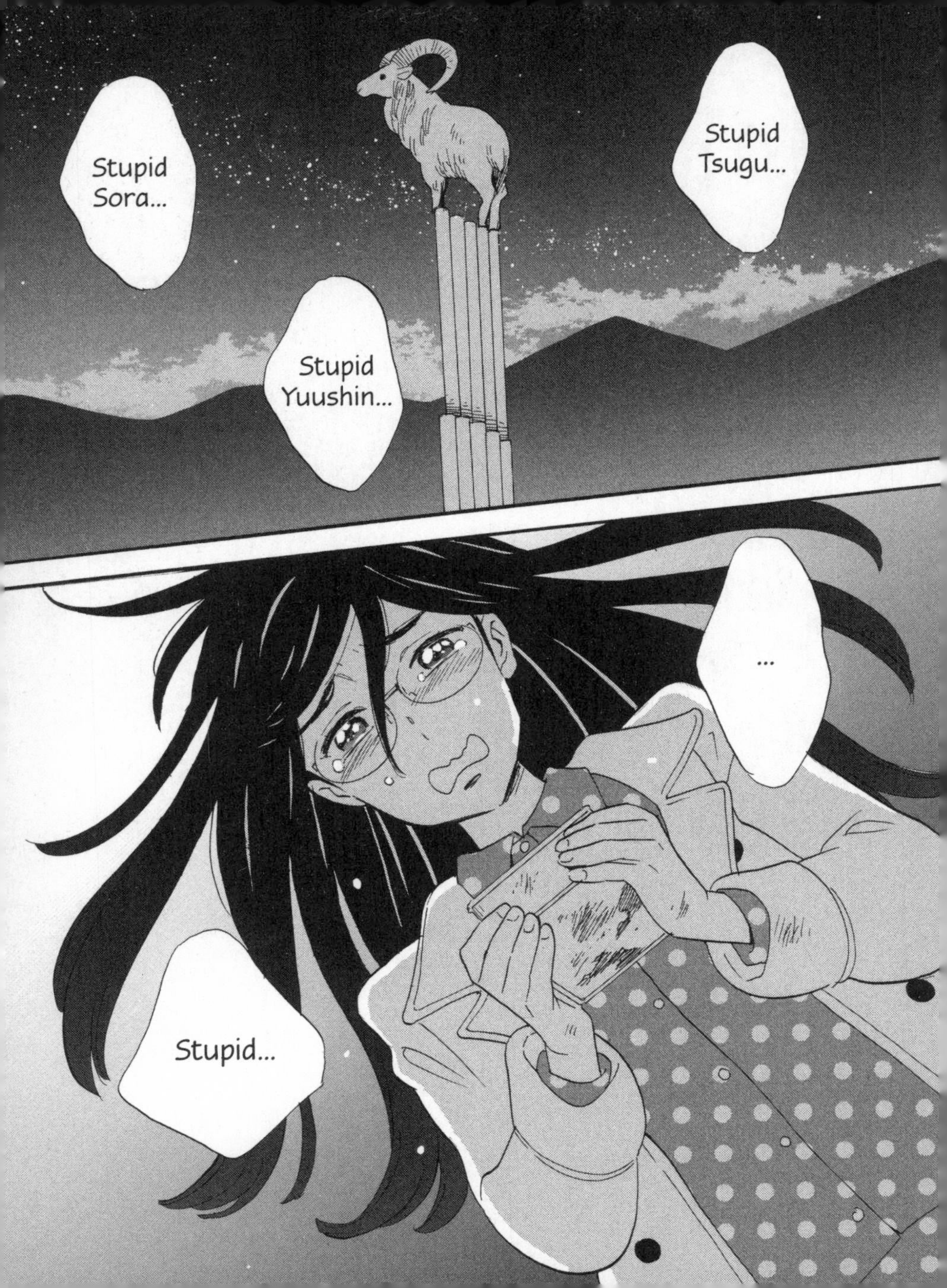
Stupid Tsugu...
Stupid Sora...
Stupid Yuushin...
...
Stupid...

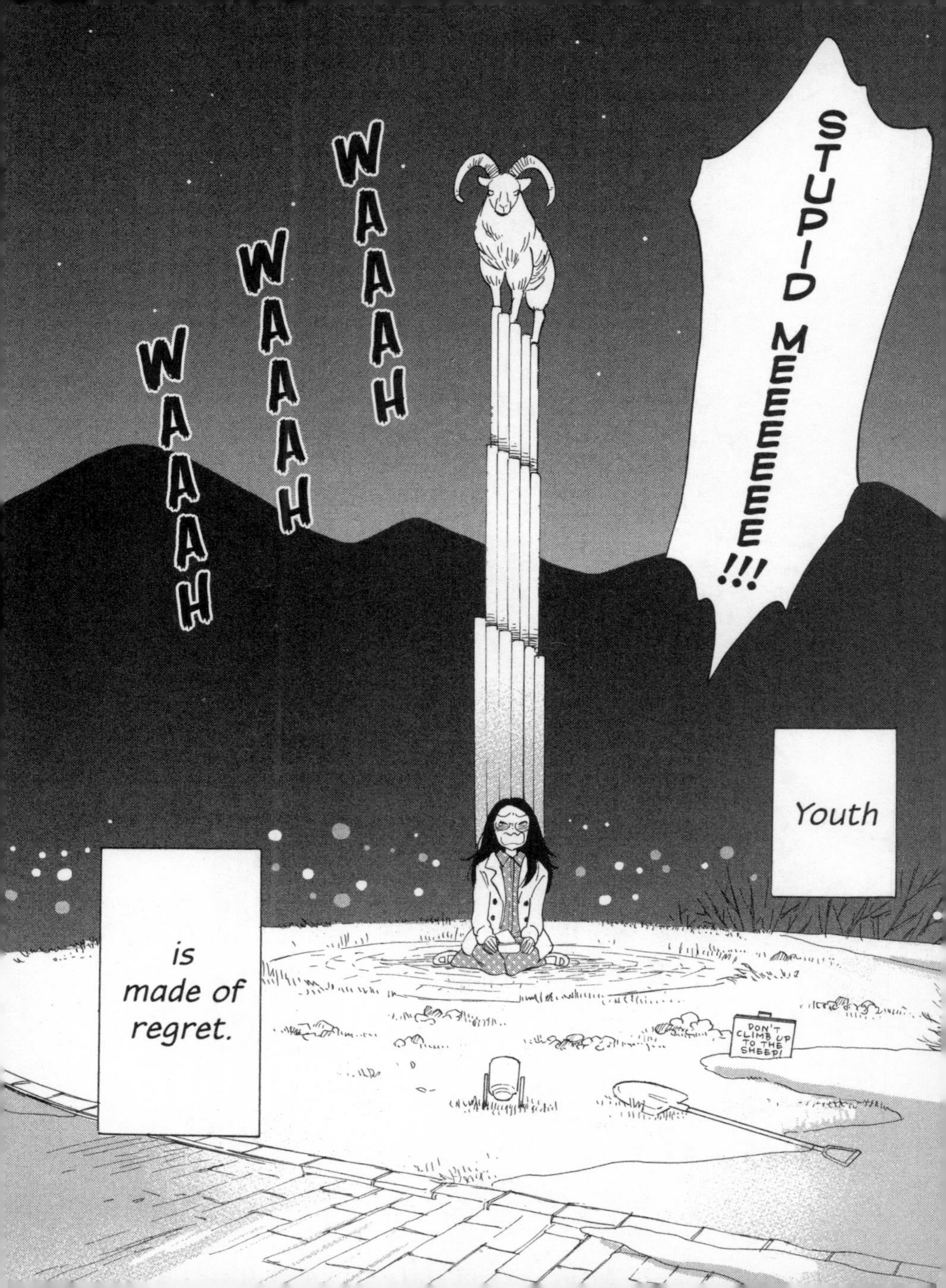
STUPID MEEEEEEE!!!
WAAAH
WAAAH
WAAAH
Youth
is made of regret.
DON'T CLIMB UP TO THE SHEEP!

THE GOLDEN SHEEP

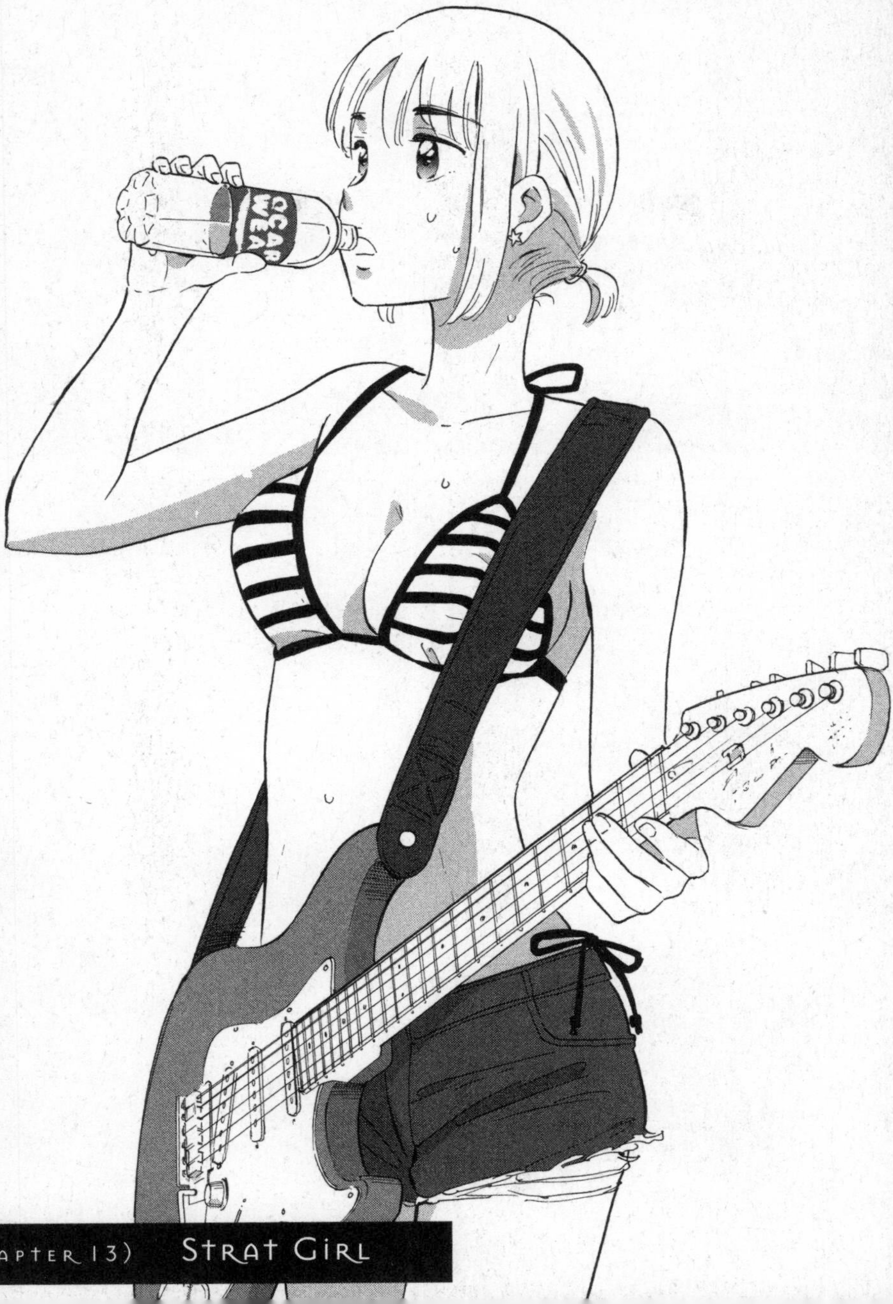

(CHAPTER 13) STRAT GIRL

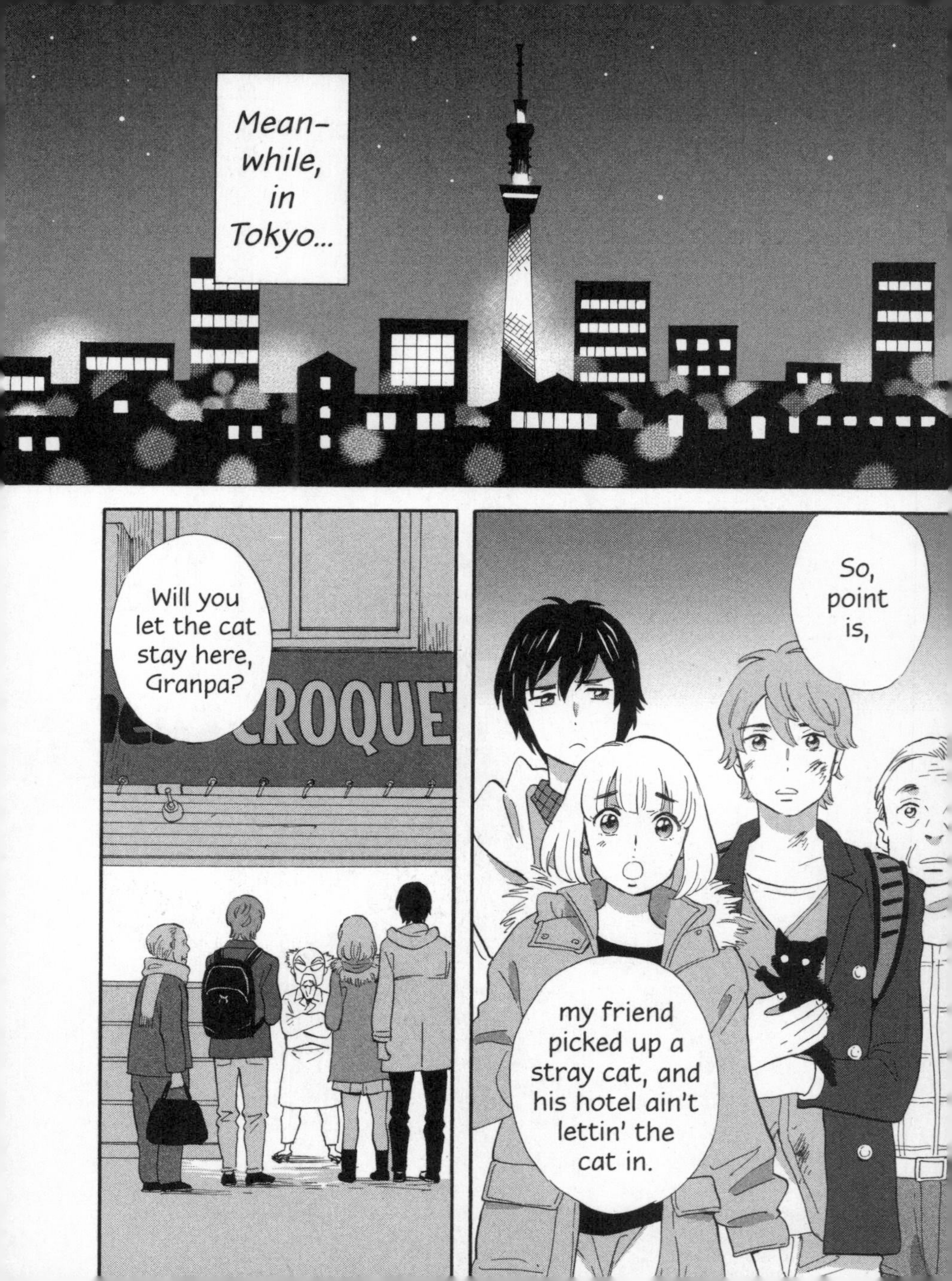
Mean-while, in Tokyo...
So, point is,
my friend picked up a stray cat, and his hotel ain't lettin' the cat in.
Will you let the cat stay here, Granpa?
CROQUE

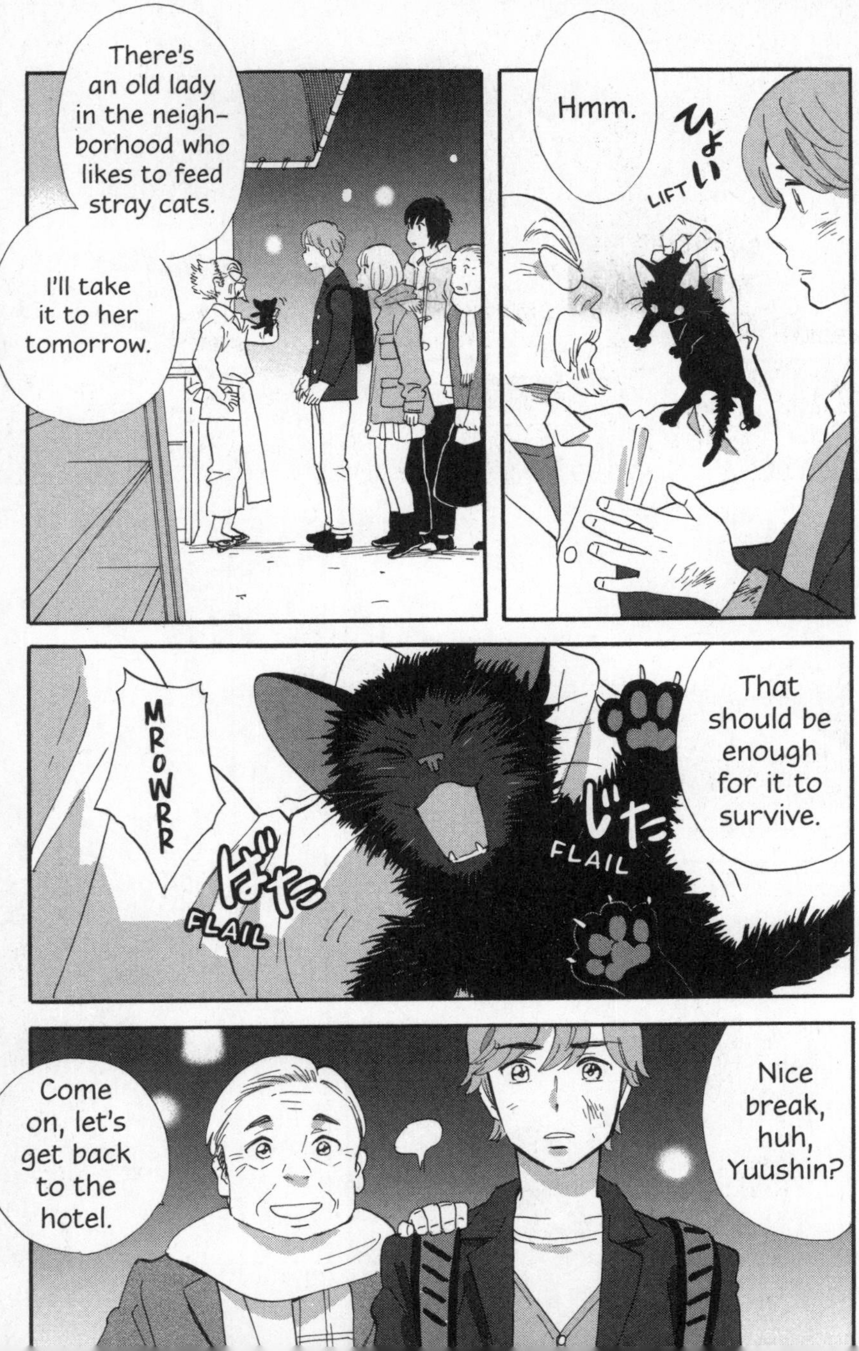
Hmm.
ひょい
LIFT
There's an old lady in the neigh-borhood who likes to feed stray cats.
I'll take it to her tomorrow.
That should be enough for it to survive.
じた
FLAIL
MROWRR
ばた
FLAIL
Nice break, huh, Yuushin?
Come on, let's get back to the hotel.

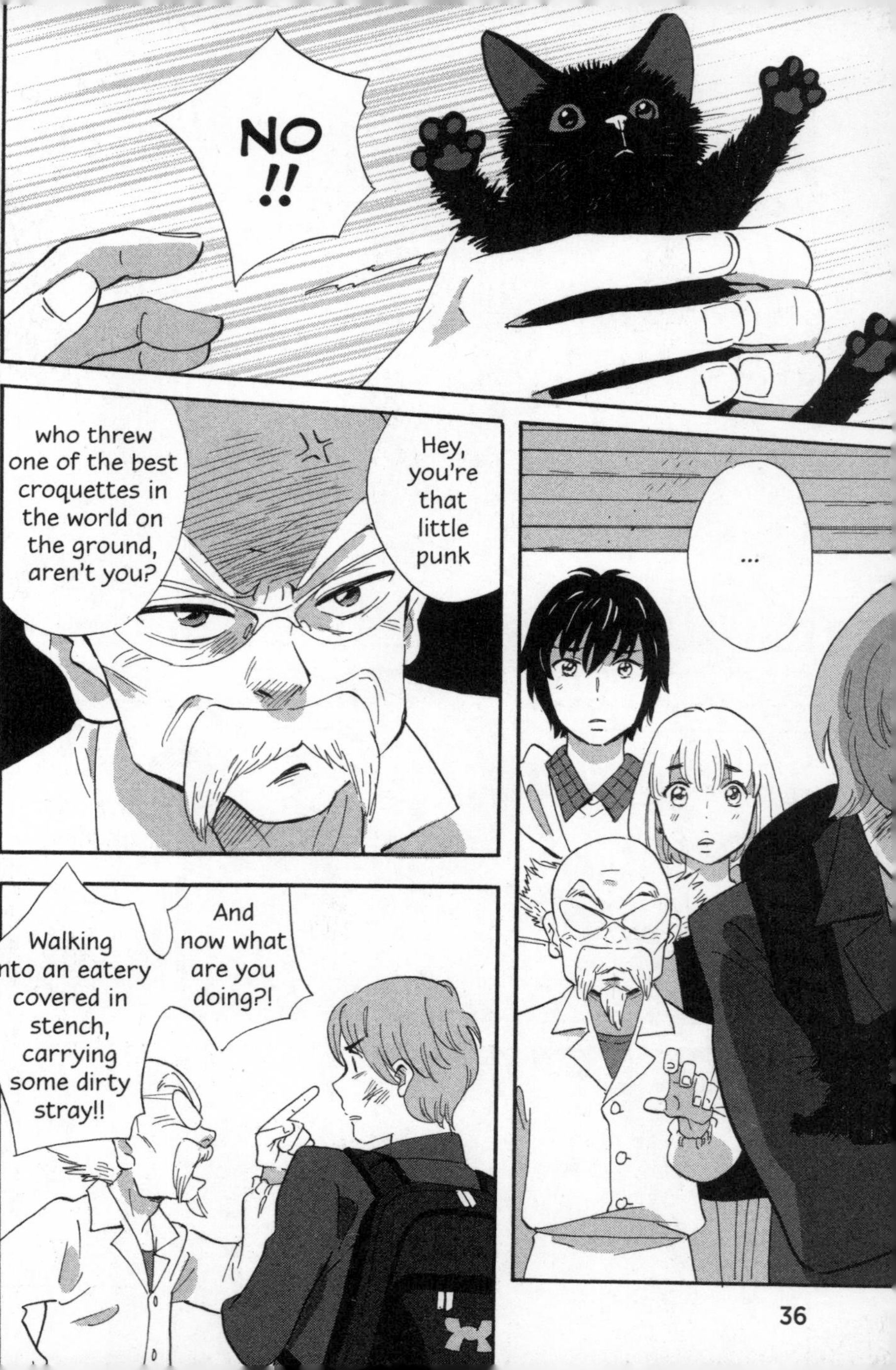
NO!!
...
Hey, you're that little punk
who threw one of the best croquettes in the world on the ground, aren't you?
And now what are you doing?!
Walking into an eatery covered in stench, carrying some dirty stray!!

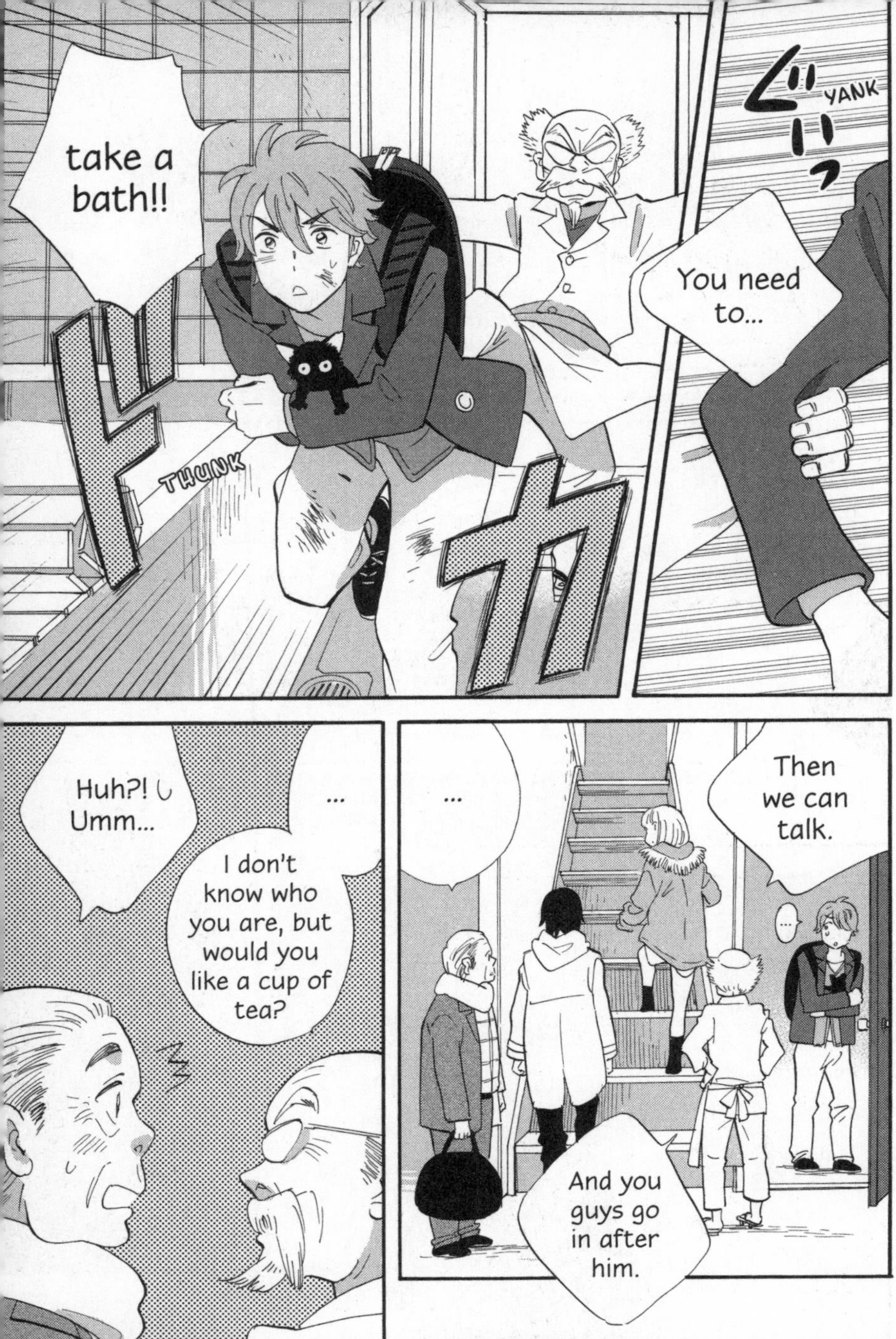
YANK
You need to...
take a bath!!
THUNK
Then we can talk.
...
...
And you guys go in after him.
...
Huh?! Umm...
I don't know who you are, but would you like a cup of tea?

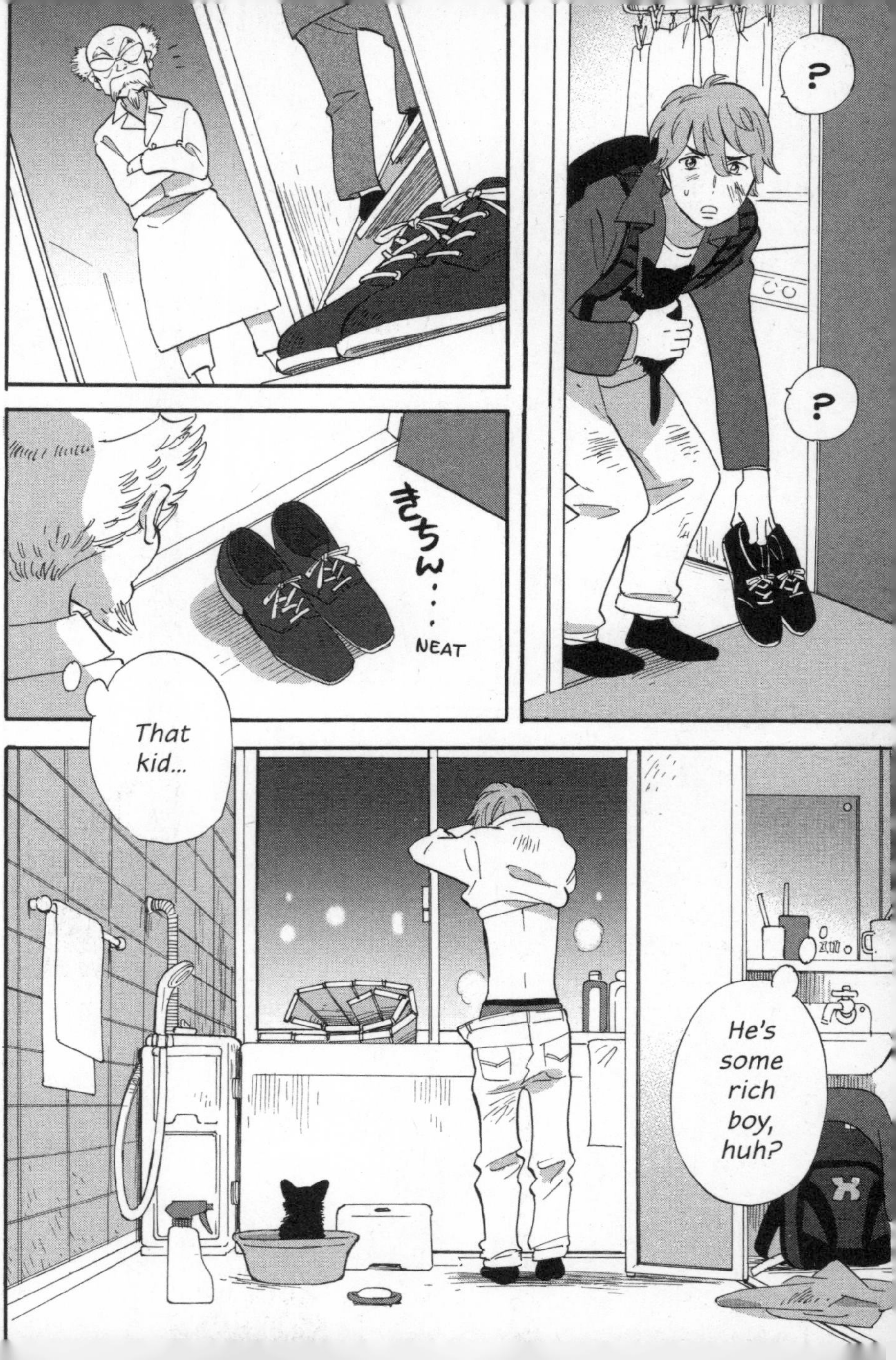
?
?
きちん・・・
NEAT
That kid...
He's some rich boy, huh?

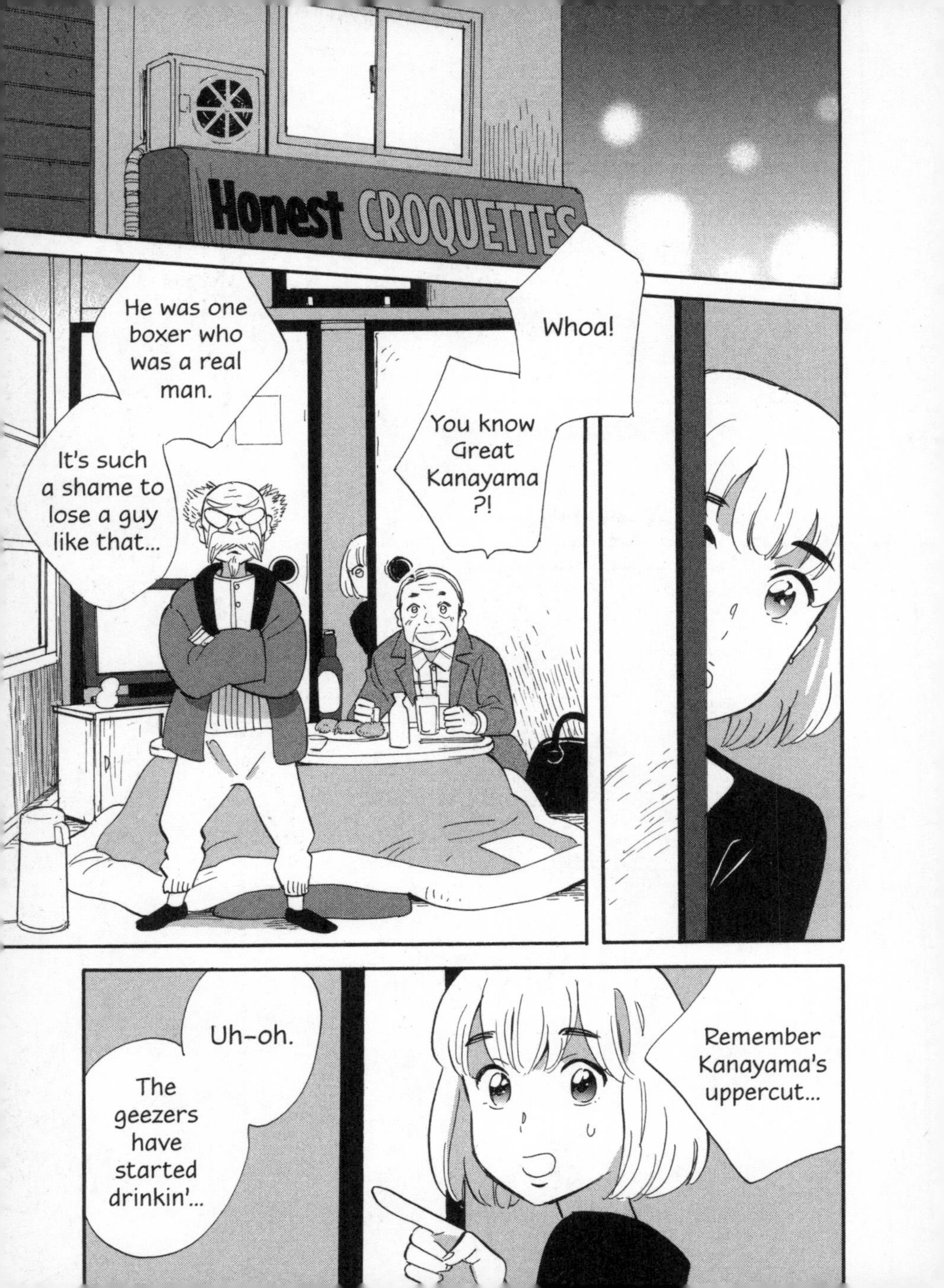
Honest CROQUETTES
Whoa!
You know Great Kanayama?!
He was one boxer who was a real man.
It's such a shame to lose a guy like that...
Remember Kanayama's uppercut...
Uh-oh.
The geezers have started drinkin'...

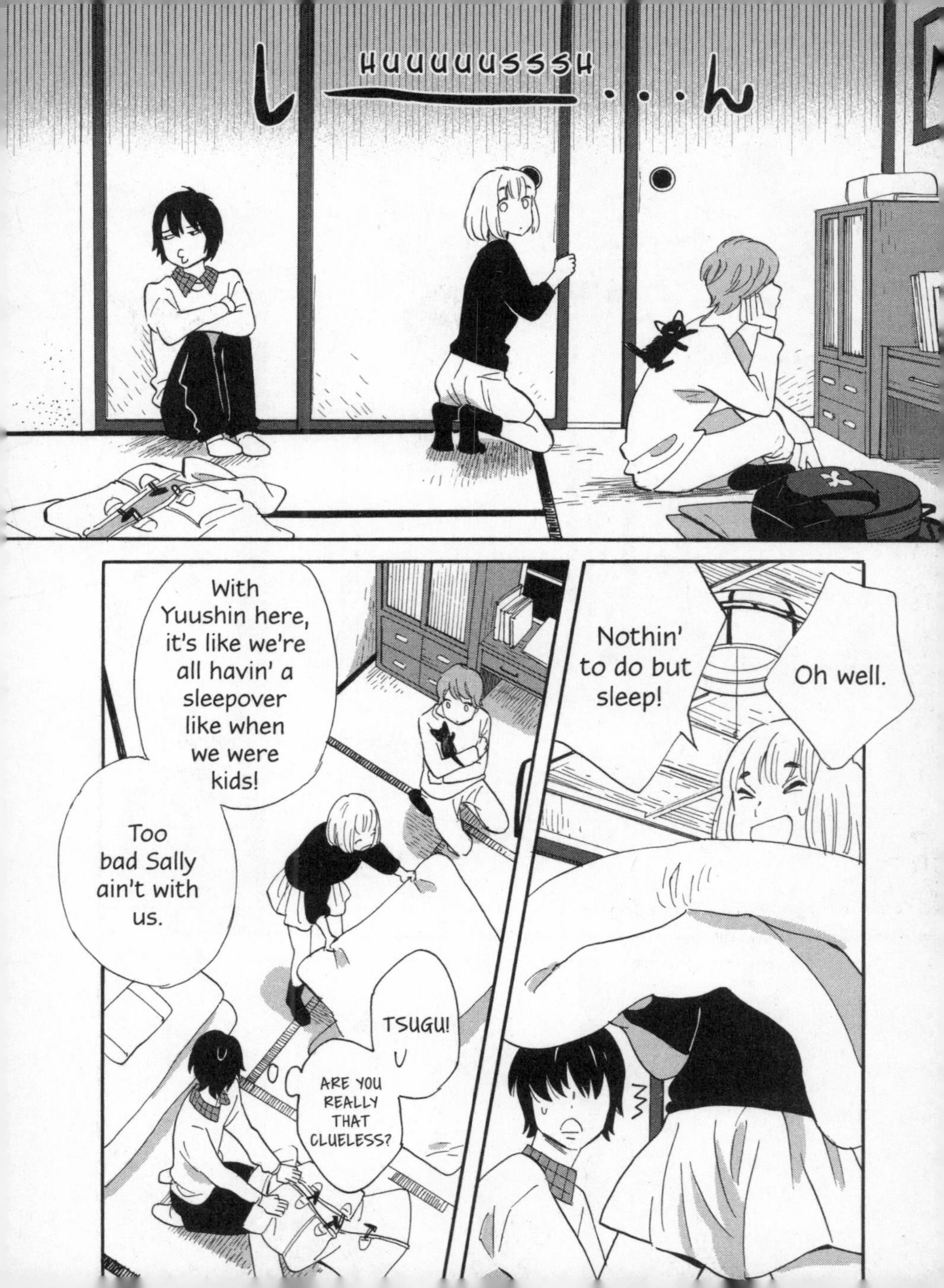
し———…ん
HUUUUUSSSH
Oh well.
Nothin' to do but sleep!
With Yuushin here, it's like we're all havin' a sleepover like when we were kids!
Too bad Sally ain't with us.
TSUGU!
ARE YOU REALLY THAT CLUELESS?

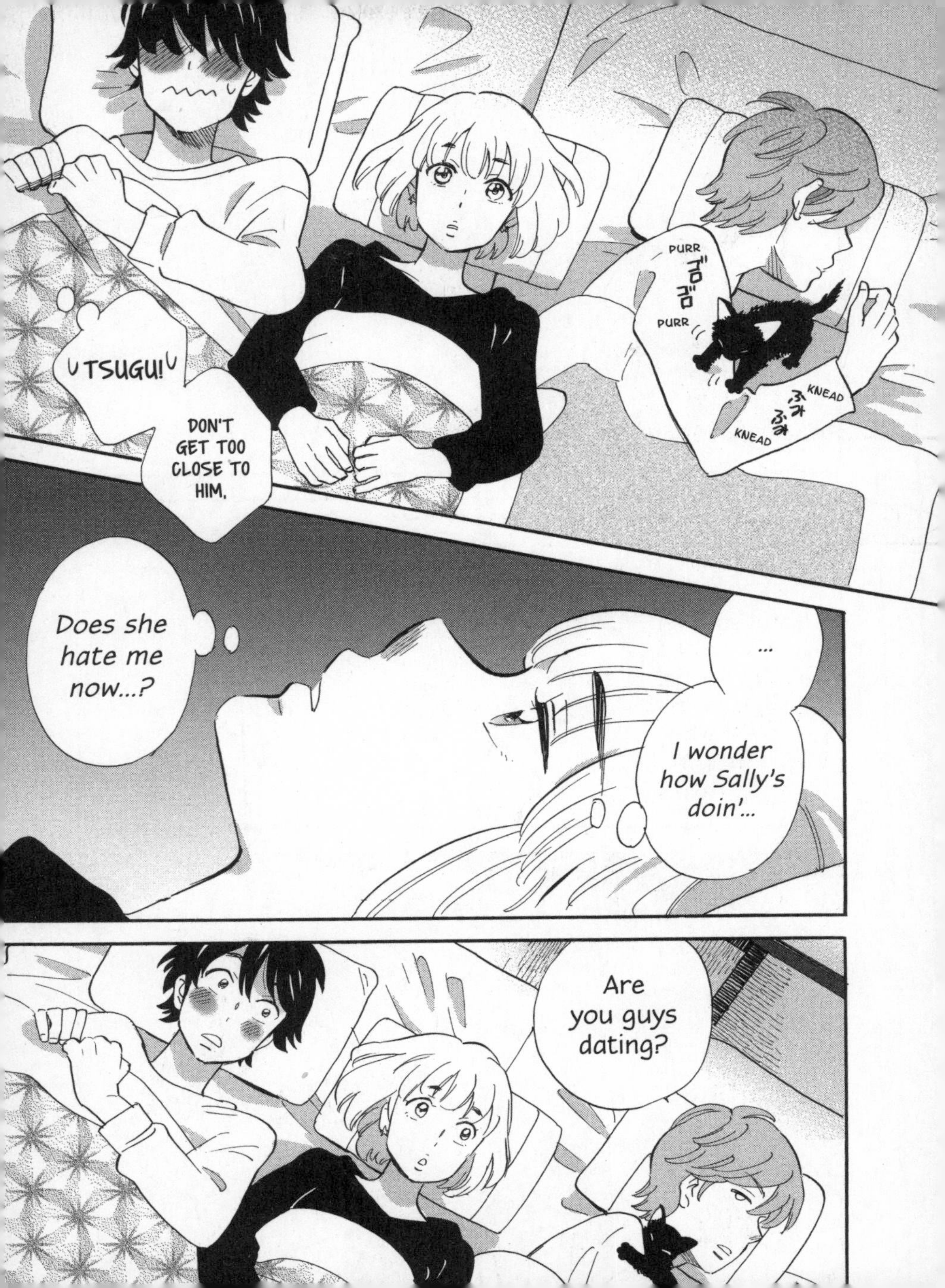
PURR
ゴロゴロ
PURR
KNEAD
ふみふみ
KNEAD
TSUGU!
DON'T GET TOO CLOSE TO HIM.
...
I wonder how Sally's doin'...
Does she hate me now...?
Are you guys dating?

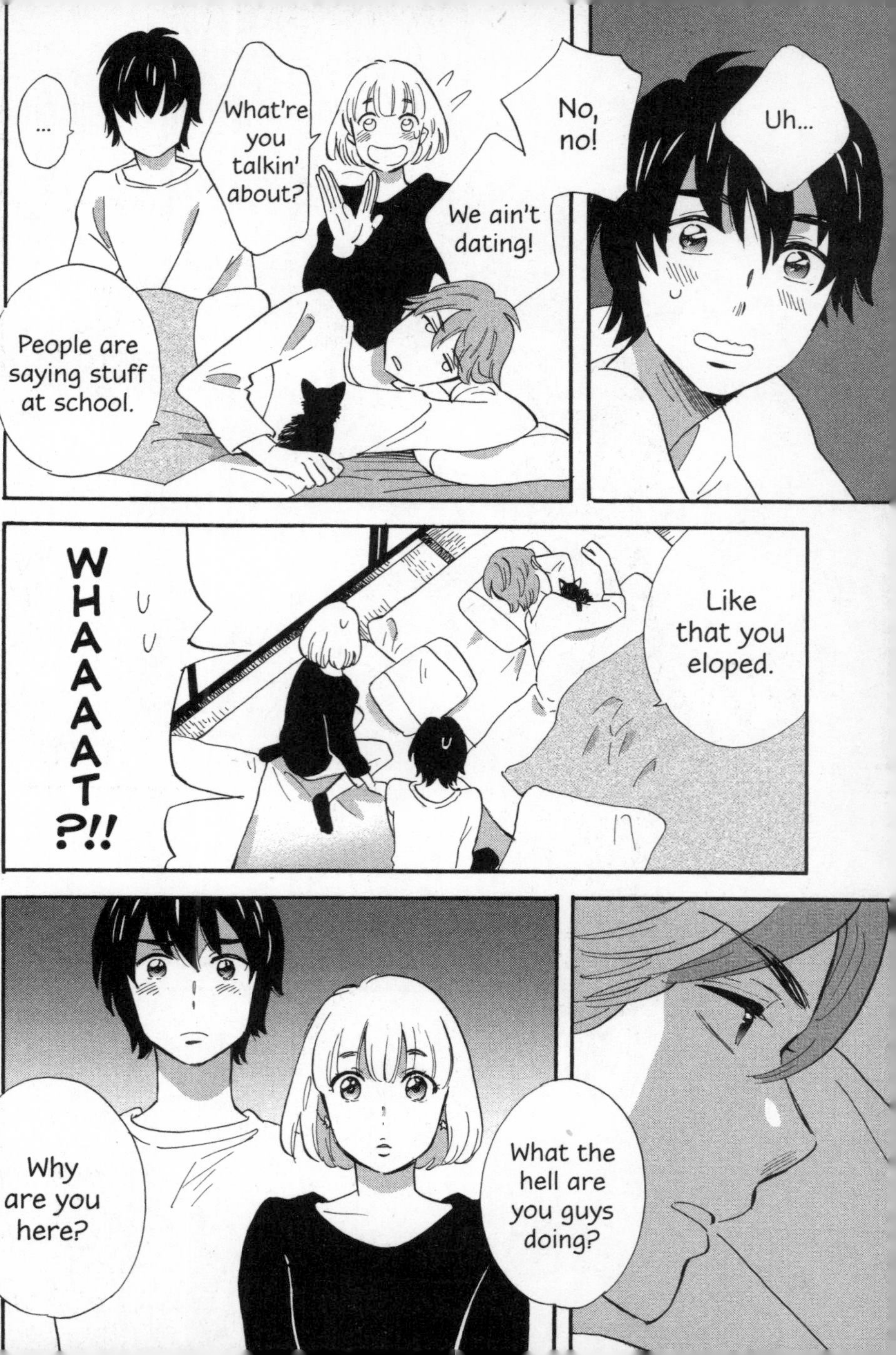
Uh...
No, no!
We ain't dating!
What're you talkin' about?
...
People are saying stuff at school.
Like that you eloped.
WHAAAAAT?!!
What the hell are you guys doing?
Why are you here?

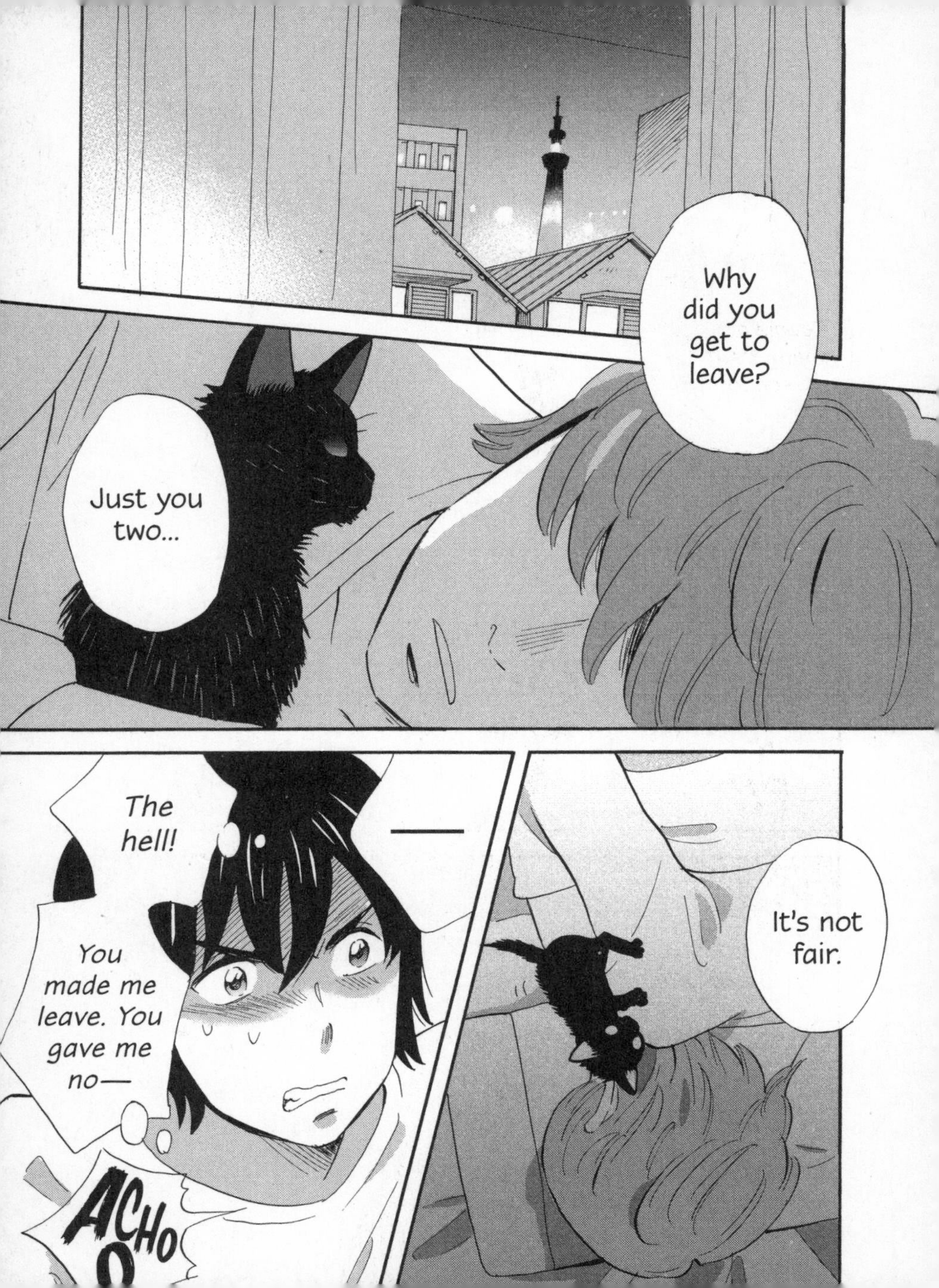
Why did you get to leave?
Just you two...
It's not fair.
The hell!
—
You made me leave. You gave me no—
ACHOO

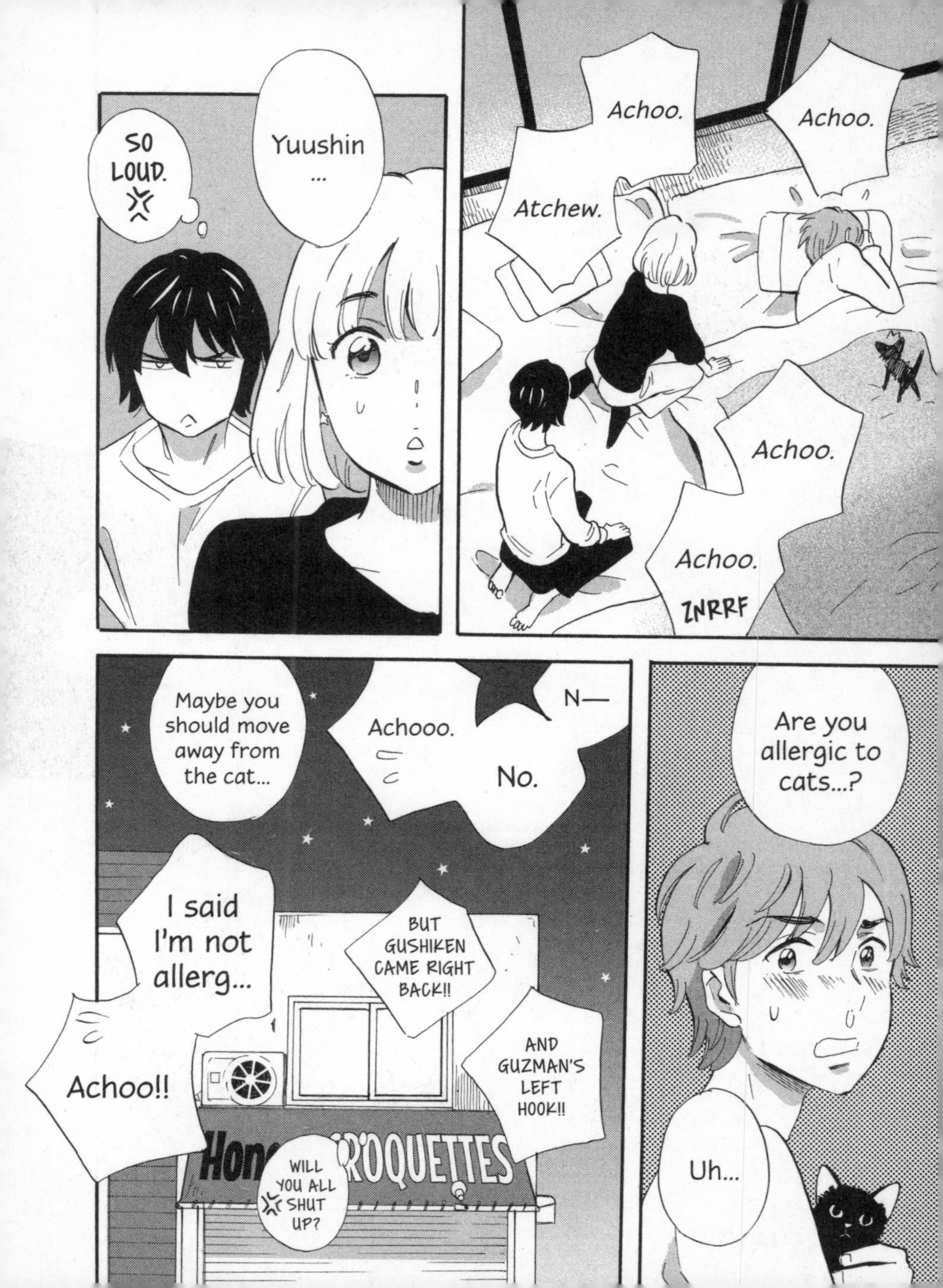

Achoo.
Achoo.
Atchew.
Achoo.
Achoo.
ZNRRF
Yuushin ...
SO LOUD.
Are you allergic to cats...?
Uh...
N—
No.
Achooo.
Maybe you should move away from the cat...
I said I'm not allerg...
Achoo!!
BUT GUSHIKEN CAME RIGHT BACK!!
AND GUZMAN'S LEFT HOOK!!
WILL YOU ALL SHUT UP?

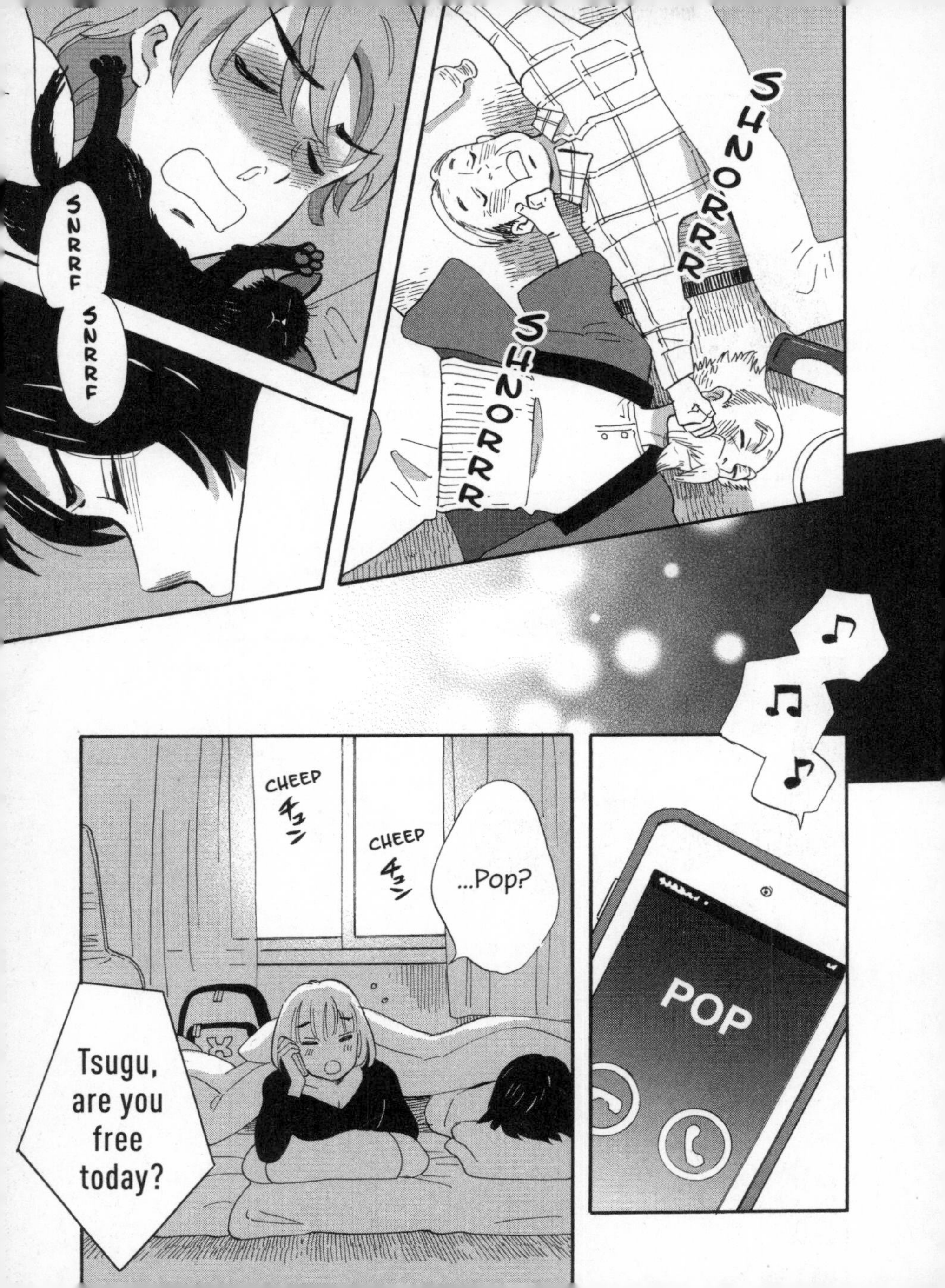
SHNORRR
SHNORRR
SNRRF
SNRRF
POP
CHEEP チュン
CHEEP チュン
...Pop?
Tsugu, are you free today?

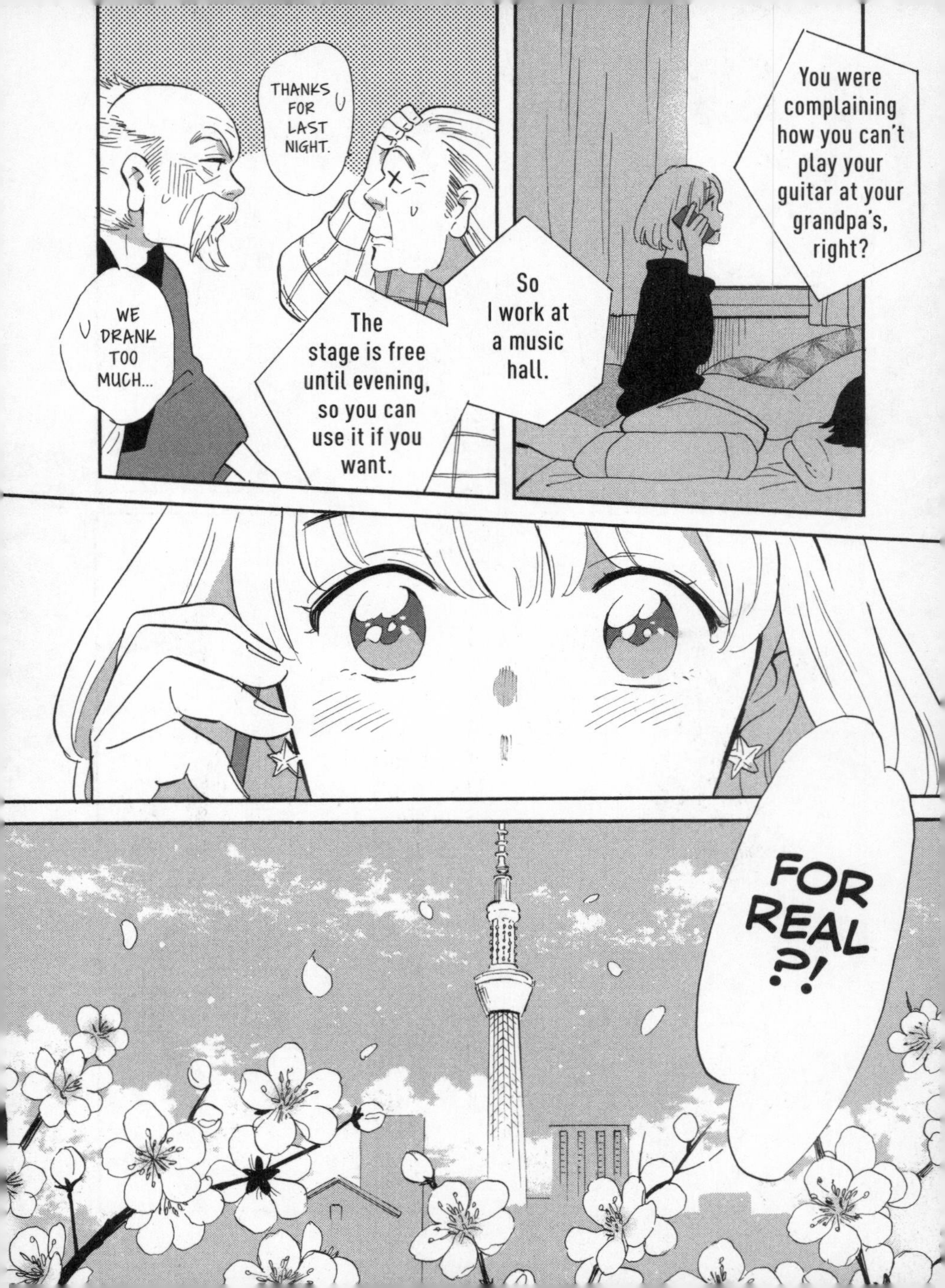
You were complaining how you can't play your guitar at your grandpa's, right?
So I work at a music hall.
The stage is free until evening, so you can use it if you want.
THANKS FOR LAST NIGHT.
WE DRANK TOO MUCH...
FOR REAL?!

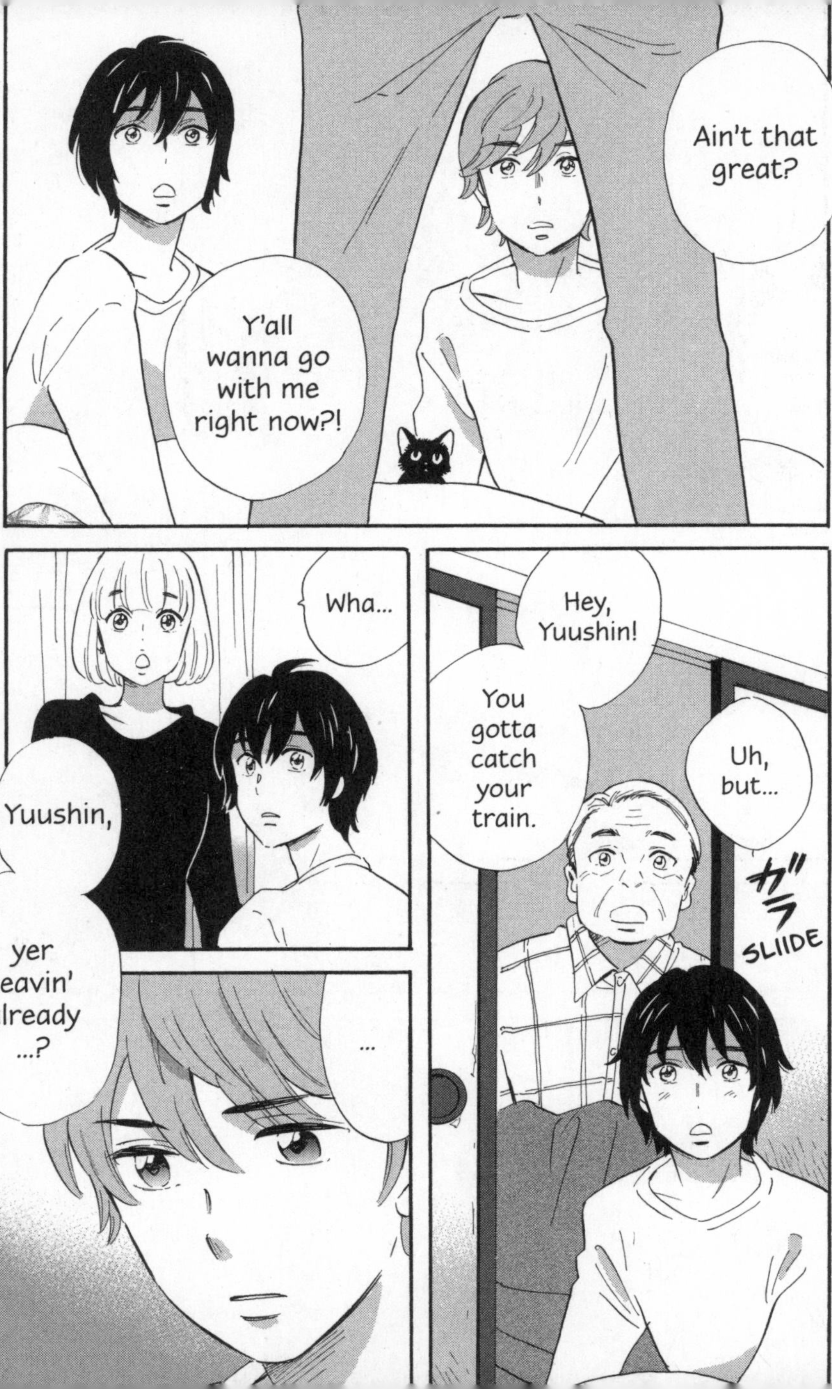
Ain't that great?
Y'all wanna go with me right now?!
Hey, Yuushin!
You gotta catch your train.
Uh, but...
ガラ
SLIIDE
Wha...
Yuushin,
yer leavin' already ...?
...

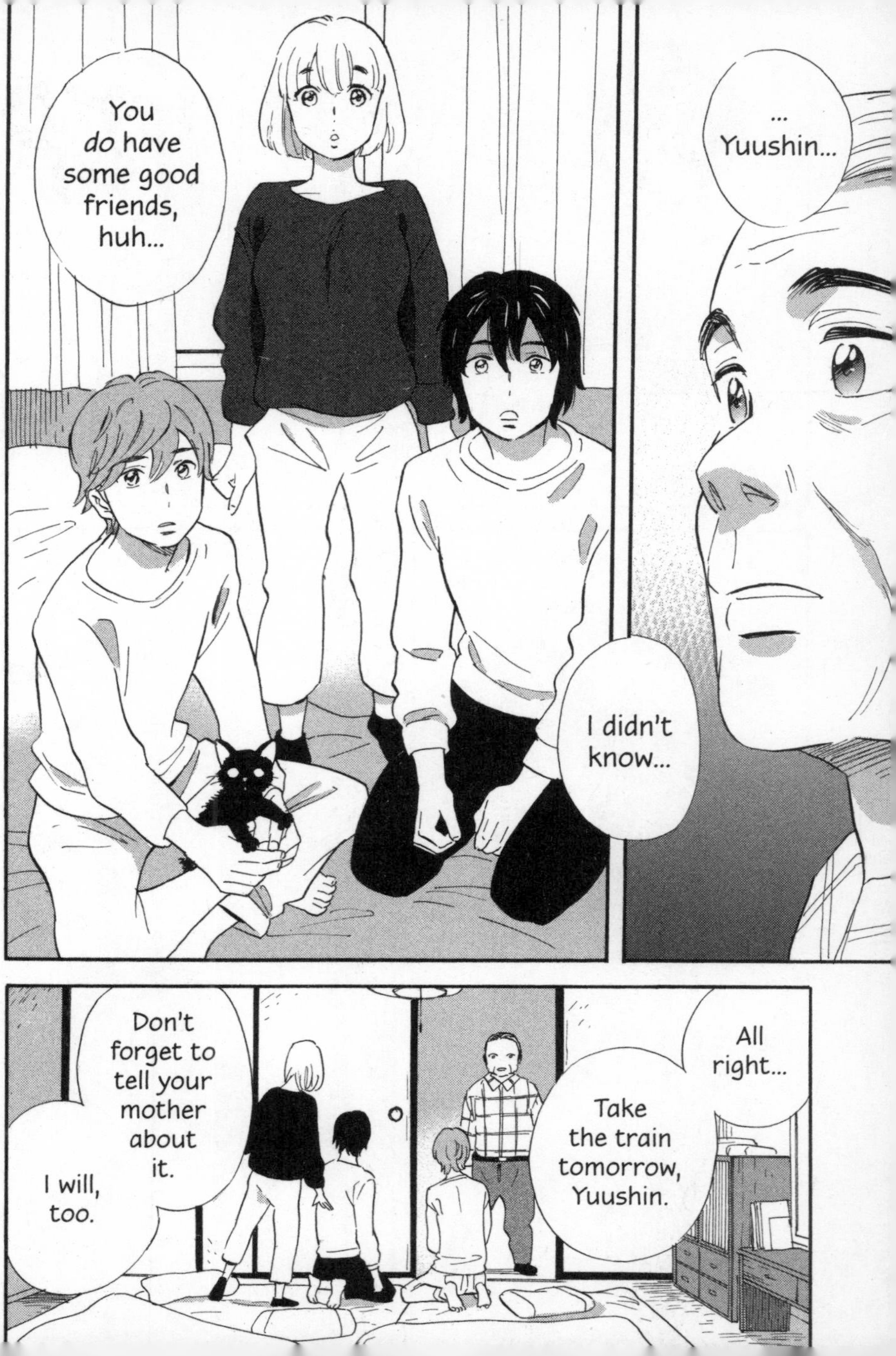
... Yuushin...
I didn't know...
You *do* have some good friends, huh...
All right...
Take the train tomorrow, Yuushin.
Don't forget to tell your mother about it.
I will, too.

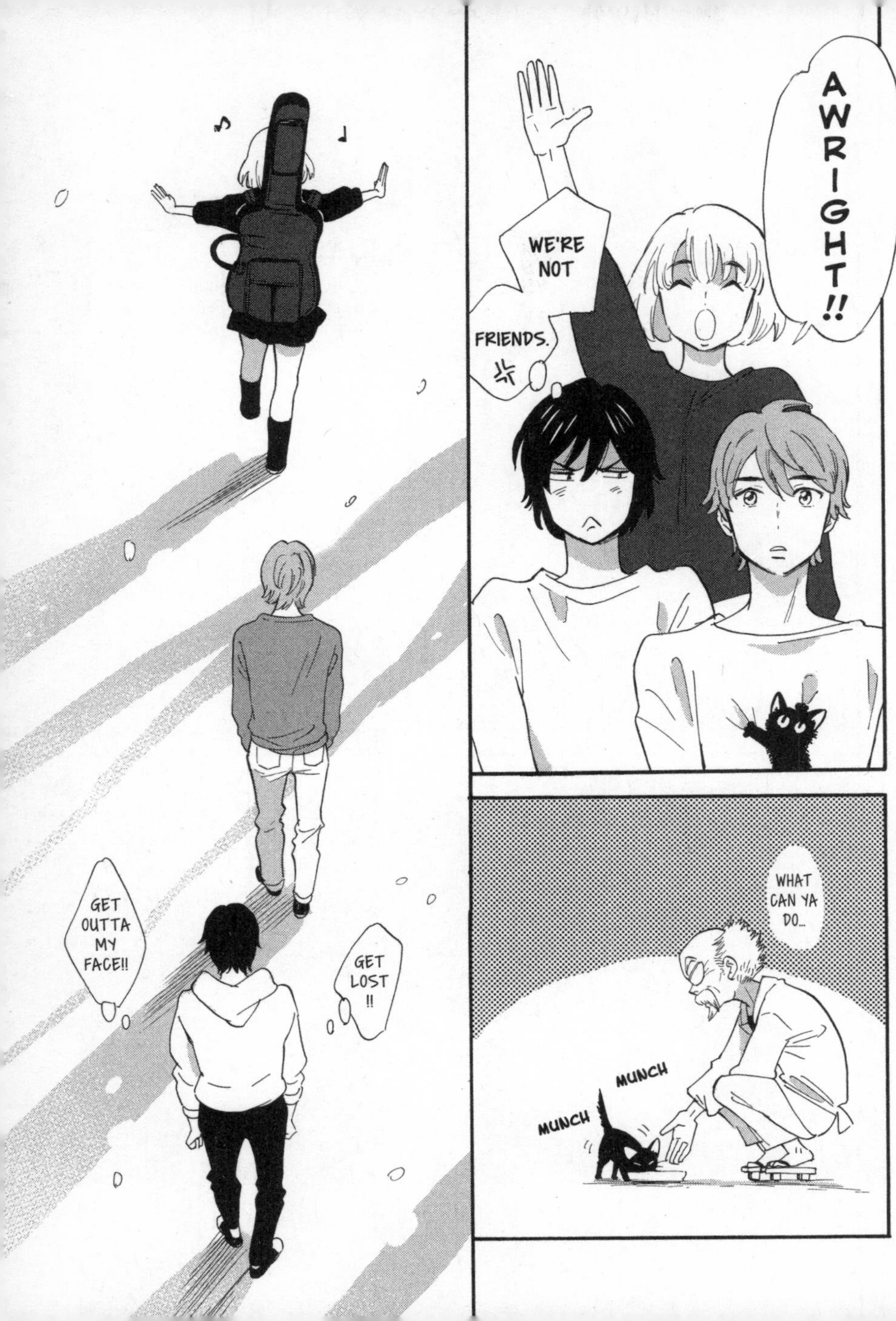
AWRIGHT!!
WE'RE NOT FRIENDS.
WHAT CAN YA DO...
MUNCH
MUNCH
GET LOST!!
GET OUTTA MY FACE!!

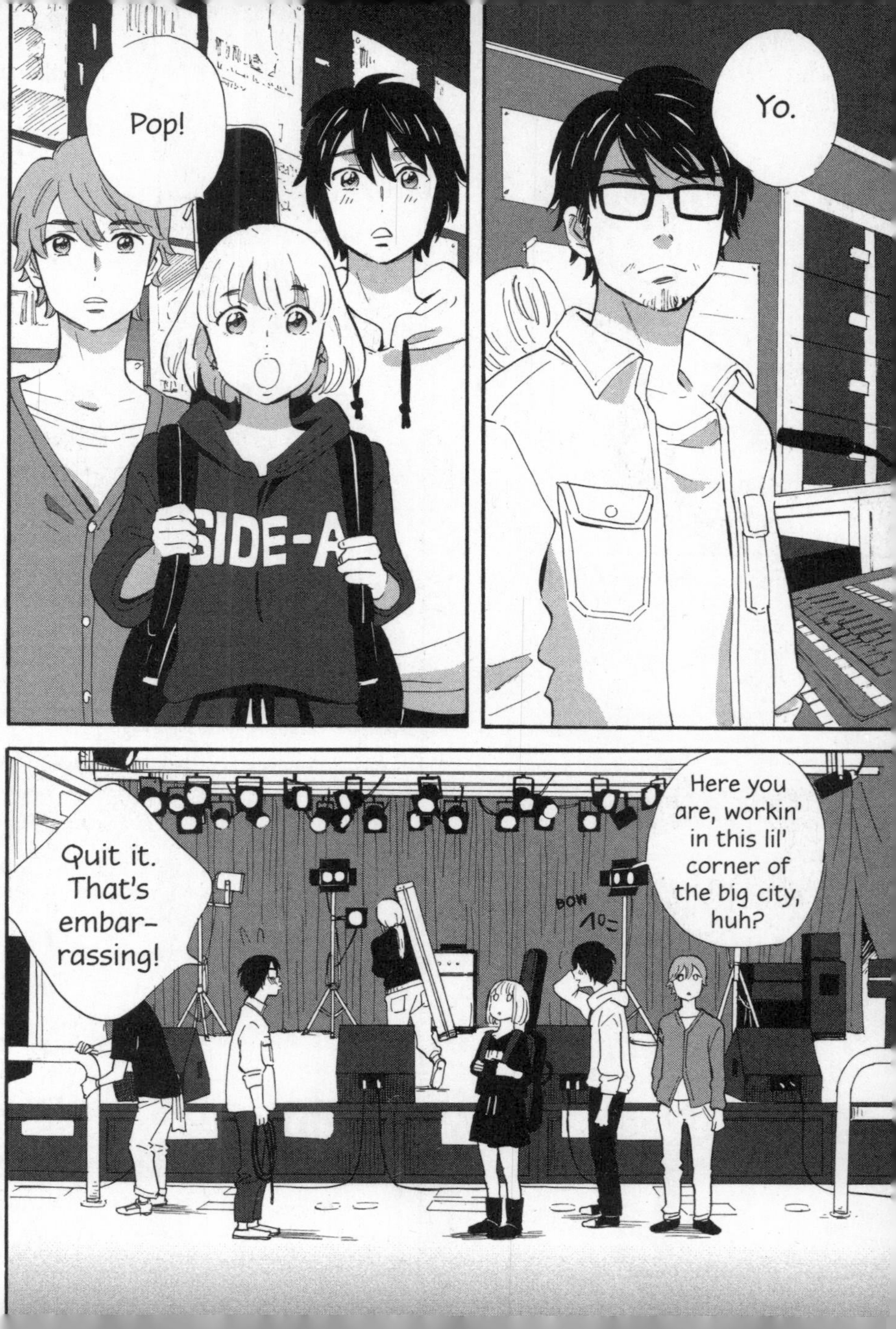
Yo.
Pop!
SIDE-A
Here you are, workin' in this lil' corner of the big city, huh?
BOW
Quit it. That's embar-rassing!

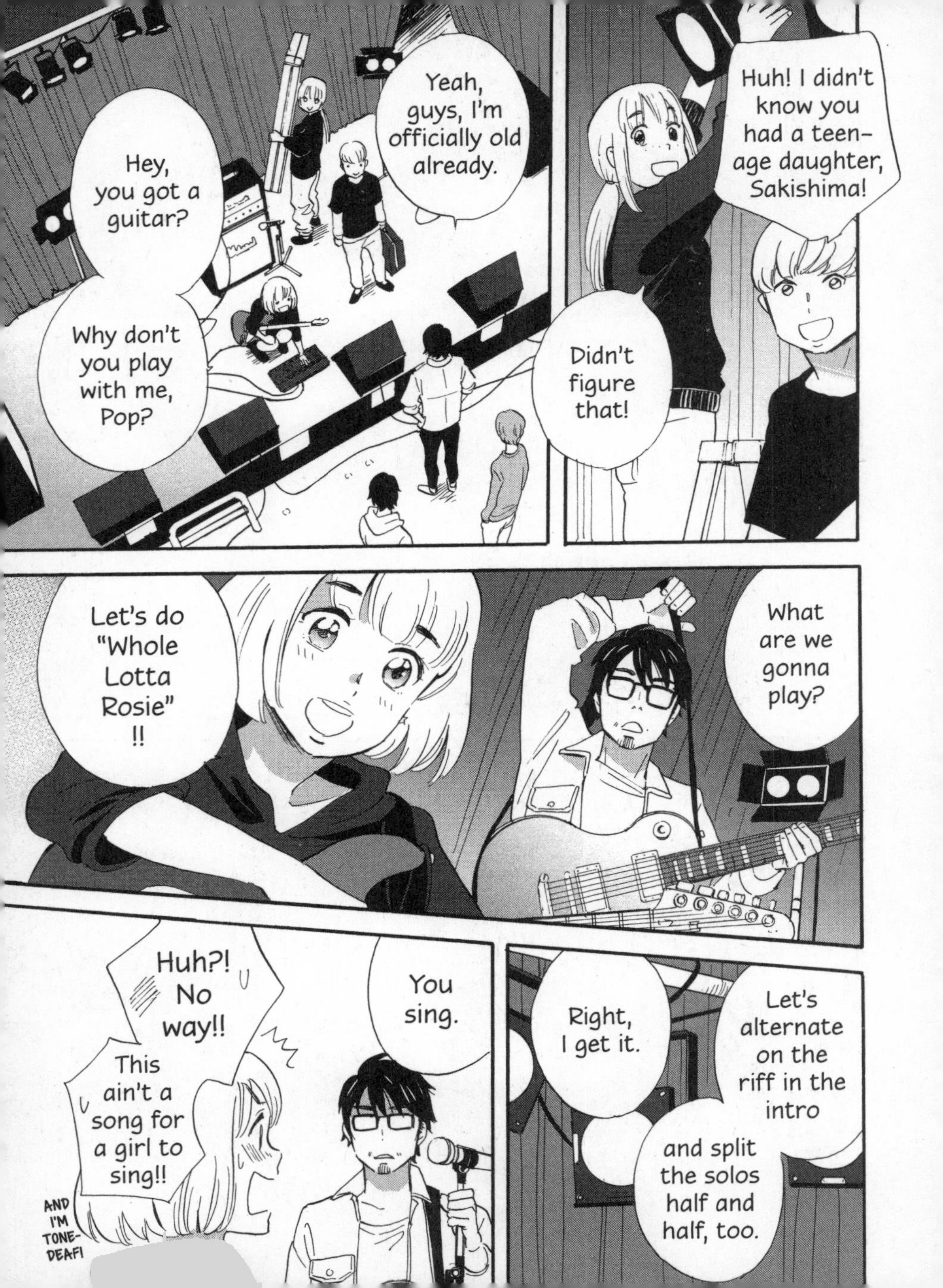
Huh! I didn't know you had a teen-age daughter, Sakishima!
Didn't figure that!
Yeah, guys, I'm officially old already.
Hey, you got a guitar?
Why don't you play with me, Pop?
What are we gonna play?
Let's do "Whole Lotta Rosie" !!
Let's alternate on the riff in the intro
Right, I get it.
and split the solos half and half, too.
You sing.
Huh?! No way!!
This ain't a song for a girl to sing!!
AND I'M TONE-DEAF!

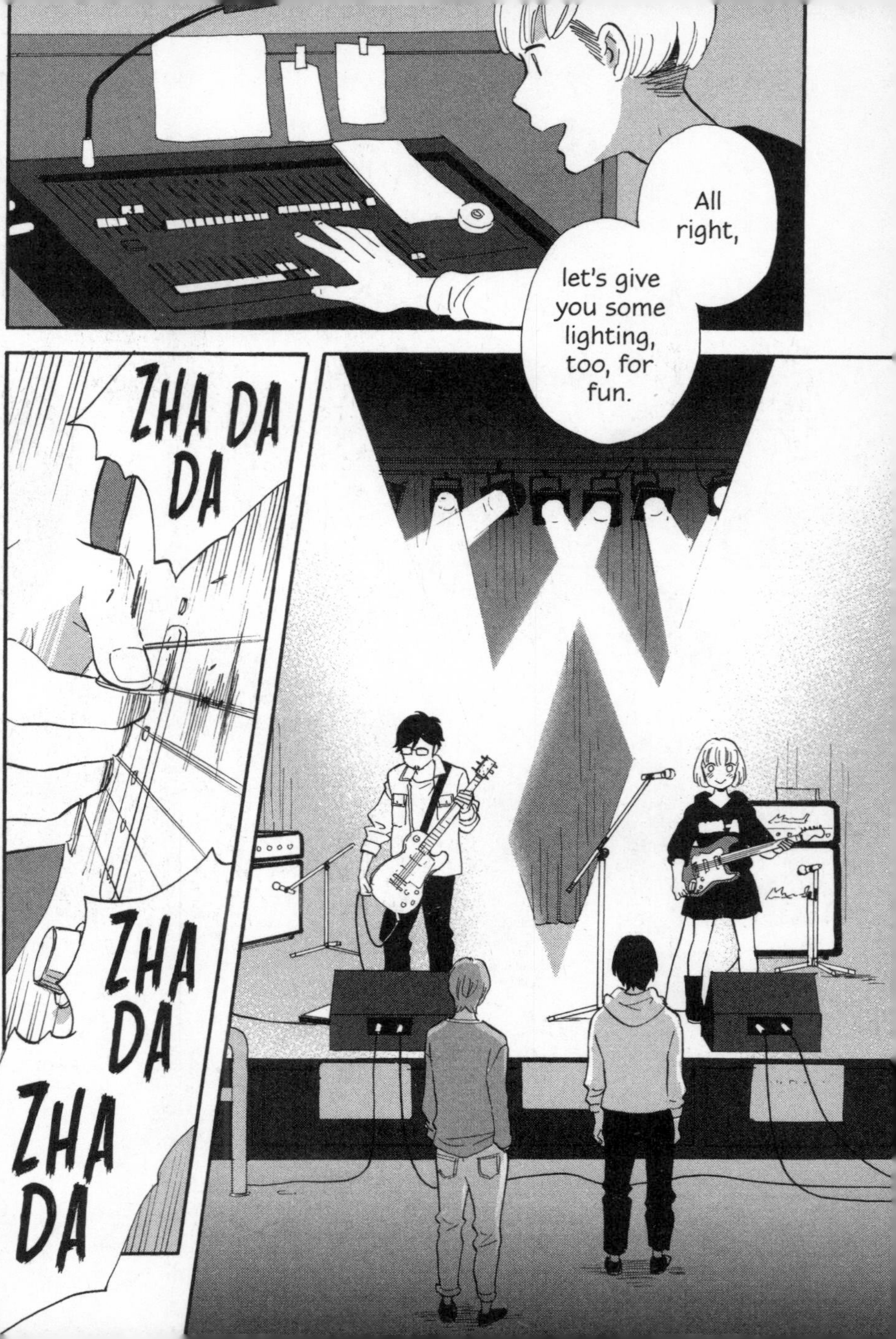
All right, let's give you some lighting, too, for fun.
ZHA DA DA
ZHA DA
ZHA DA

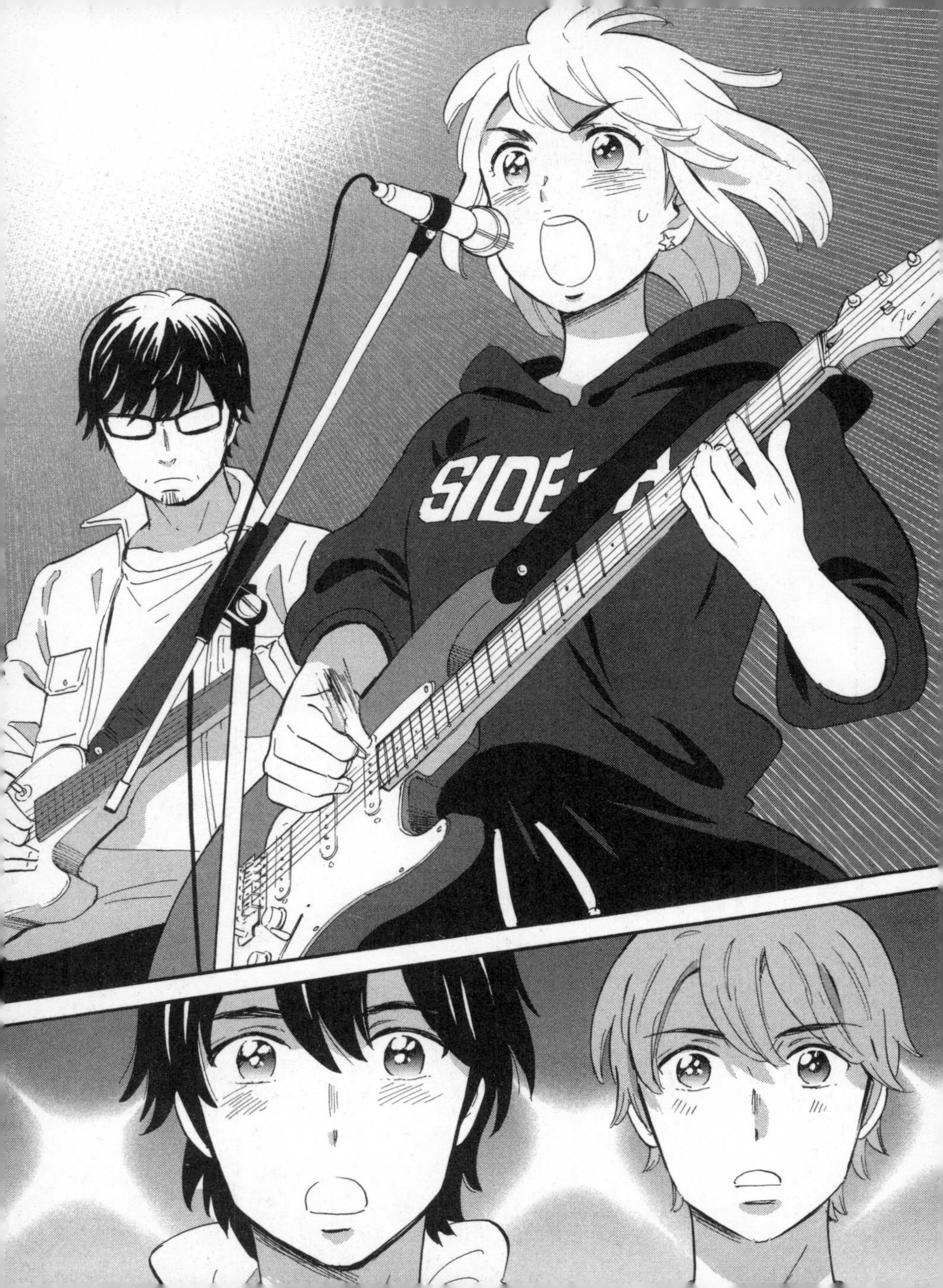

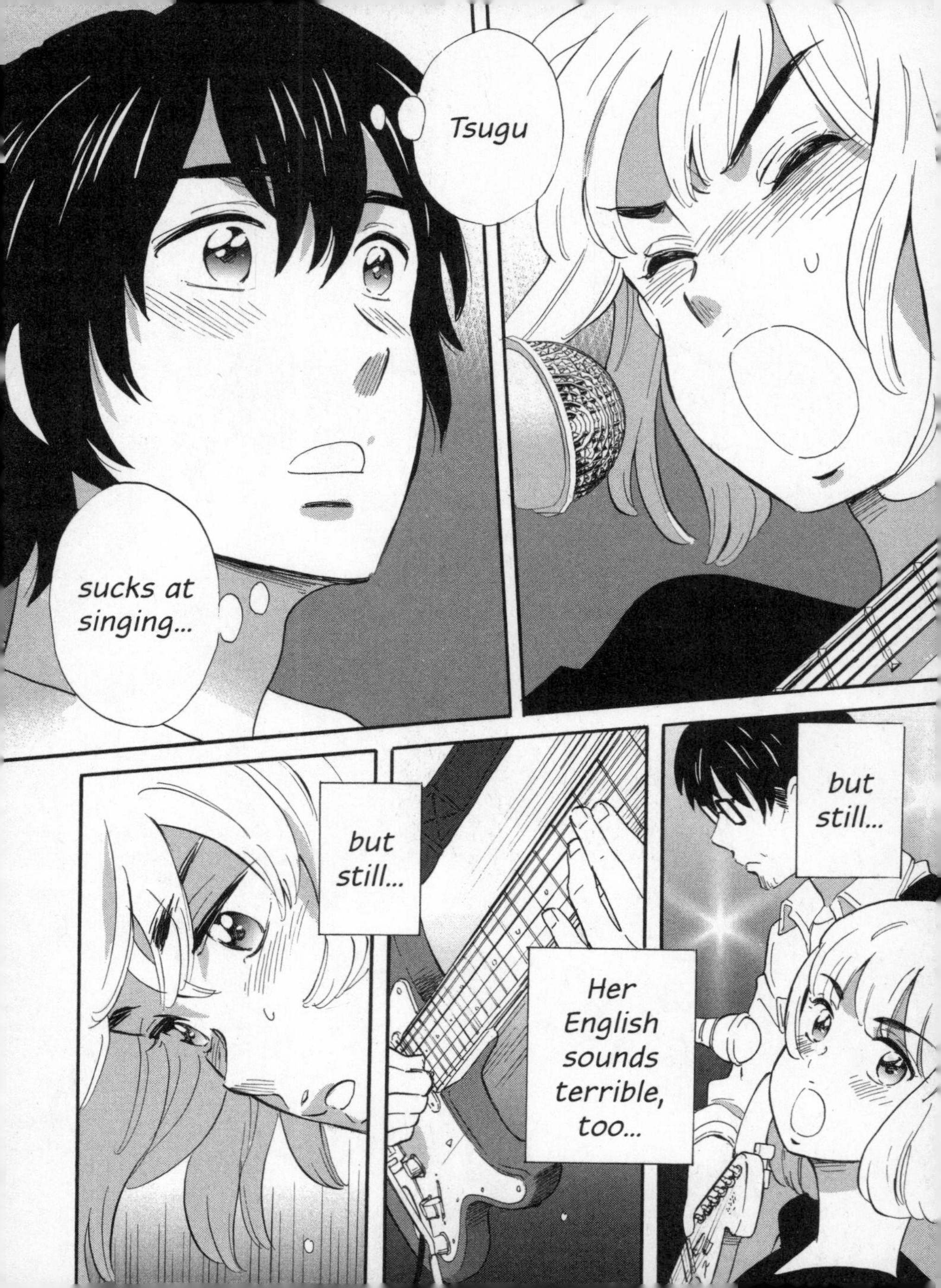
Tsugu
sucks at singing...
but still...
Her English sounds terrible, too...
but still...

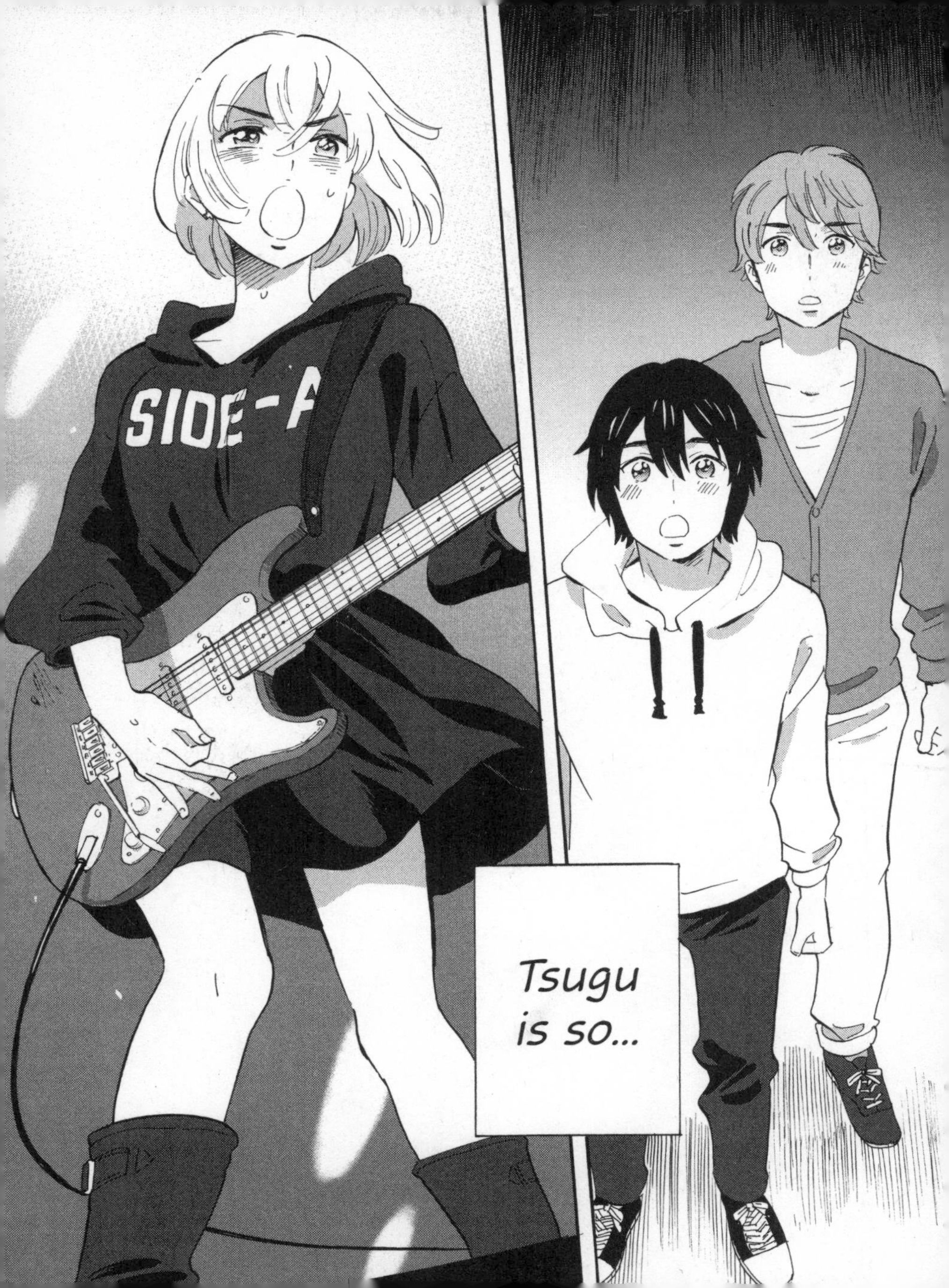
Tsugu is so...

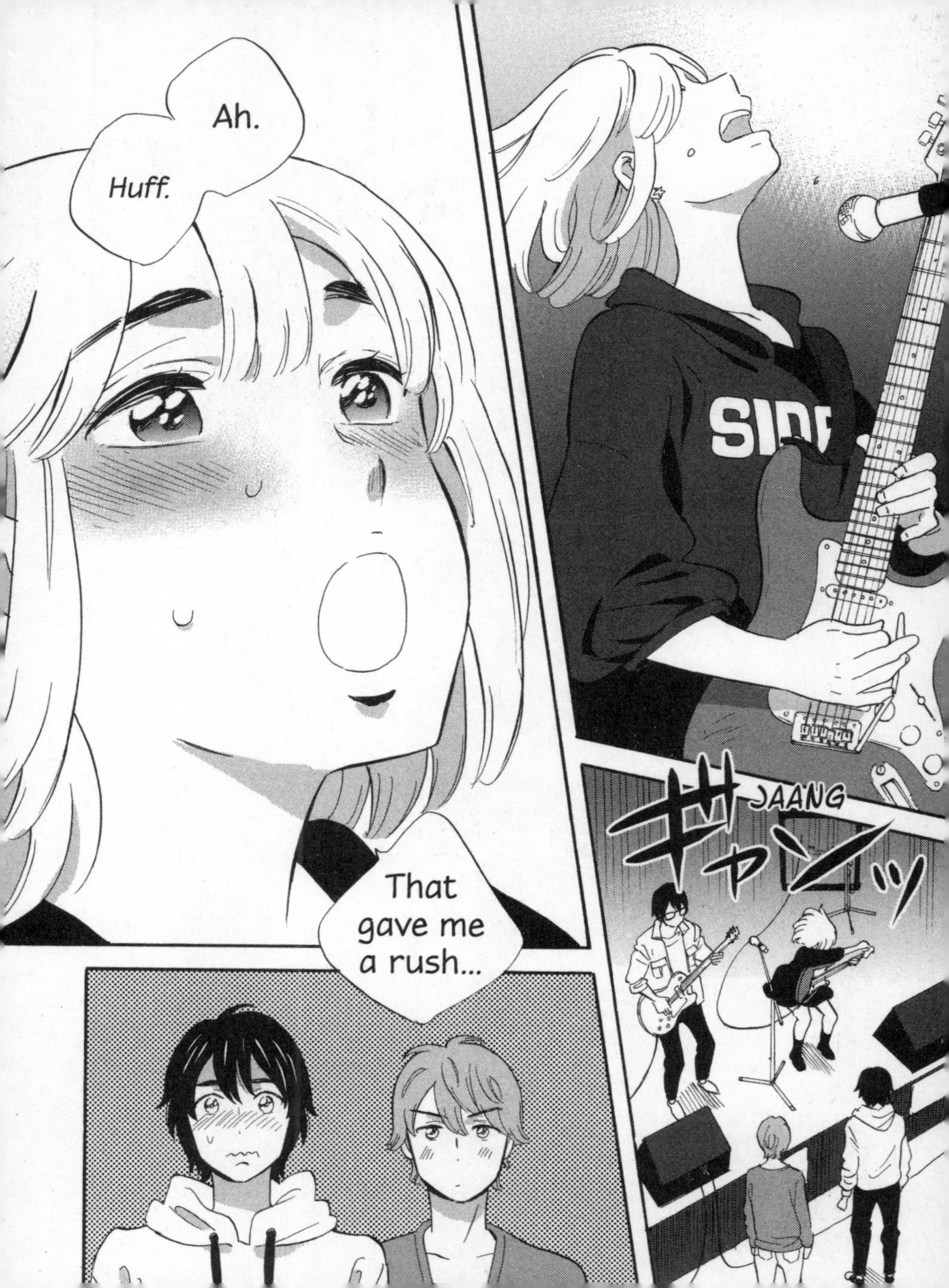
ギャンッ
JAANG
Ah.
Huff.
That gave me a rush...

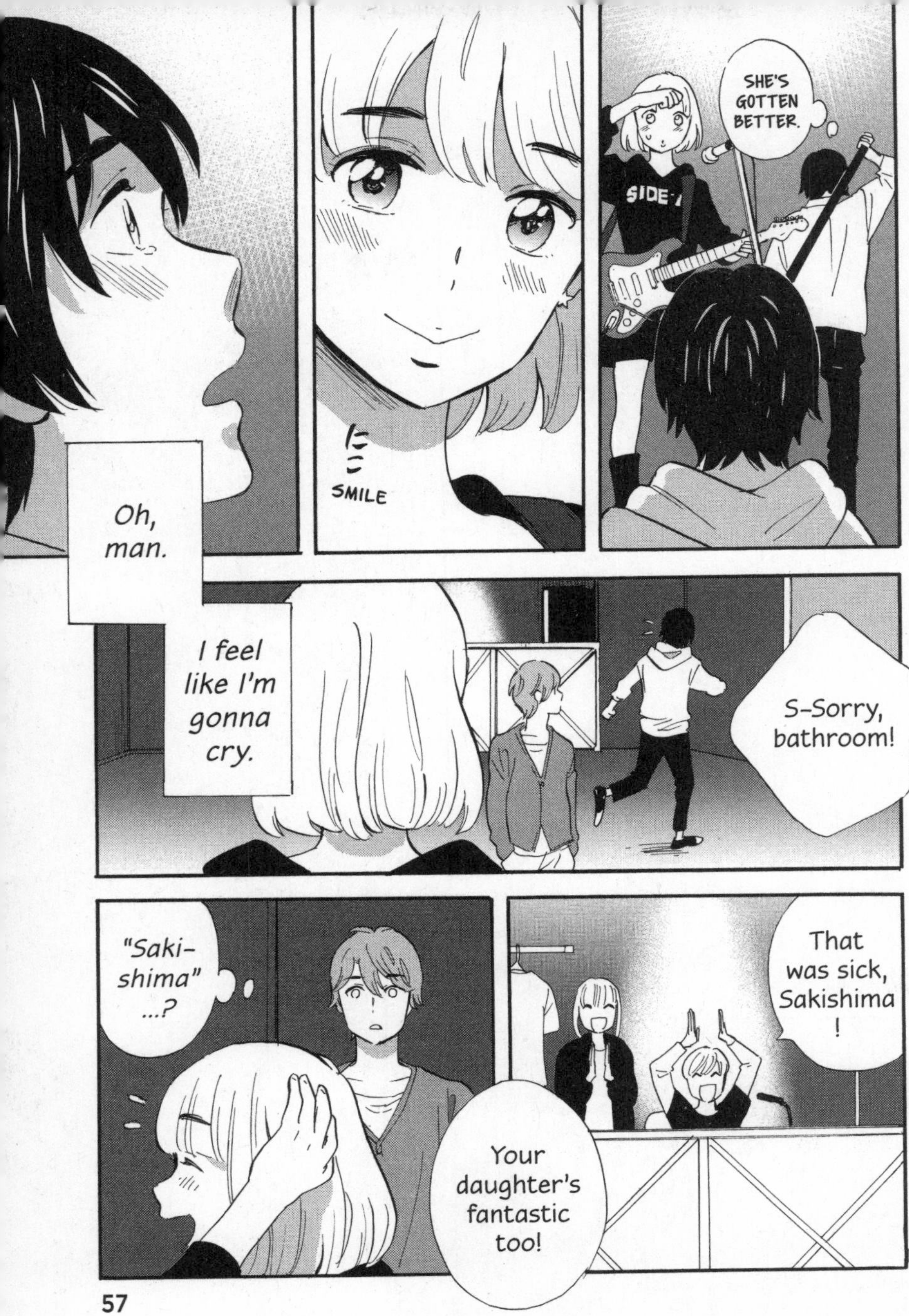

SHE'S GOTTEN BETTER.
SMILE
Oh, man.
I feel like I'm gonna cry.
S-Sorry, bathroom!
That was sick, Sakishima!
Your daughter's fantastic too!
"Saki-shima" ...?

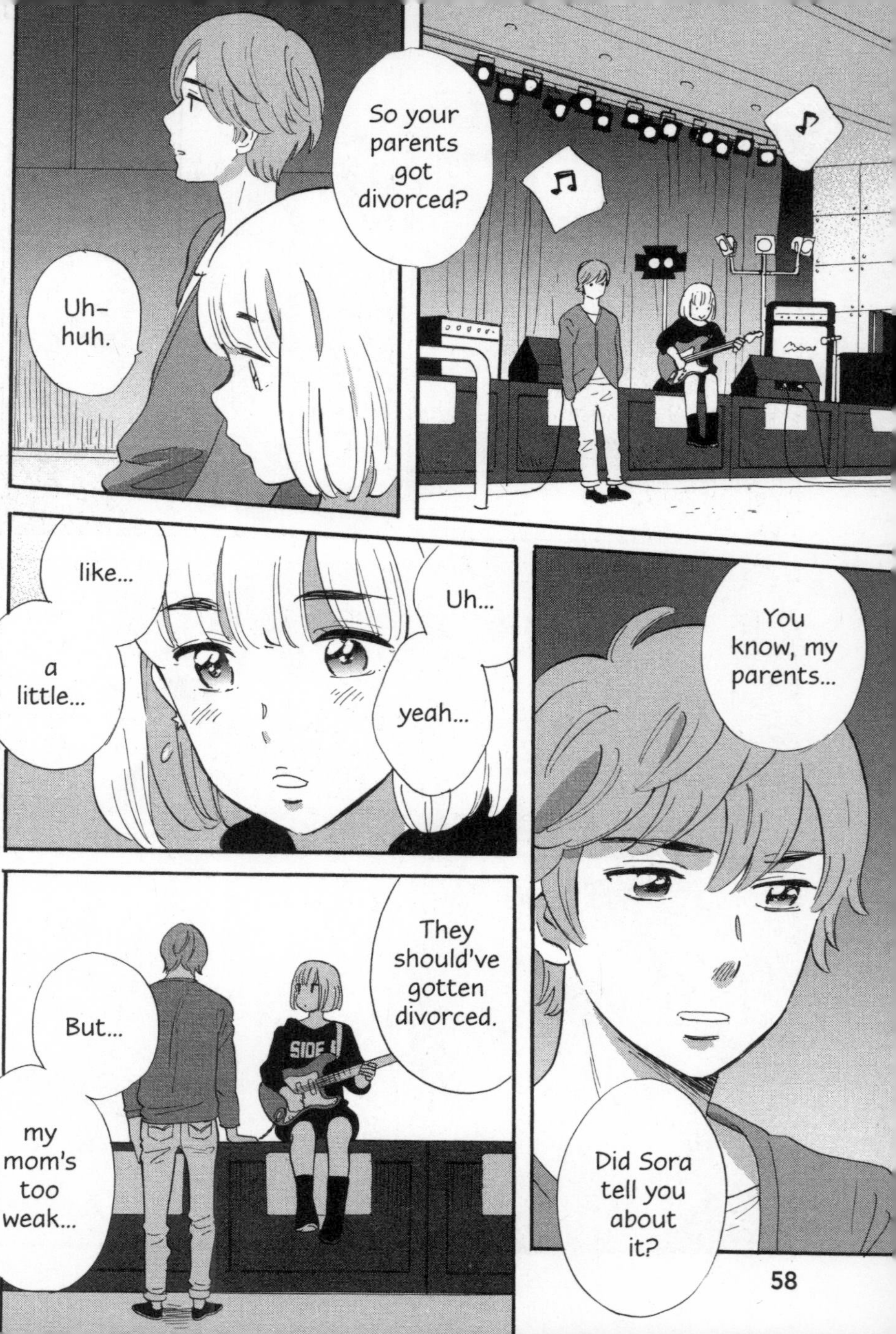
So your parents got divorced?
Uh-huh.
You know, my parents...
Did Sora tell you about it?
Uh...
yeah...
like...
a little...
They should've gotten divorced.
But...
my mom's too weak...
SIDE

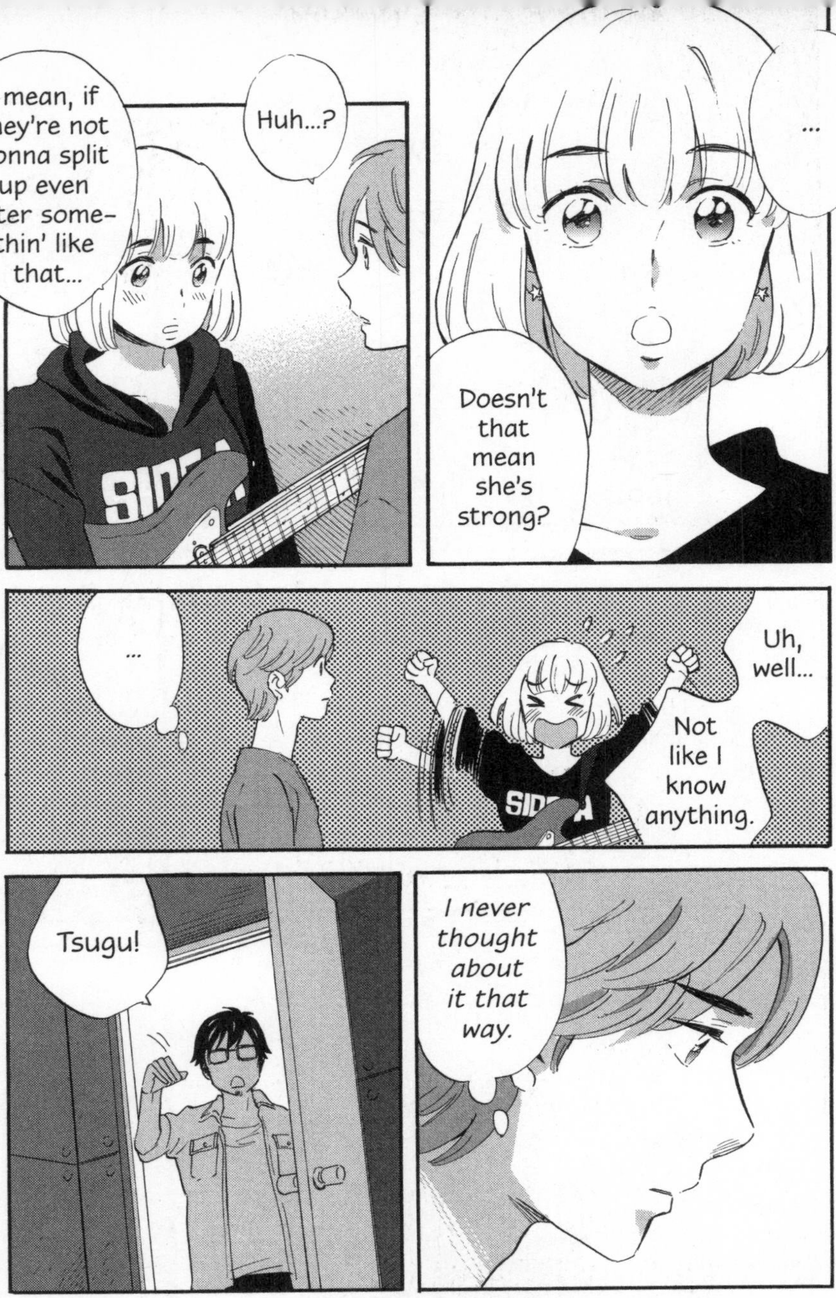
...
Doesn't that mean she's strong?
Huh...?
I mean, if they're not gonna split up even after some-thin' like that...
Uh, well...
Not like I know anything.
...
I never thought about it that way.
Tsugu!

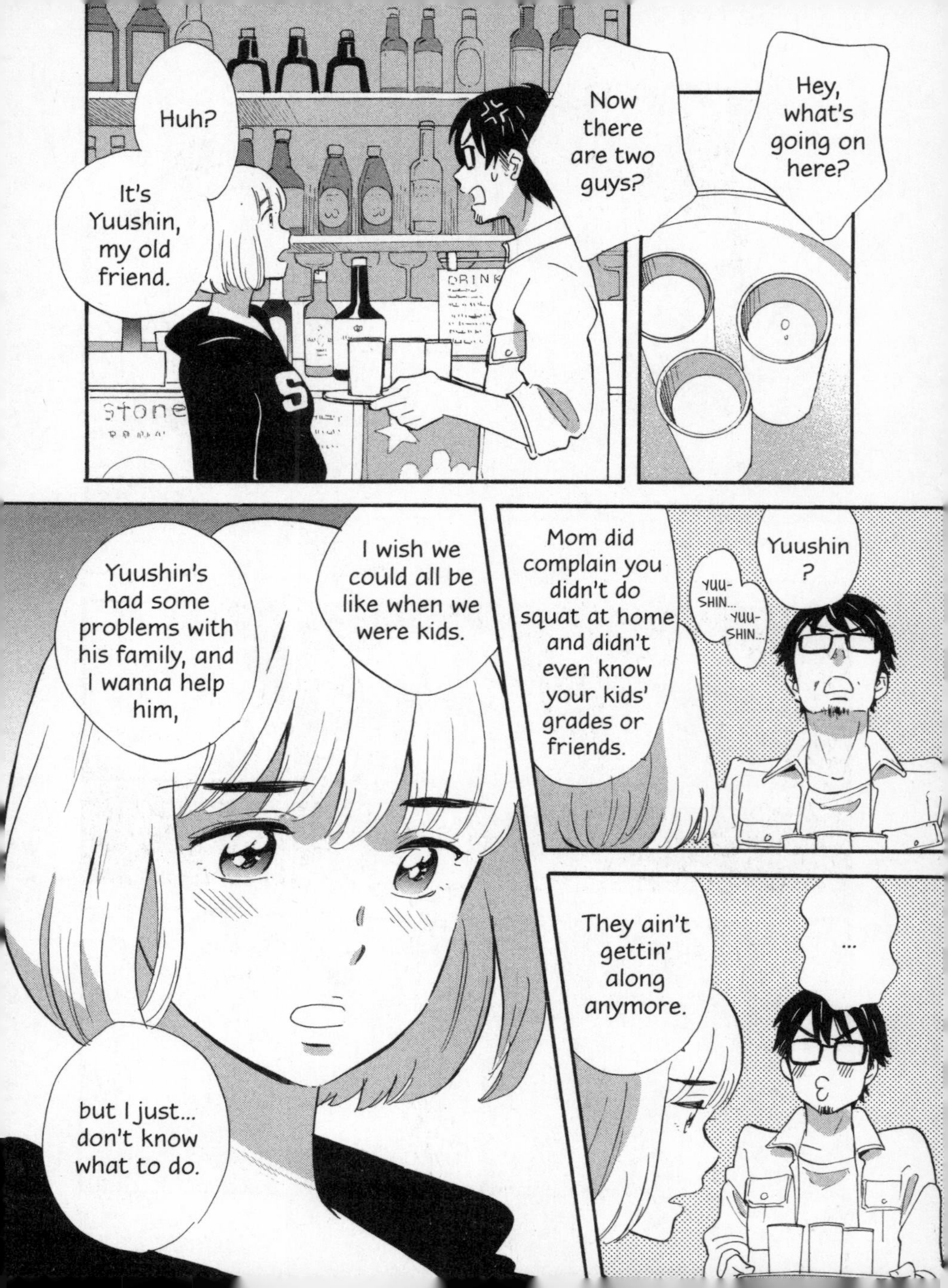
Hey, what's going on here?
Now there are two guys?
Huh?
It's Yuushin, my old friend.
DRINK
Stone
Yuushin?
YUU-SHIN... YUU-SHIN...
Mom did complain you didn't do squat at home and didn't even know your kids' grades or friends.
...
They ain't gettin' along anymore.
I wish we could all be like when we were kids.
Yuushin's had some problems with his family, and I wanna help him,
but I just... don't know what to do.

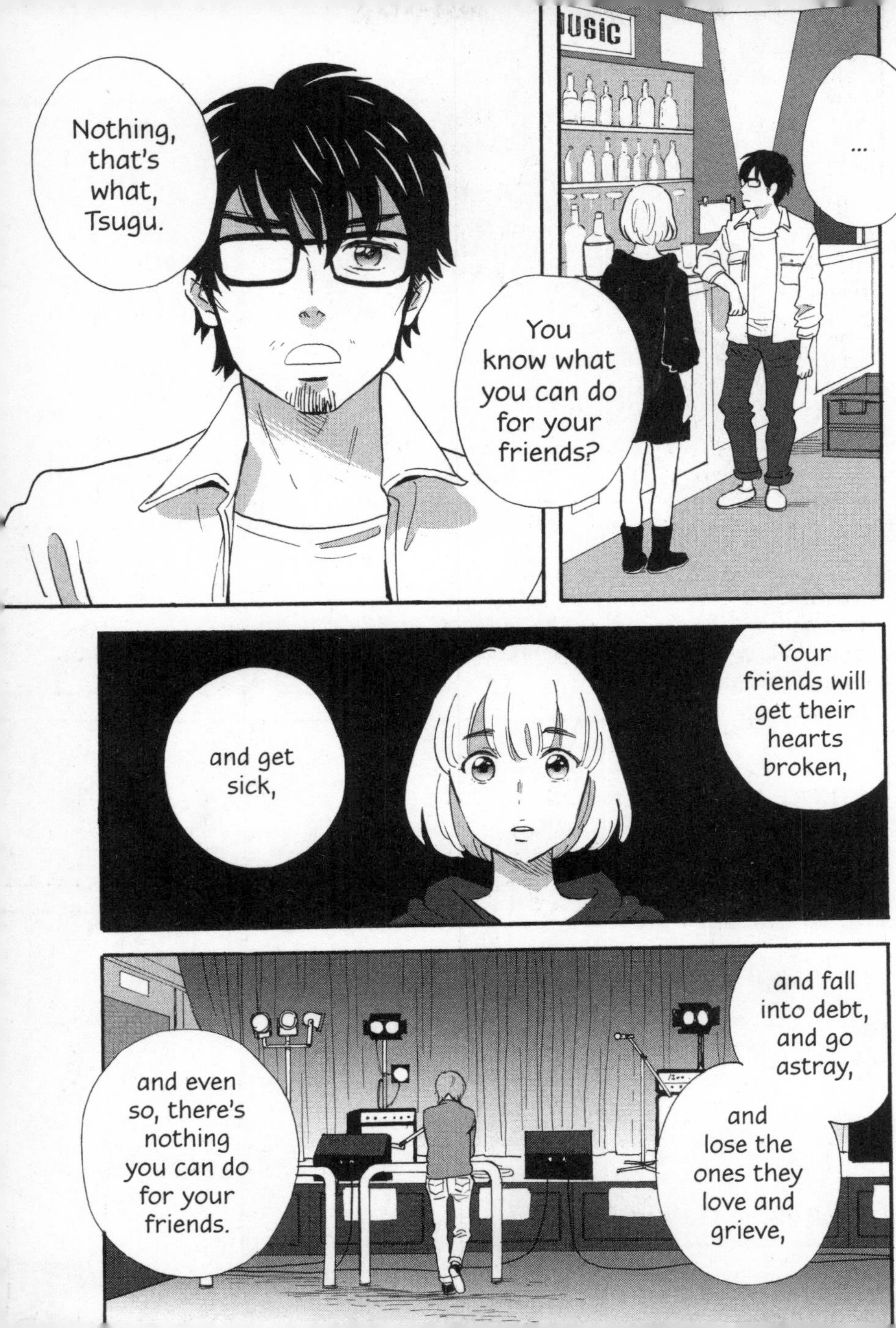
You know what you can do for your friends?
...
Nothing, that's what, Tsugu.
Your friends will get their hearts broken,
and get sick,
and fall into debt, and go astray,
and lose the ones they love and grieve,
and even so, there's nothing you can do for your friends.

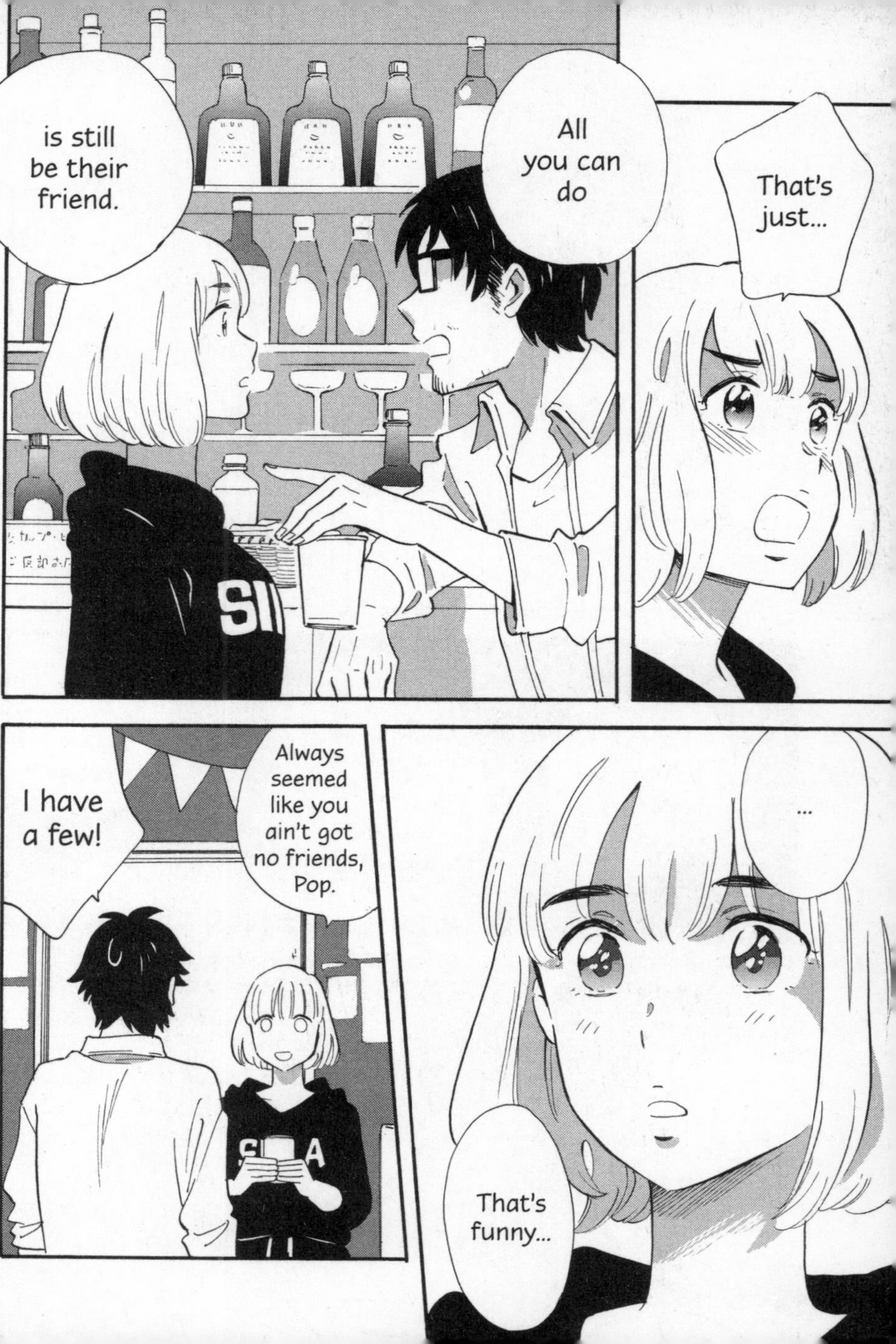
That's just...
All you can do
is still be their friend.
...
That's funny...
Always seemed like you ain't got no friends, Pop.
I have a few!

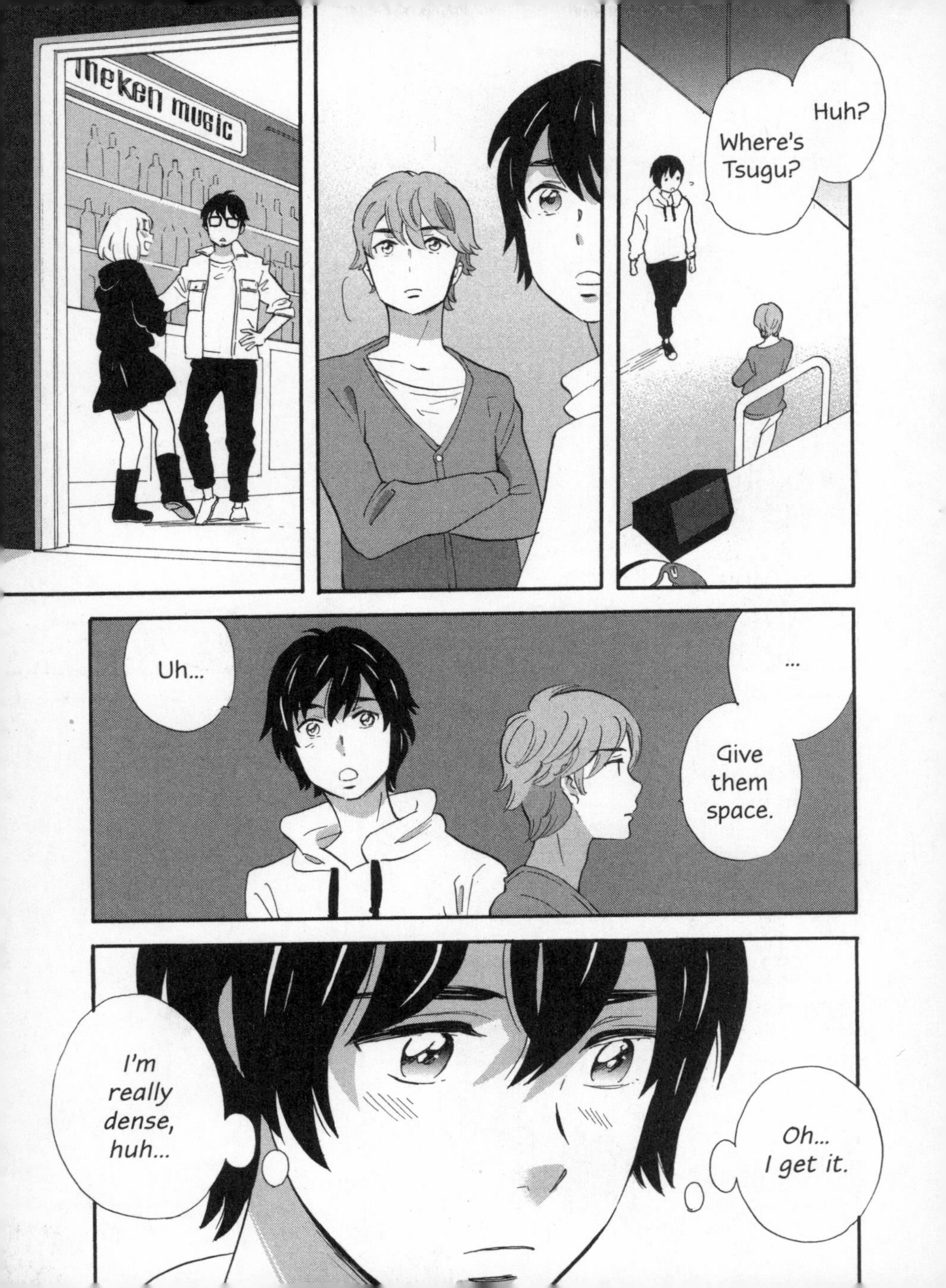
Huh? Where's Tsugu?
... Give them space.
Uh...
Oh... I get it.
I'm really dense, huh...

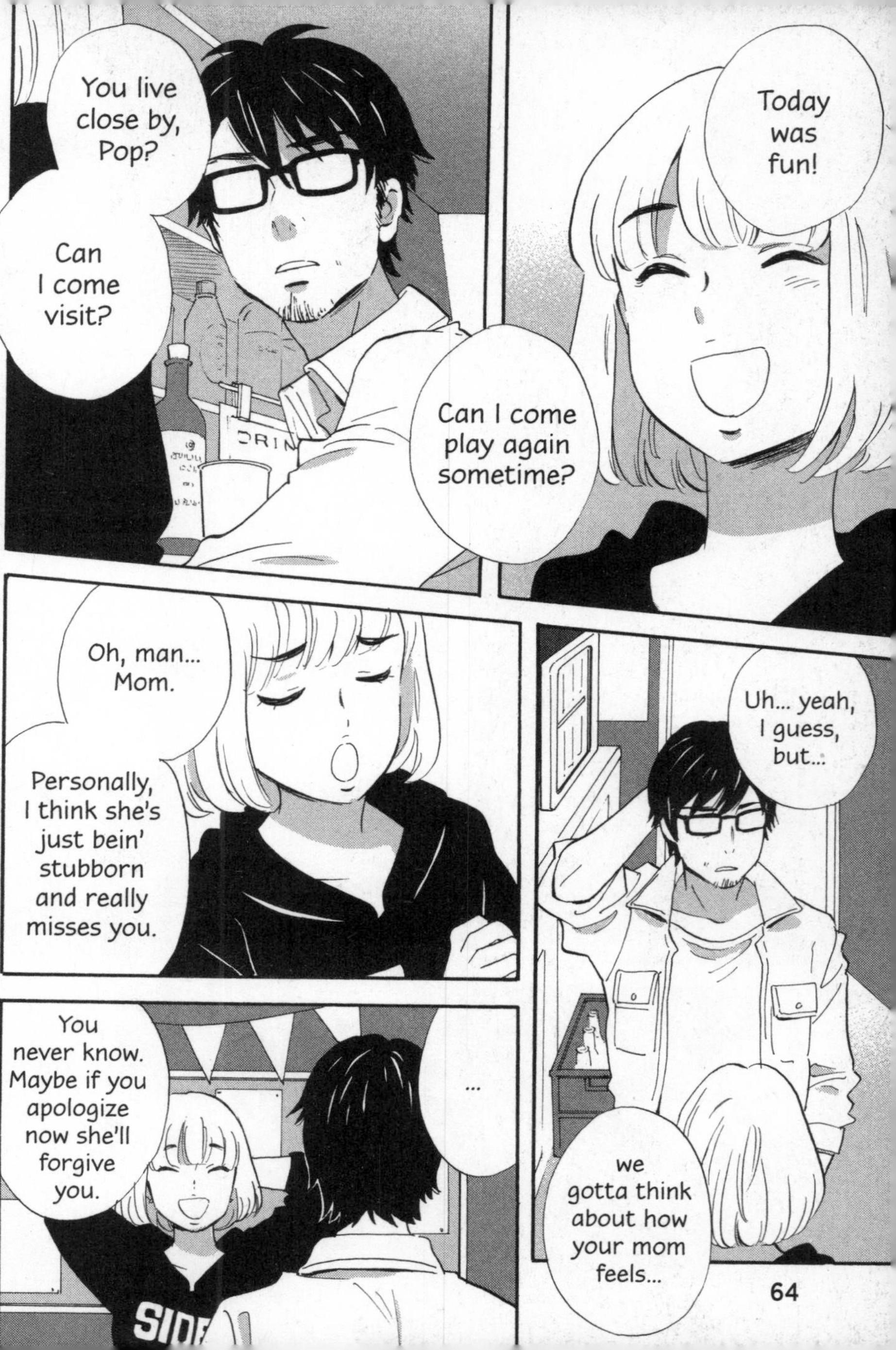
Today was fun!
Can I come play again sometime?
You live close by, Pop?
Can I come visit?
Uh... yeah, I guess, but...
we gotta think about how your mom feels...
Oh, man... Mom.
Personally, I think she's just bein' stubborn and really misses you.
...
You never know. Maybe if you apologize now she'll forgive you.

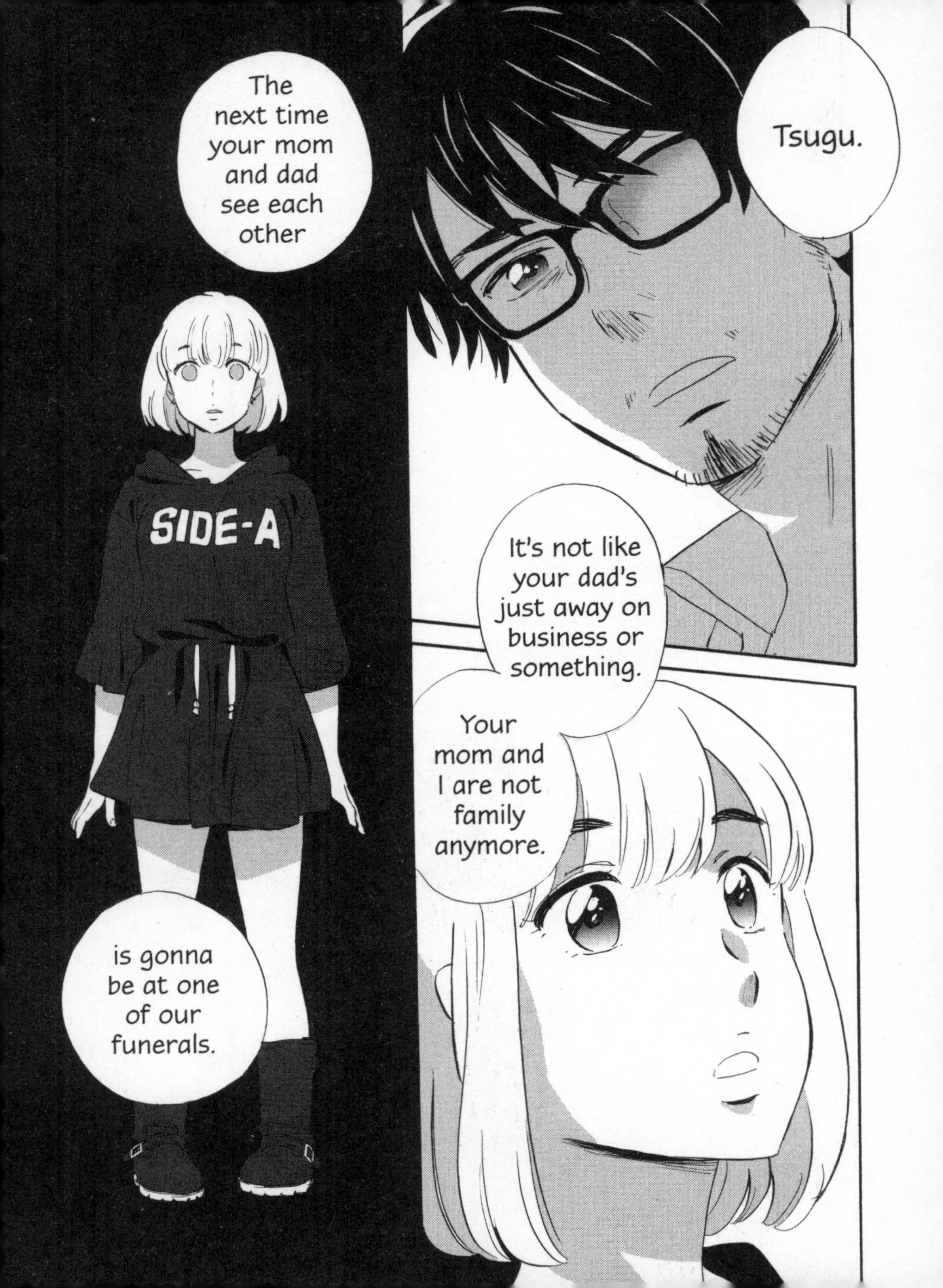
Tsugu.
It's not like your dad's just away on business or something.
Your mom and I are not family anymore.
The next time your mom and dad see each other
SIDE-A
is gonna be at one of our funerals.

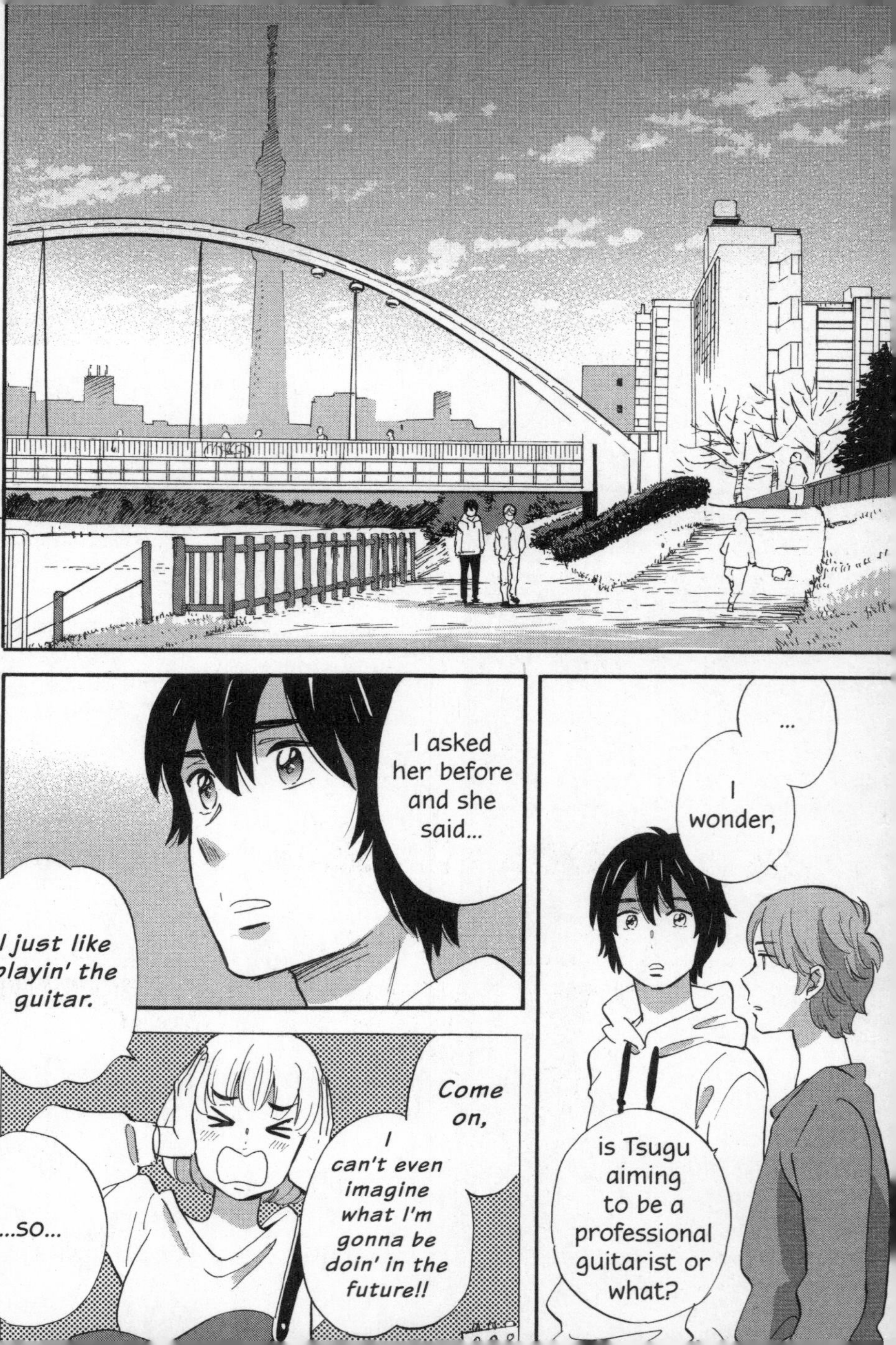
...
I wonder,
is Tsugu aiming to be a professional guitarist or what?
I asked her before and she said...
I just like playin' the guitar.
Come on,
I can't even imagine what I'm gonna be doin' in the future!!
...so...

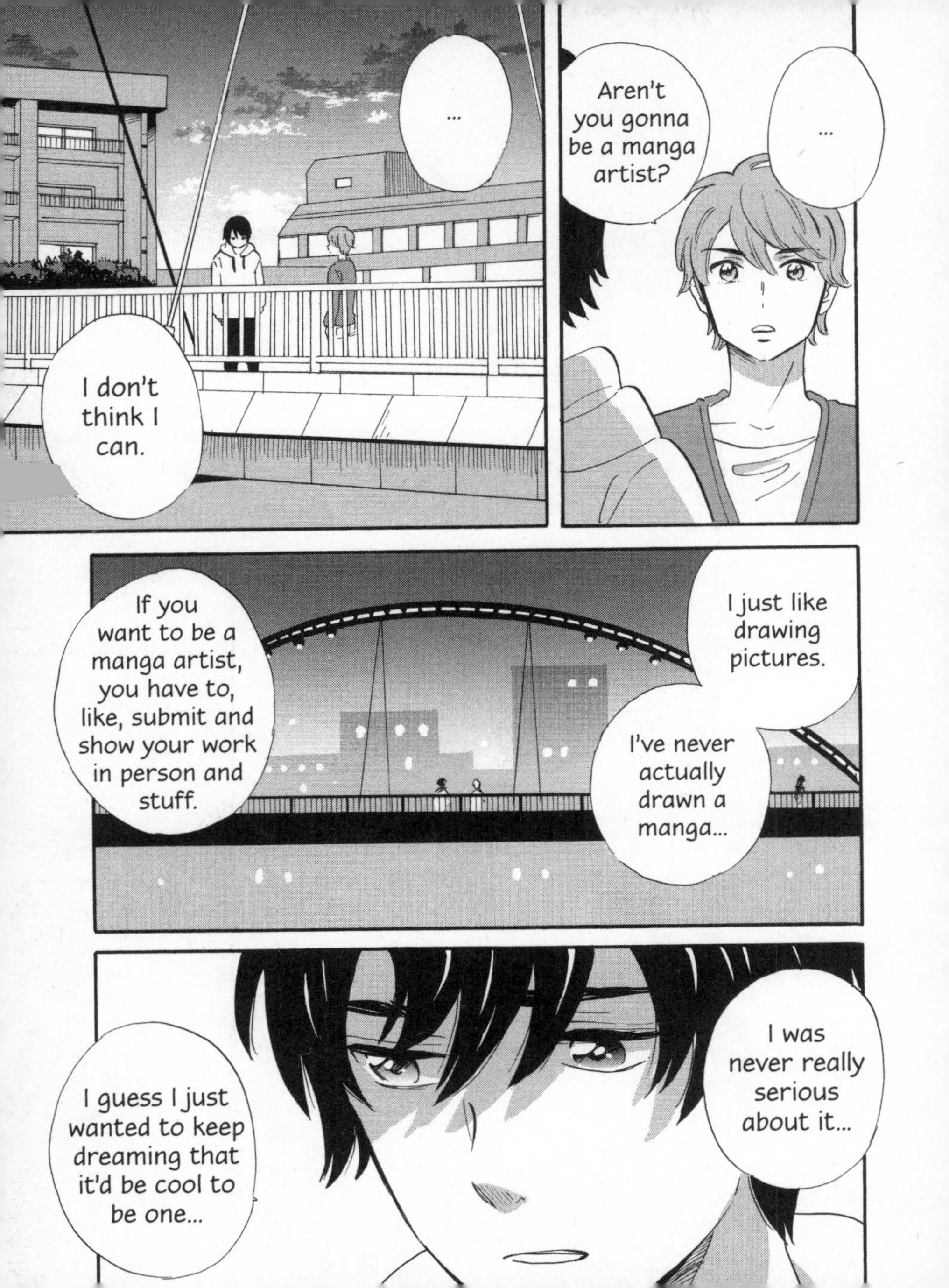
Aren't you gonna be a manga artist?
...
...
I don't think I can.
I just like drawing pictures.
I've never actually drawn a manga...
If you want to be a manga artist, you have to, like, submit and show your work in person and stuff.
I was never really serious about it...
I guess I just wanted to keep dreaming that it'd be cool to be one...

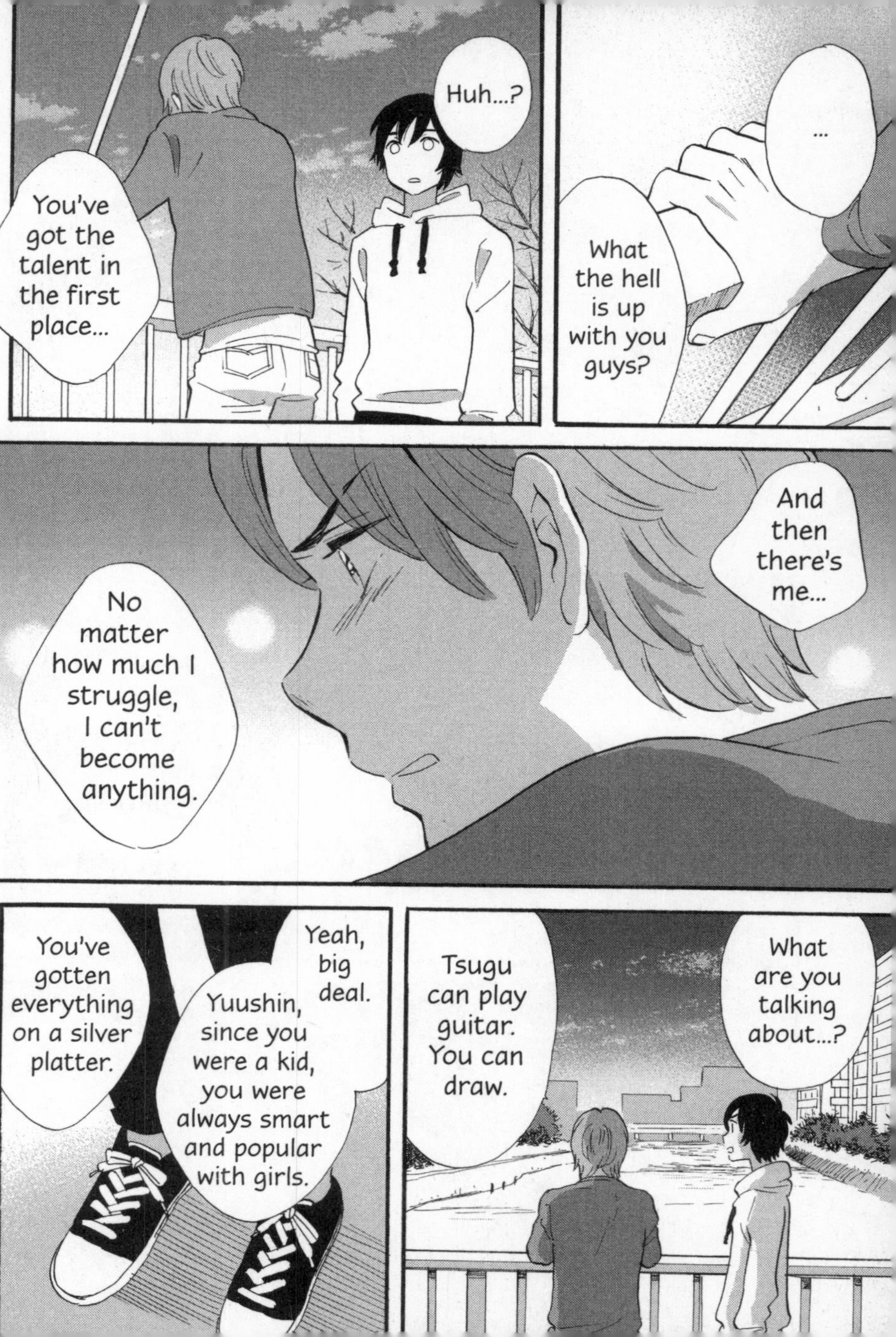
...
What the hell is up with you guys?
Huh...?
You've got the talent in the first place...
And then there's me...
No matter how much I struggle, I can't become anything.
What are you talking about...?
Tsugu can play guitar. You can draw.
Yeah, big deal.
Yuushin, since you were a kid, you were always smart and popular with girls.
You've gotten everything on a silver platter.

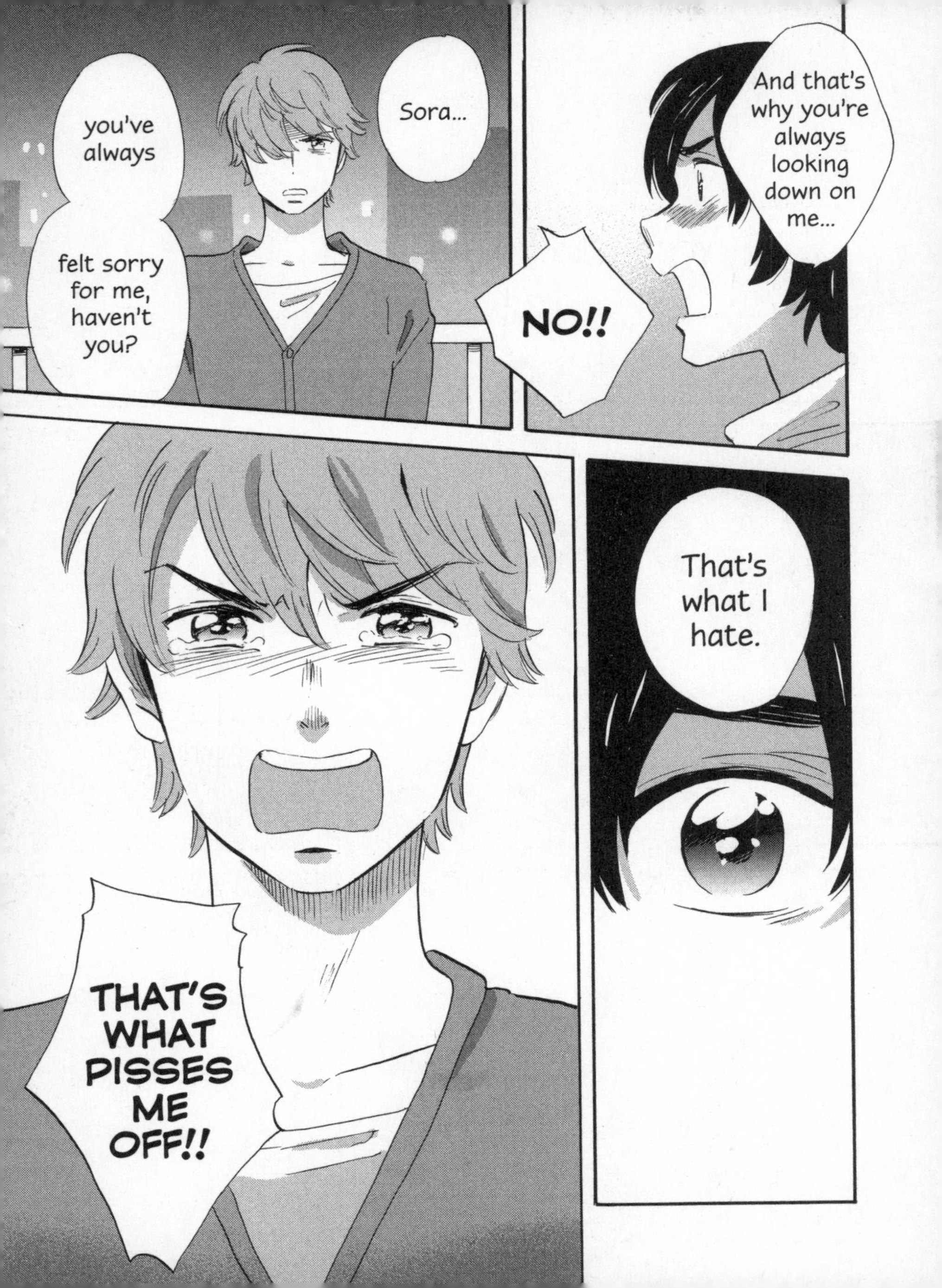
And that's why you're always looking down on me...
NO!!
Sora...
you've always
felt sorry for me, haven't you?
That's what I hate.
THAT'S WHAT PISSES ME OFF!!

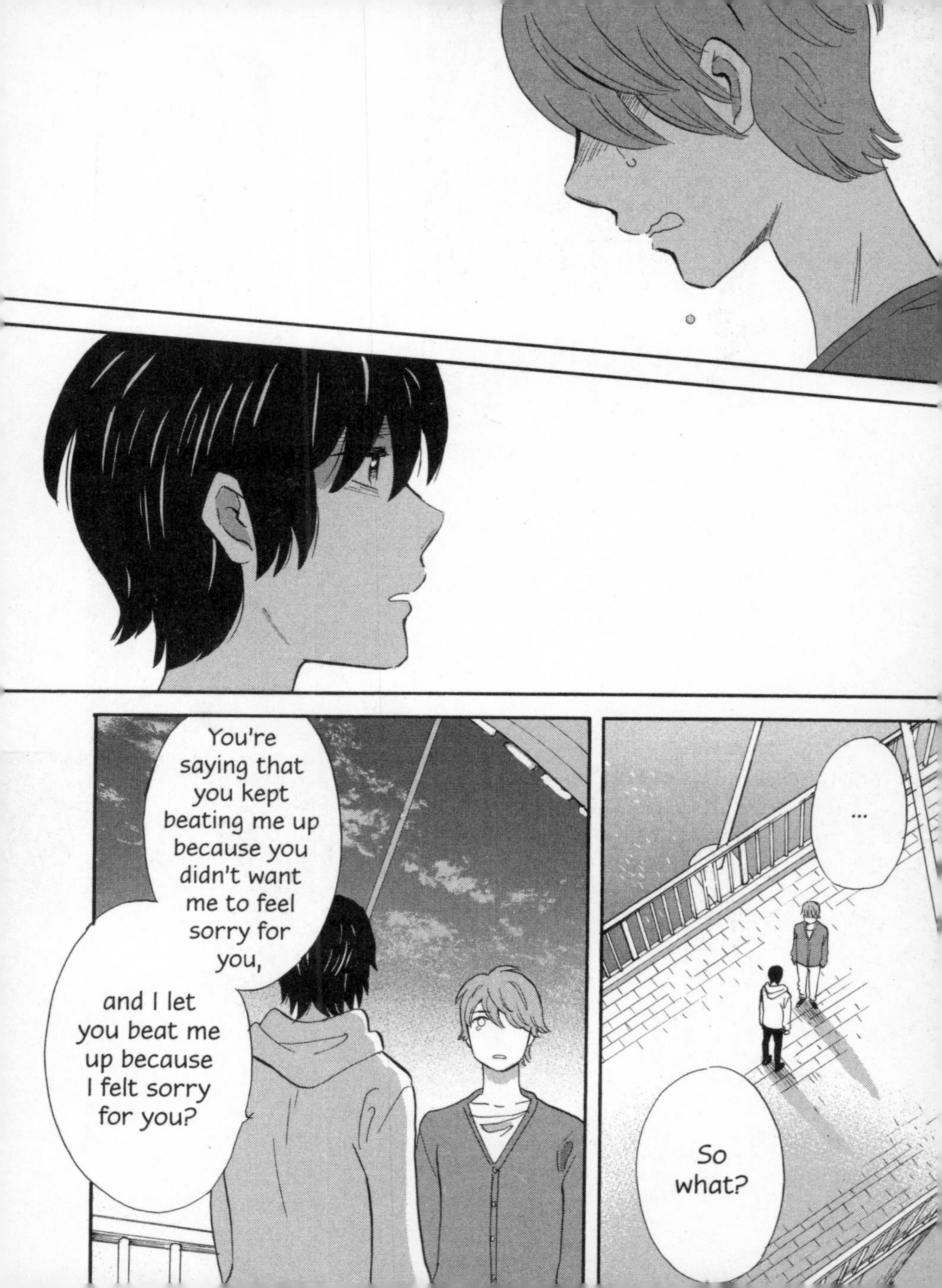
You're saying that you kept beating me up because you didn't want me to feel sorry for you,
and I let you beat me up because I felt sorry for you?
...
So what?

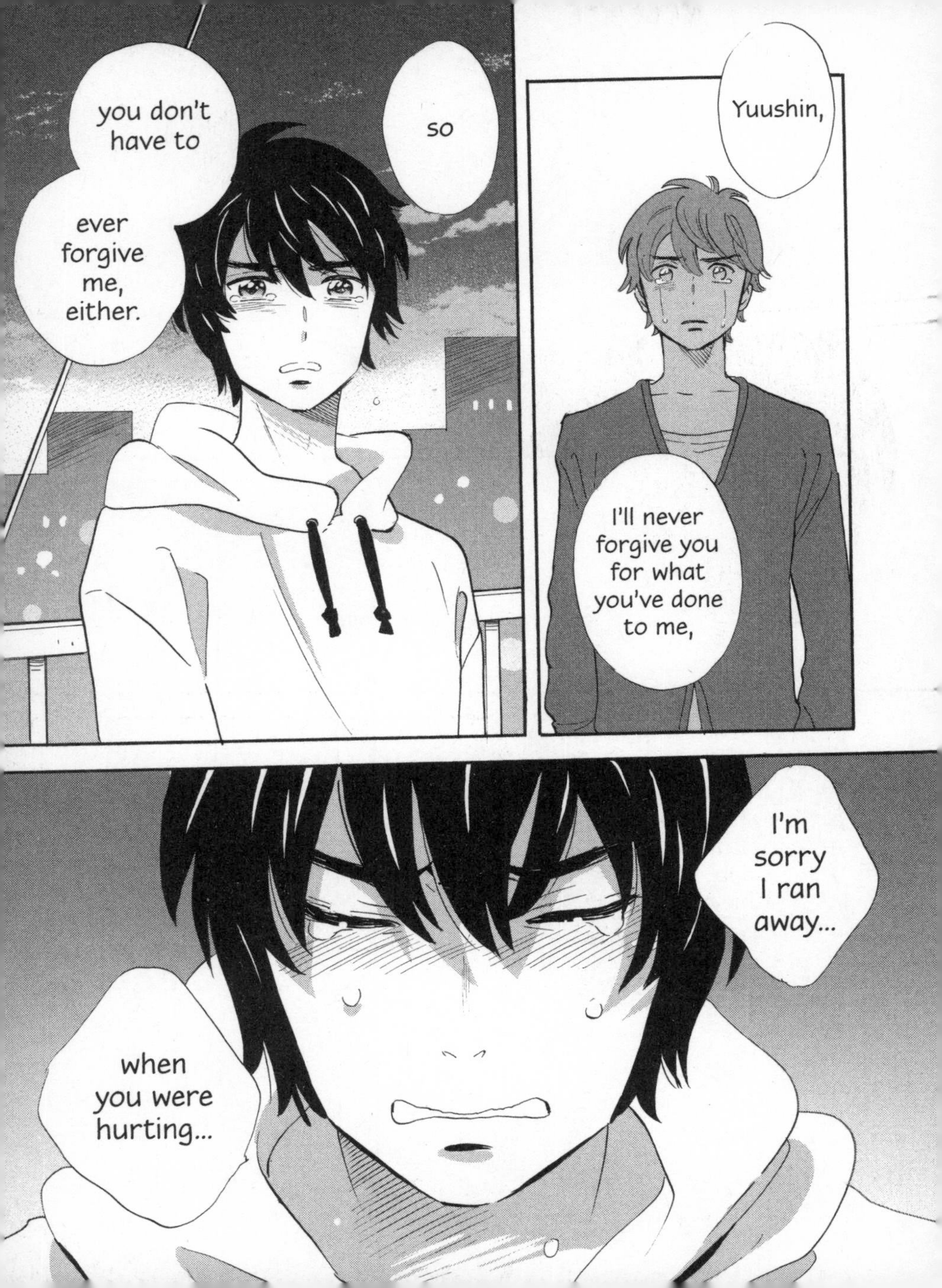
Yuushin,
I'll never forgive you for what you've done to me,
so
you don't have to
ever forgive me, either.
I'm sorry I ran away...
when you were hurting...

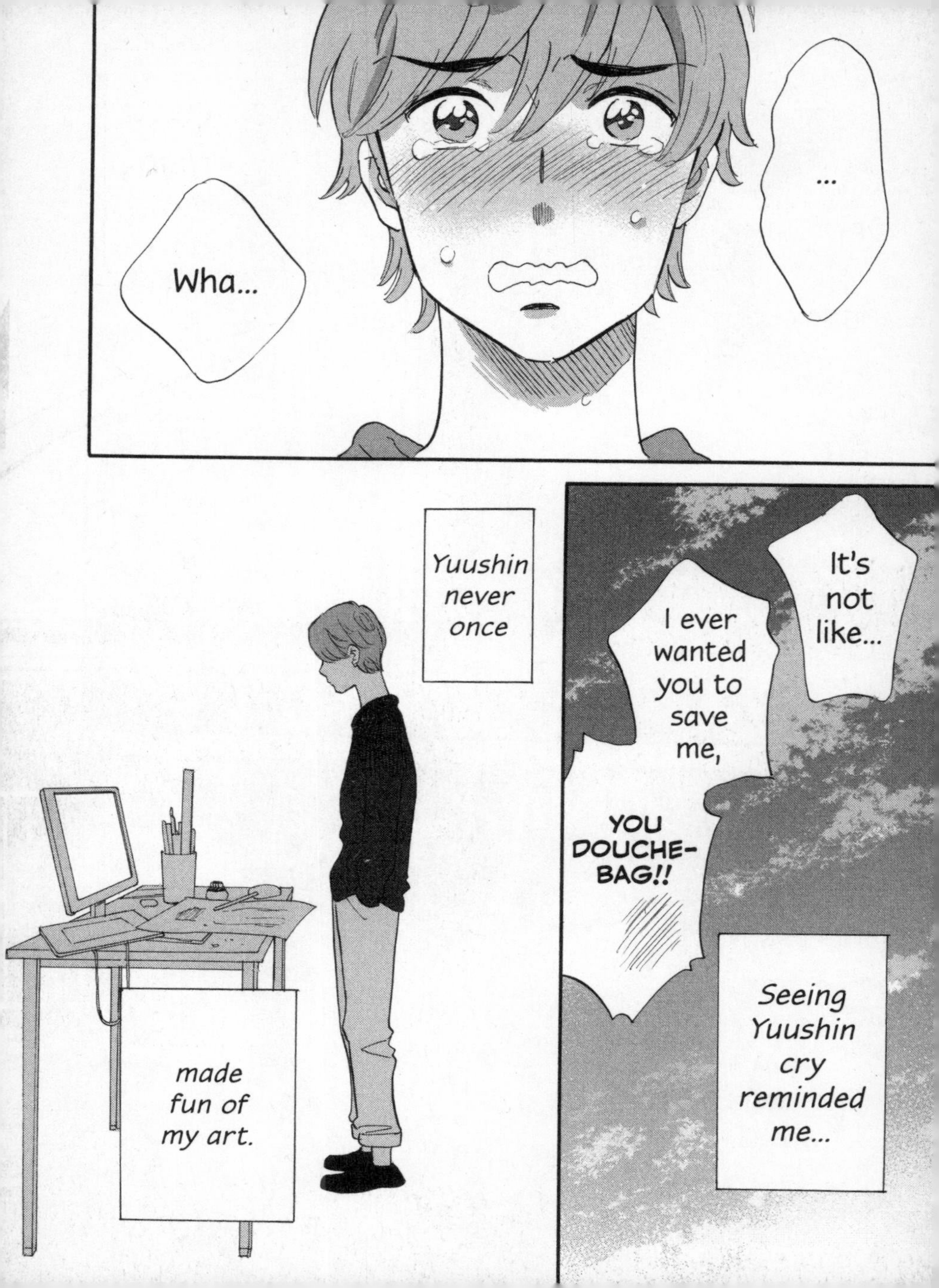
...
Wha...
It's not like...
I ever wanted you to save me,
YOU DOUCHE-BAG!!
Seeing Yuushin cry reminded me...
Yuushin never once
made fun of my art.

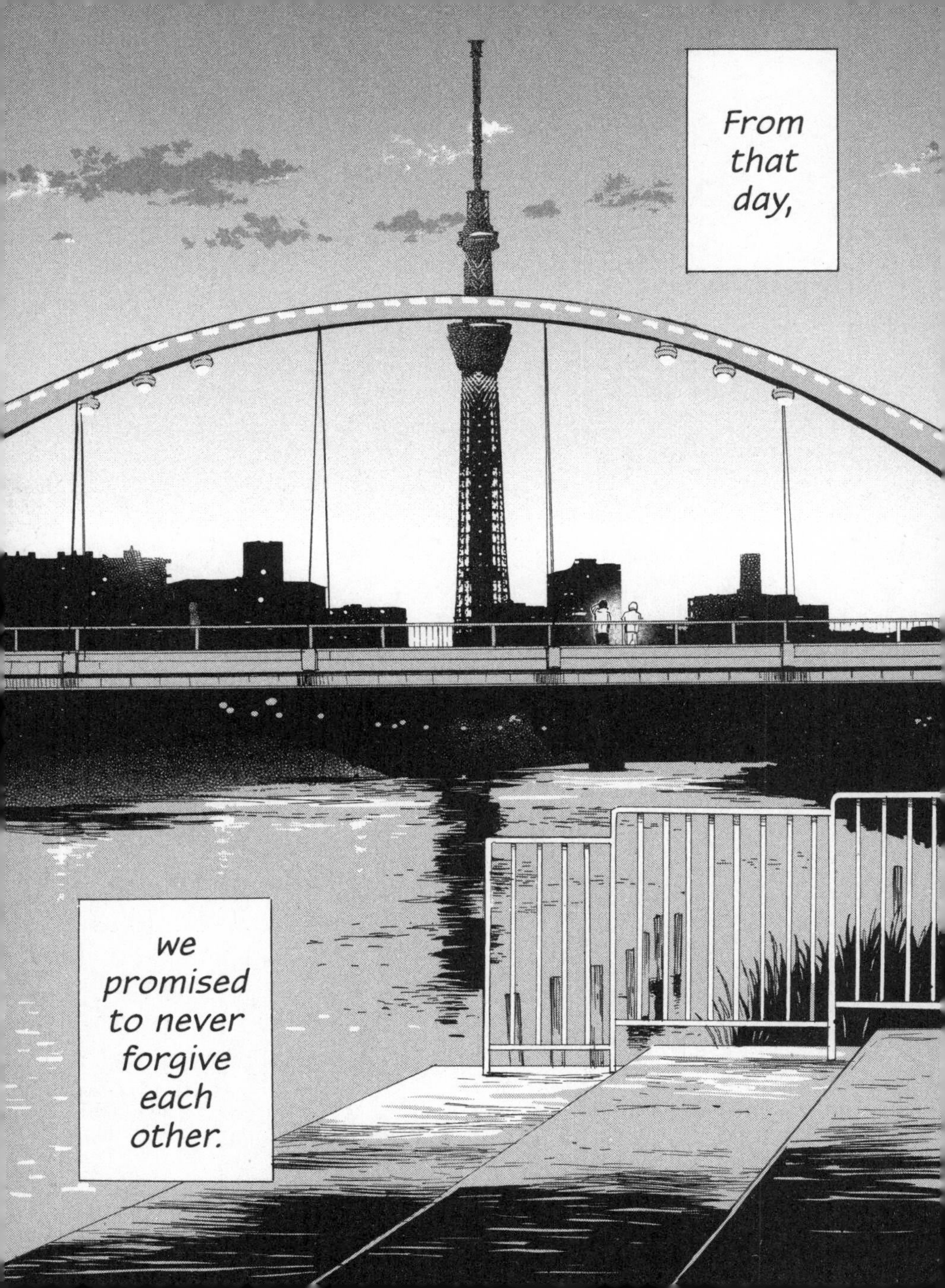
From that day,
we promised to never forgive each other.

(CHAPTER 14) ADIEU L'AMI

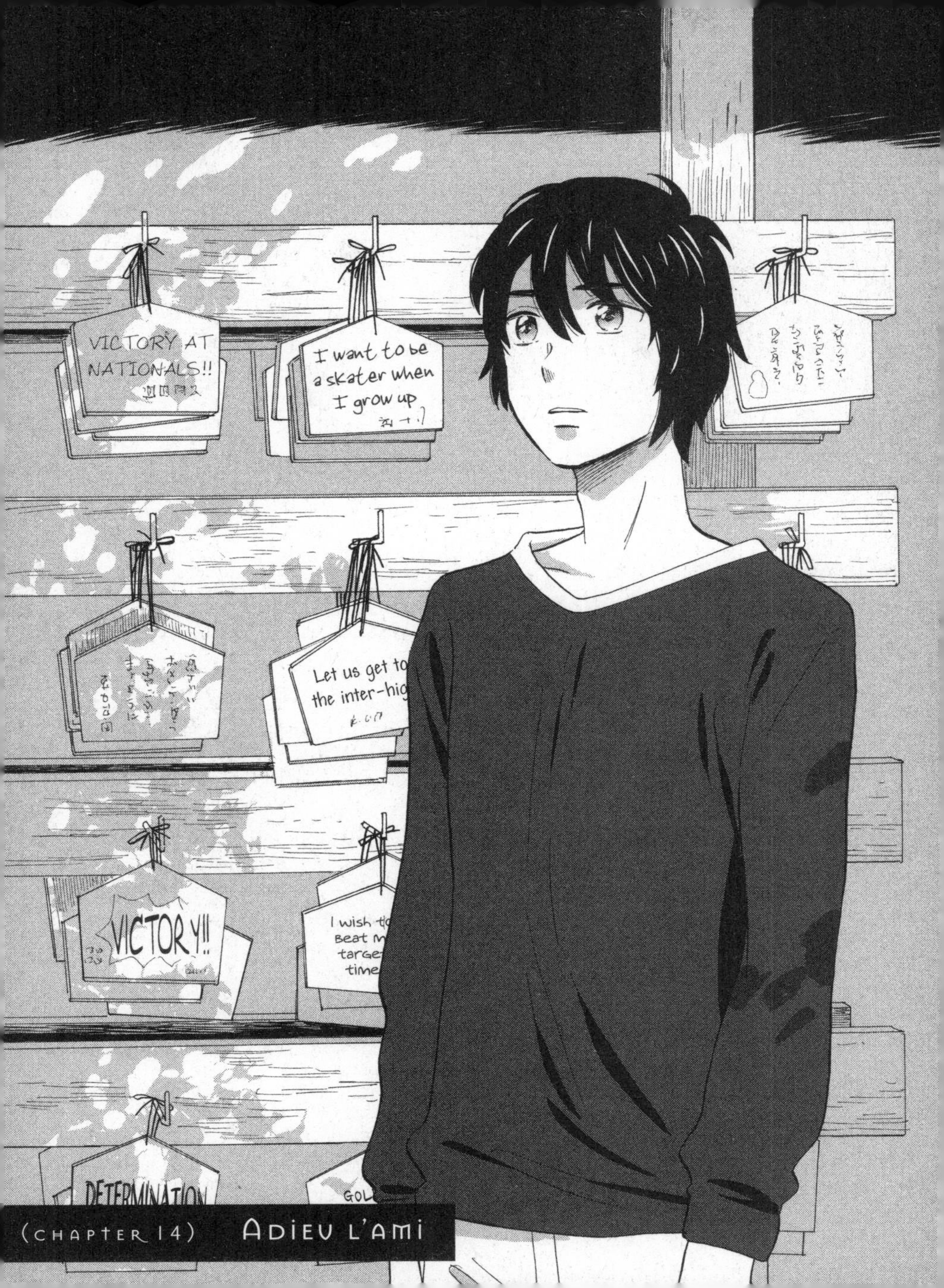

VICTORY AT NATIONALS!!
I want to be a skater when I grow up
VICTORY!!
DETERMINATION

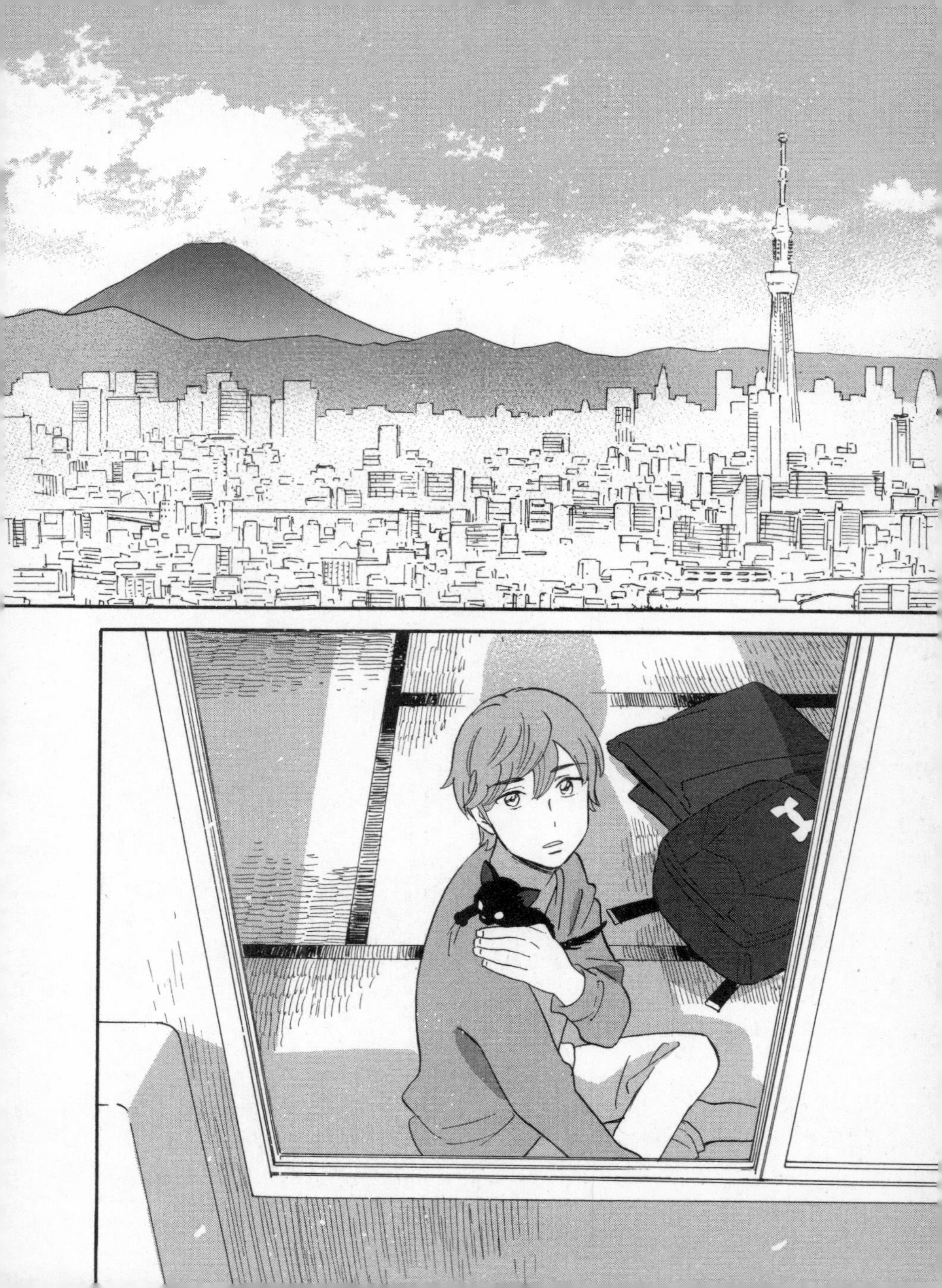

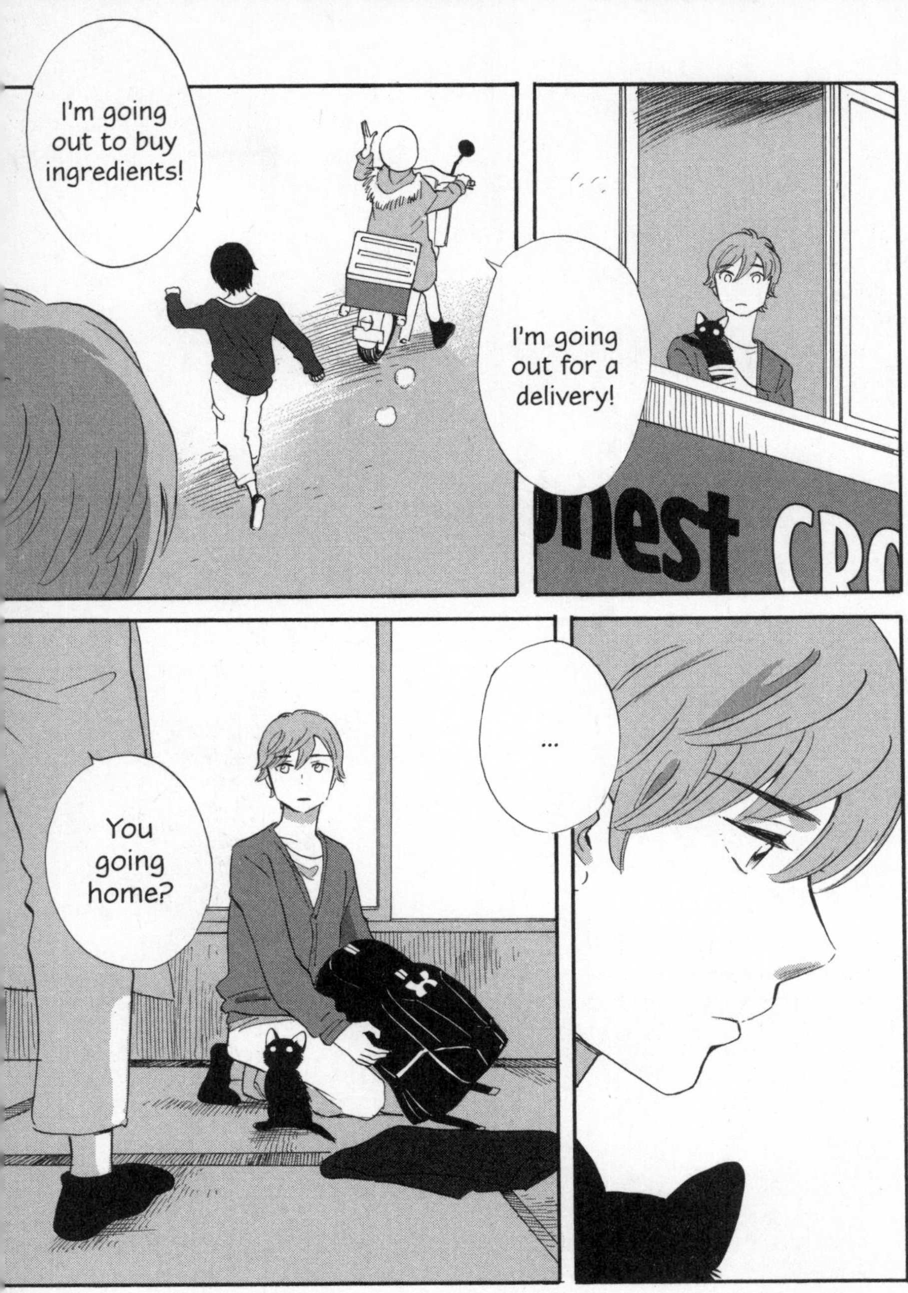
I'm going out for a delivery!
I'm going out to buy ingredients!
...
You going home?

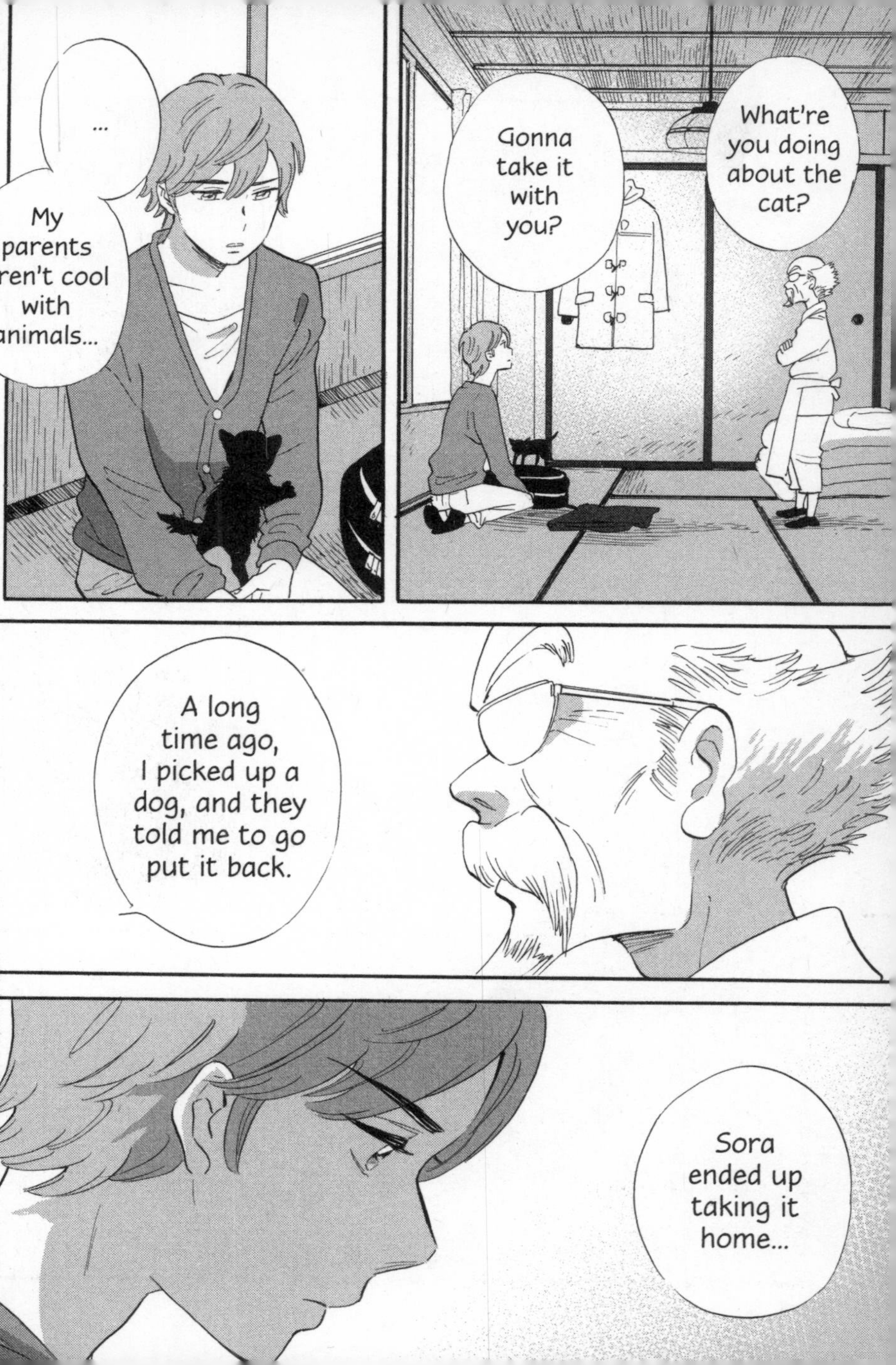
What're you doing about the cat?
Gonna take it with you?
...
My parents aren't cool with animals...
A long time ago, I picked up a dog, and they told me to go put it back.
Sora ended up taking it home...

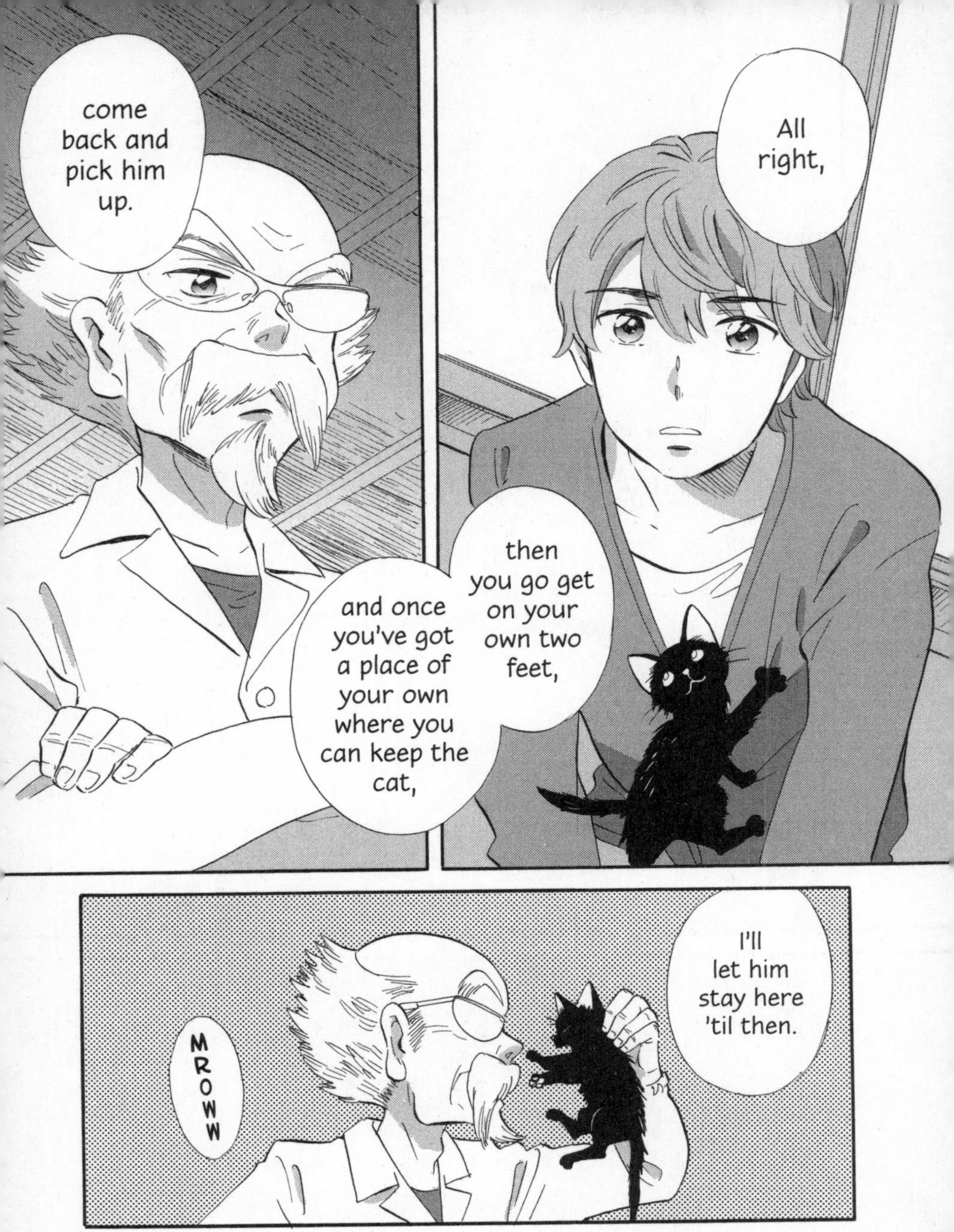
All right,
then you go get on your own two feet,
and once you've got a place of your own where you can keep the cat,
come back and pick him up.
I'll let him stay here 'til then.
MROWW

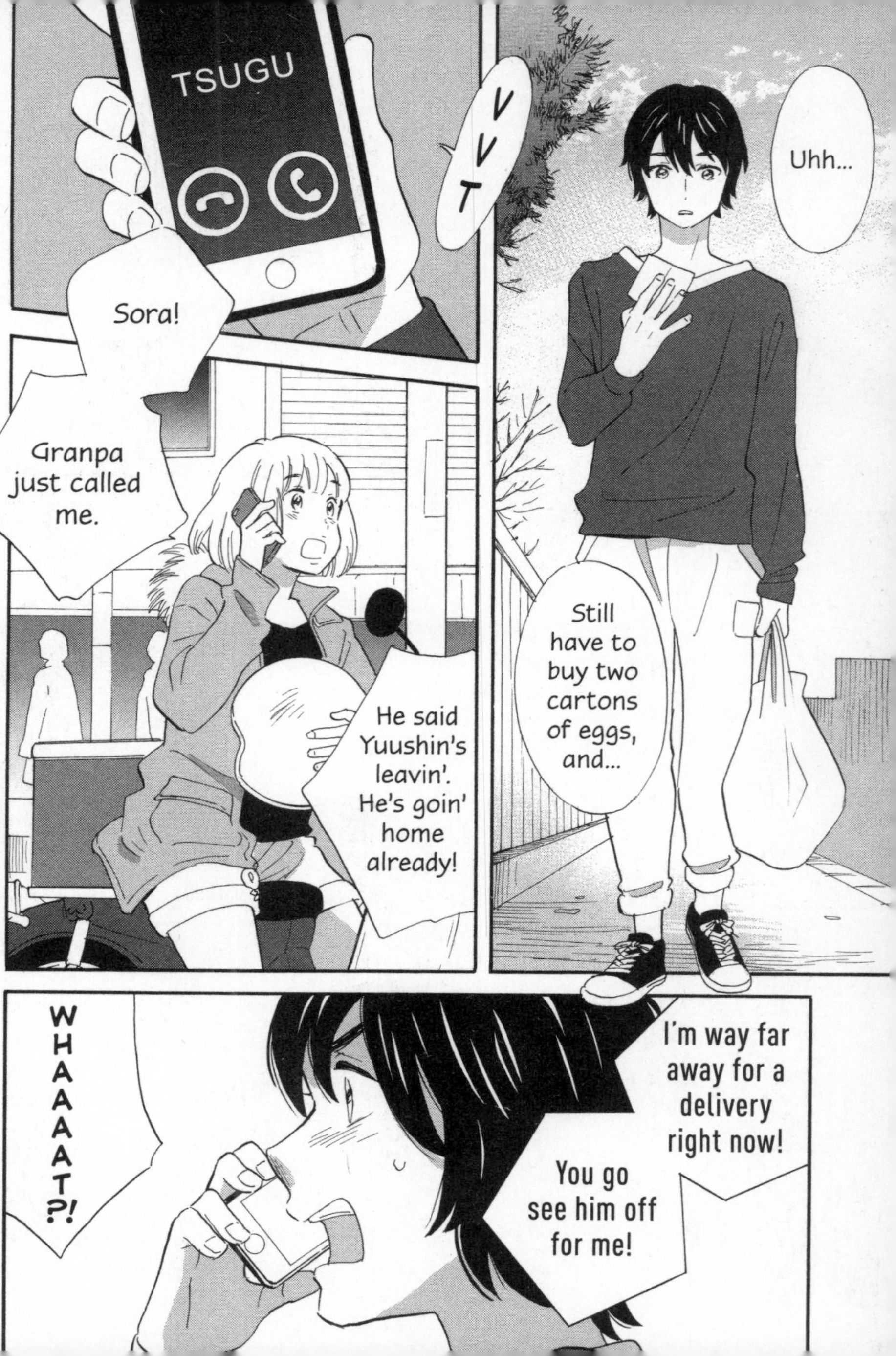
Uhh...
Still have to buy two cartons of eggs, and...
TSUGU
VVVT
Sora!
Granpa just called me.
He said Yuushin's leavin'. He's goin' home already!
I'm way far away for a delivery right now!
You go see him off for me!
WHAAAAT?!

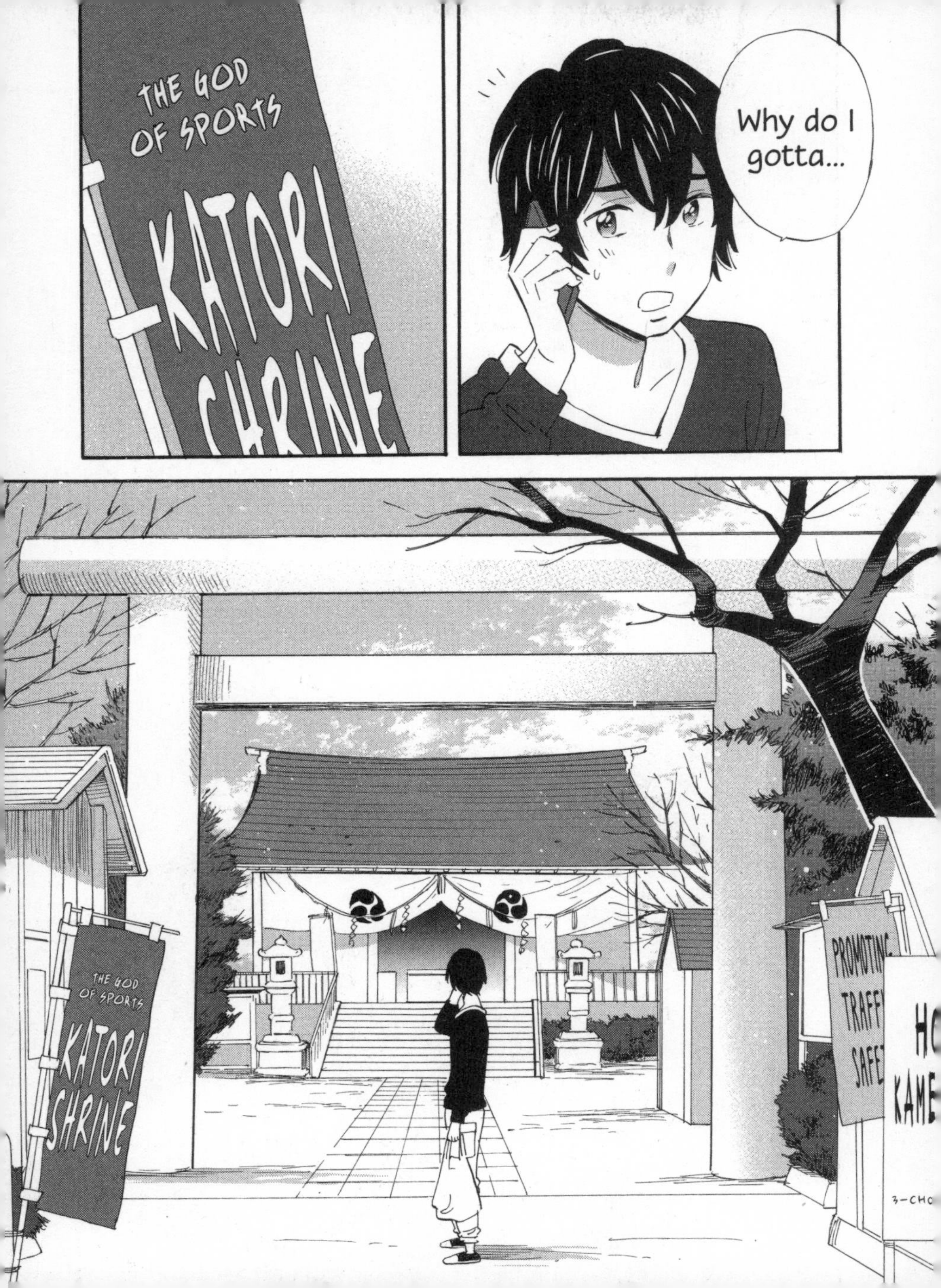
Why do I gotta...
THE GOD OF SPORTS
KATORI SHRINE
PROMOTIN TRAFF SAFE
HO KAME
3-CHO
THE GOD OF SPORTS
KATORI SHRINE

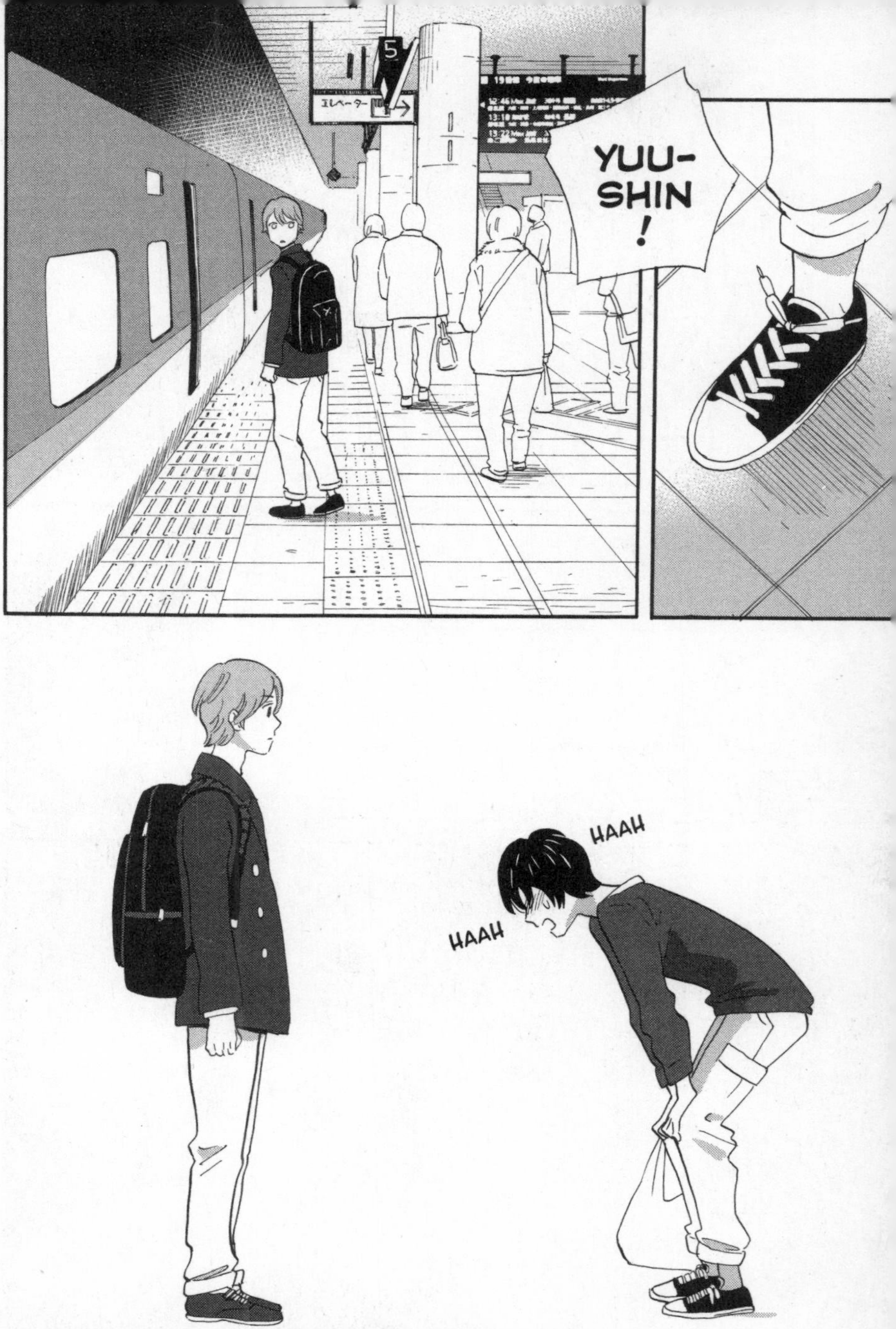
YUU-SHIN!
5
エレベーター
HAAH
HAAH

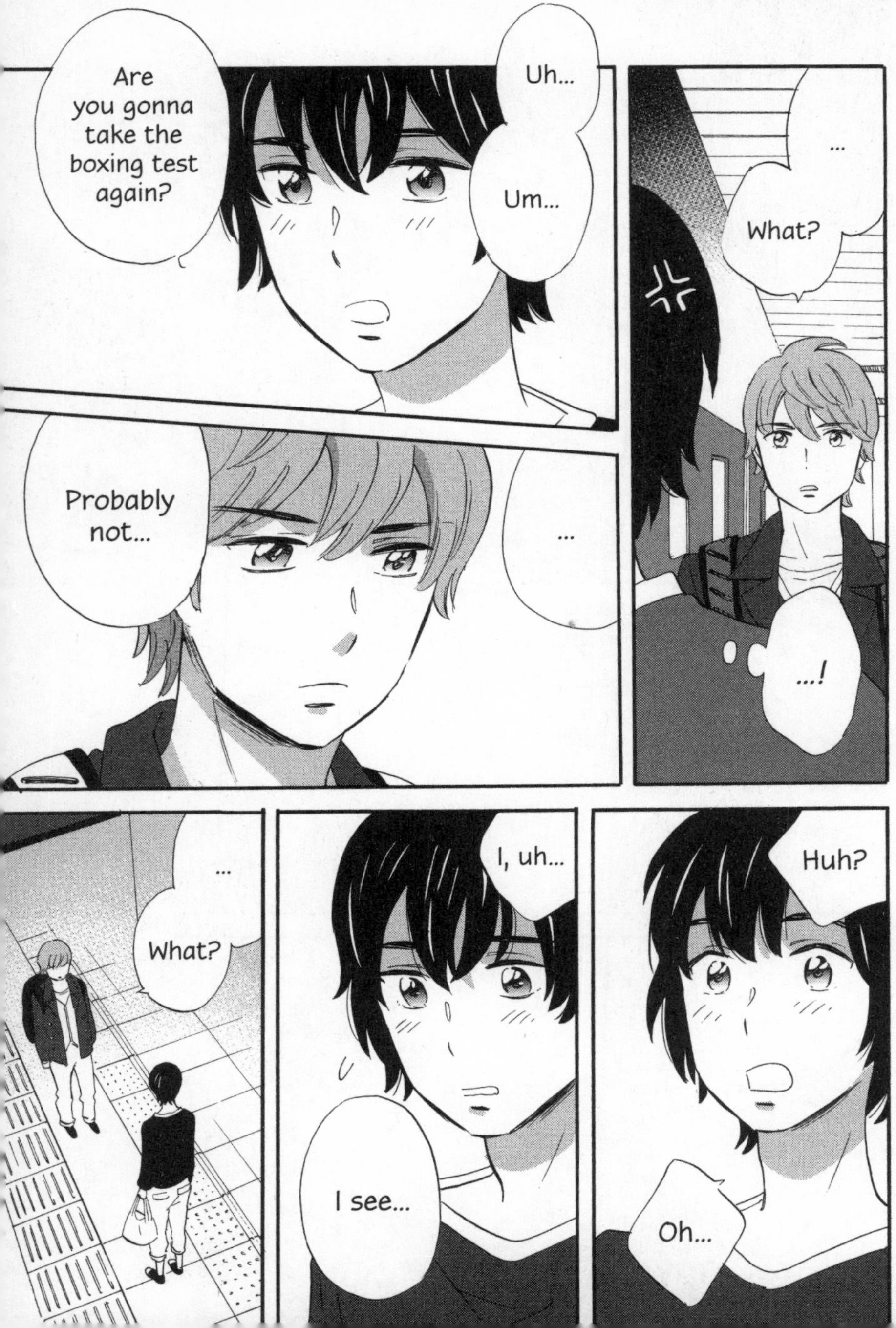
...
What?
...!
Uh...
Um...
Are you gonna take the boxing test again?
...
Probably not...
Huh?
Oh...
I, uh...
I see...
...
What?

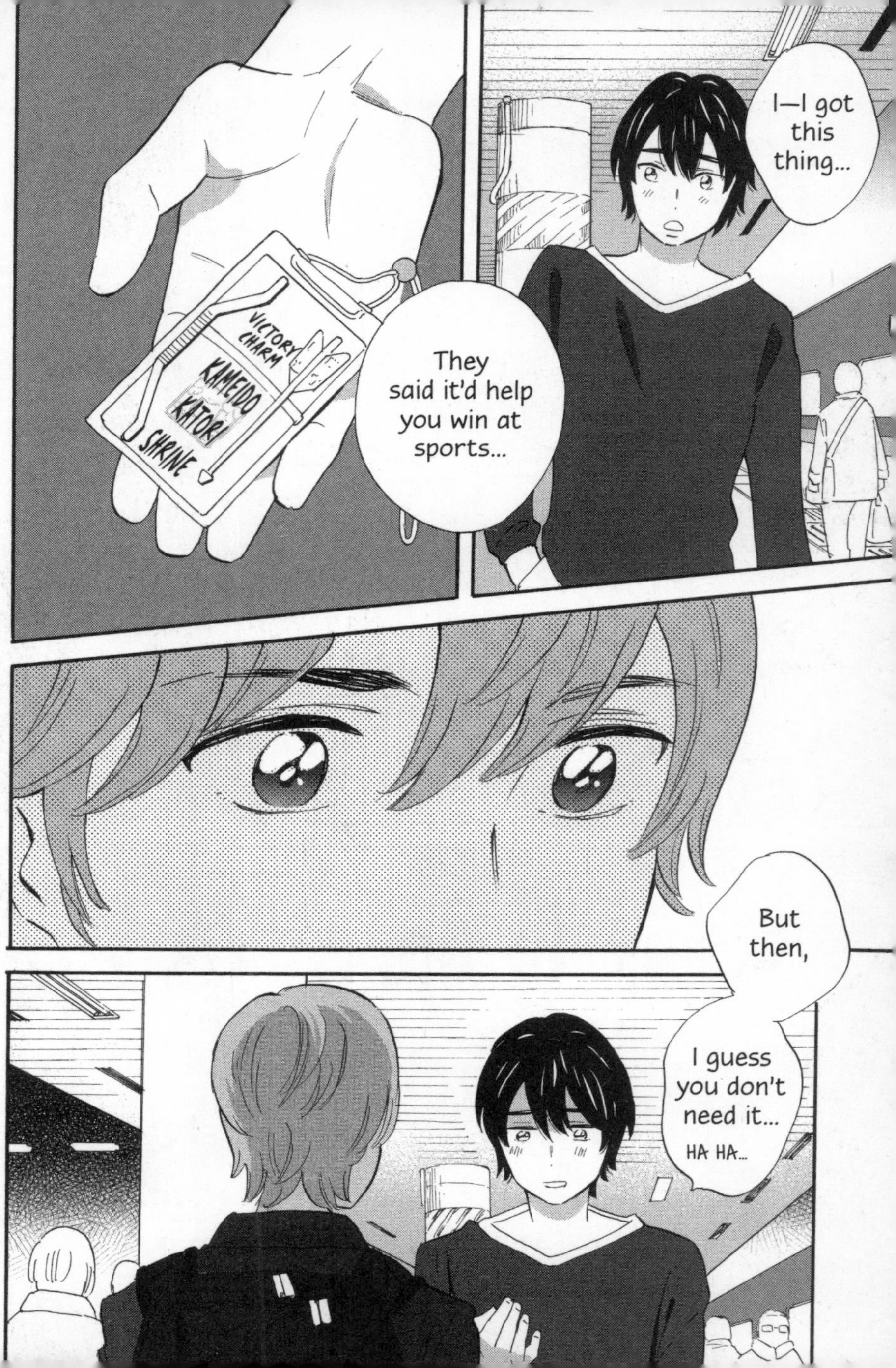
I—I got this thing...
VICTORY CHARM
KAMEIDO KATORI SHRINE
They said it'd help you win at sports...
But then,
I guess you don't need it...
HA HA...

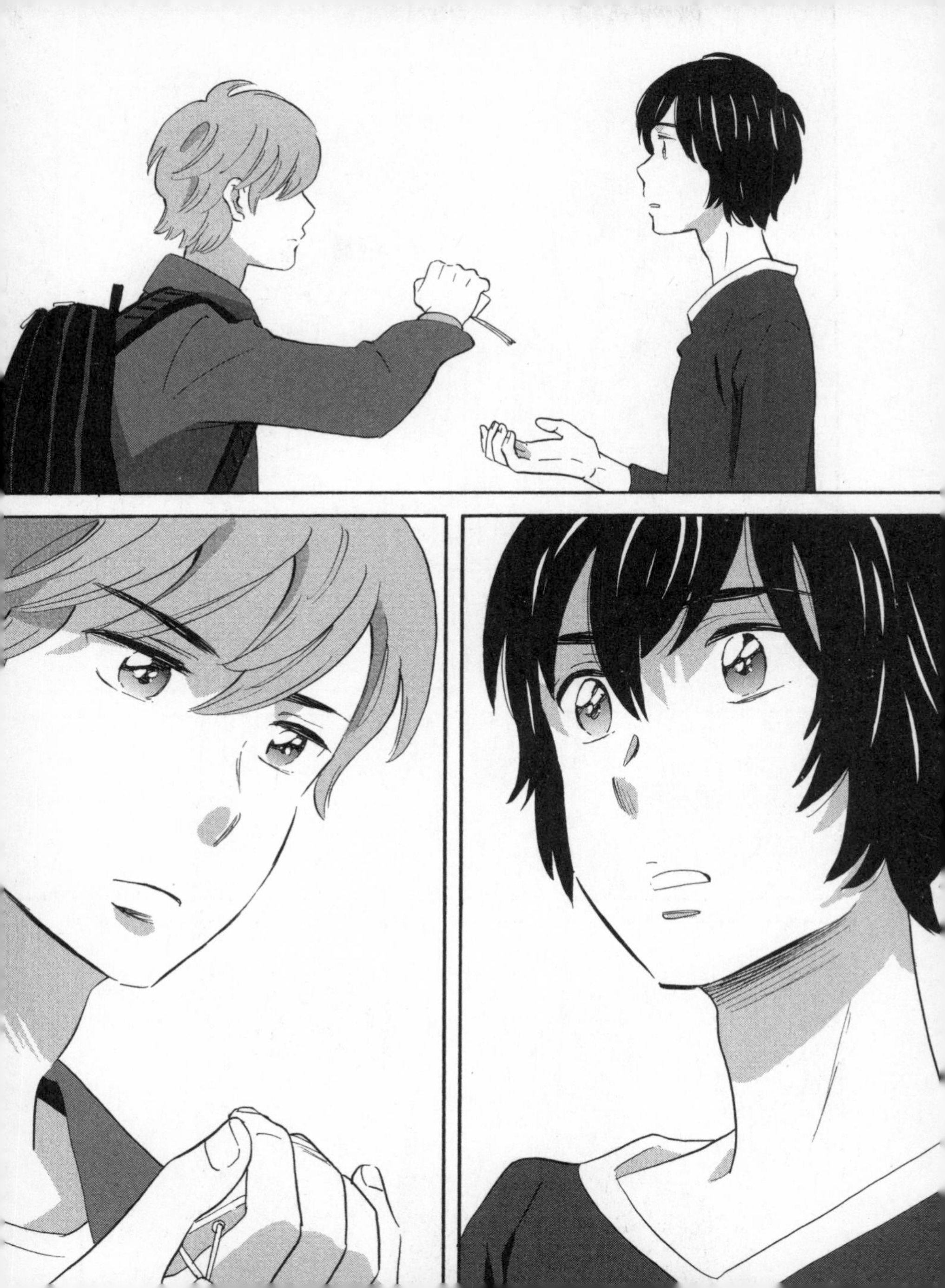

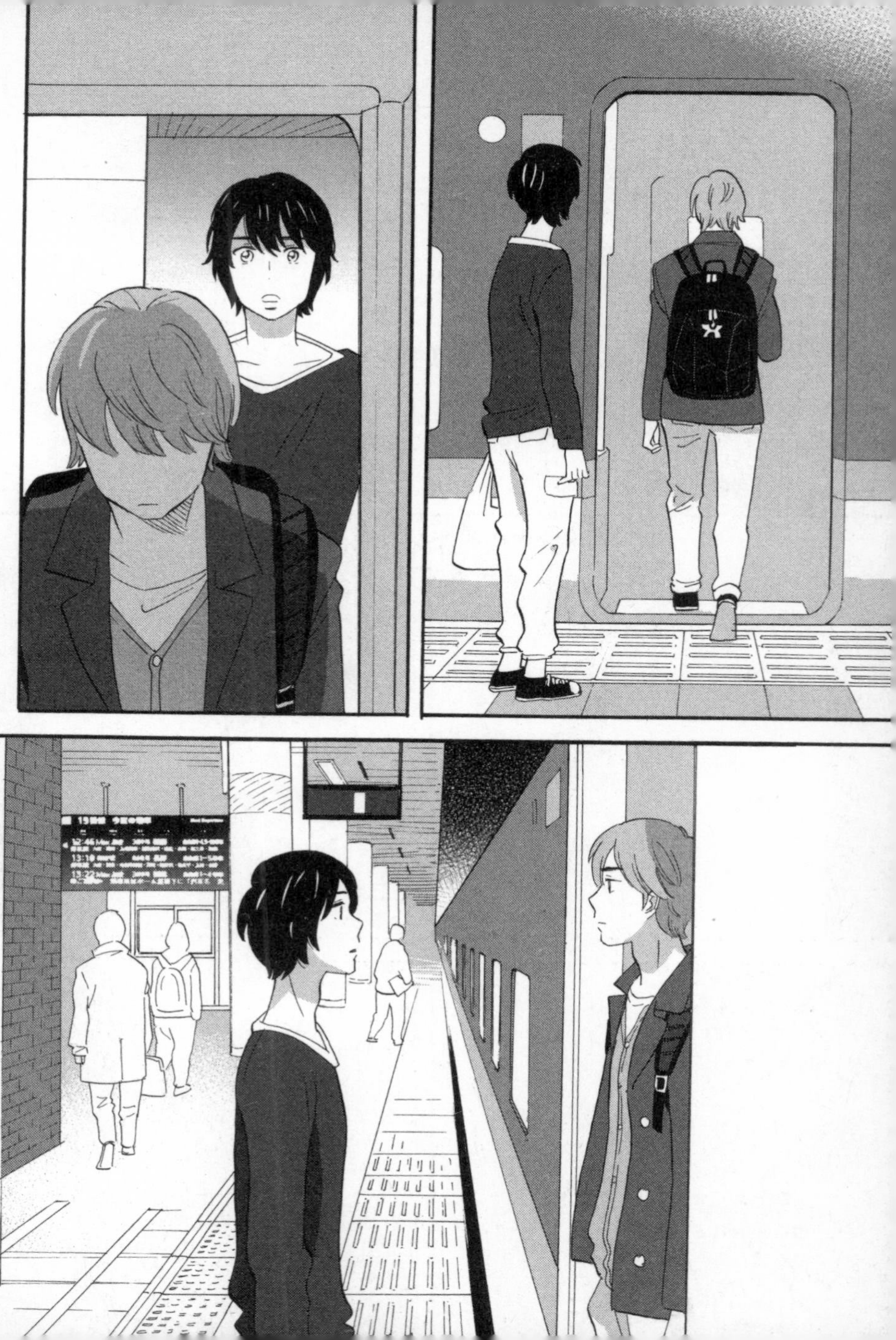

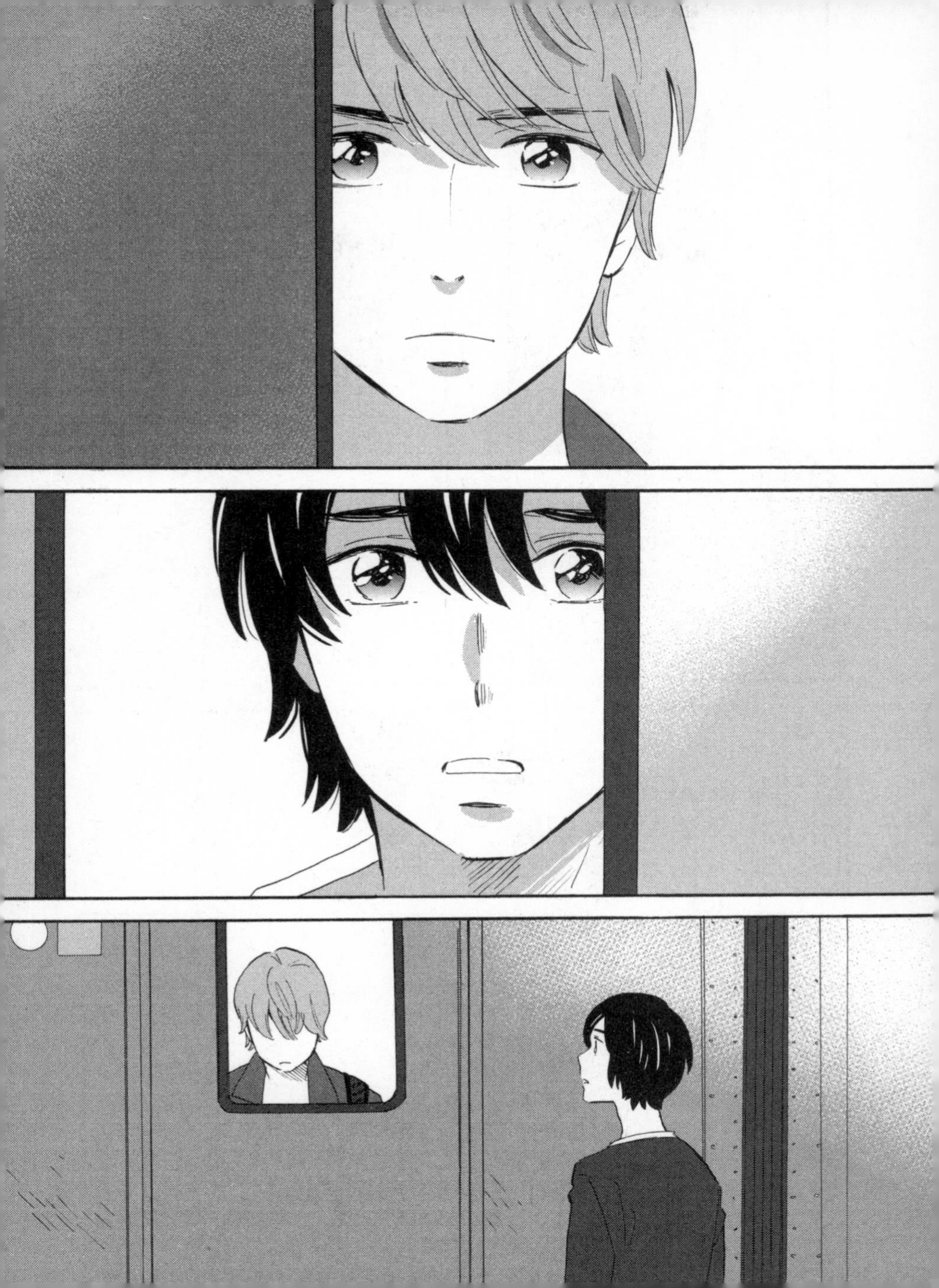

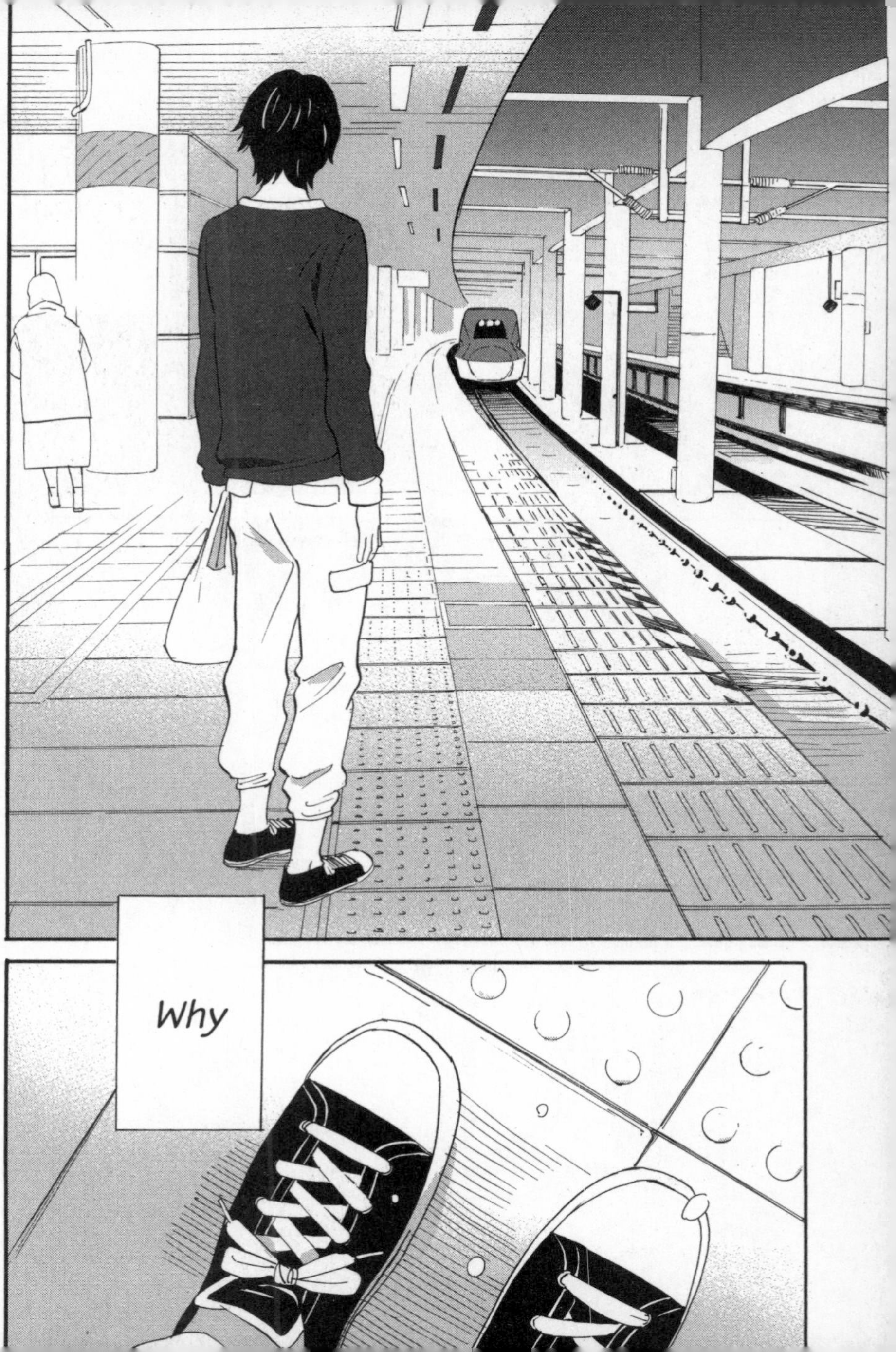
Why

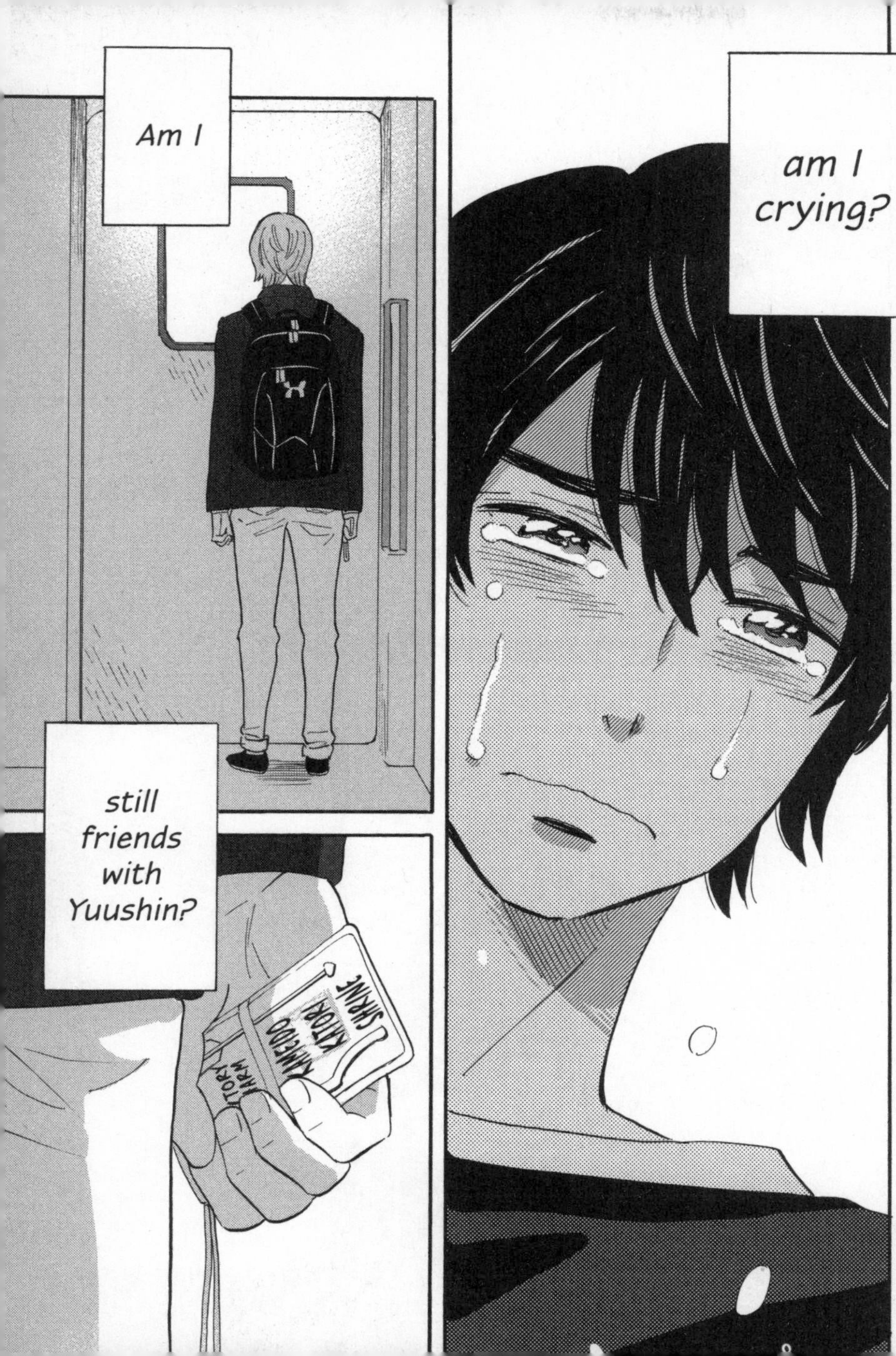
am I crying?
Am I
still friends with Yuushin?
KAMEIDO KATORI SHRINE

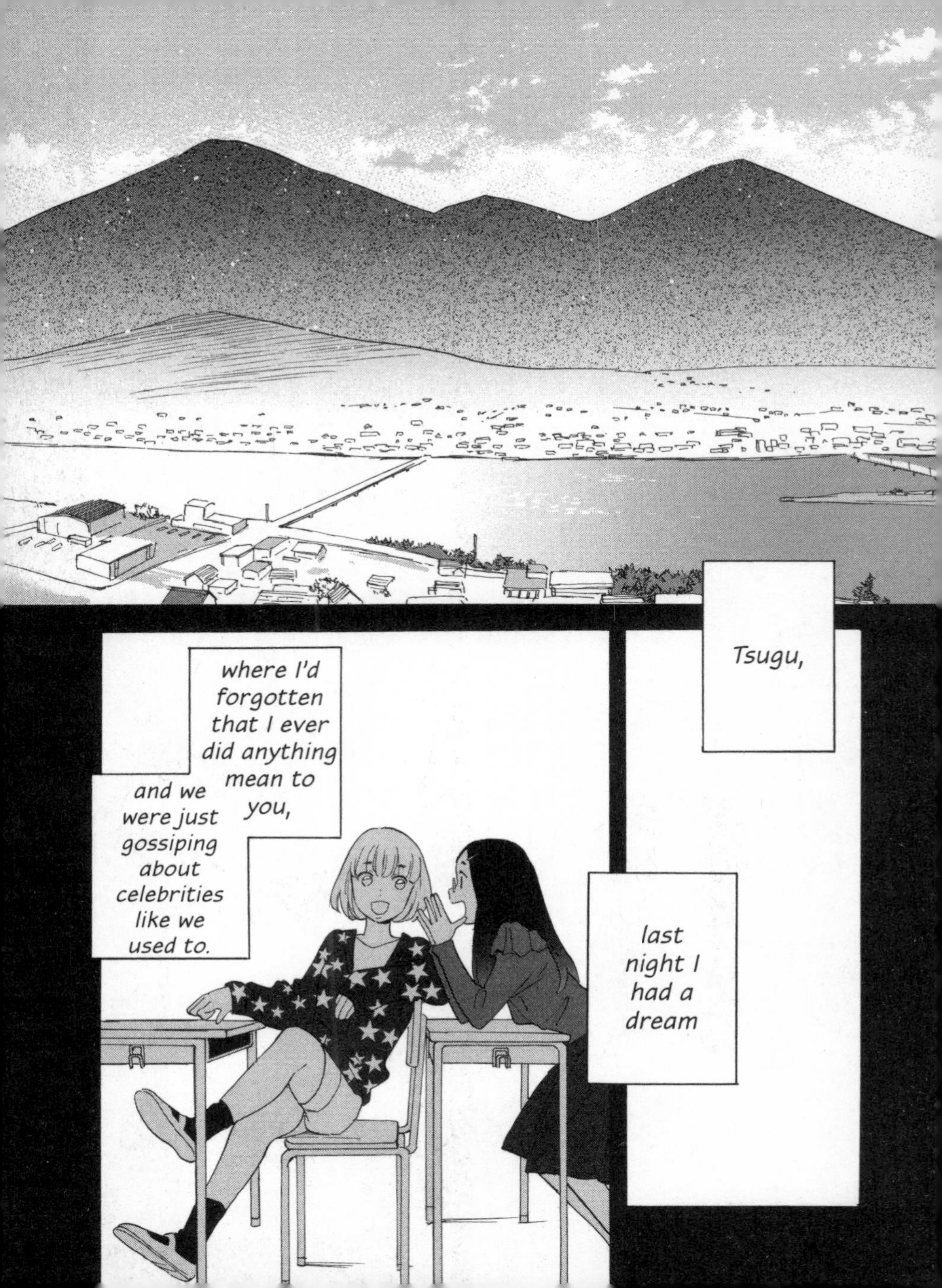
Tsugu,
last night I had a dream
where I'd forgotten that I ever did anything mean to you,
and we were just gossiping about celebrities like we used to.

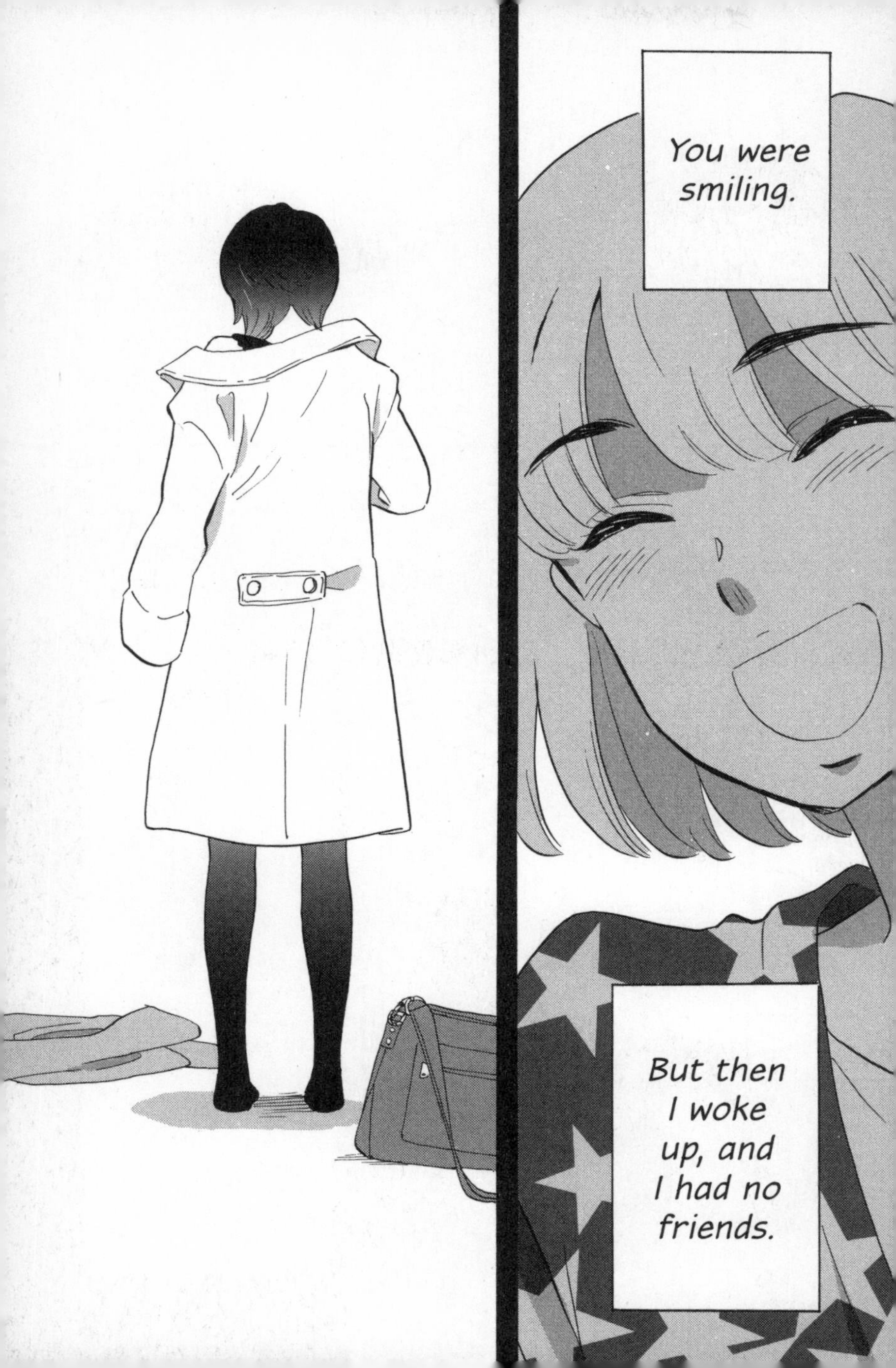
You were smiling.
But then I woke up, and I had no friends.

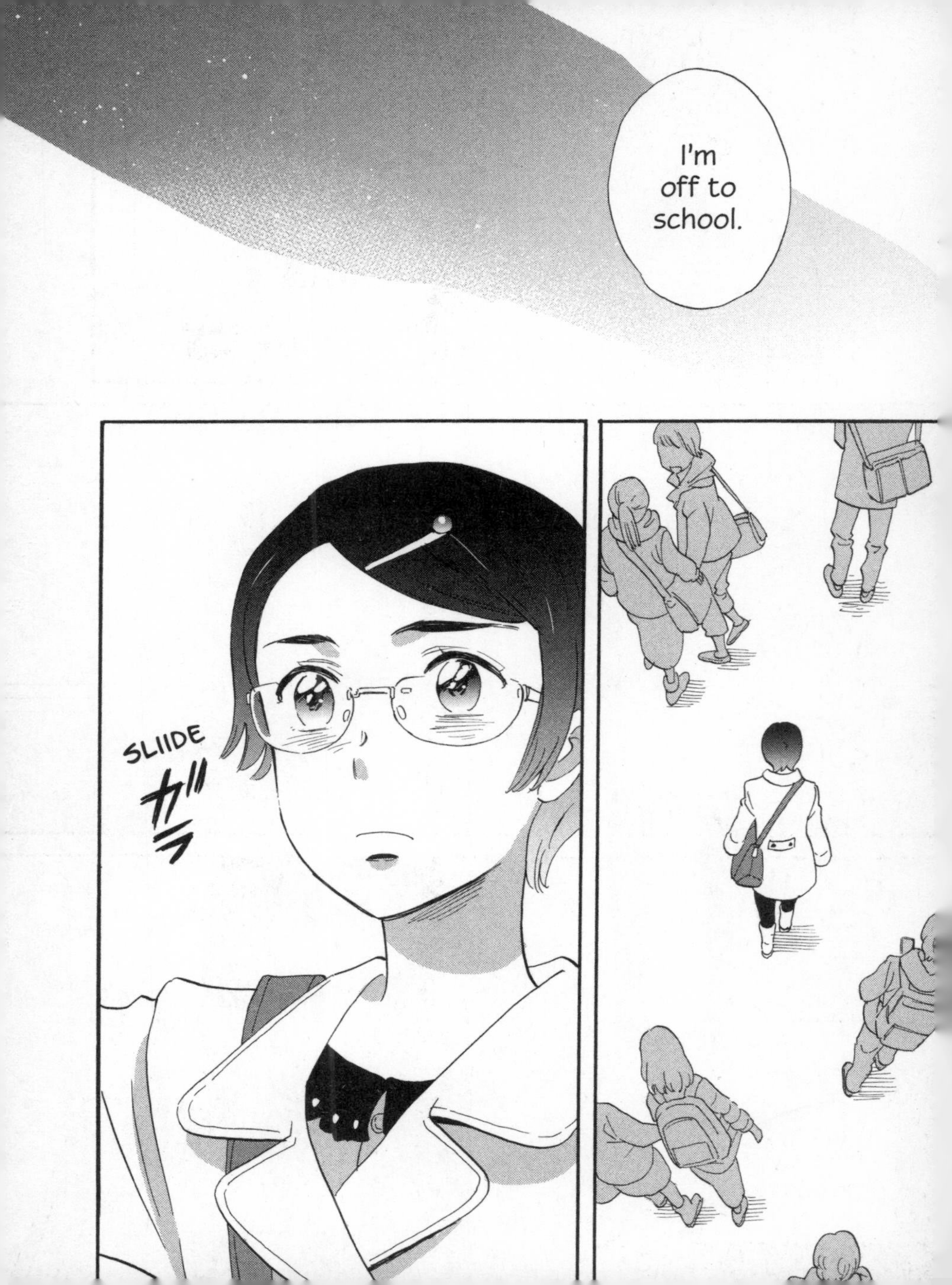
I'm off to school.
SLIIDE
ガラ

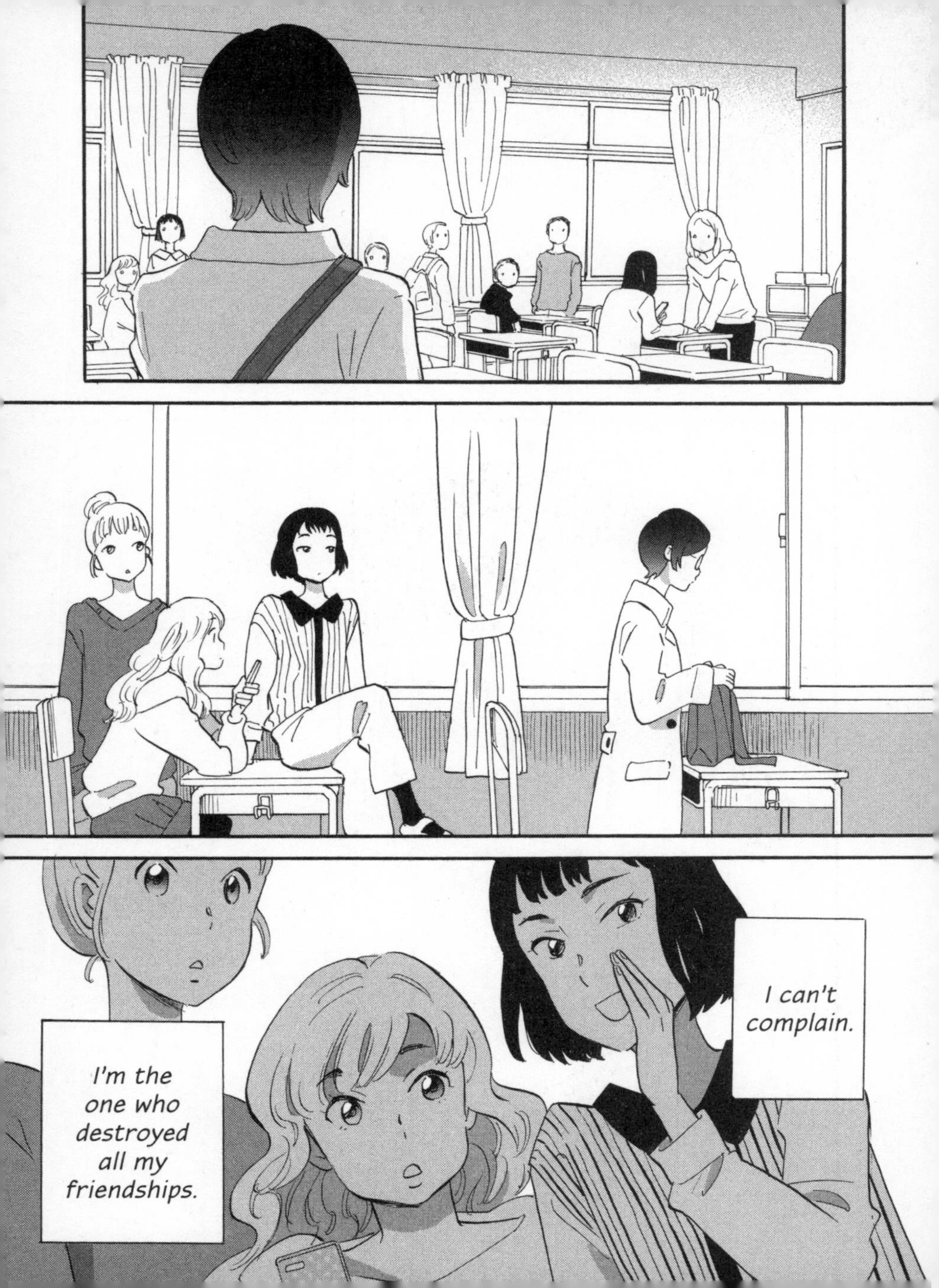
I can't complain.
I'm the one who destroyed all my friendships.

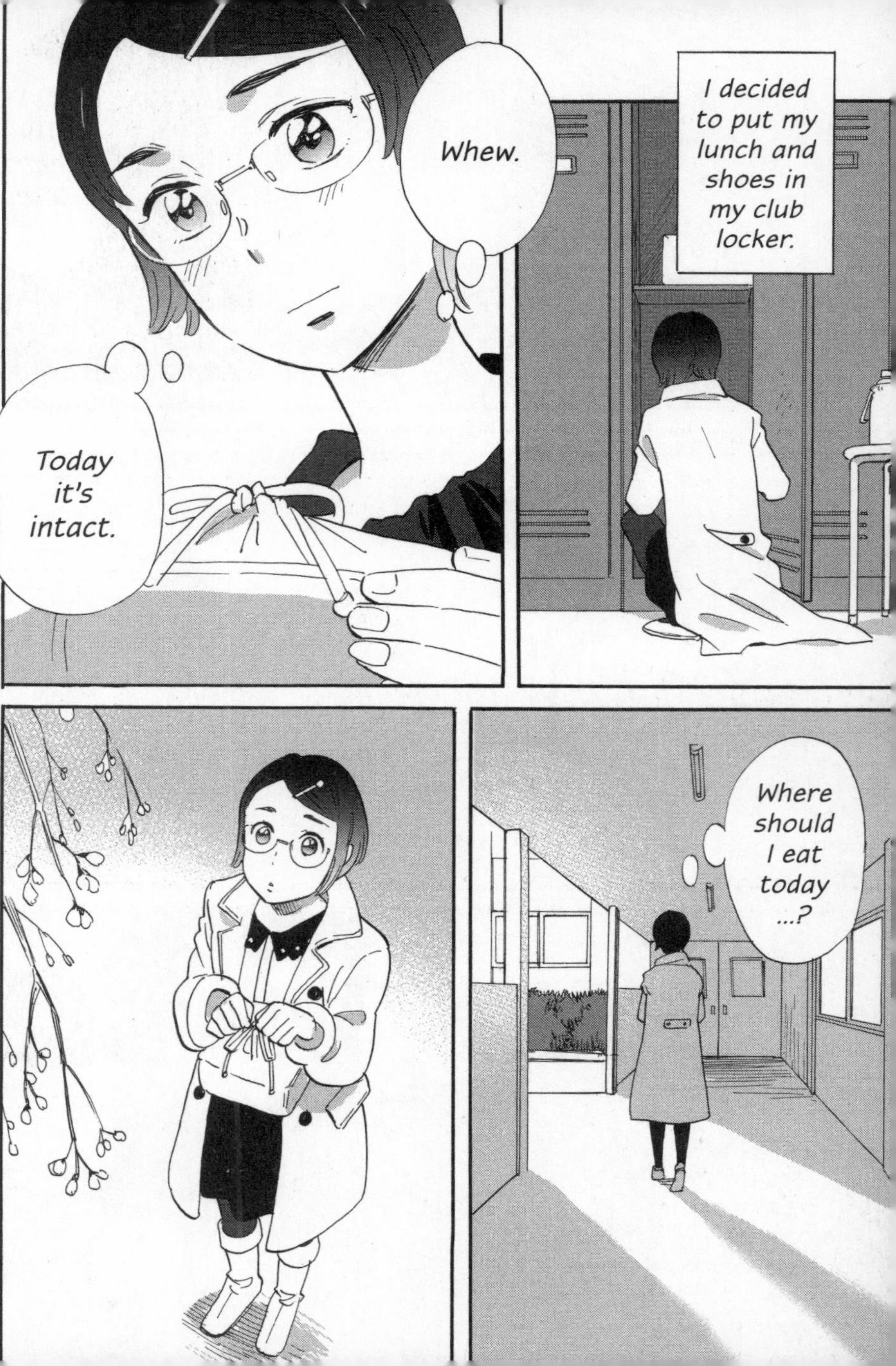
I decided to put my lunch and shoes in my club locker.
Whew.
Today it's intact.
Where should I eat today ...?

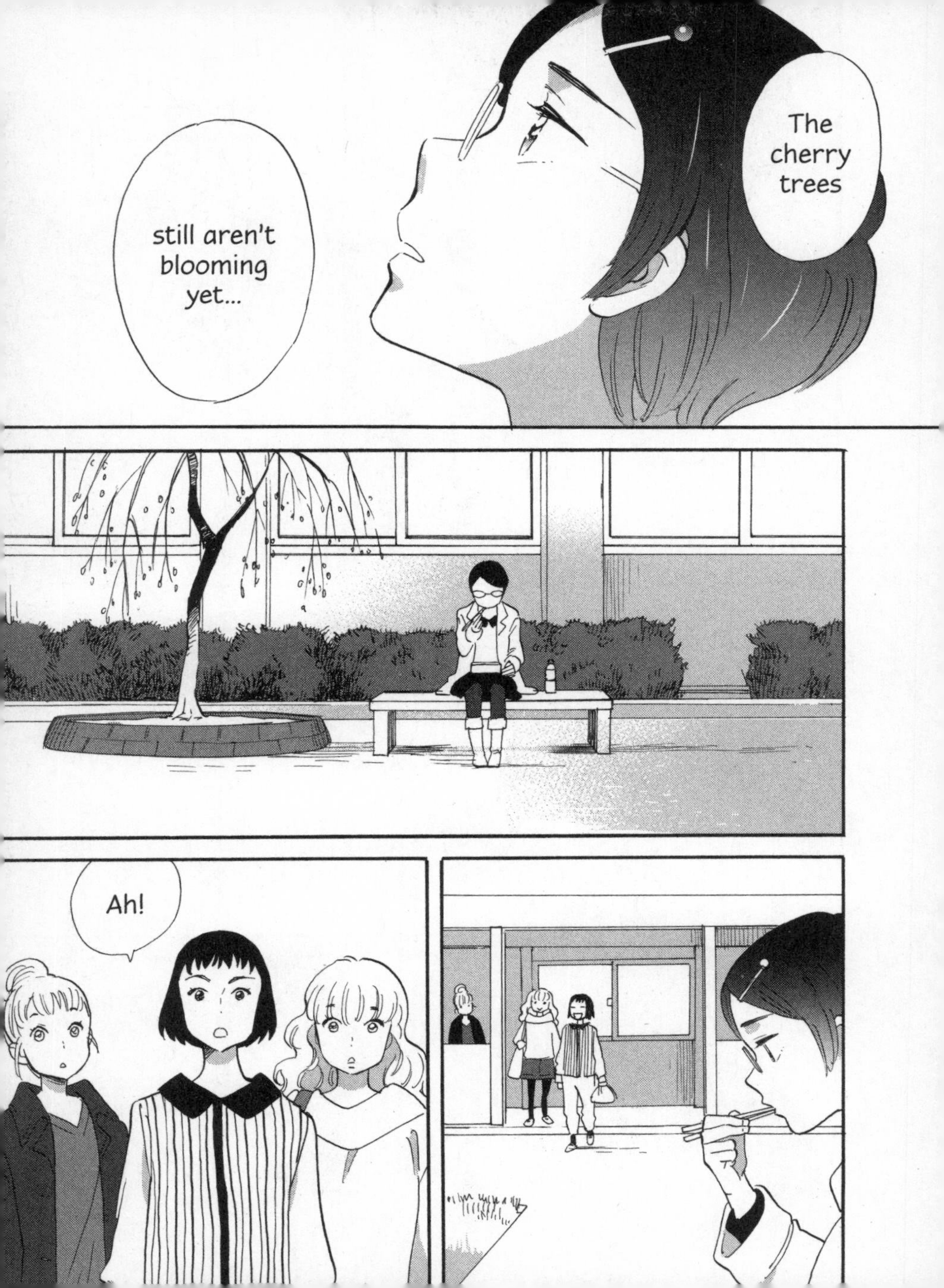
The cherry trees
still aren't blooming yet...
Ah!

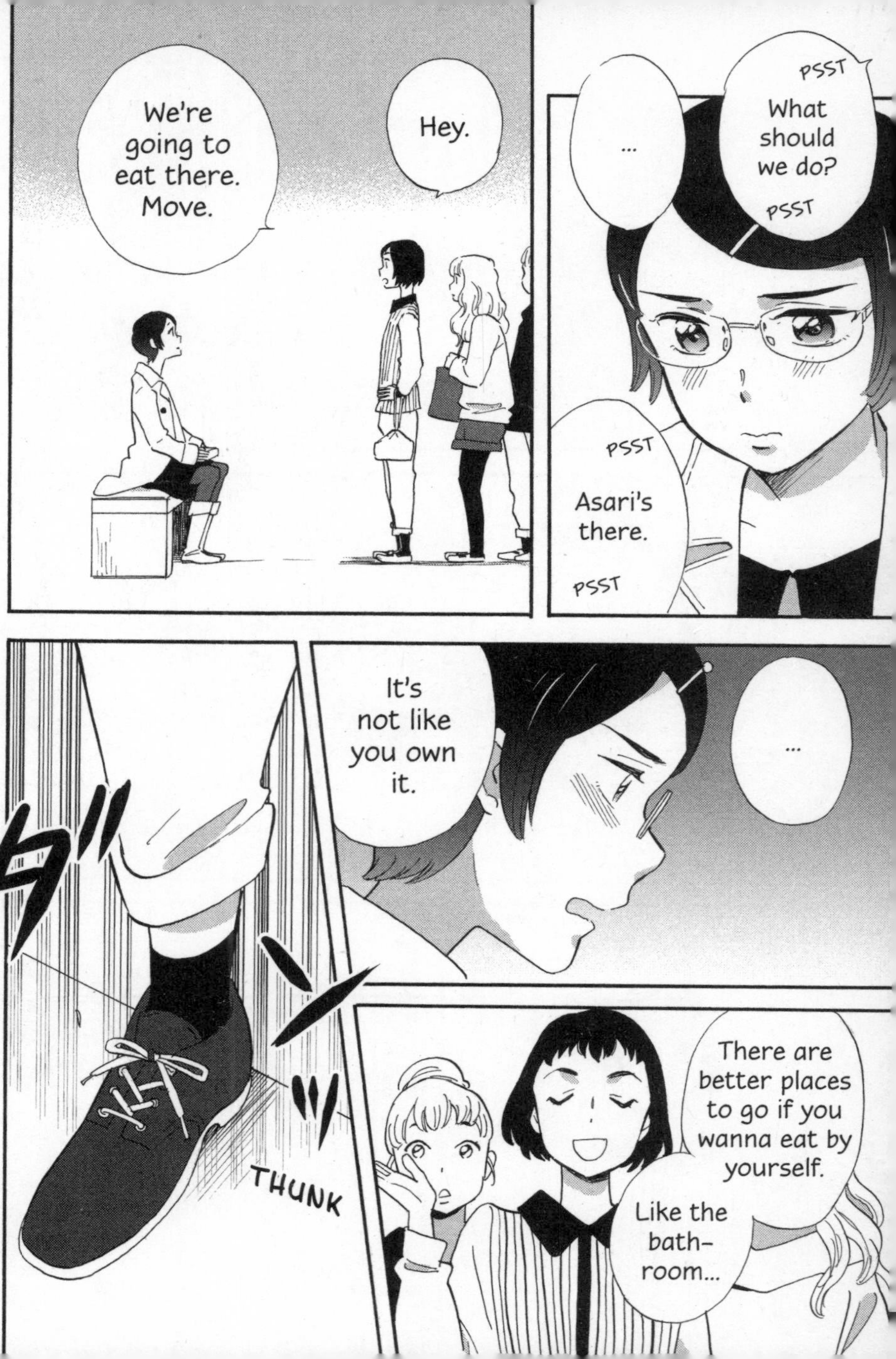
PSST
What should we do?
PSST
...
PSST
Asari's there.
PSST
Hey.
We're going to eat there. Move.
...
It's not like you own it.
There are better places to go if you wanna eat by yourself.
Like the bath-room...
THUNK

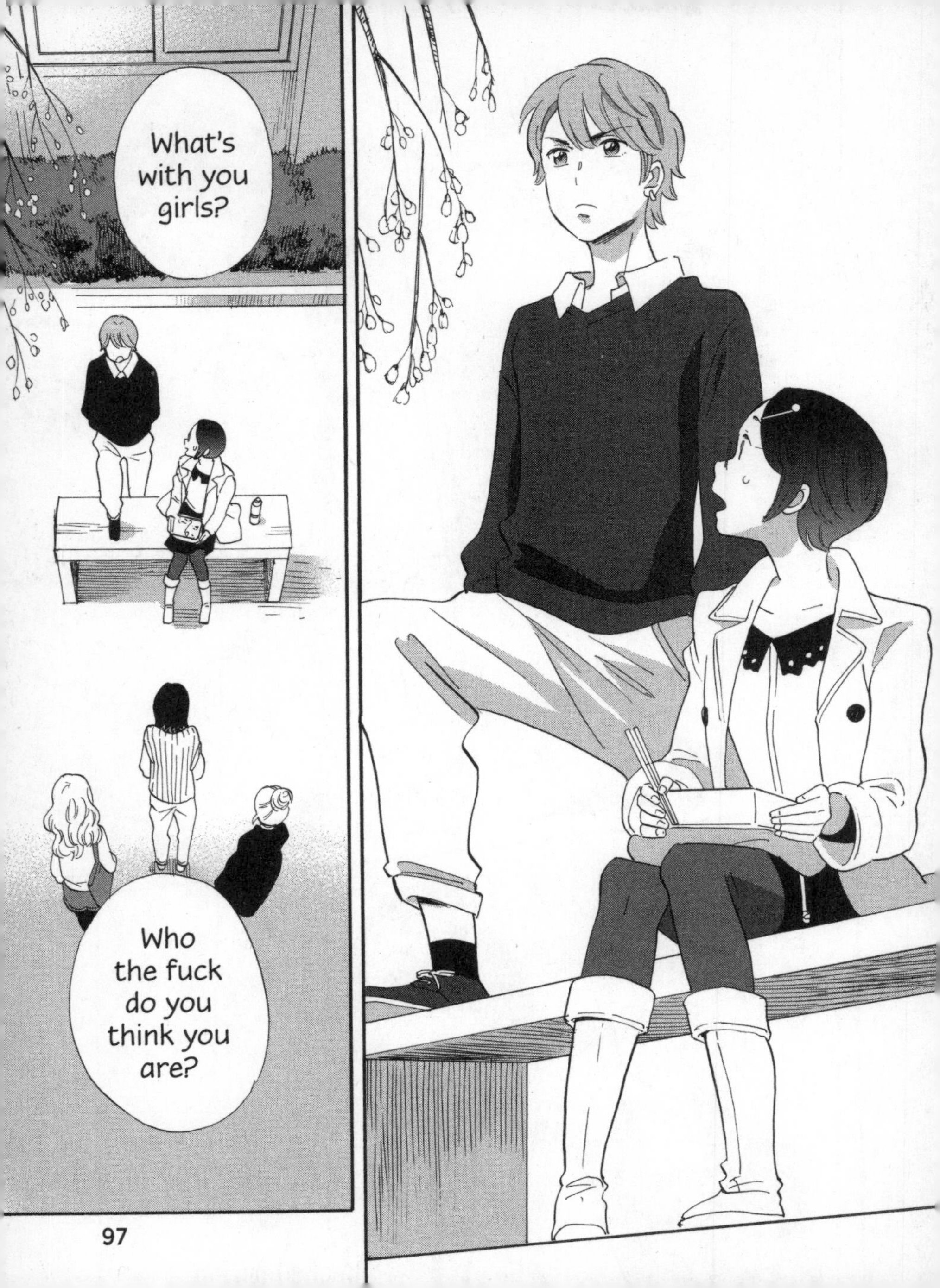
What's with you girls?
Who the fuck do you think you are?

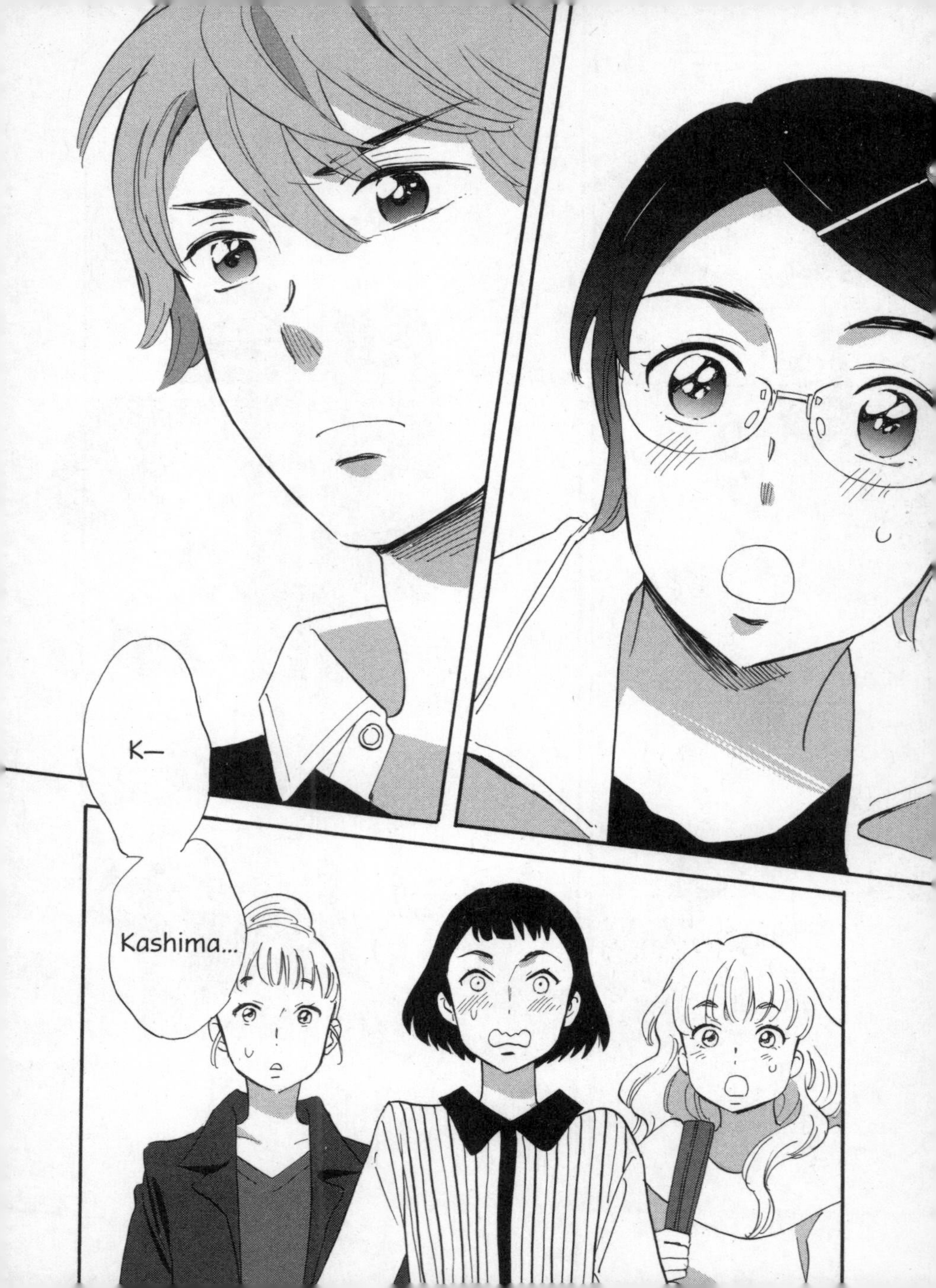
K—
Kashima...

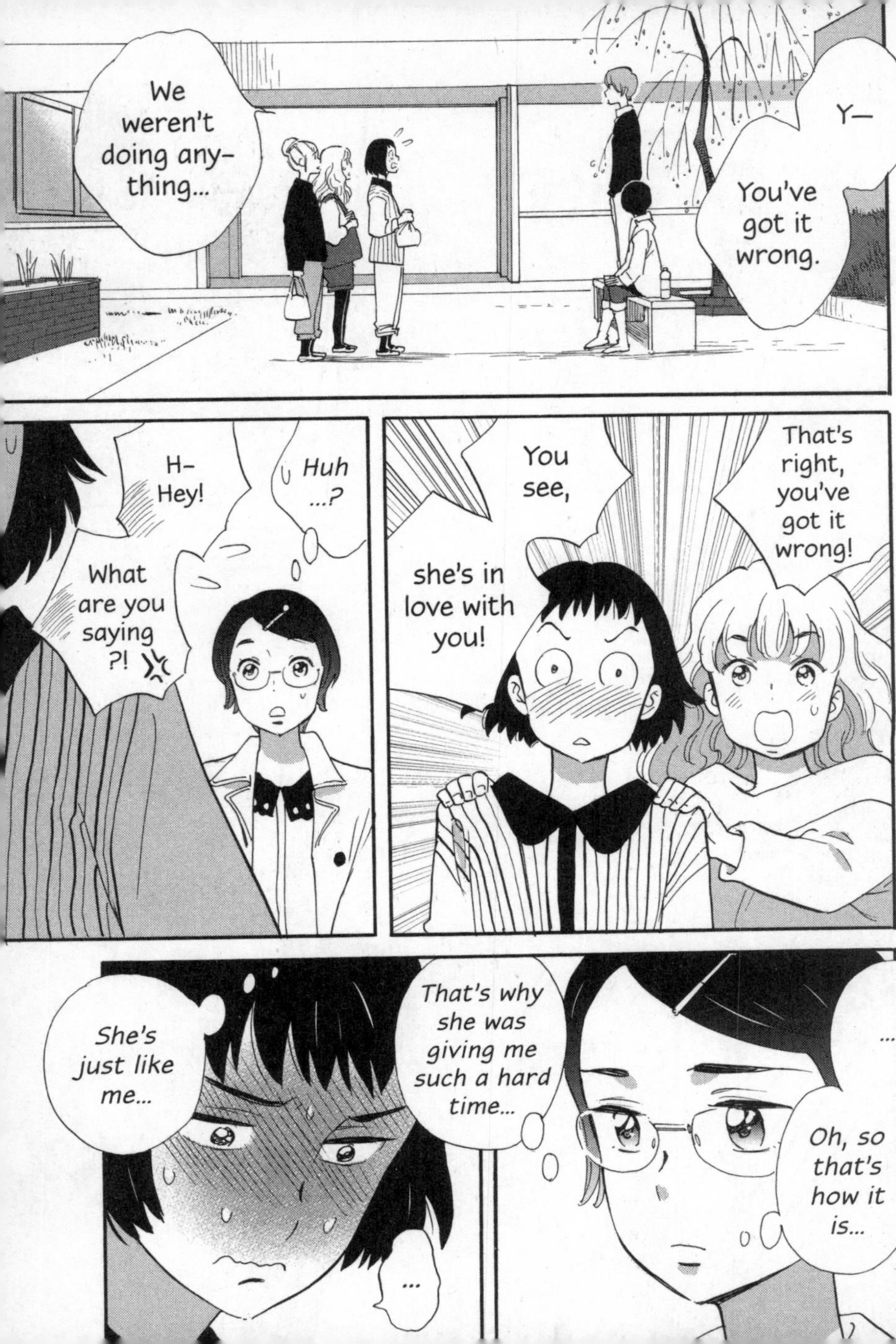
Y—
You've got it wrong.
We weren't doing anything...
That's right, you've got it wrong!
You see, she's in love with you!
Huh ...?
H- Hey! What are you saying?!
...
Oh, so that's how it is...
That's why she was giving me such a hard time...
She's just like me...
...

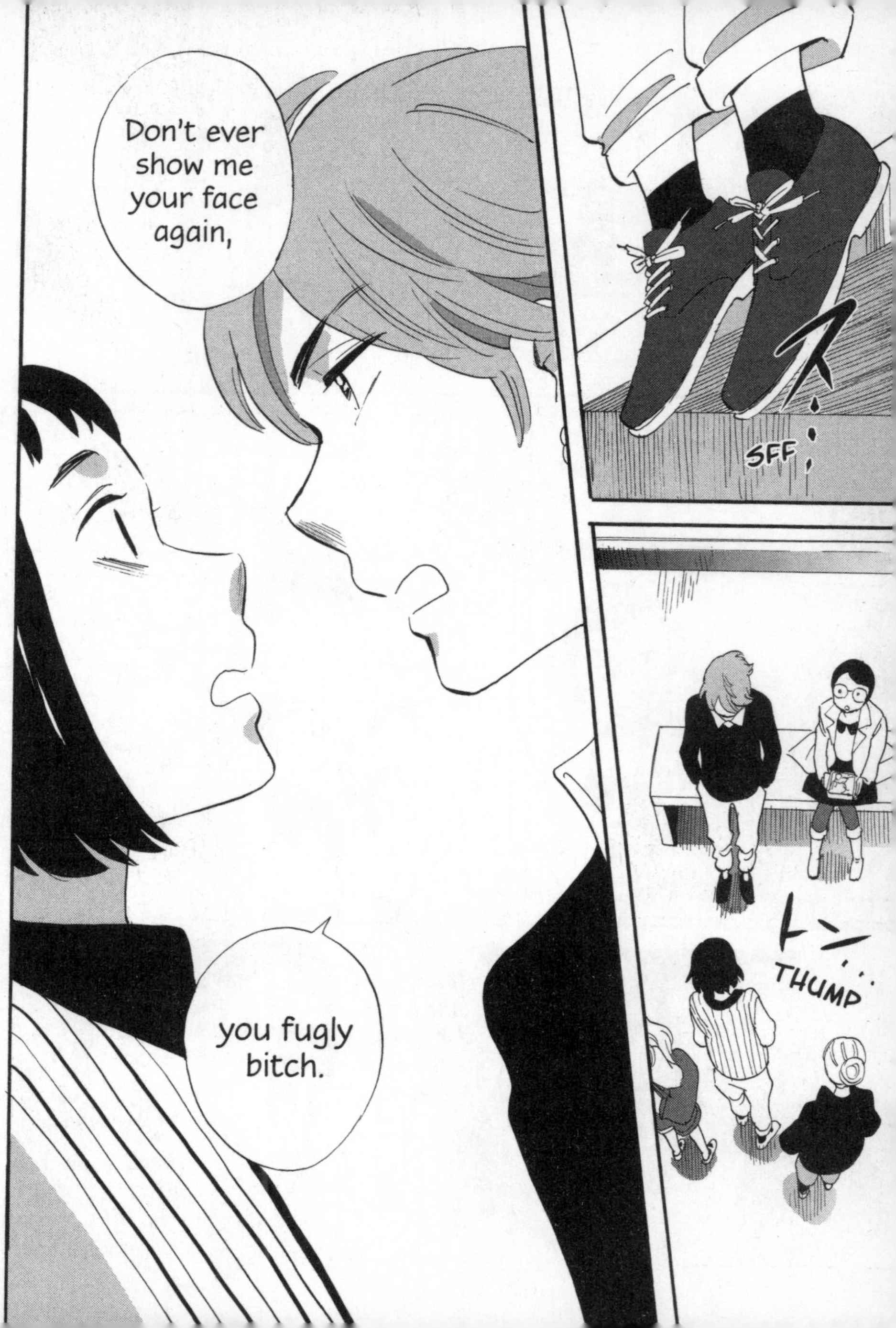

ス
SFF
トン
THUMP
Don't ever show me your face again,
you fugly bitch.

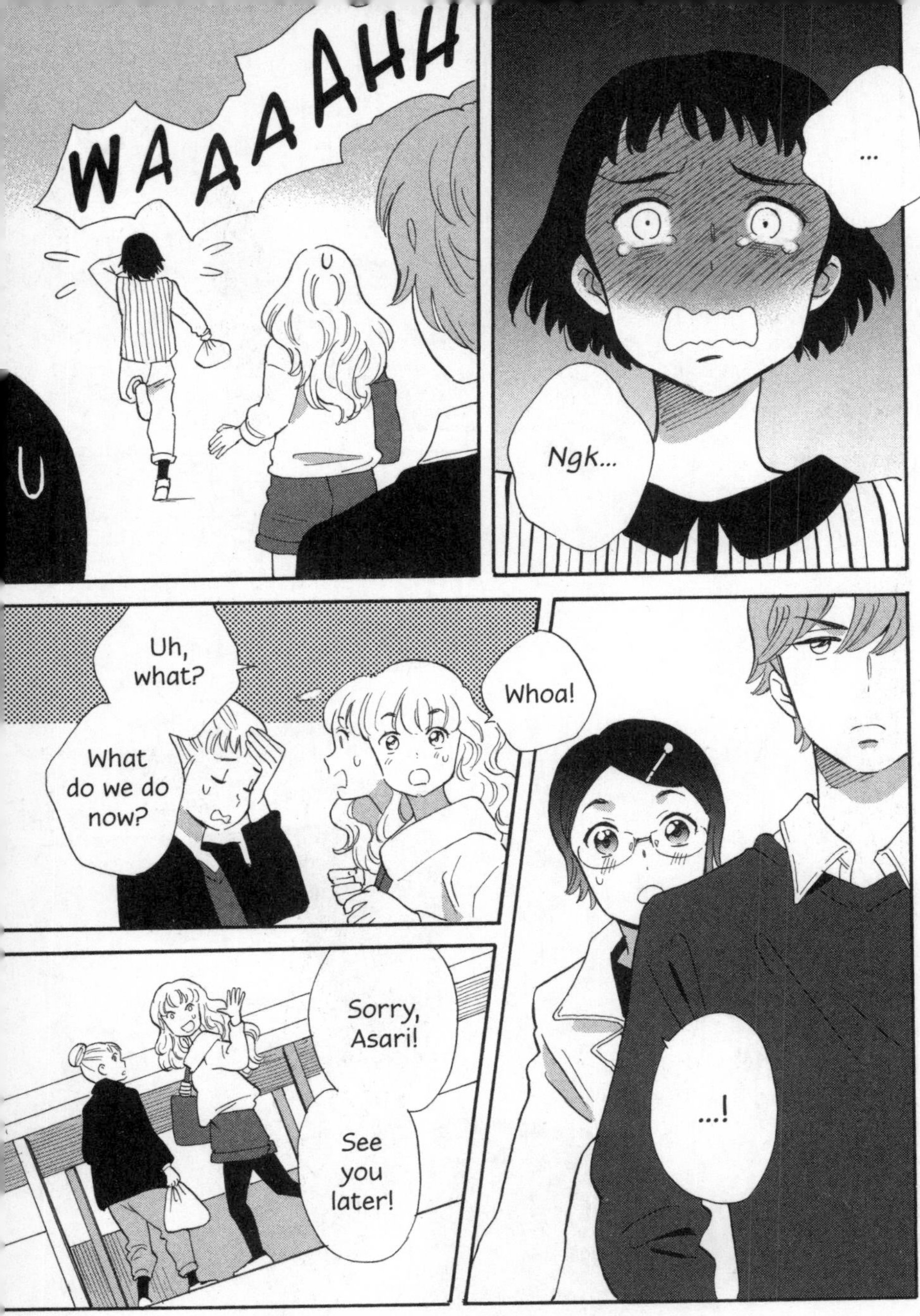
...
Ngk...
WAAAAHH
...!
Whoa!
Uh, what?
What do we do now?
Sorry, Asari!
See you later!

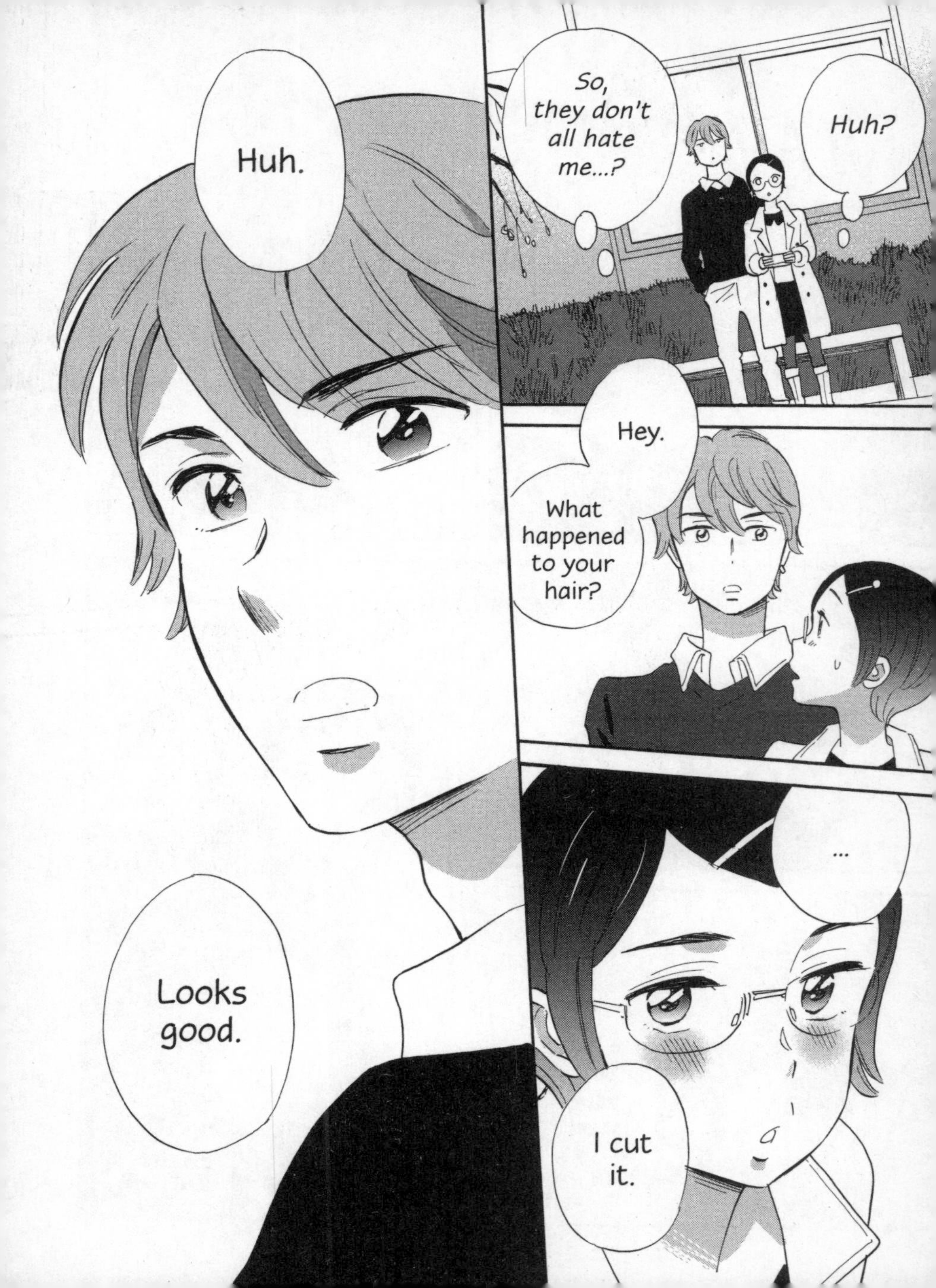
Huh?
So, they don't all hate me...?
Hey.
What happened to your hair?
...
I cut it.
Huh.
Looks good.

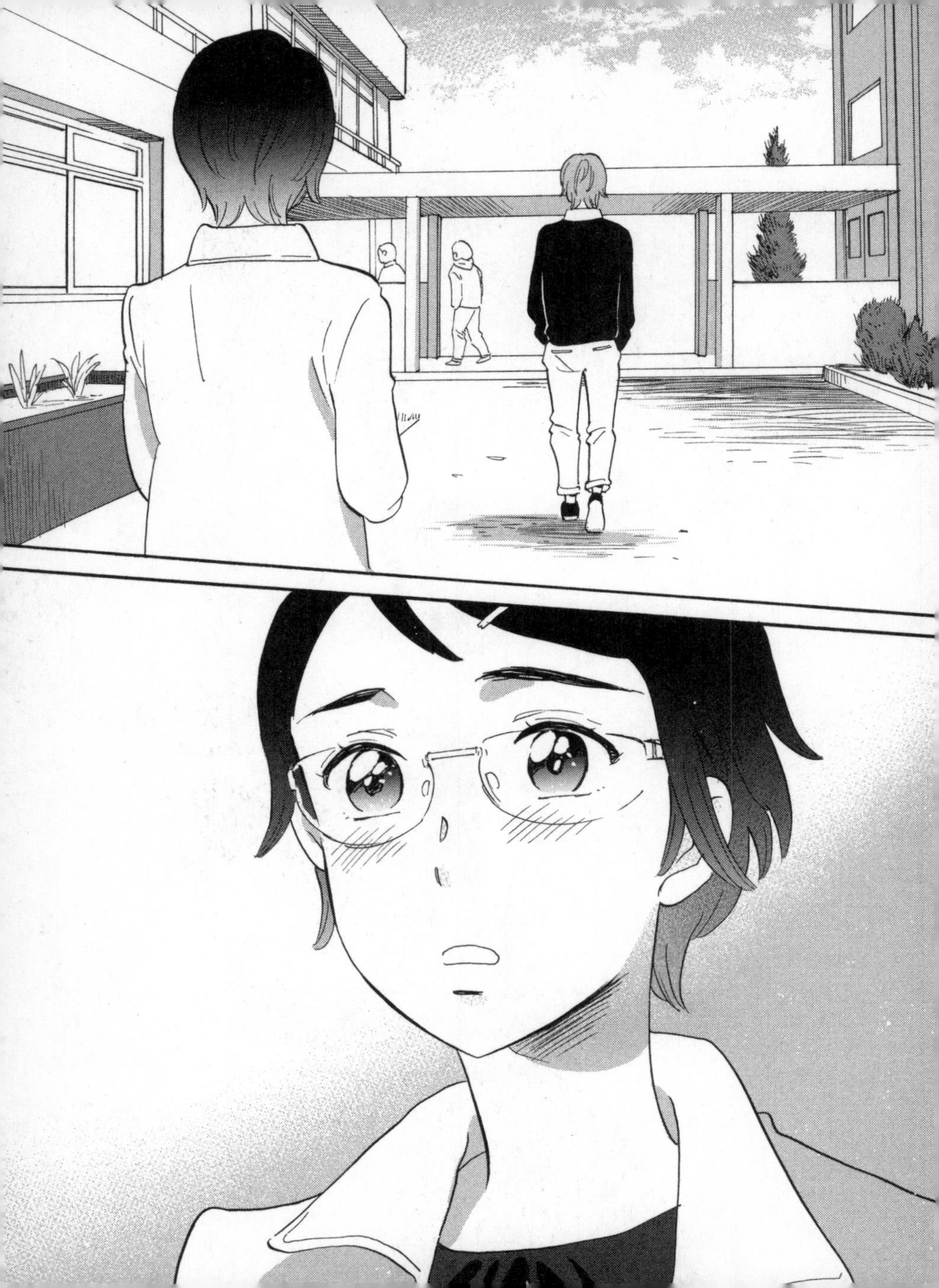

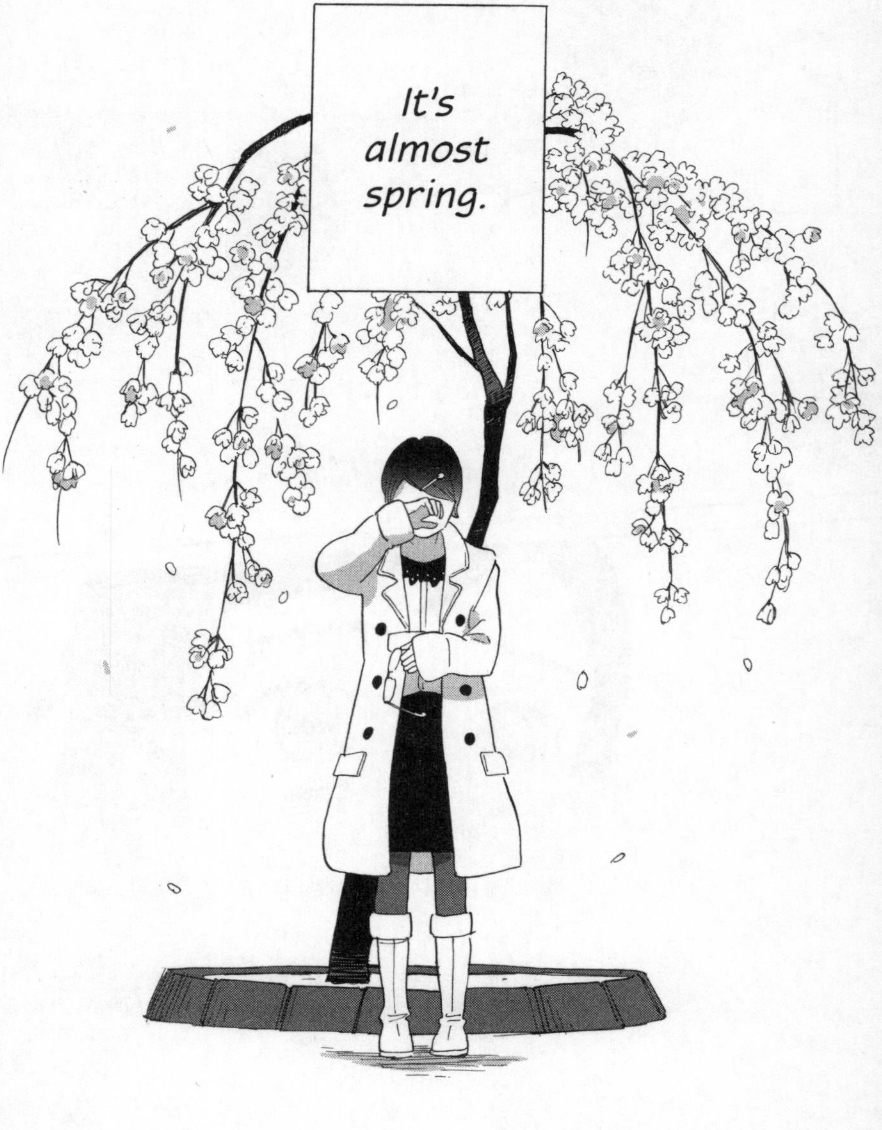
It's almost spring.

THE GOLDEN SHEEP

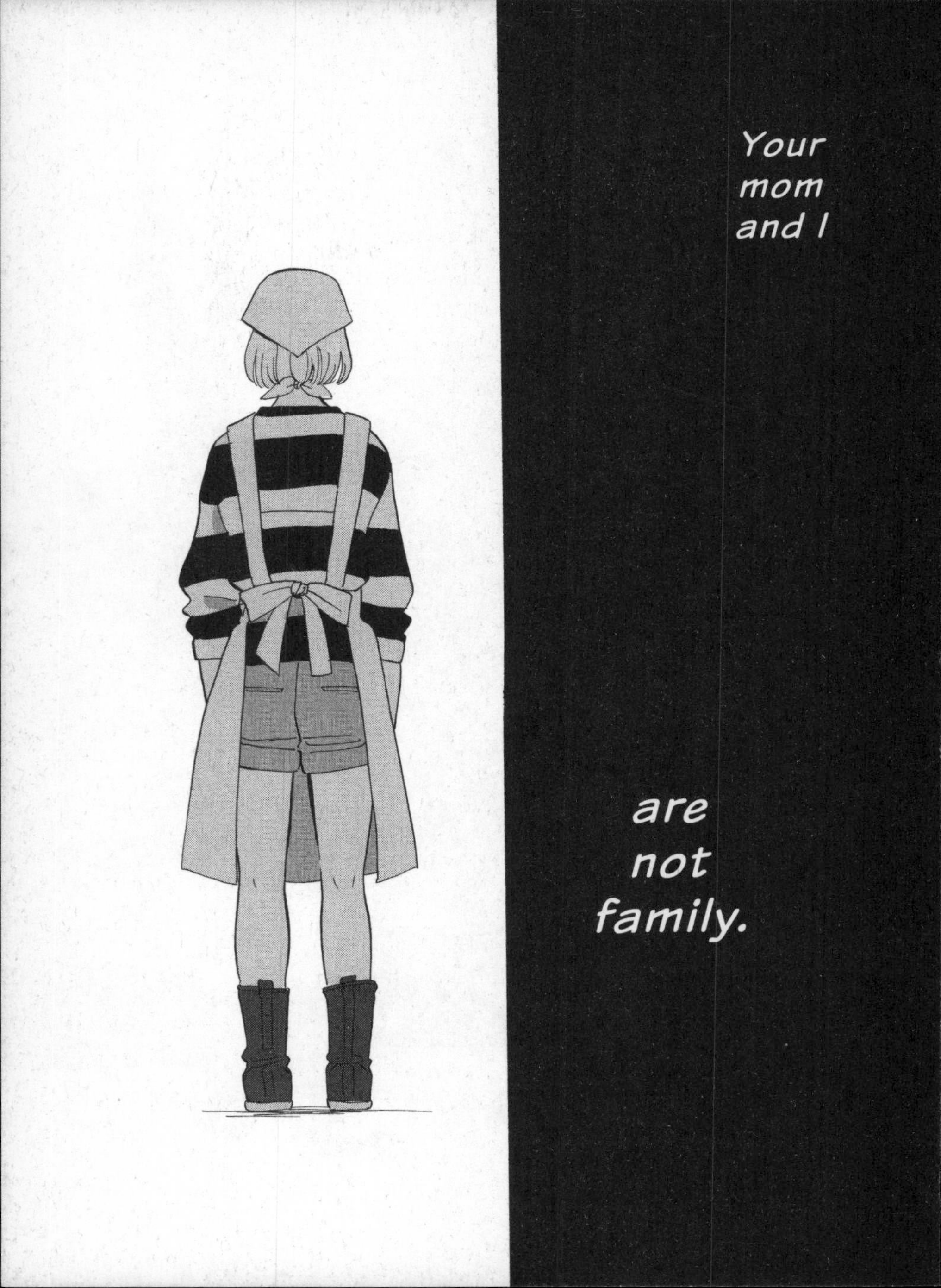
Your mom and I
are not family.

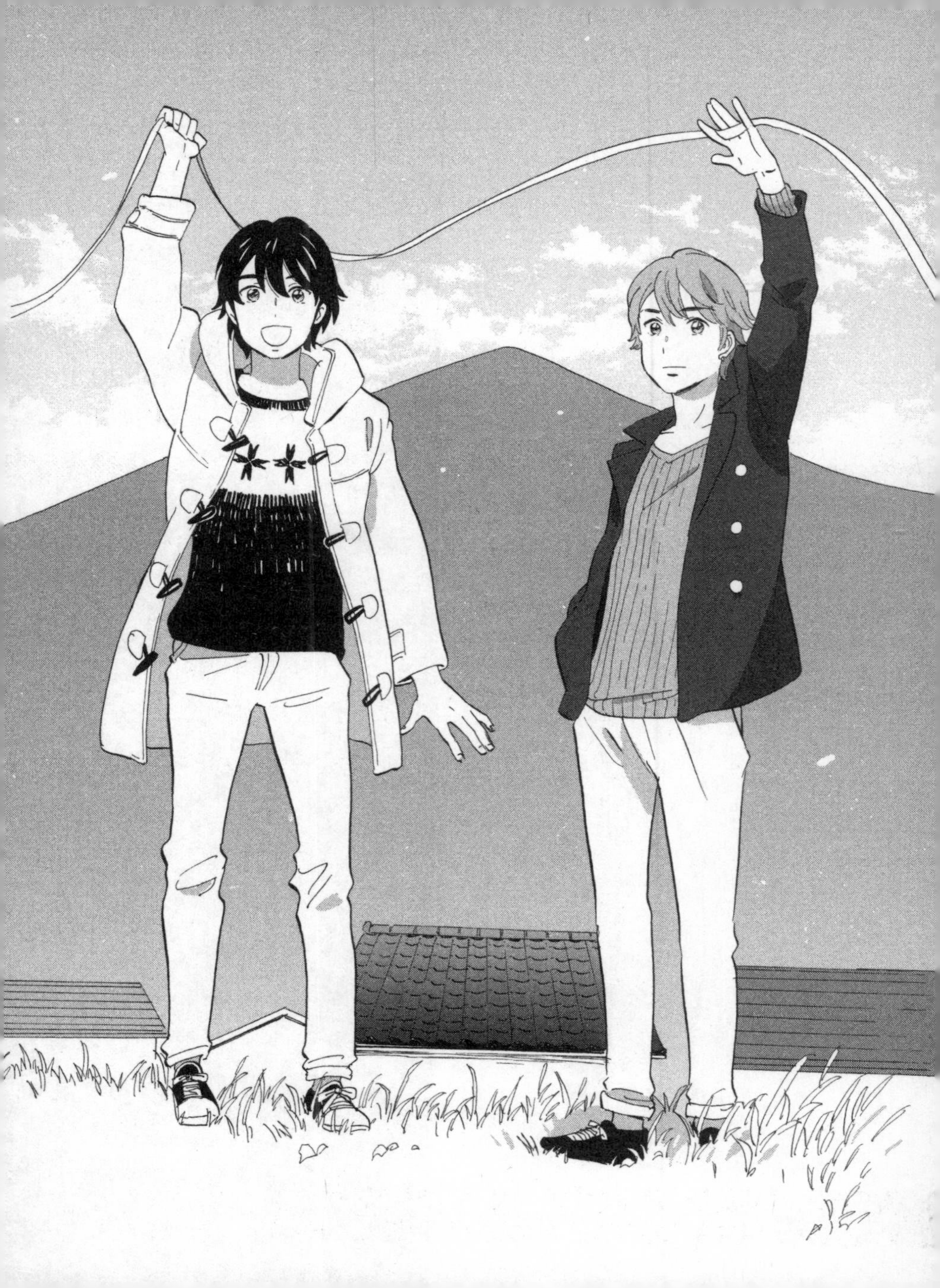

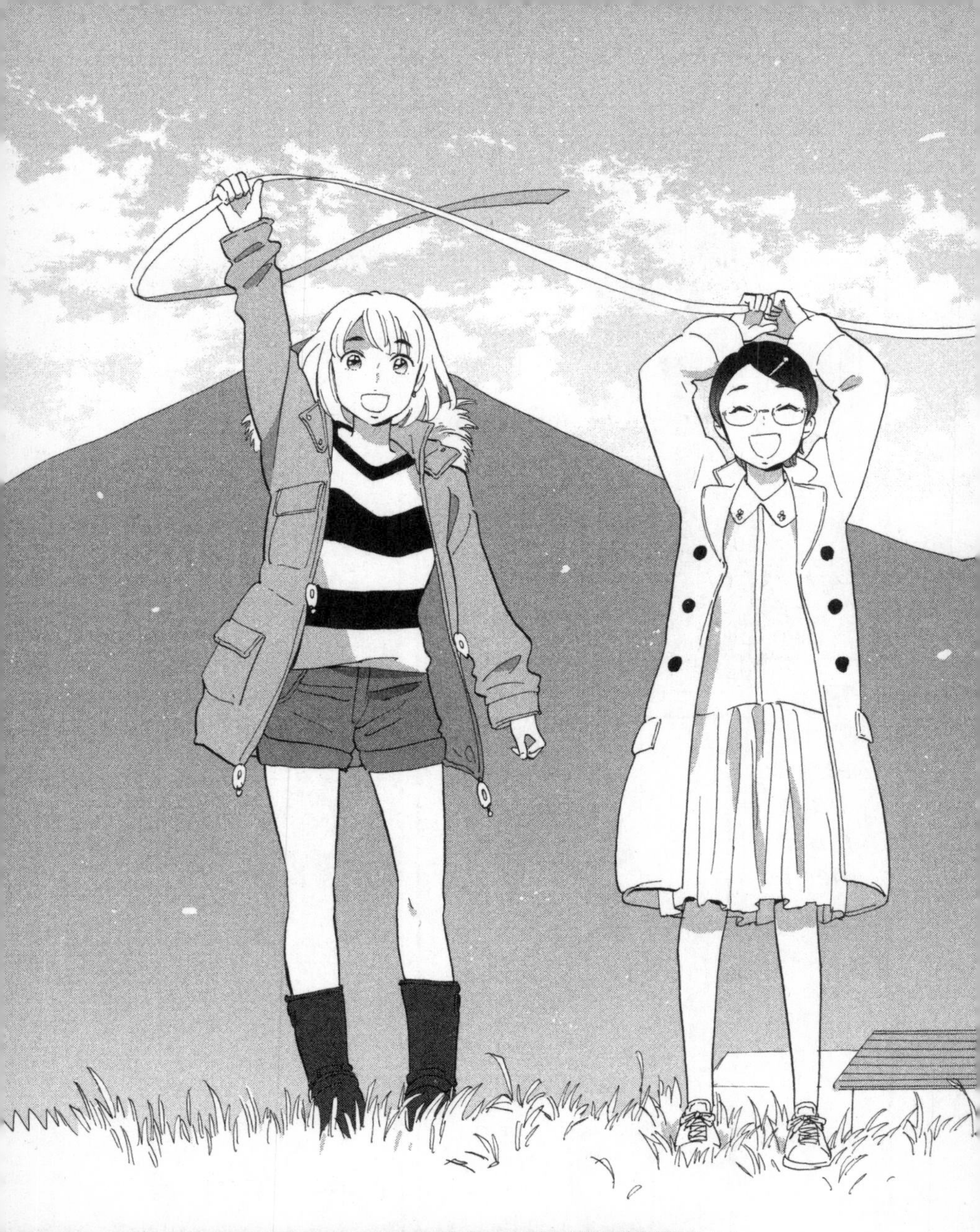

(Final chapter) The Time Has Come!

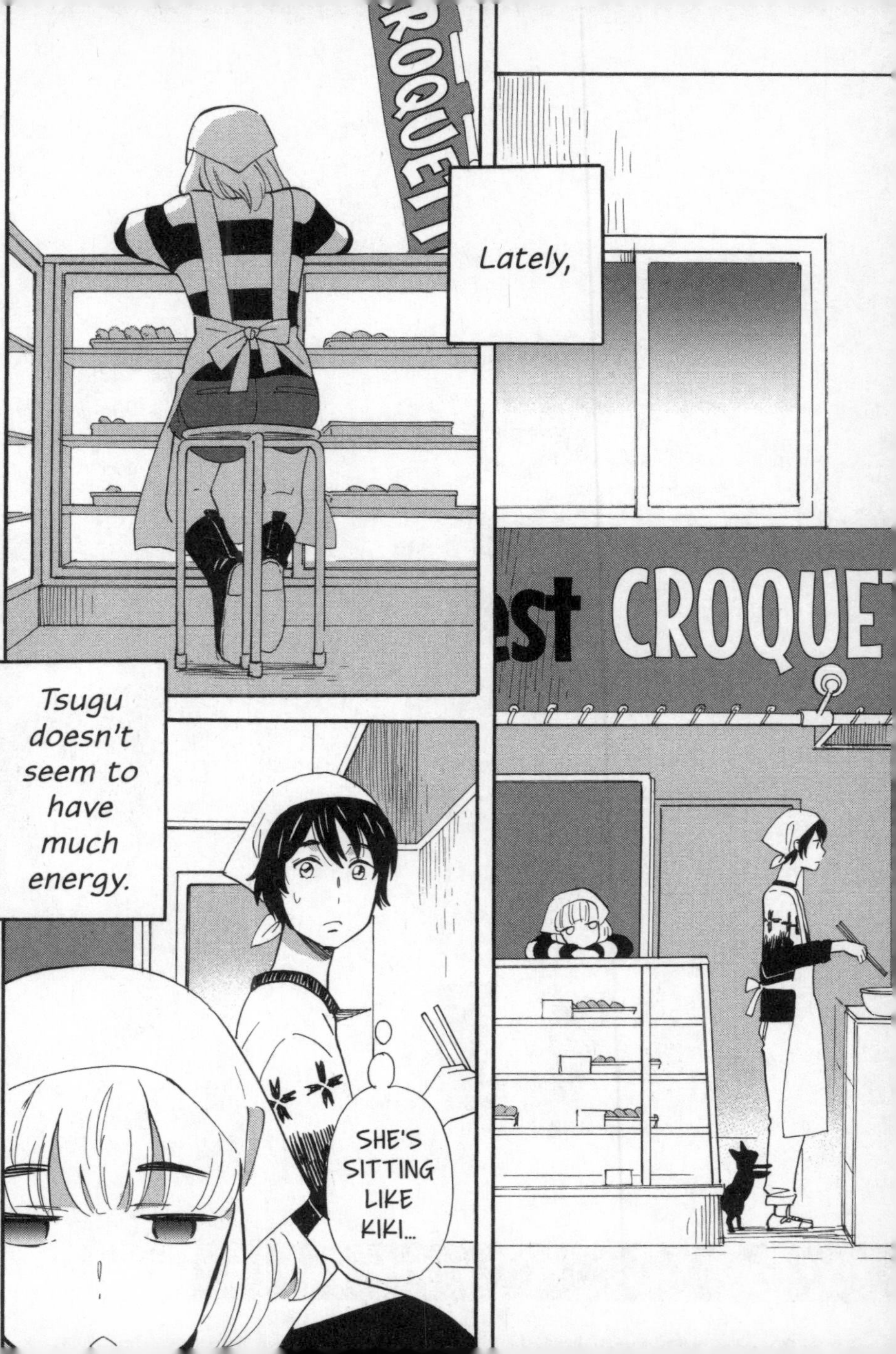
Lately,
Tsugu doesn't seem to have much energy.
SHE'S SITTING LIKE KIKI...

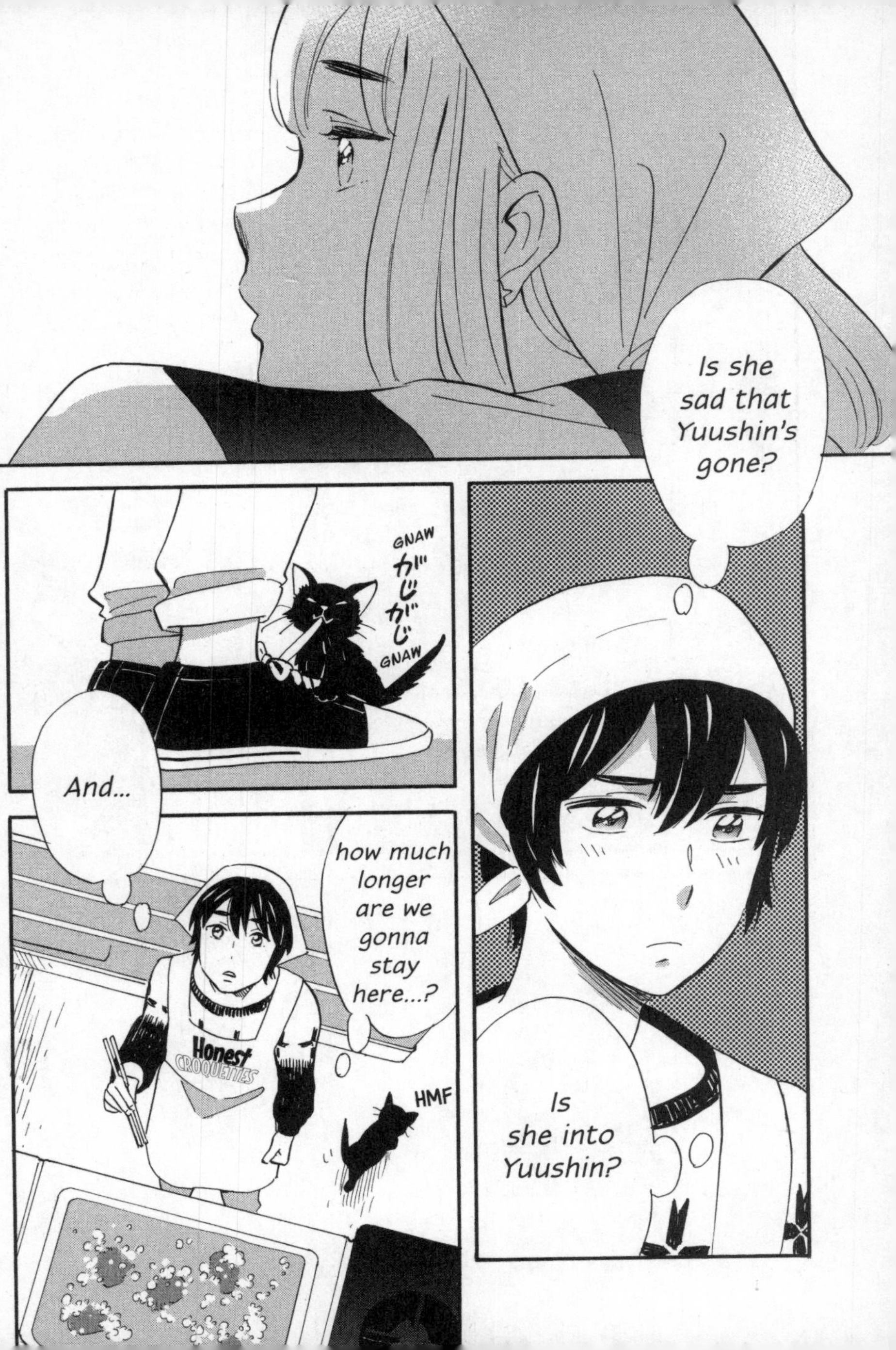
Is she sad that Yuushin's gone?
Is she into Yuushin?
GNAW
がじがじ
GNAW
And...
how much longer are we gonna stay here...?
Honest CROQUETTES
HMF

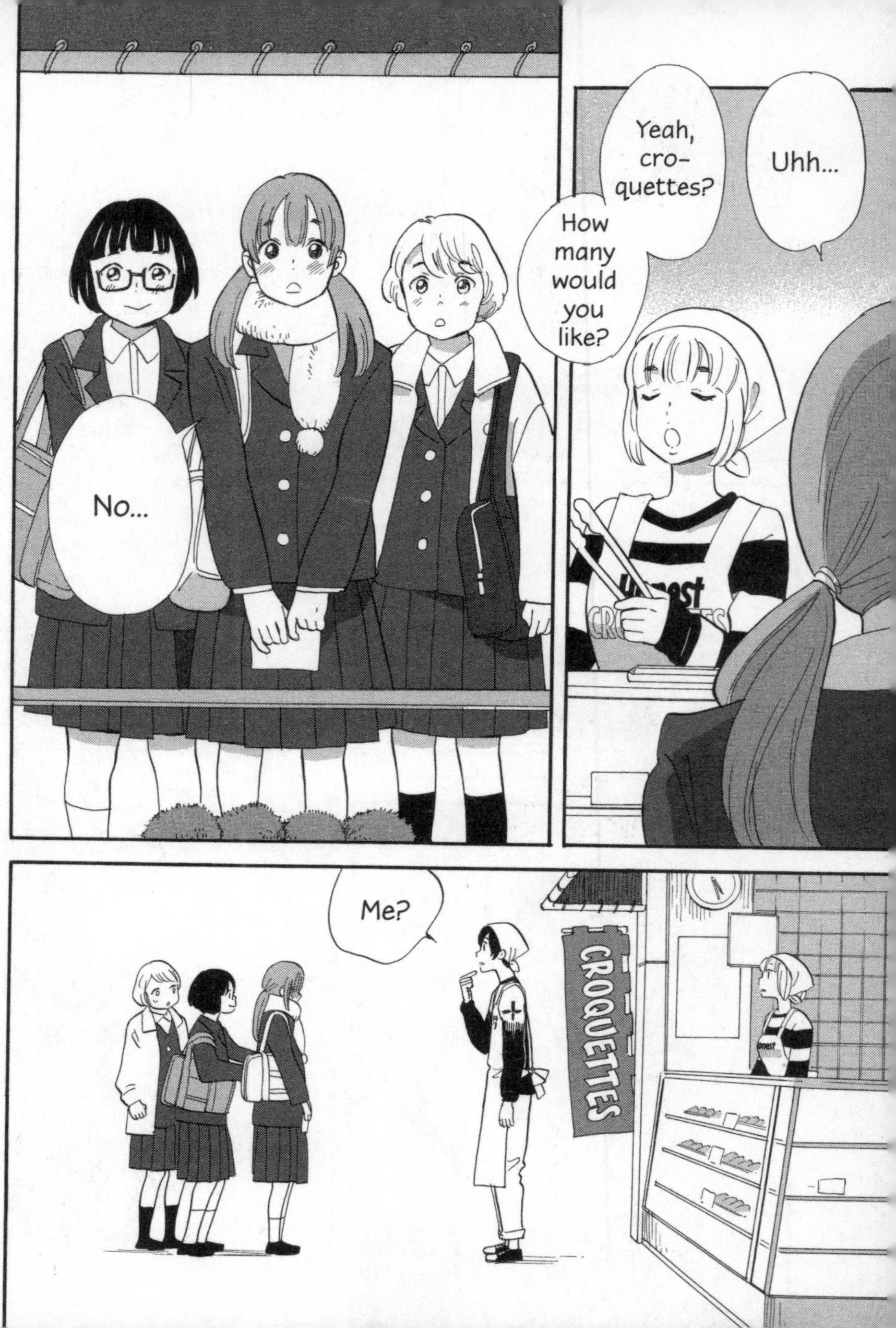
Uhh...
Yeah, cro-quettes?
How many would you like?
No...
Me?
CROQUETTES

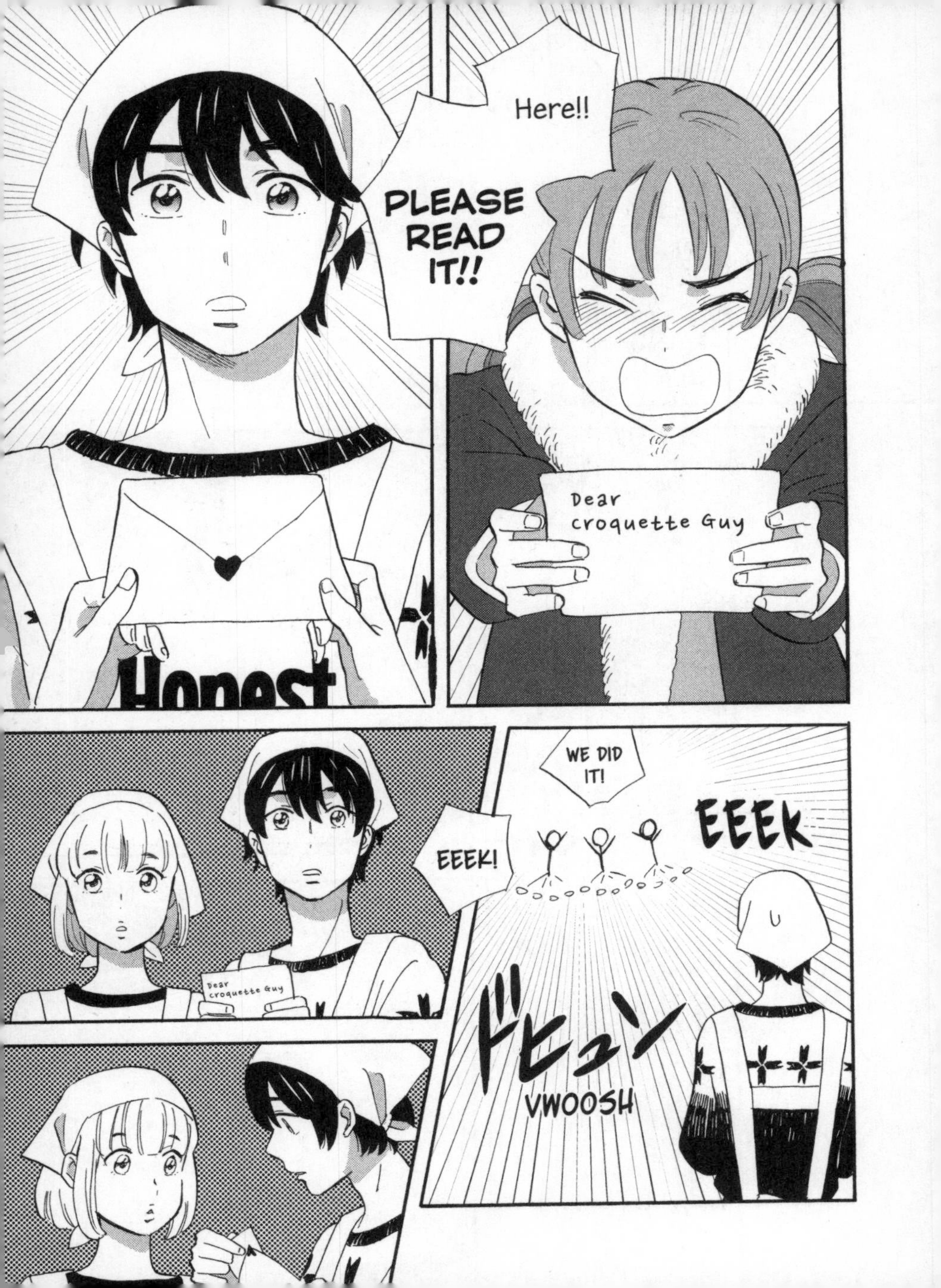
Here!!
PLEASE READ IT!!
Dear croquette Guy
Honest
WE DID IT!
EEEK
ドヒュン
VWOOSH
EEEK!
Dear croquette Guy

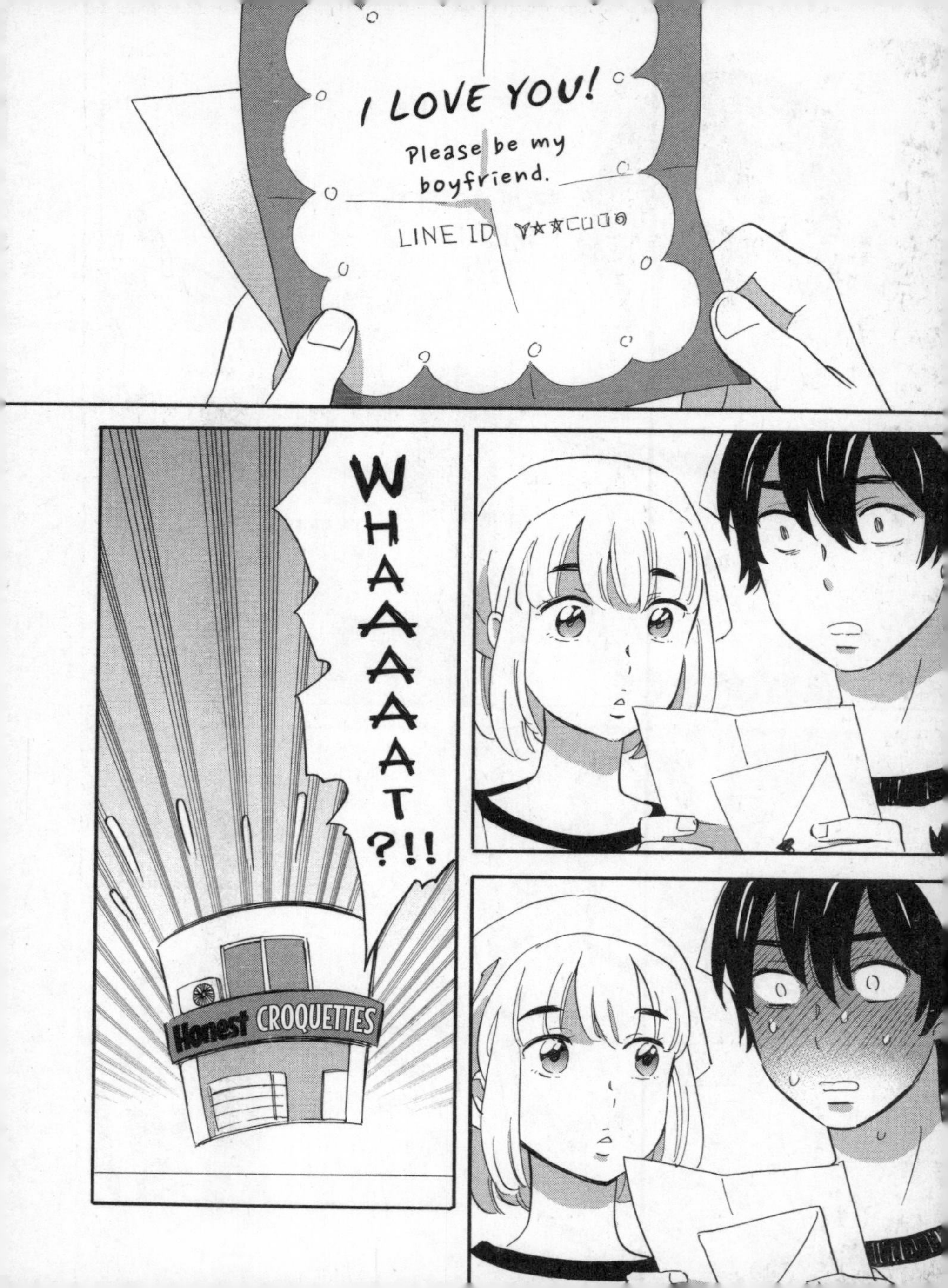
I LOVE YOU!
Please be my boyfriend.
LINE ID
Honest CROQUETTES
WHAAAAT?!!

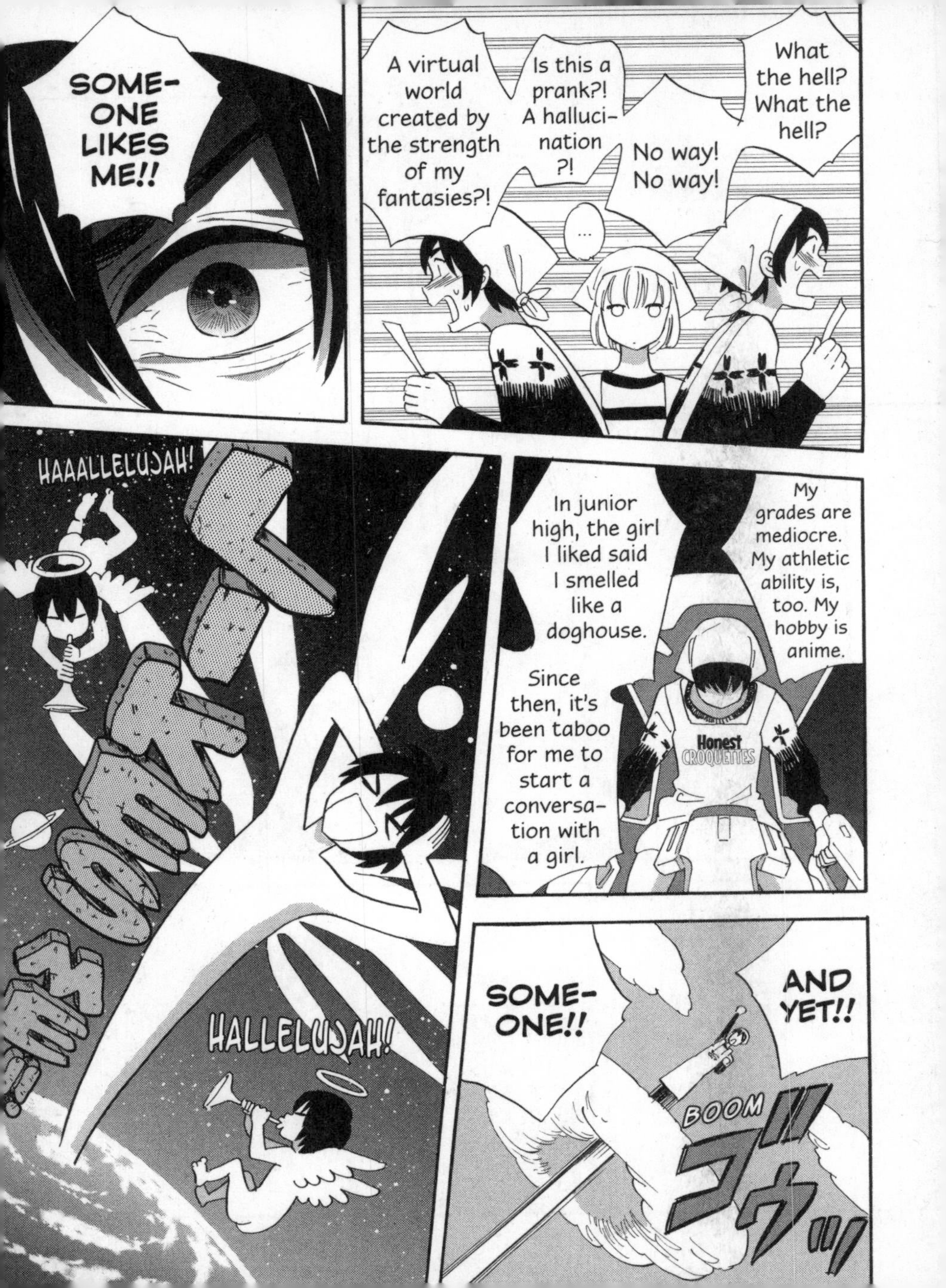
What the hell? What the hell?
No way! No way!
Is this a prank?! A halluci-nation?!
A virtual world created by the strength of my fantasies?!
...
SOME-ONE LIKES ME!!
My grades are mediocre. My athletic ability is, too. My hobby is anime.
In junior high, the girl I liked said I smelled like a doghouse.
Since then, it's been taboo for me to start a conversation with a girl.
Honest CROQUETTES
AND YET!!
SOME-ONE!!
BOOM
HAAALLELUJAH!
HALLELUJAH!

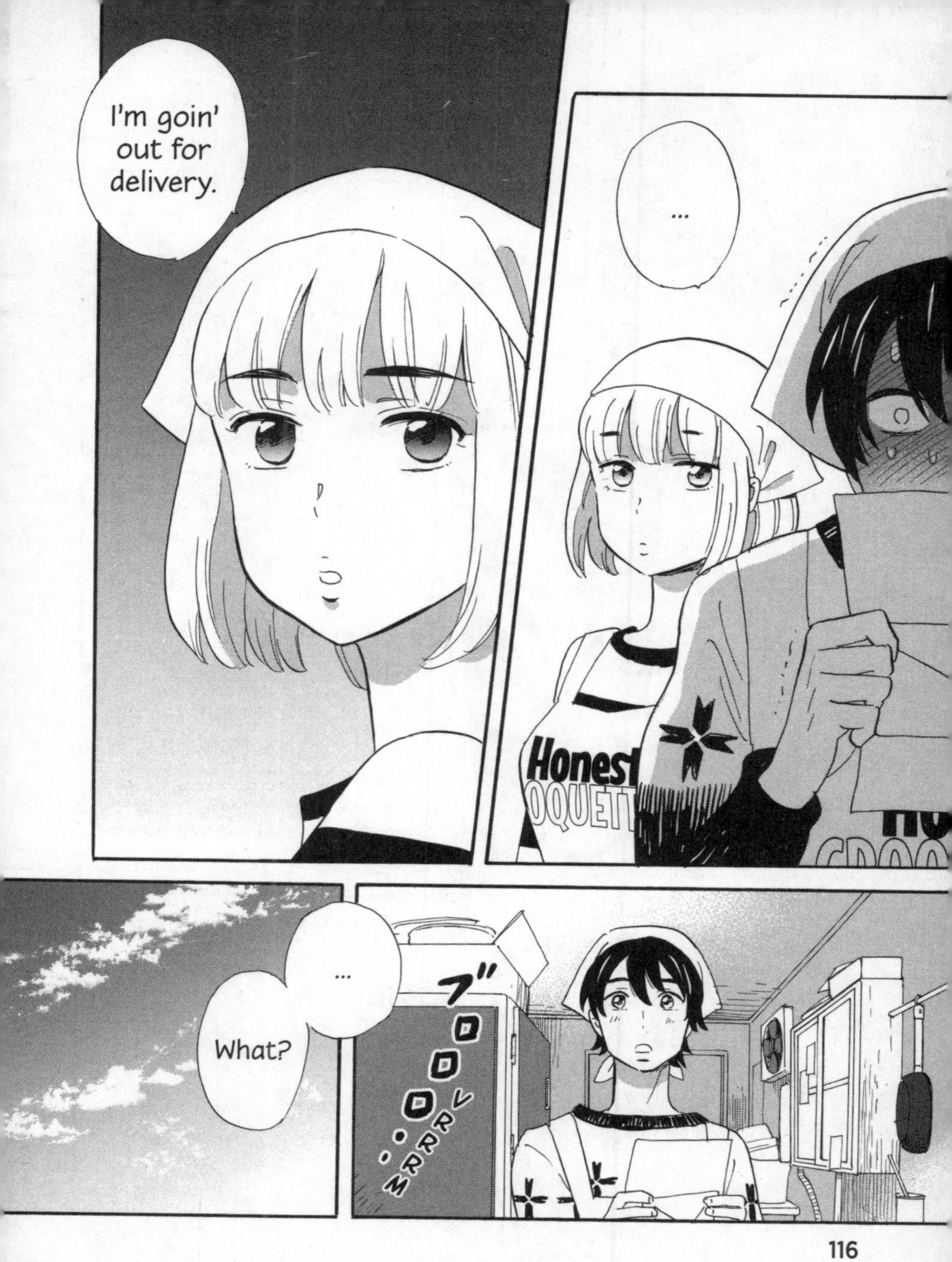
...
I'm goin' out for delivery.
Honest
OQUETT
ブ
DDDVRRRM..
...
What?

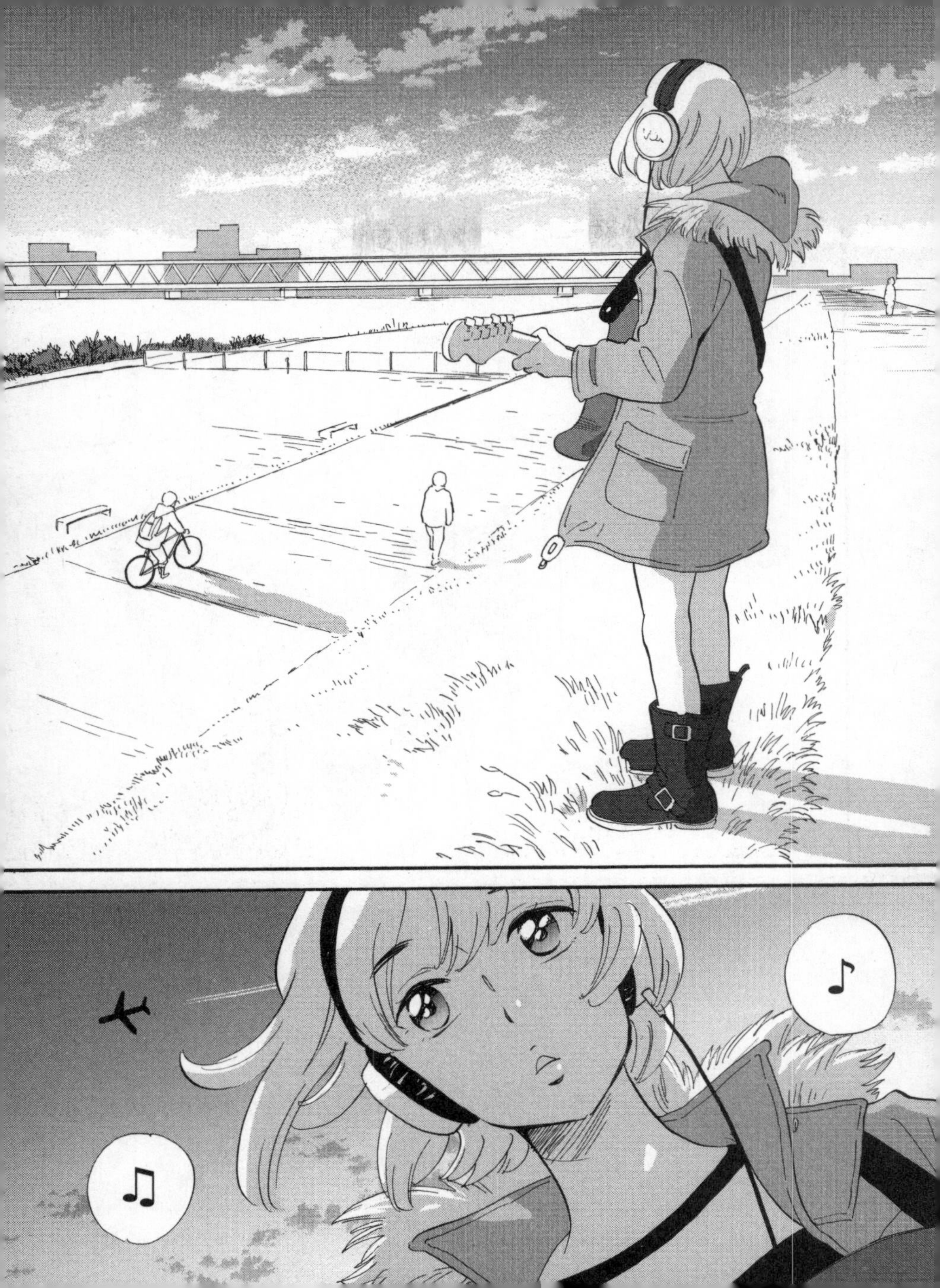
♪
♫

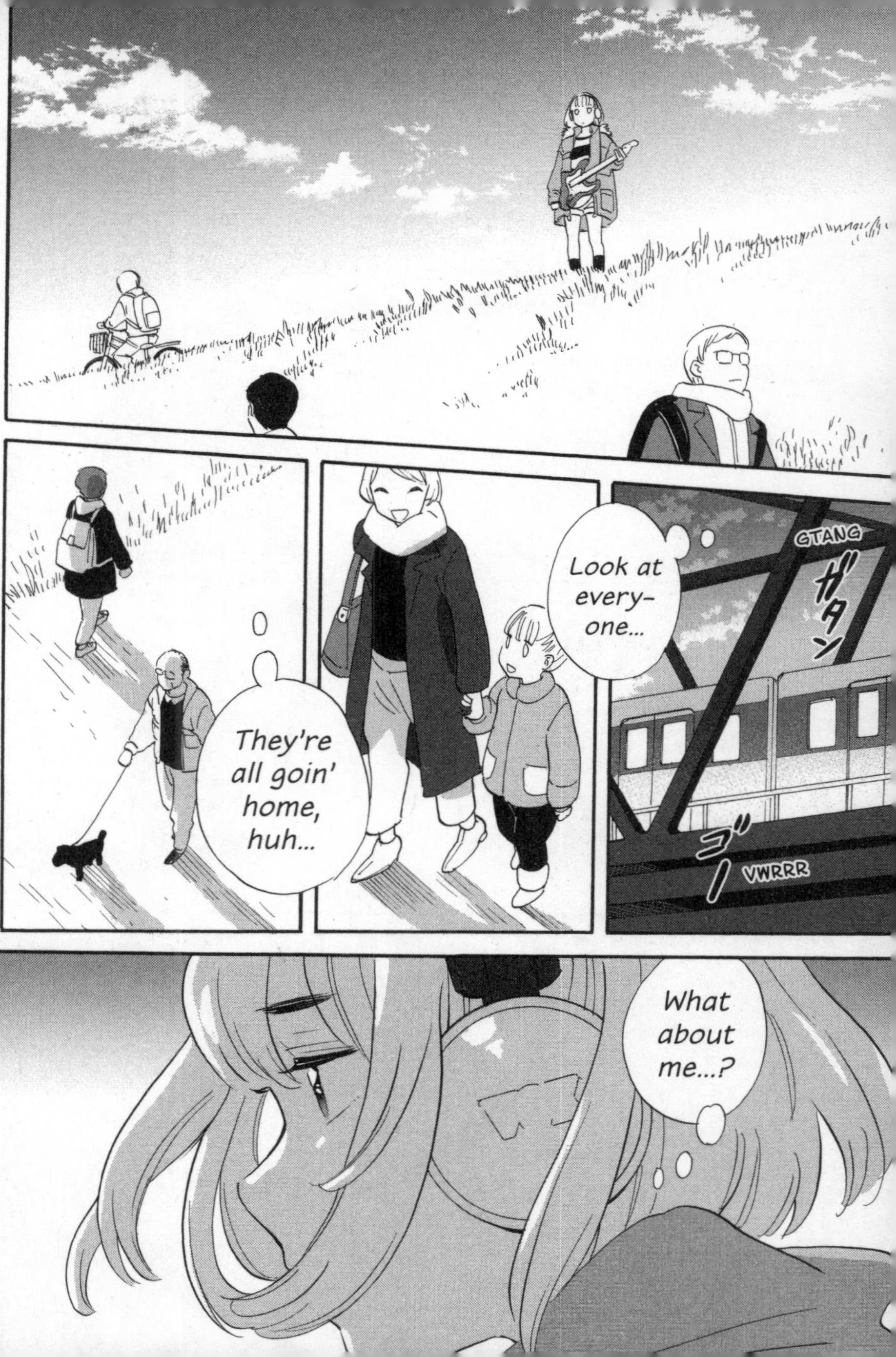
GTANG
ガタン
ゴー
VWRRR
Look at every-one...
They're all goin' home, huh...
What about me...?

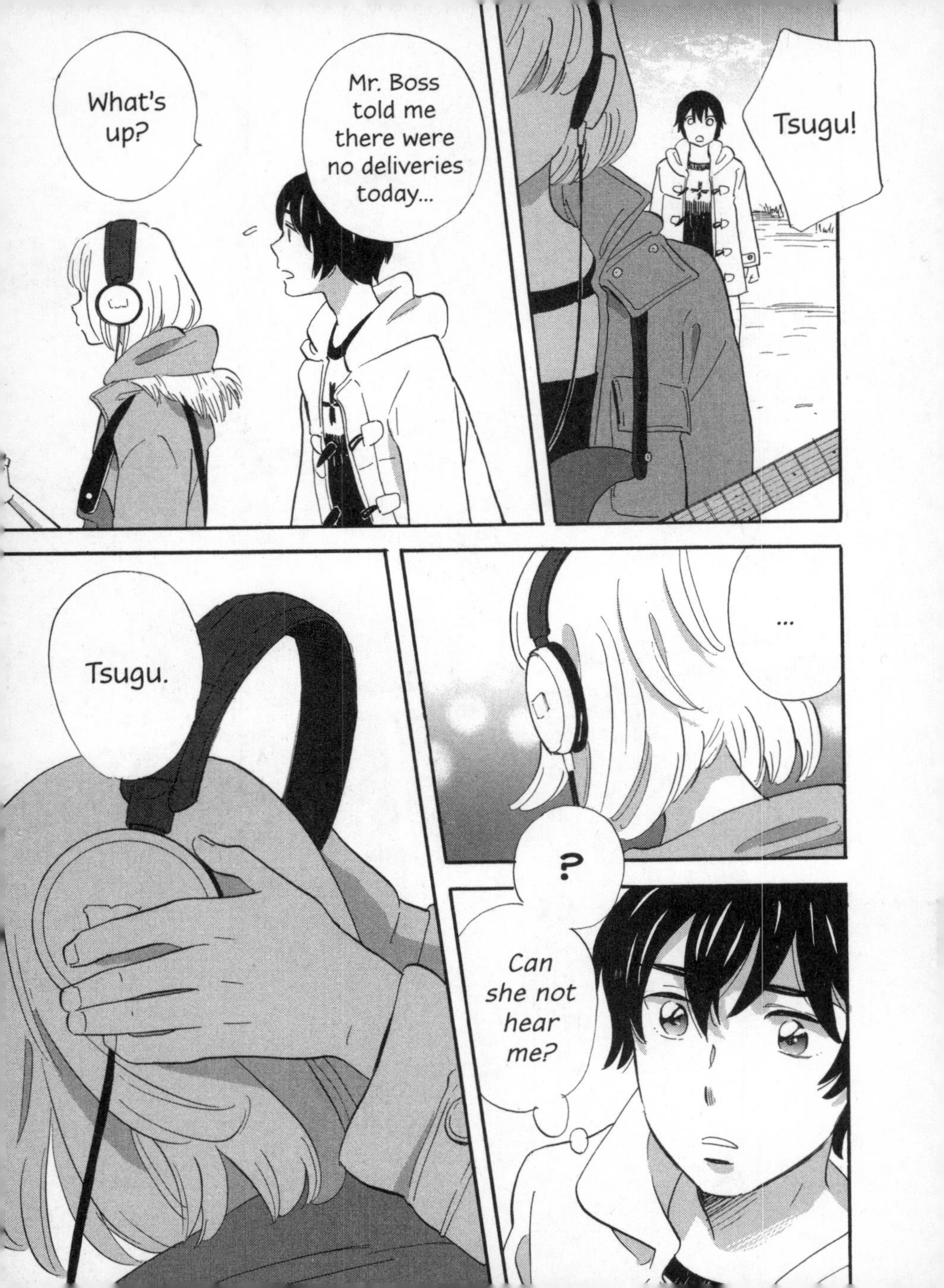
Tsugu!
Mr. Boss told me there were no deliveries today...
What's up?
...
?
Can she not hear me?
Tsugu.

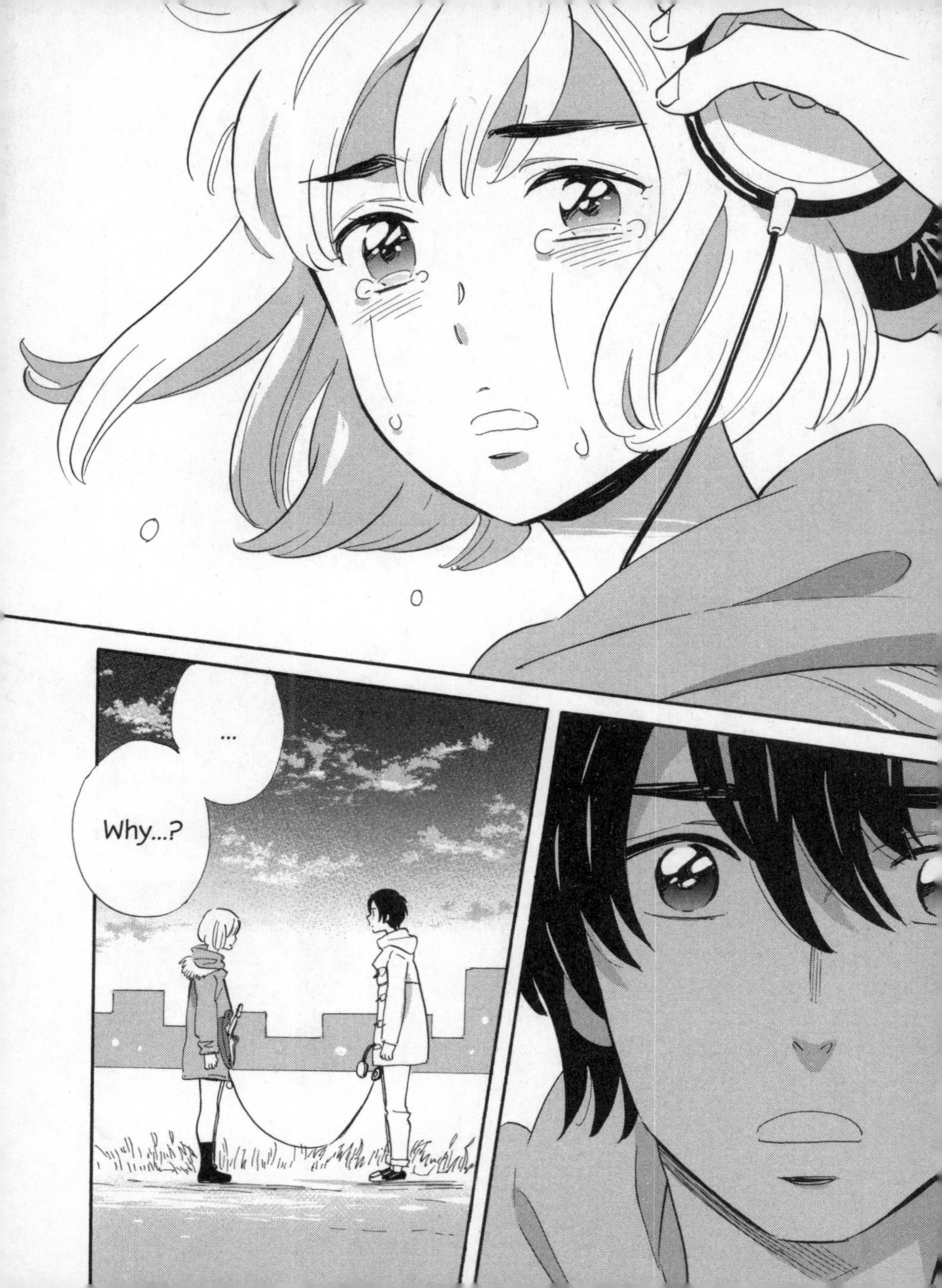
...
Why...?

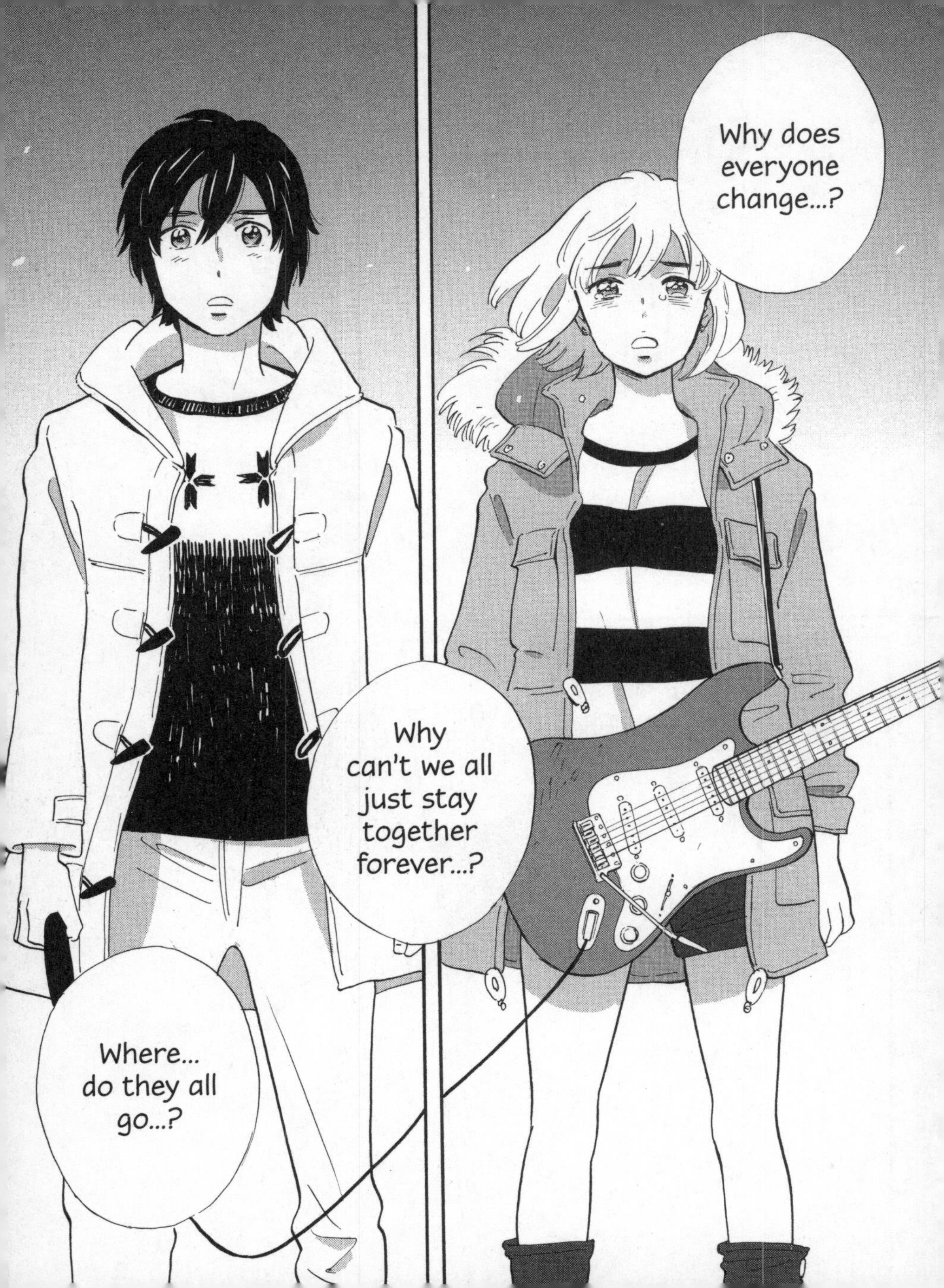
Why does everyone change...?
Why can't we all just stay together forever...?
Where... do they all go...?

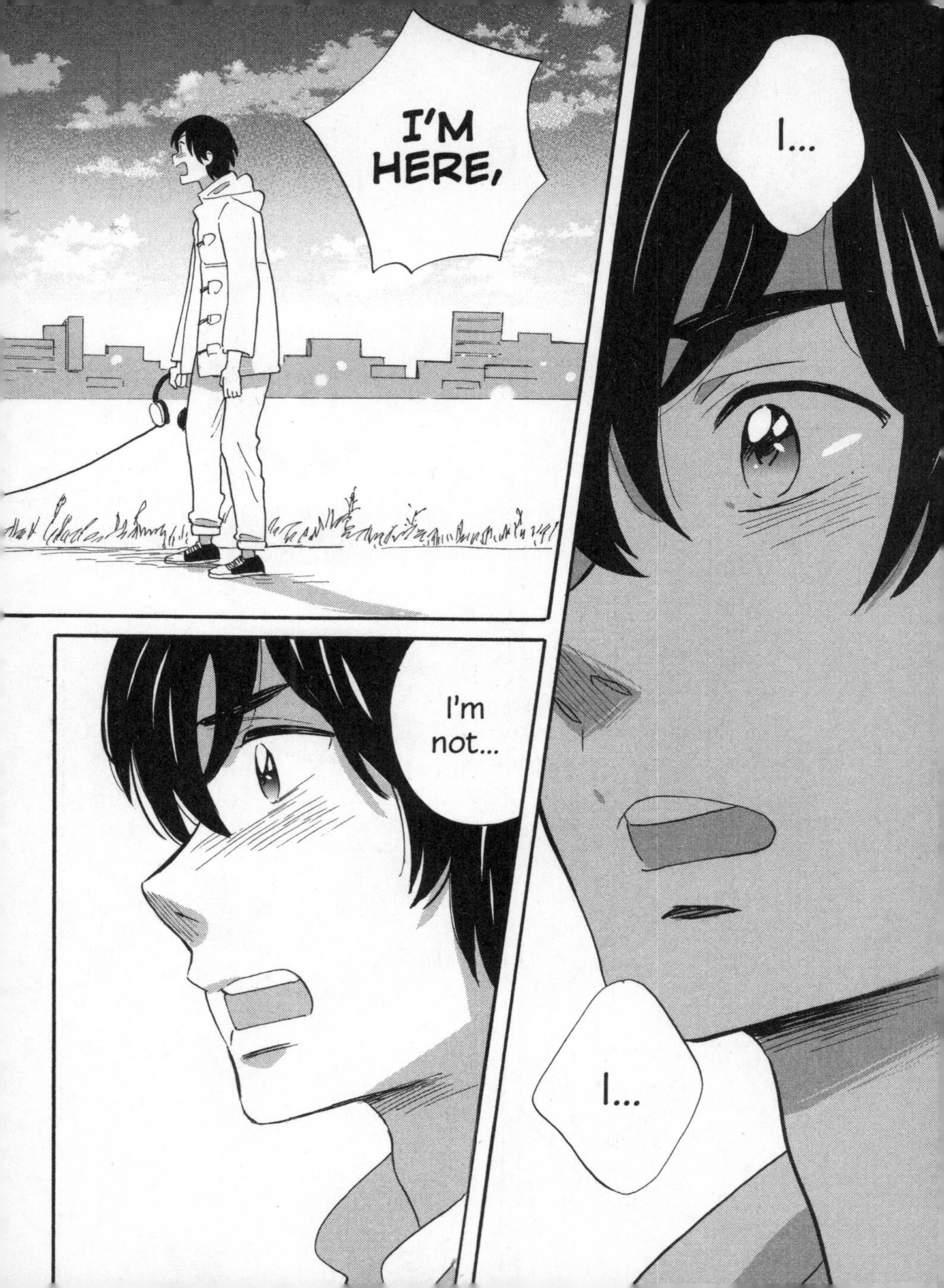
I...
I...
I'M HERE,
I'm not...

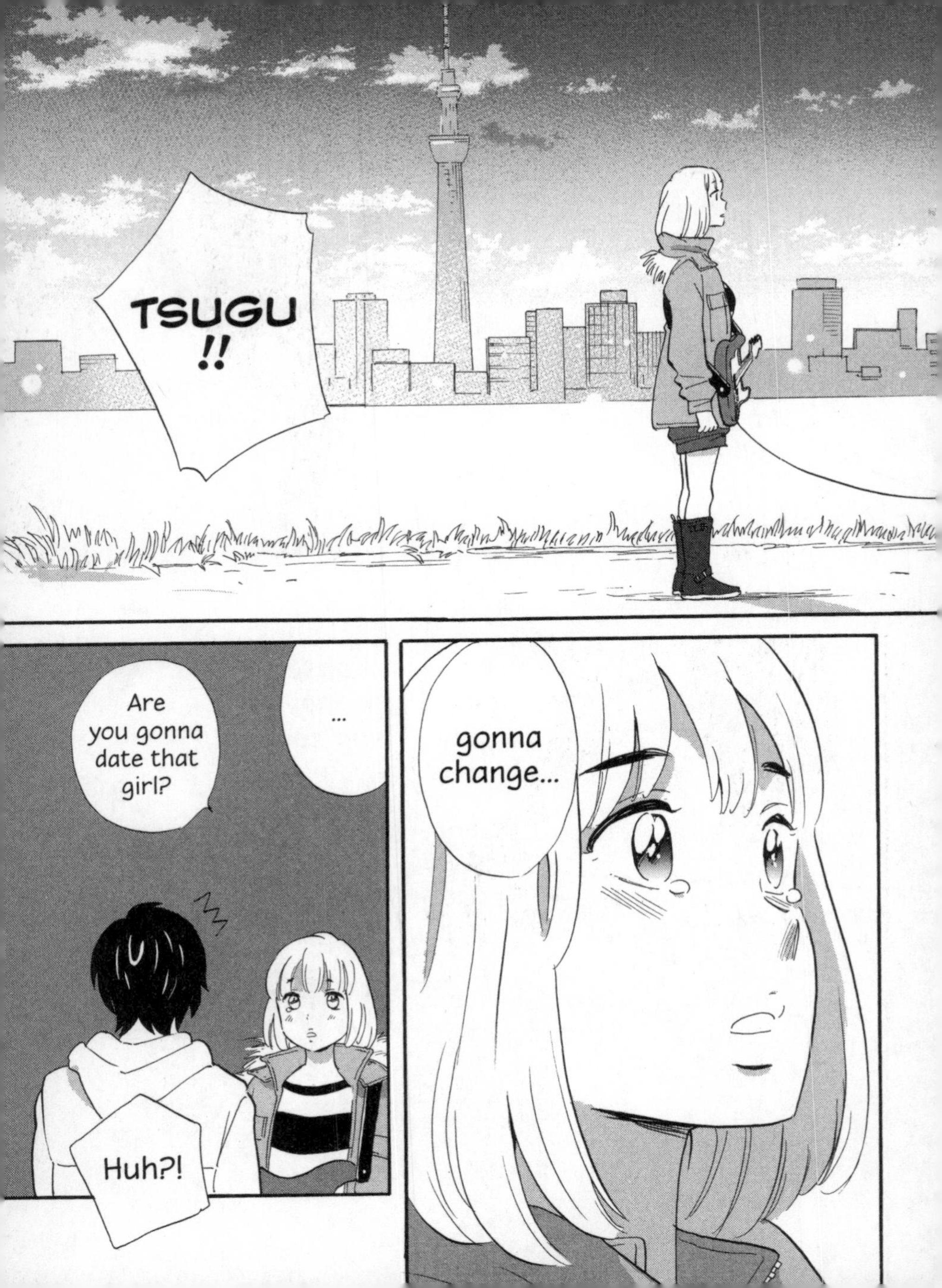
TSUGU!!
gonna change...
...
Are you gonna date that girl?
Huh?!

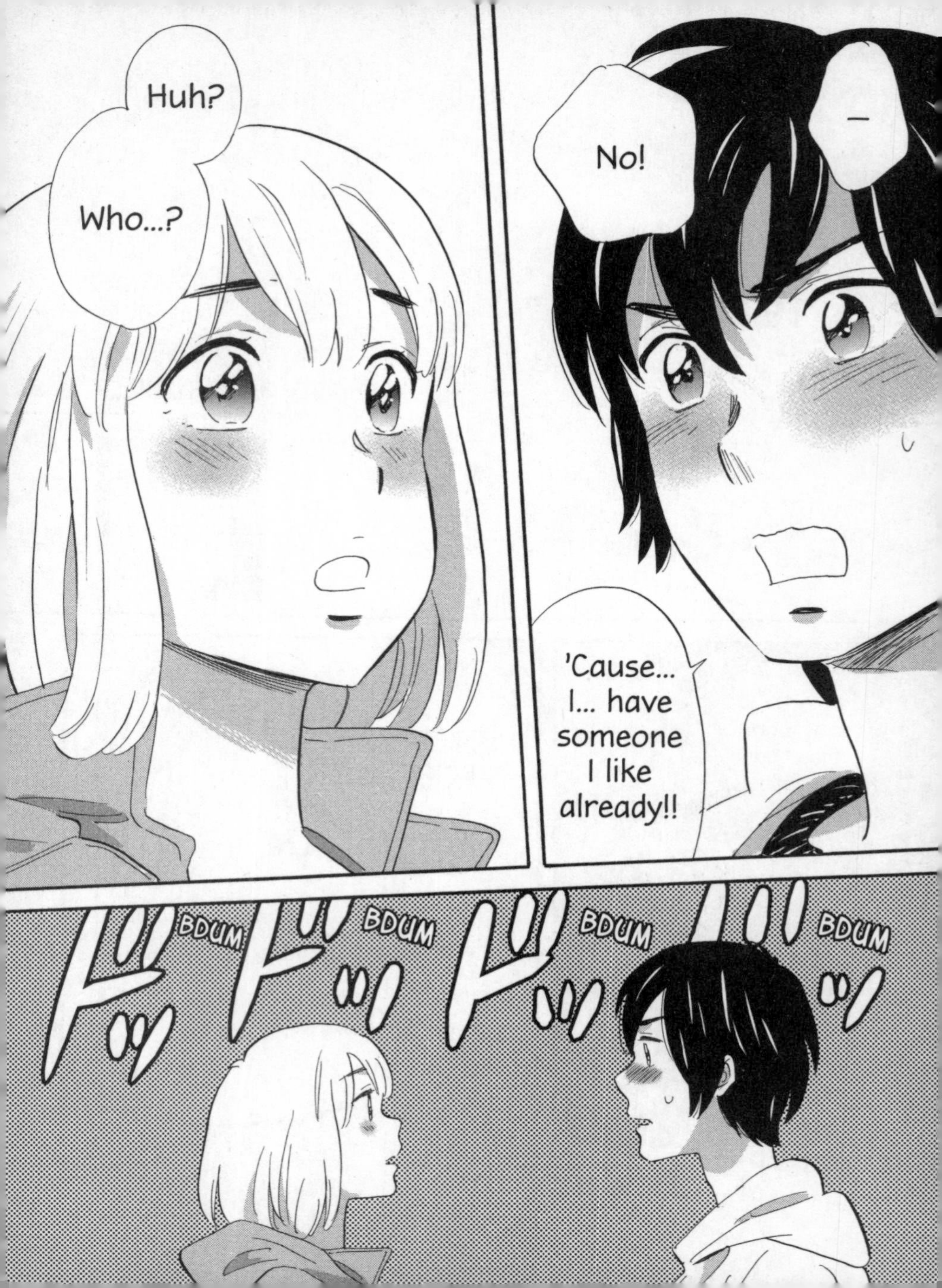
—
No!
'Cause... I... have someone I like already!!
Huh?
Who...?
BDUM
BDUM
BDUM
BDUM

I'm not gonna say.

she's a really strong person.

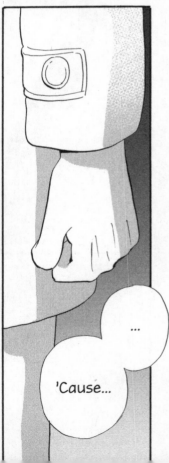

I'm not remotely worthy of her yet.

...

'Cause...

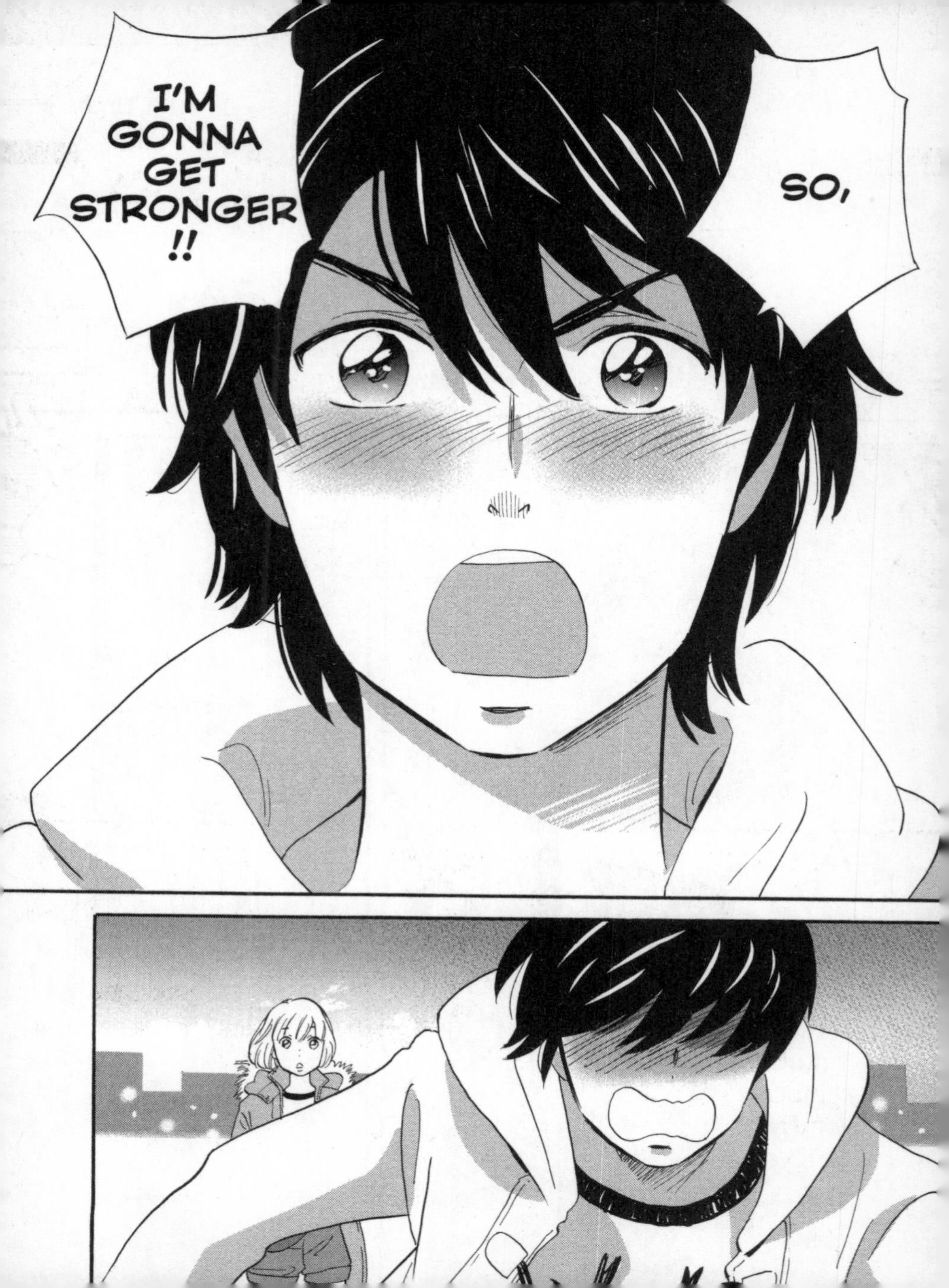
SO,
I'M GONNA GET STRONGER!!

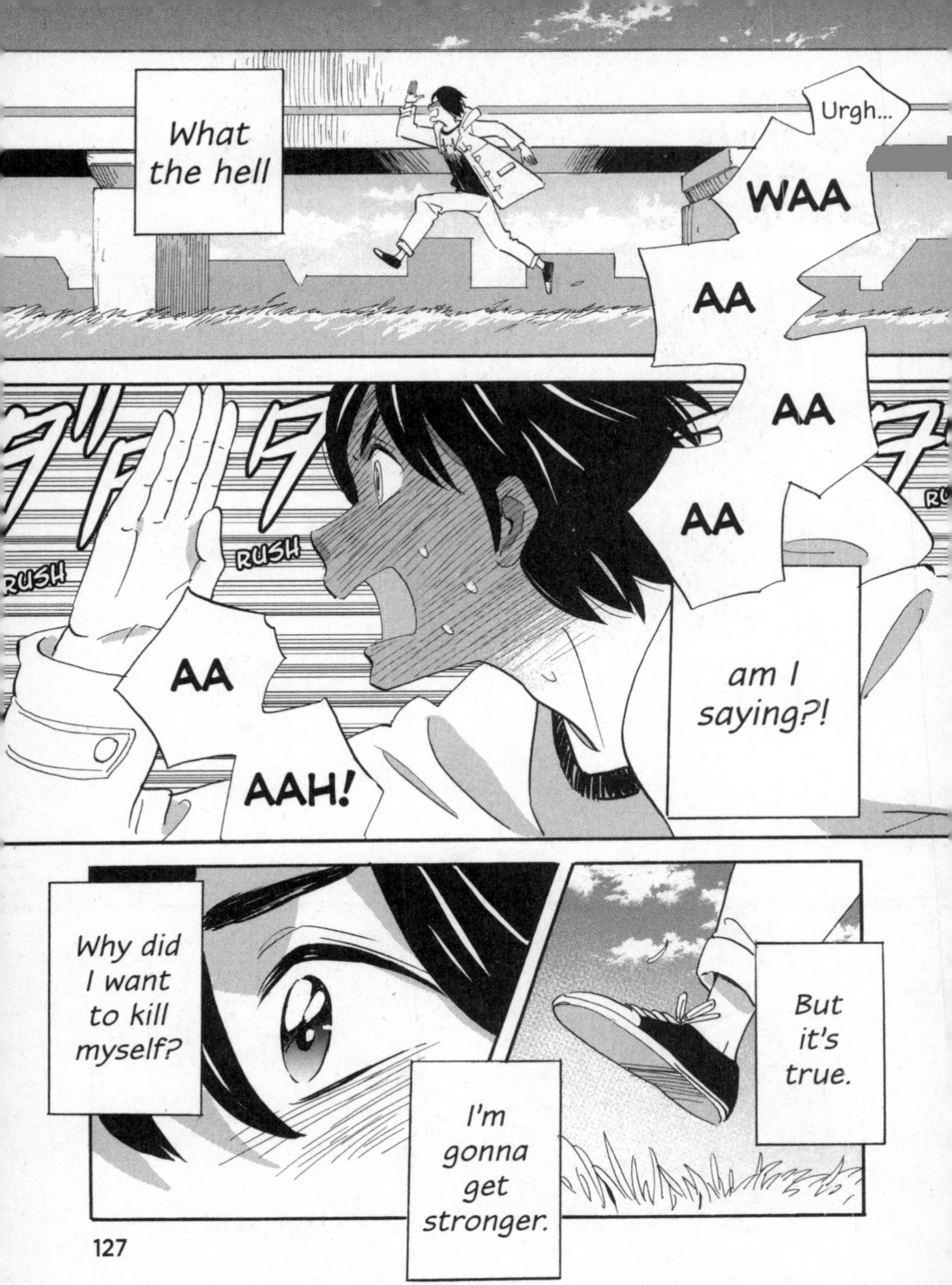
Urgh...
WAA AA AA AA
What the hell
am I saying?!
AA AAH!
RUSH
RUSH
RUSH
But it's true.
I'm gonna get stronger.
Why did I want to kill myself?

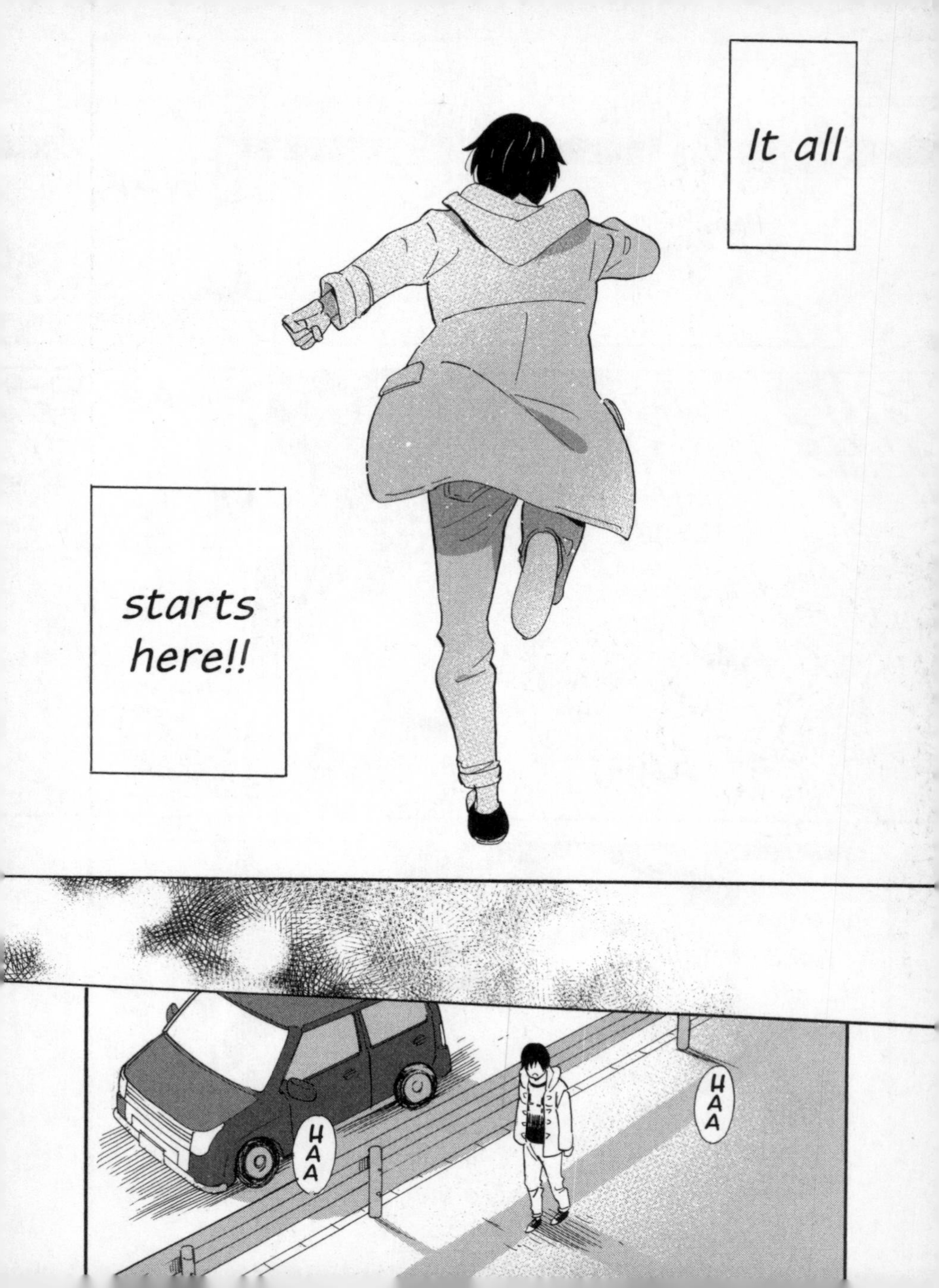
It all
starts here!!
HAA
HAA

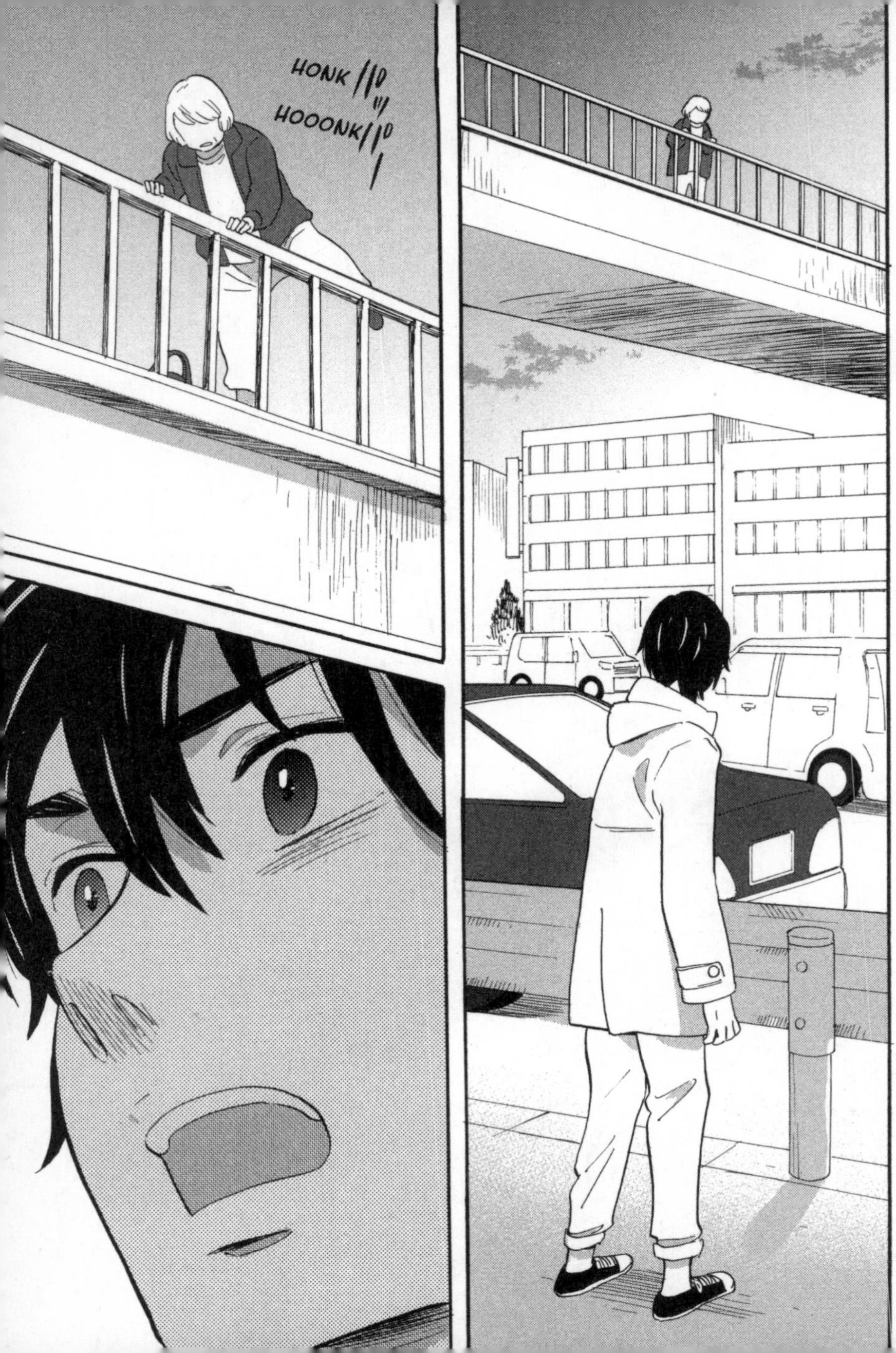
HONK
HOOONK

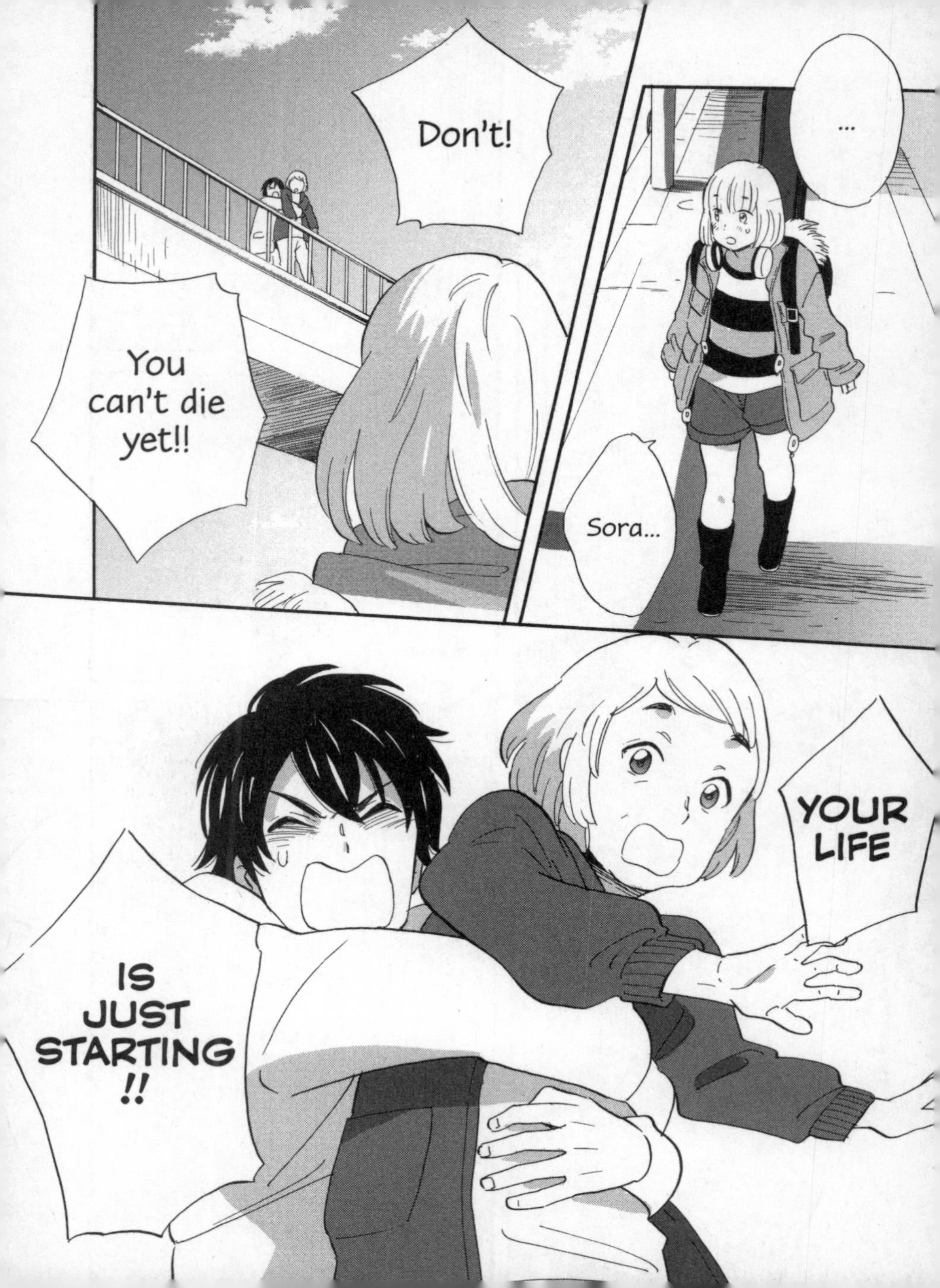
...
Sora...
Don't!
You can't die yet!!
YOUR LIFE
IS JUST STARTING!!

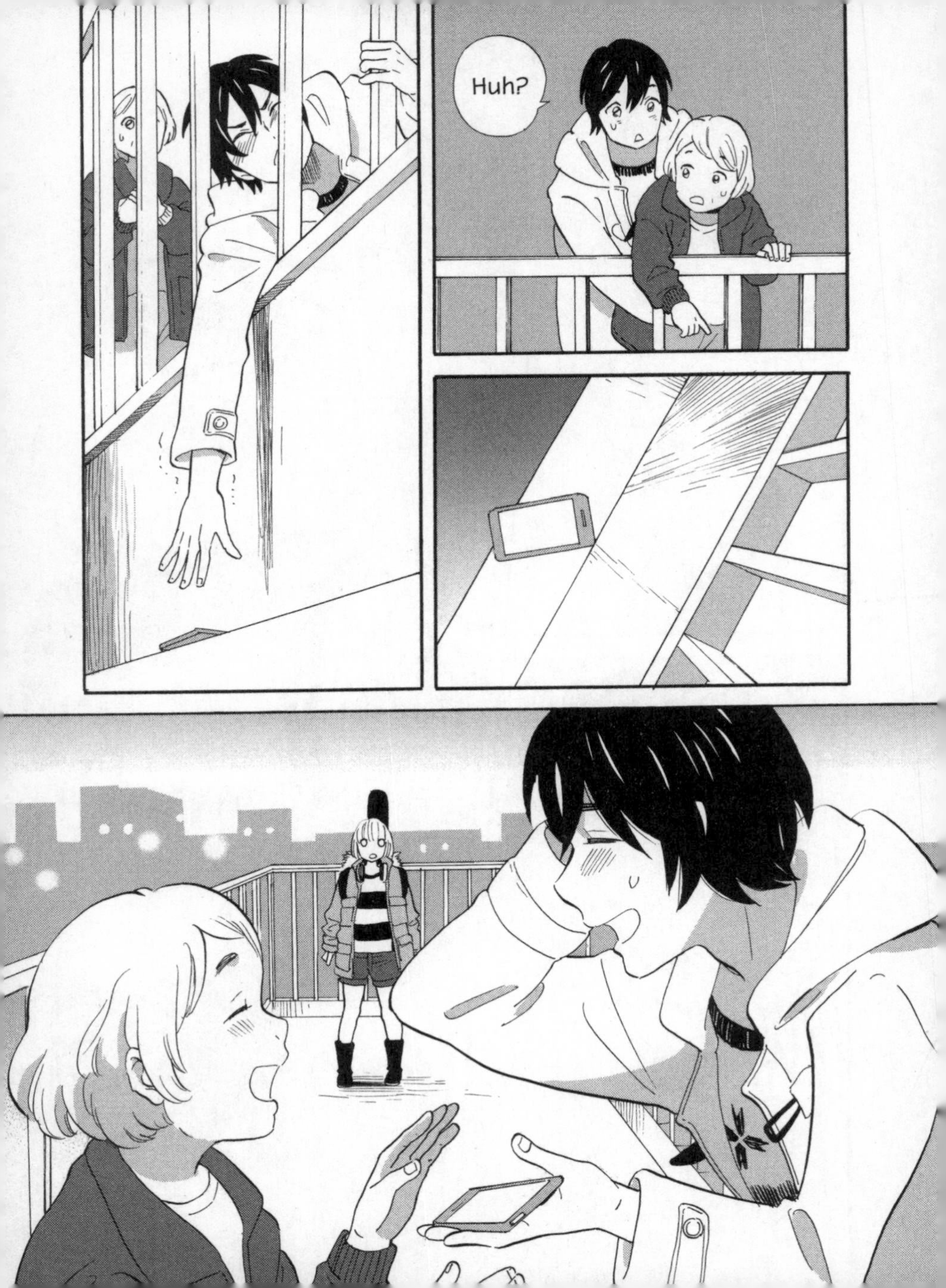
Huh?

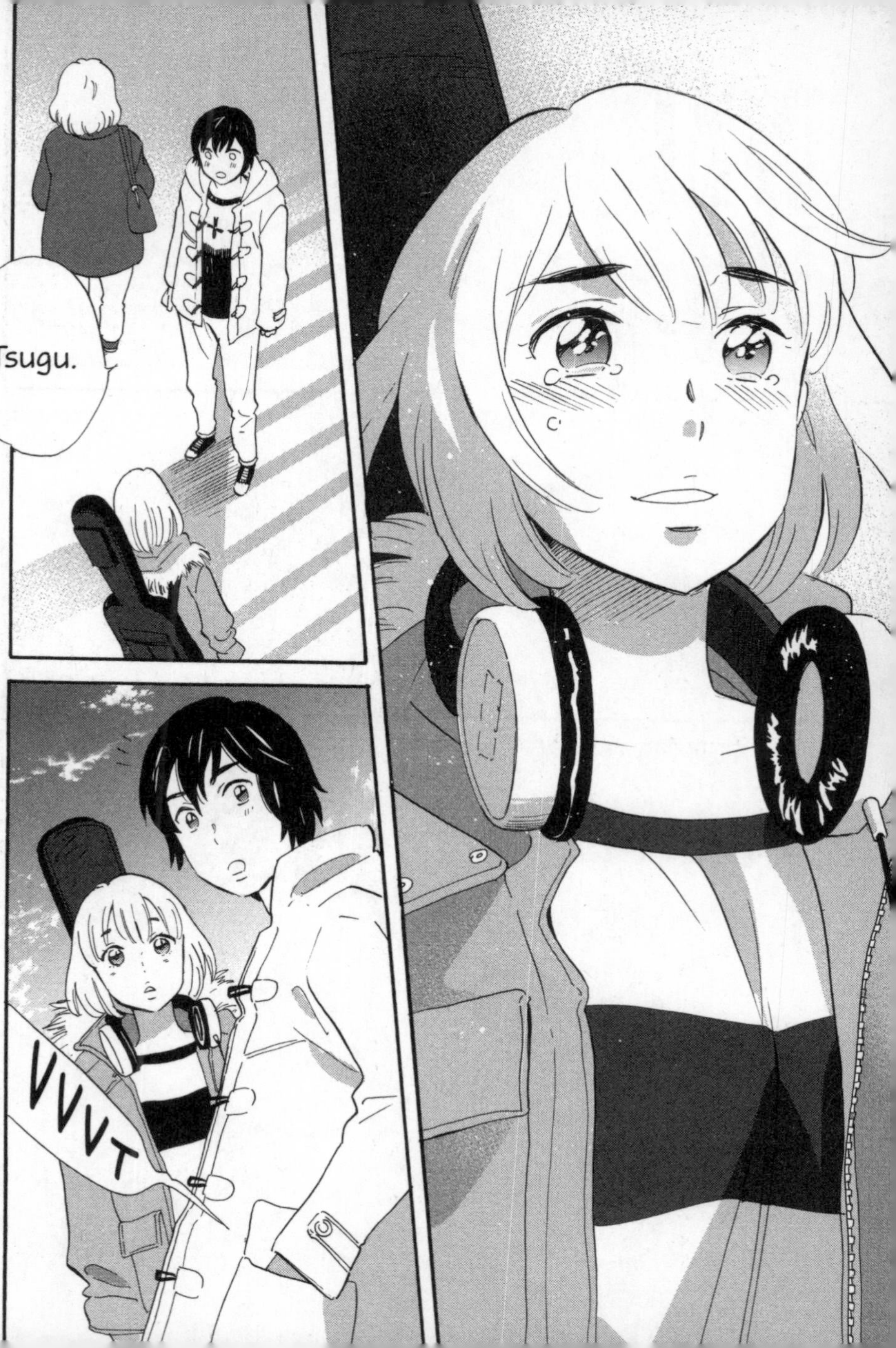
Tsugu.
VVVT

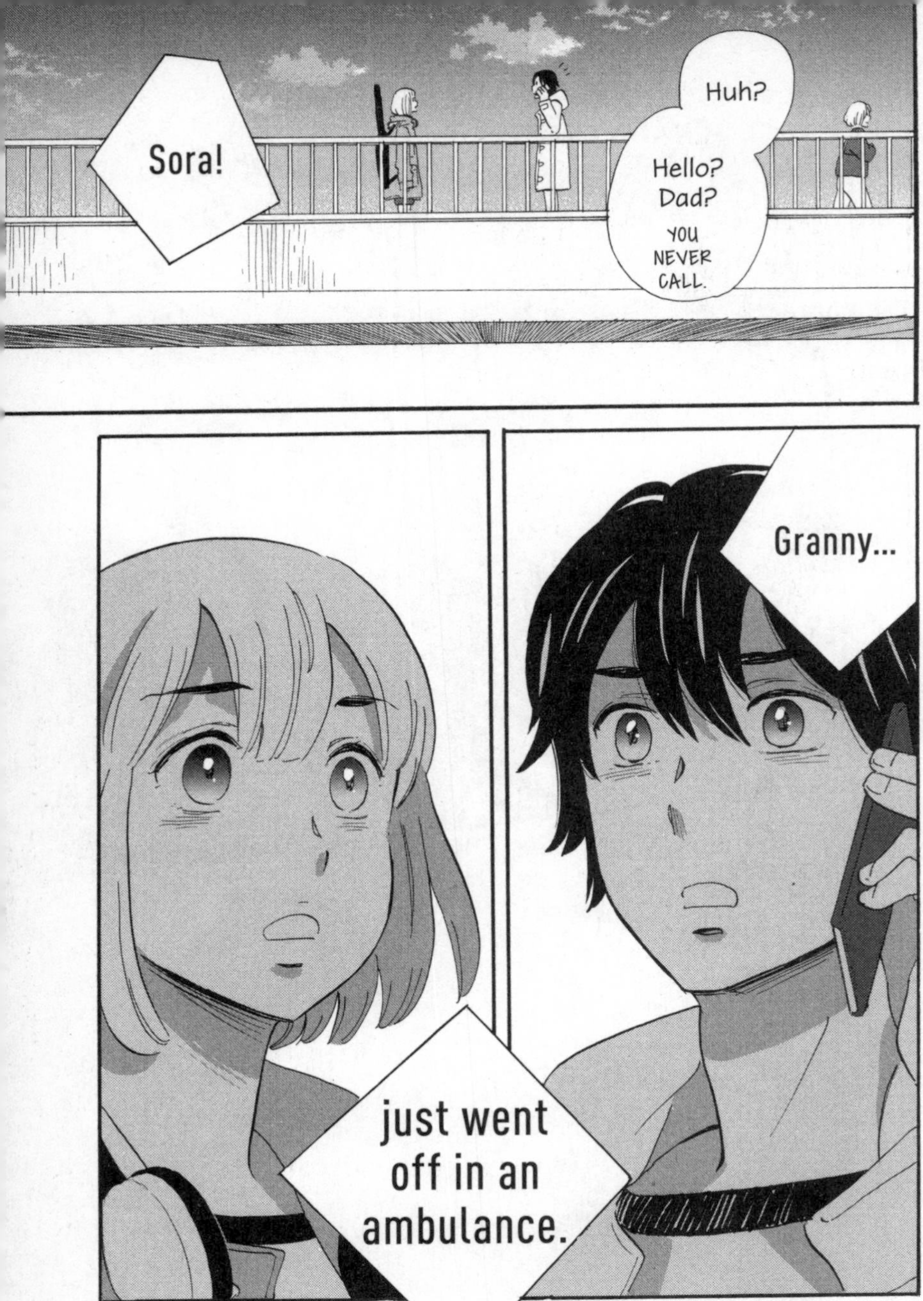
Huh?
Hello? Dad?
YOU NEVER CALL.
Sora!
Granny...
just went off in an ambulance.

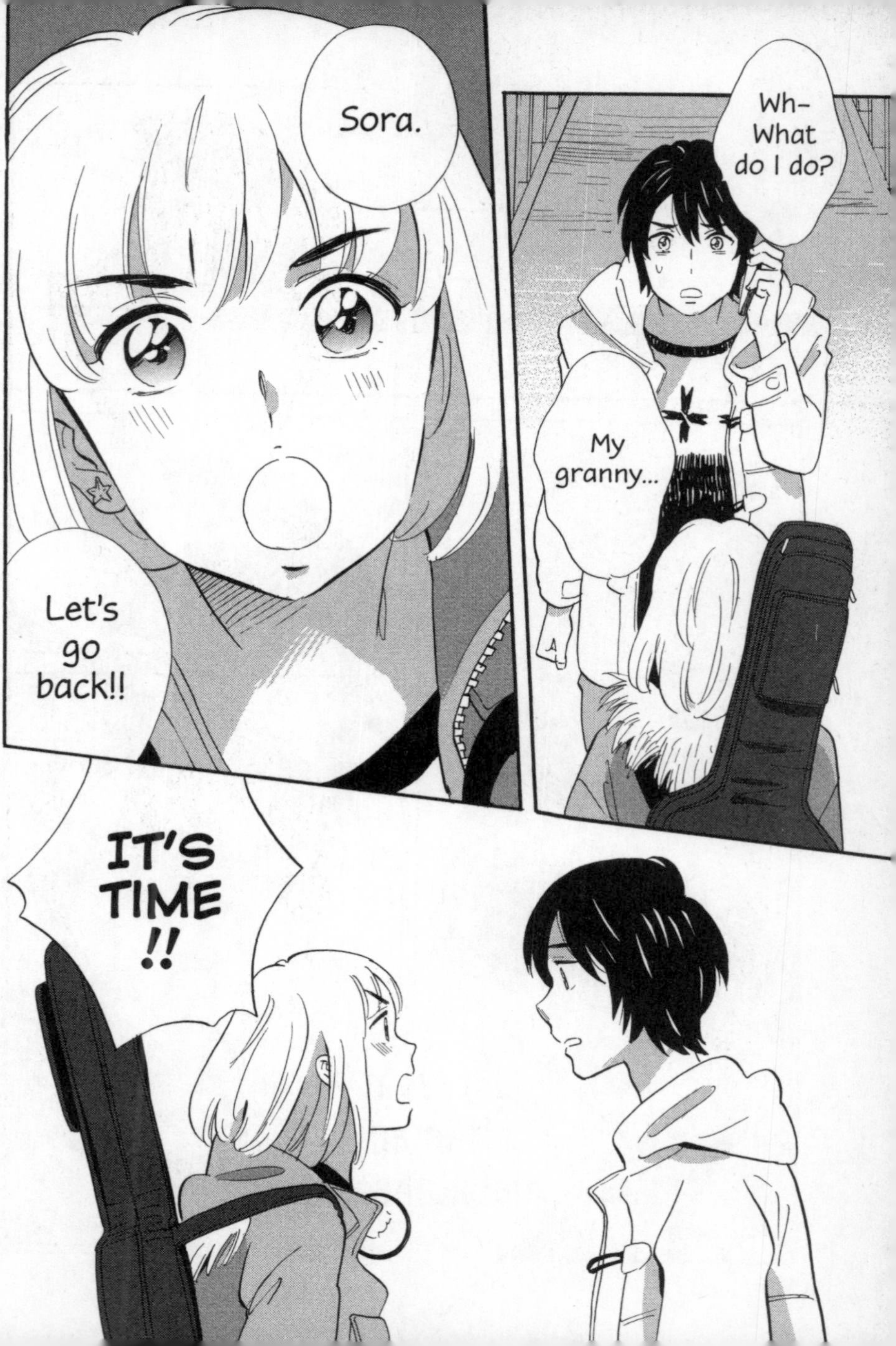
Wh- What do I do?
My granny...
Sora.
Let's go back!!
IT'S TIME!!

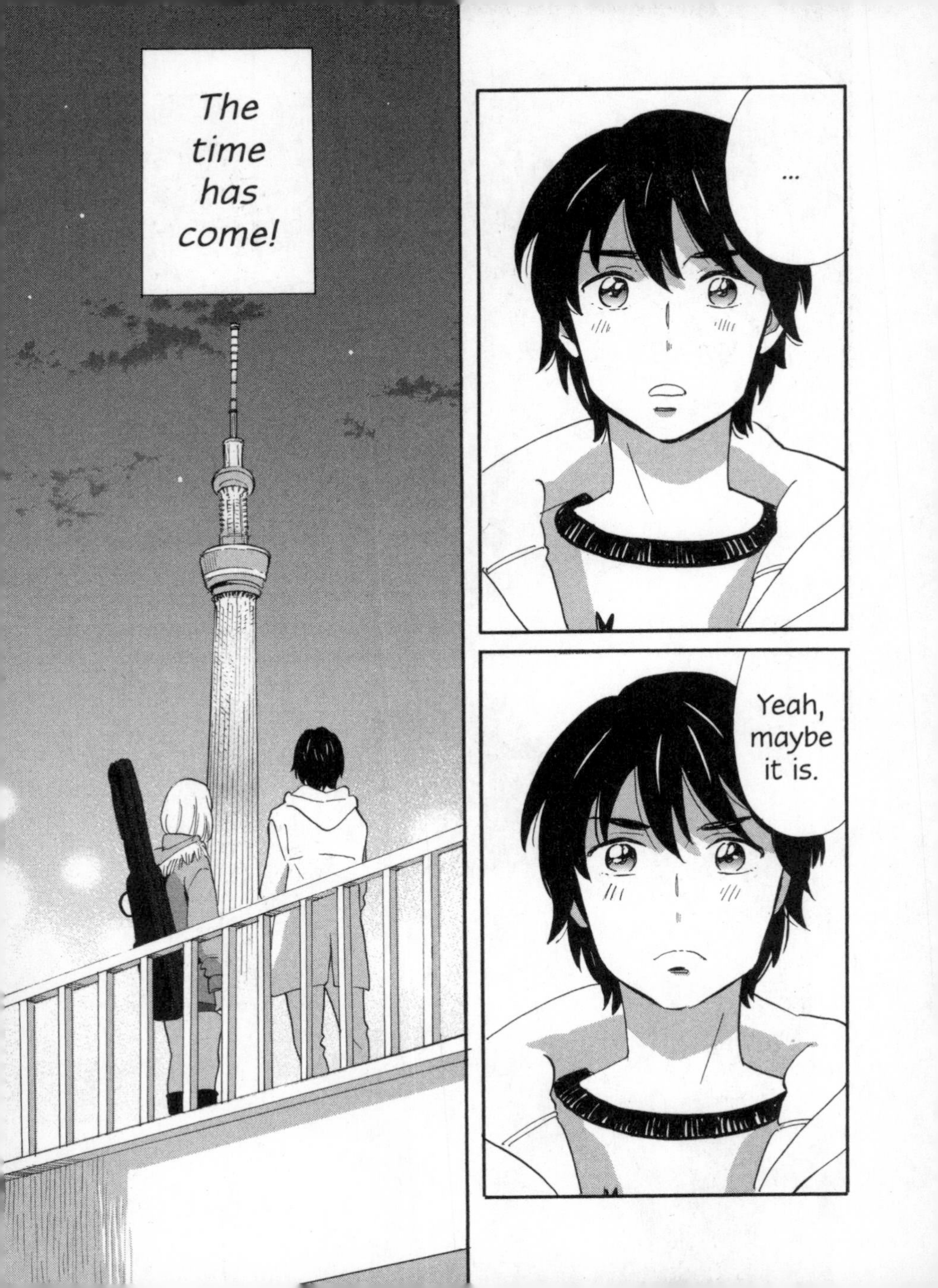
...
Yeah, maybe it is.
The time has come!

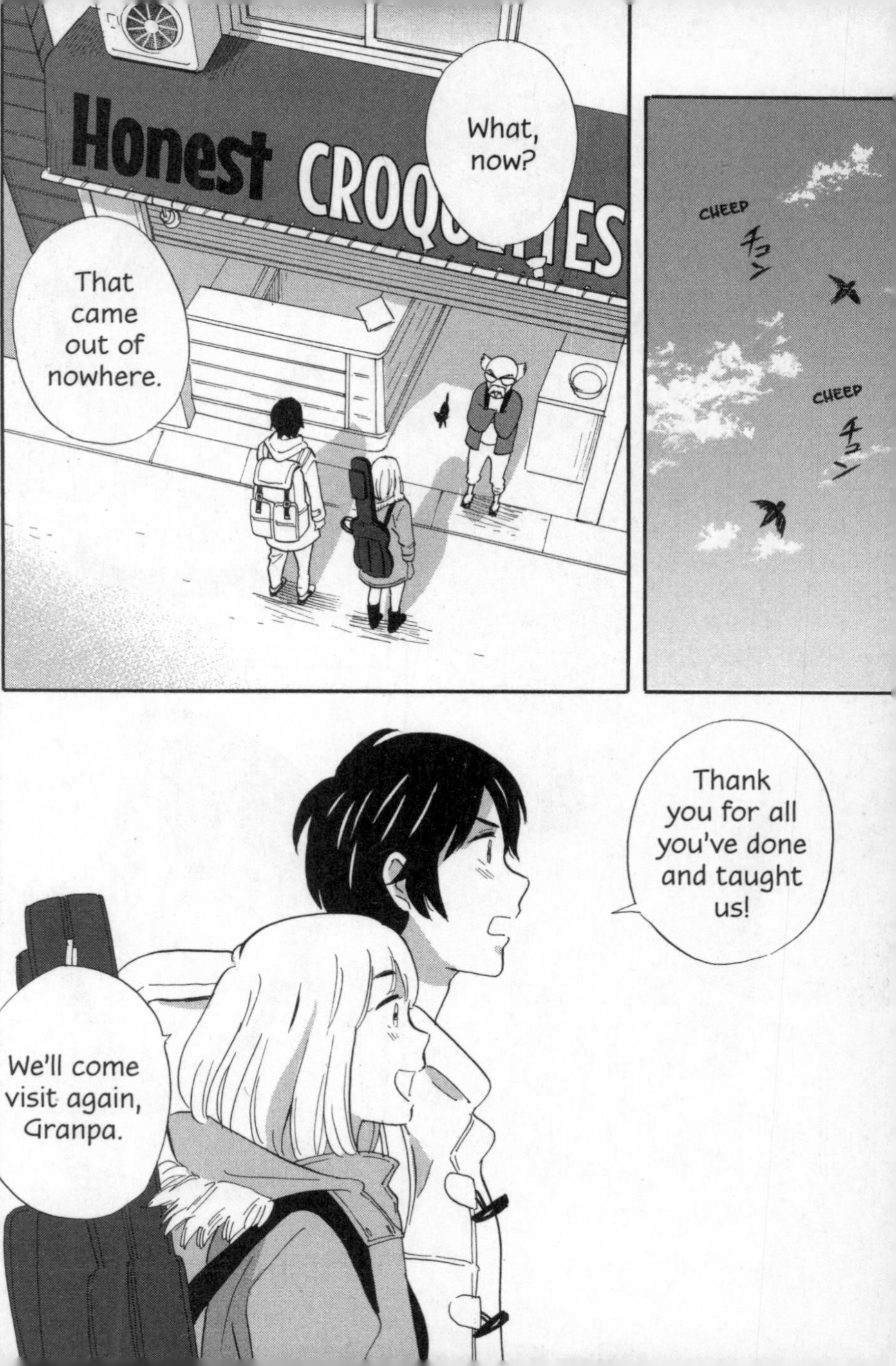
CHEEP
チュン
CHEEP
チュン
What, now?
Honest
That came out of nowhere.
Thank you for all you've done and taught us!
We'll come visit again, Granpa.

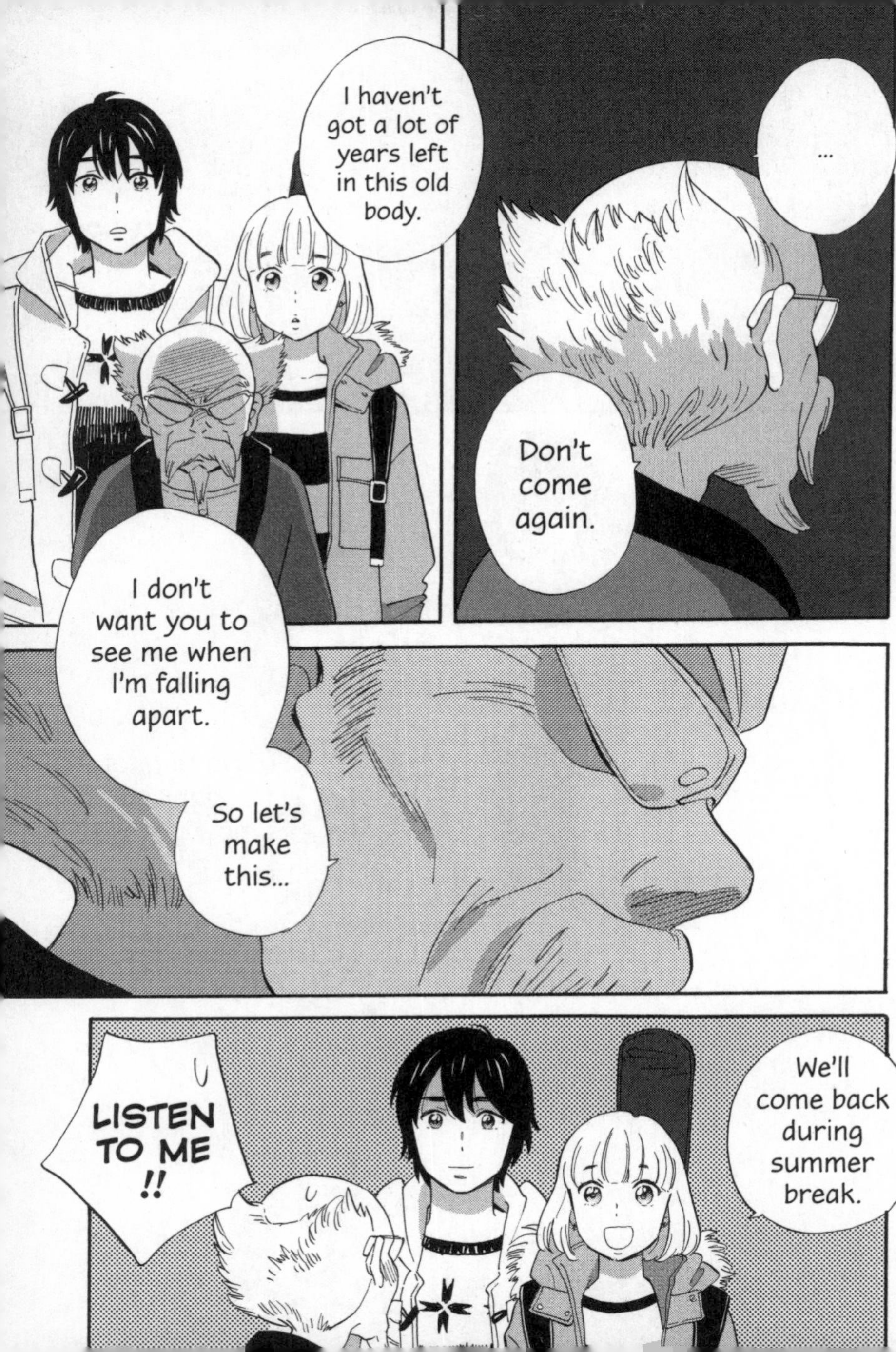
...
Don't come again.
I haven't got a lot of years left in this old body.
I don't want you to see me when I'm falling apart.
So let's make this...
We'll come back during summer break.
LISTEN TO ME!!

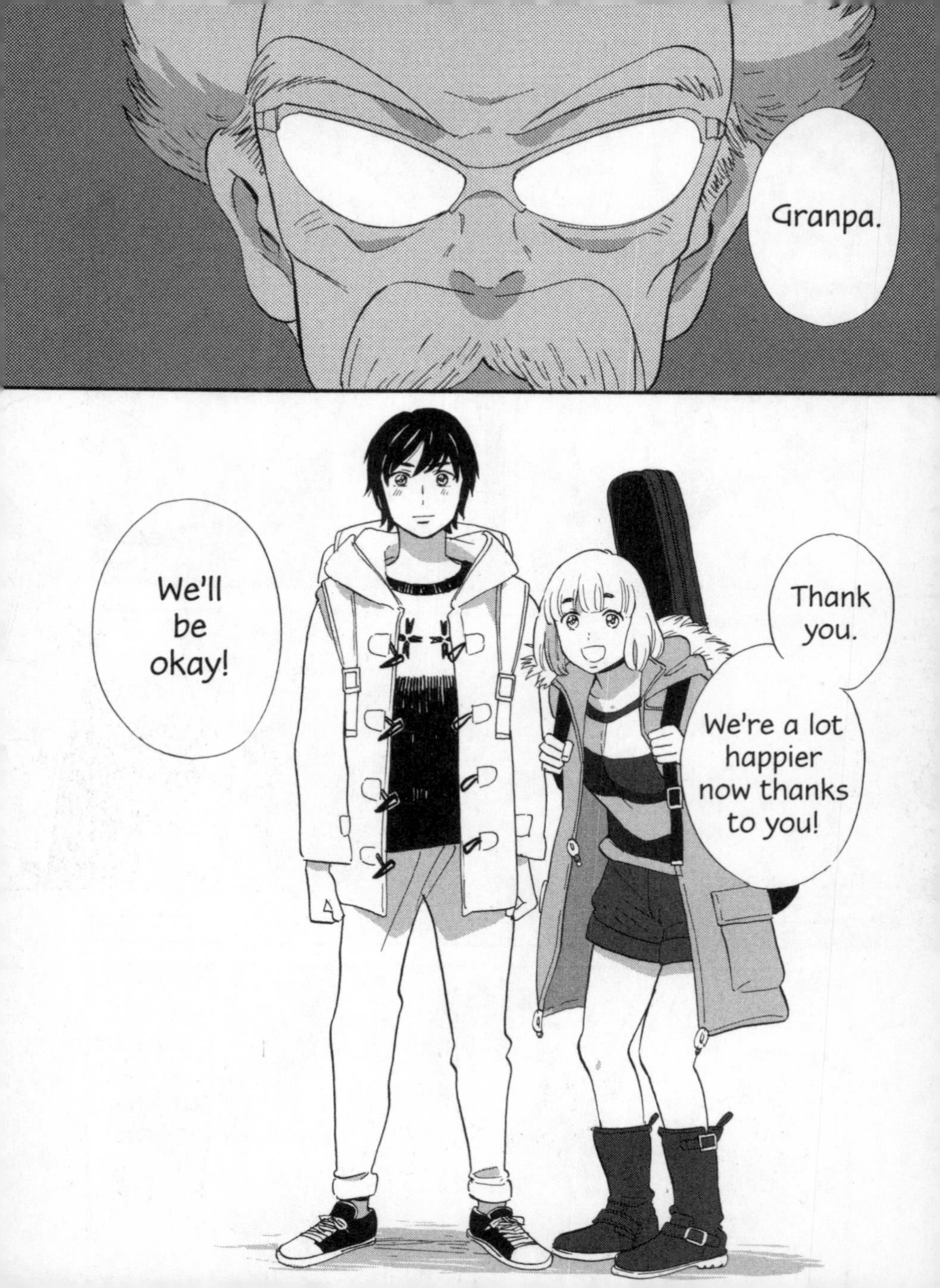
Granpa.
Thank you.
We're a lot happier now thanks to you!
We'll be okay!

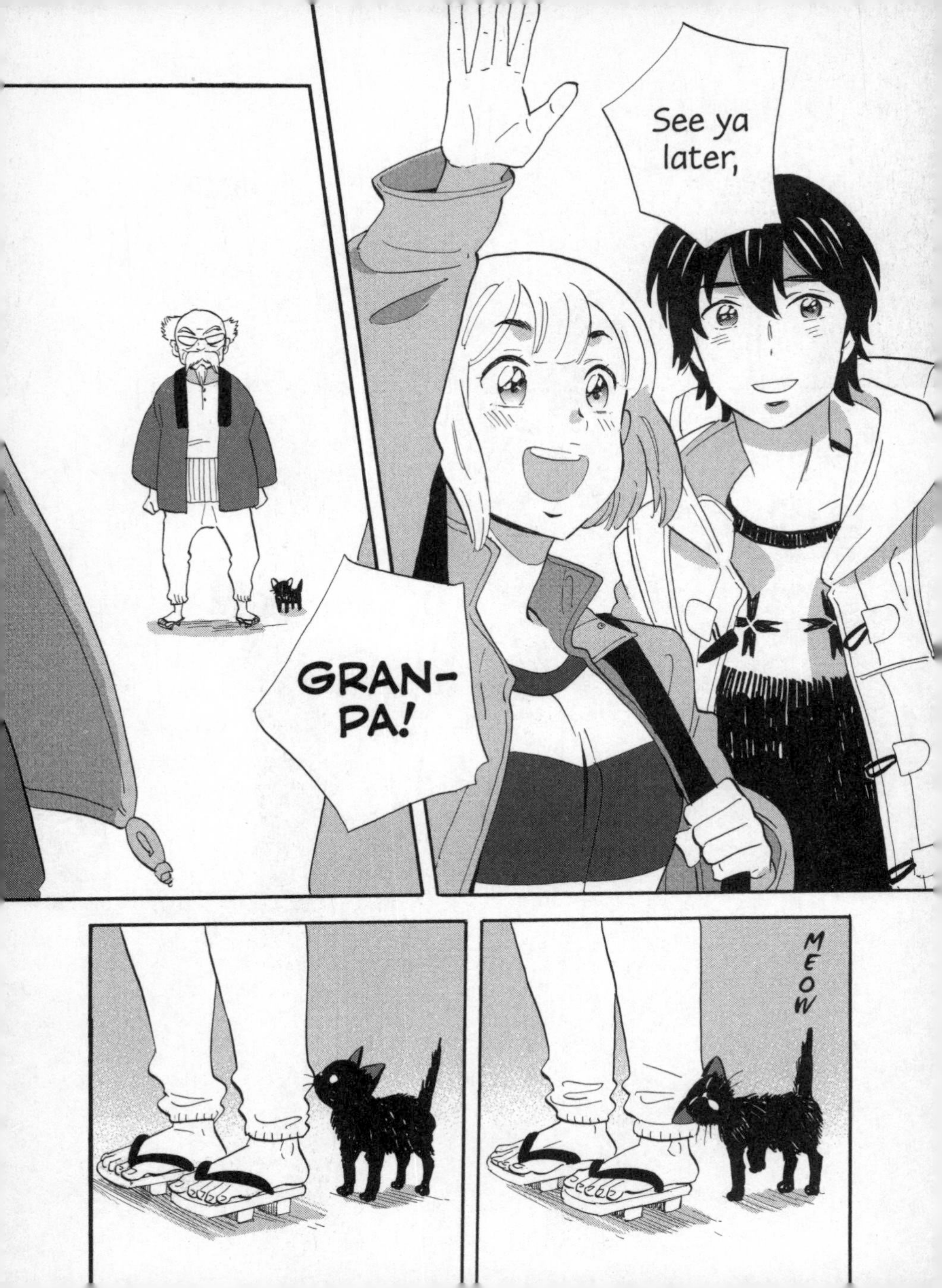
See ya later,
GRAN-PA!
MEOW

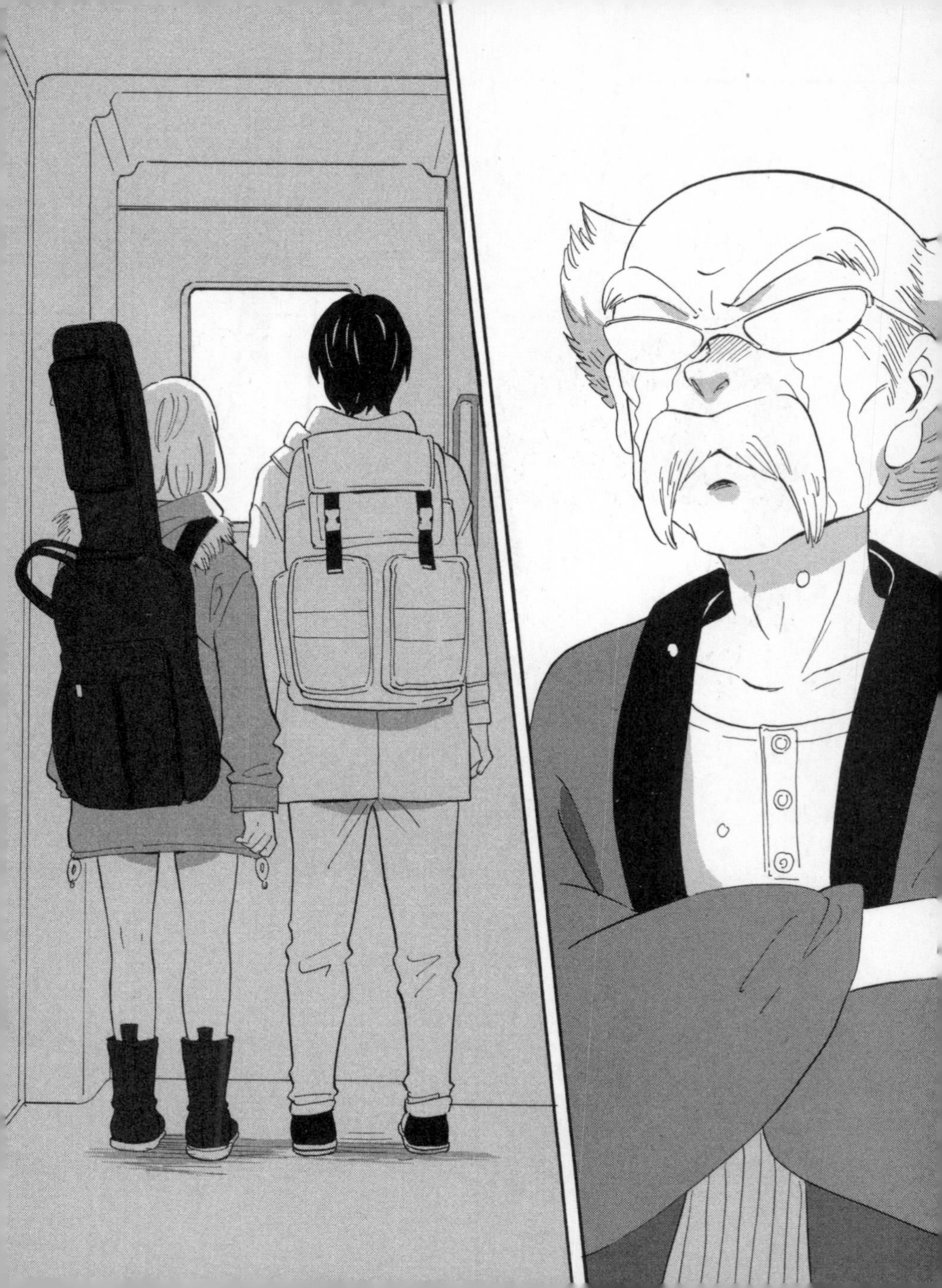

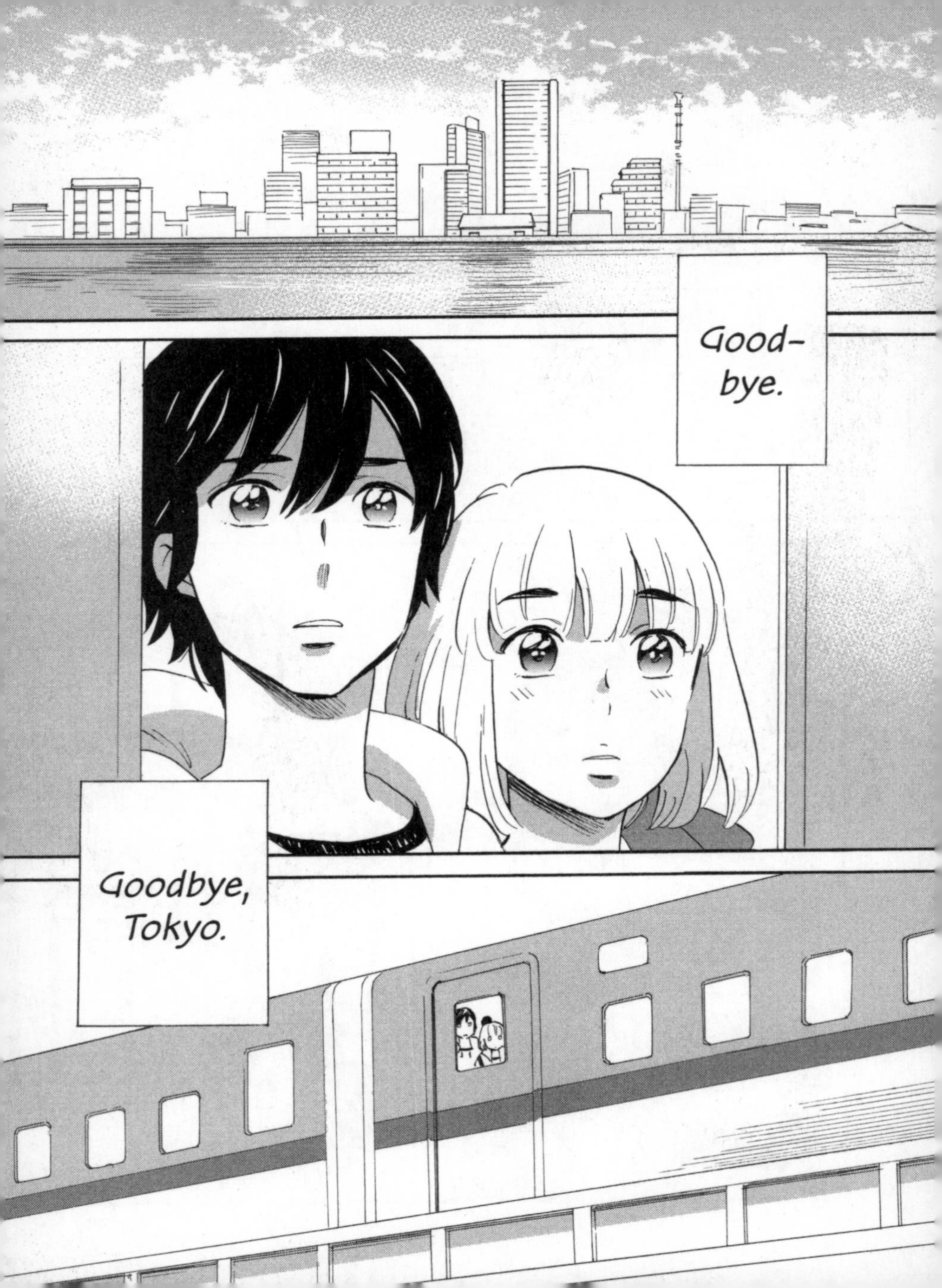
Good-
bye.
Goodbye,
Tokyo.

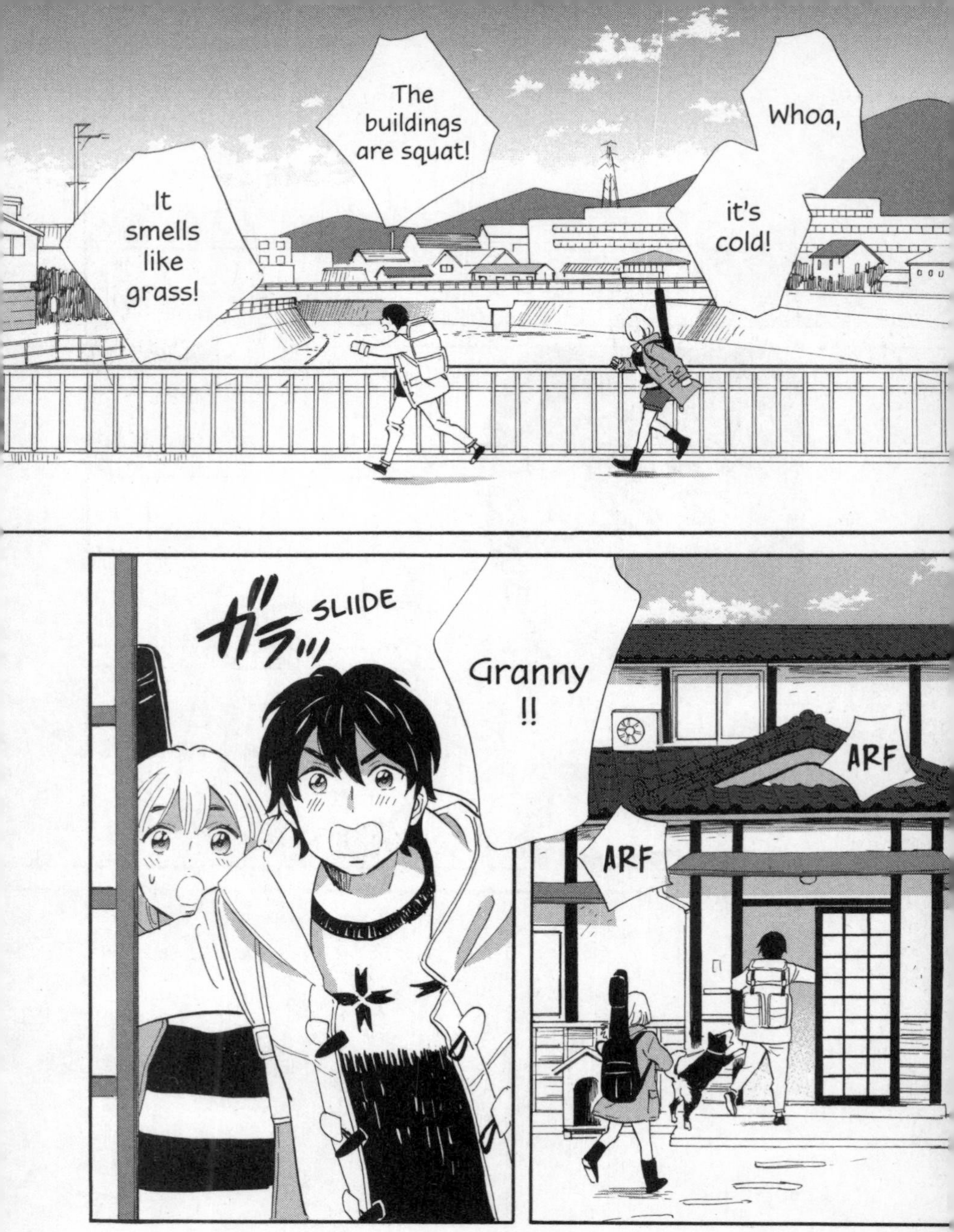
Whoa, it's cold!
The buildings are squat!
It smells like grass!
ARF
ARF
Granny !!
ガラッ
SLIIDE

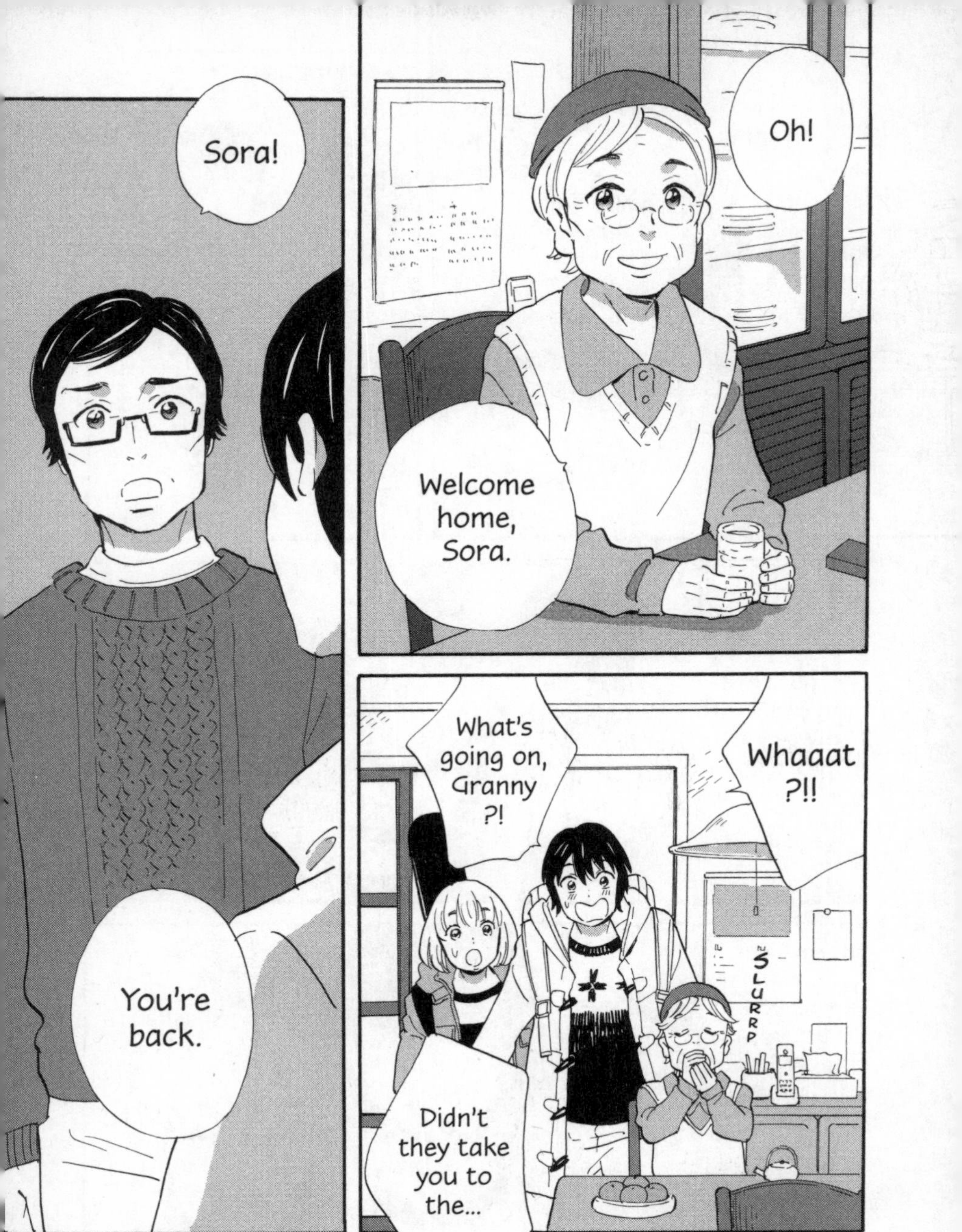
Oh!
Welcome home, Sora.
Whaaat ?!!
What's going on, Granny ?!
SLURRP
Didn't they take you to the...
Sora!
You're back.

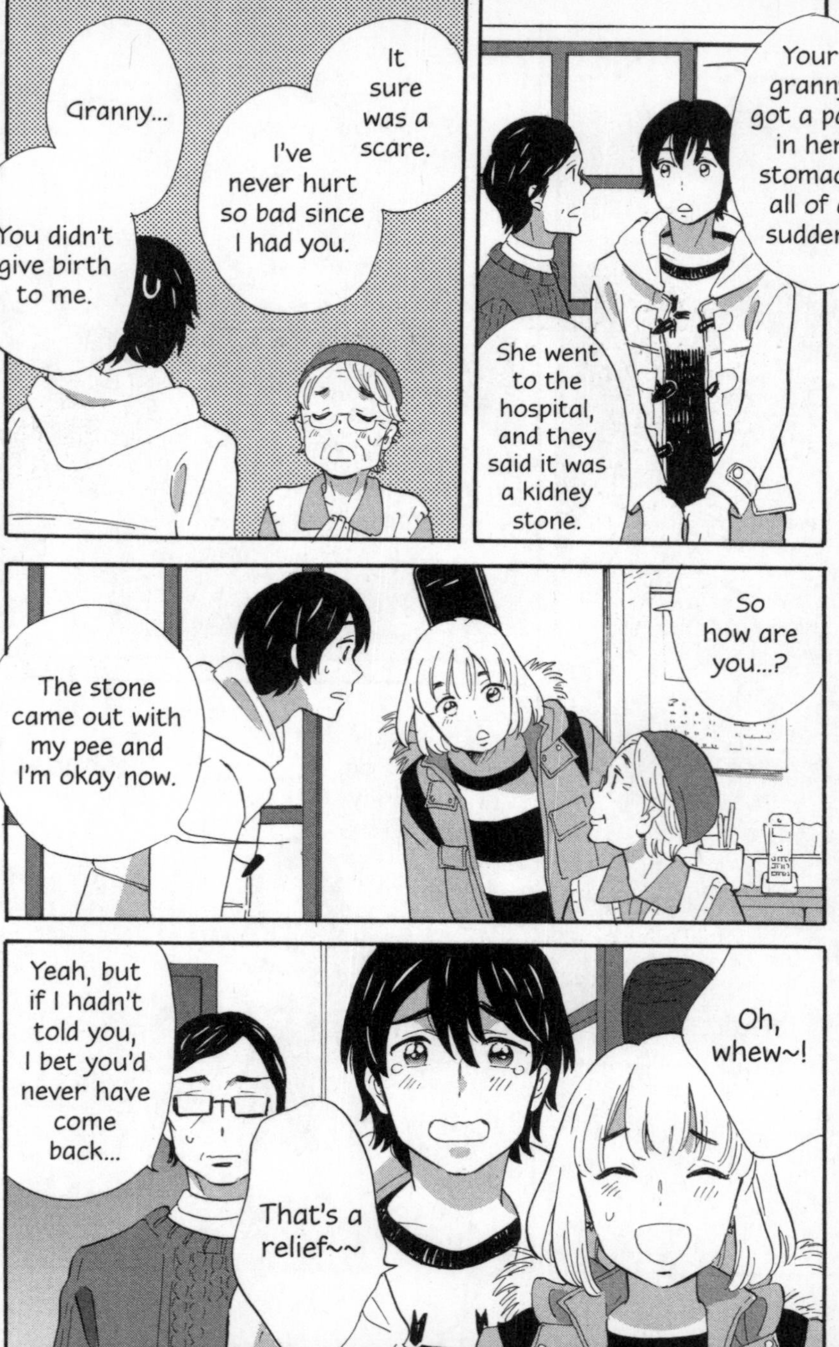
Your granny got a pain in her stomach all of a sudden.
She went to the hospital, and they said it was a kidney stone.
It sure was a scare.
I've never hurt so bad since I had you.
Granny...
You didn't give birth to me.
So how are you...?
The stone came out with my pee and I'm okay now.
Oh, whew~!
Yeah, but if I hadn't told you, I bet you'd never have come back...
That's a relief~~

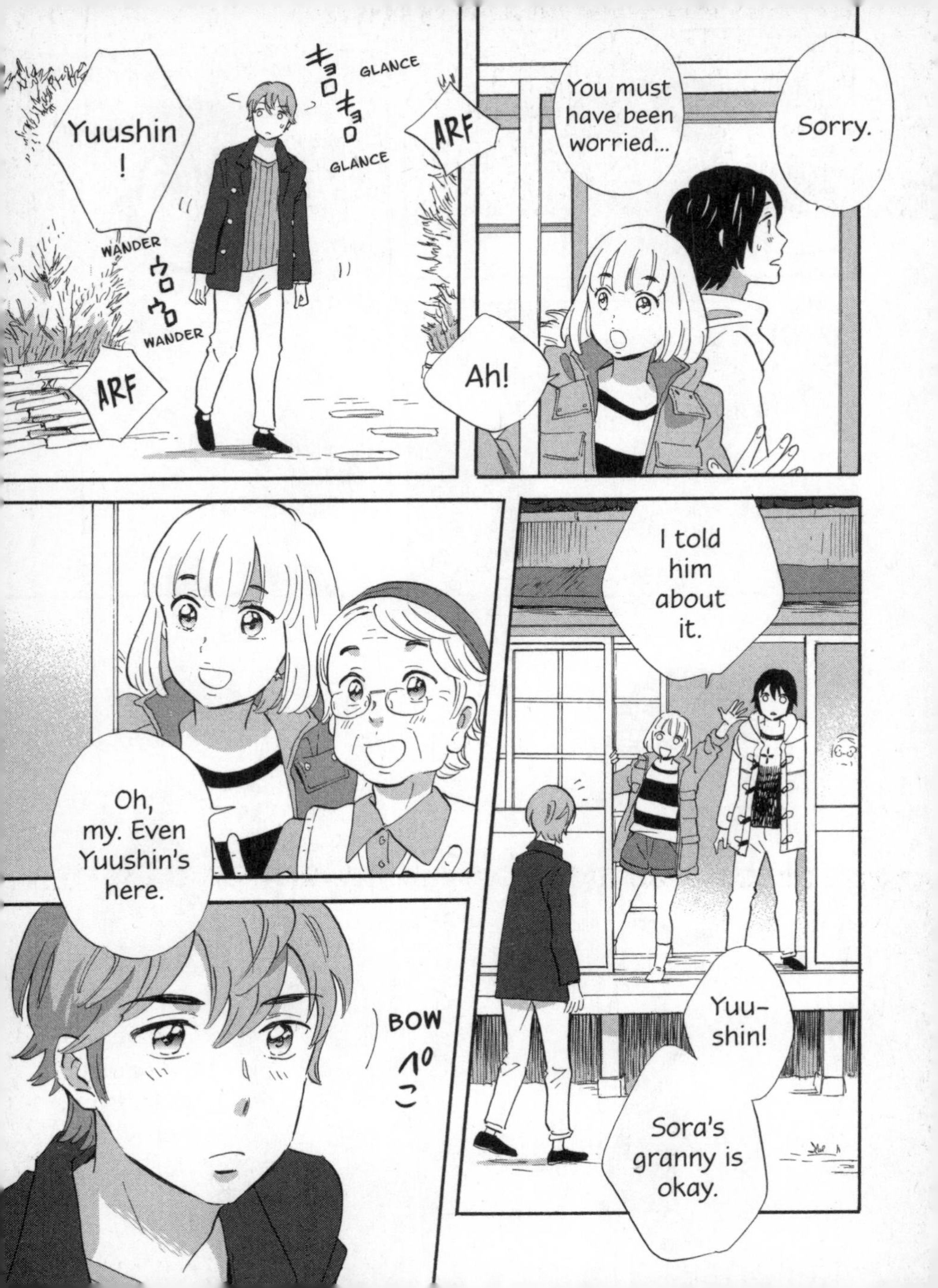
Sorry.
You must have been worried...
Ah!
Yuushin!
キョロキョロ
GLANCE GLANCE
ARF
ウロウロ
WANDER WANDER
ARF
I told him about it.
Yuu-shin!
Sora's granny is okay.
Oh, my. Even Yuushin's here.
ペコ
BOW

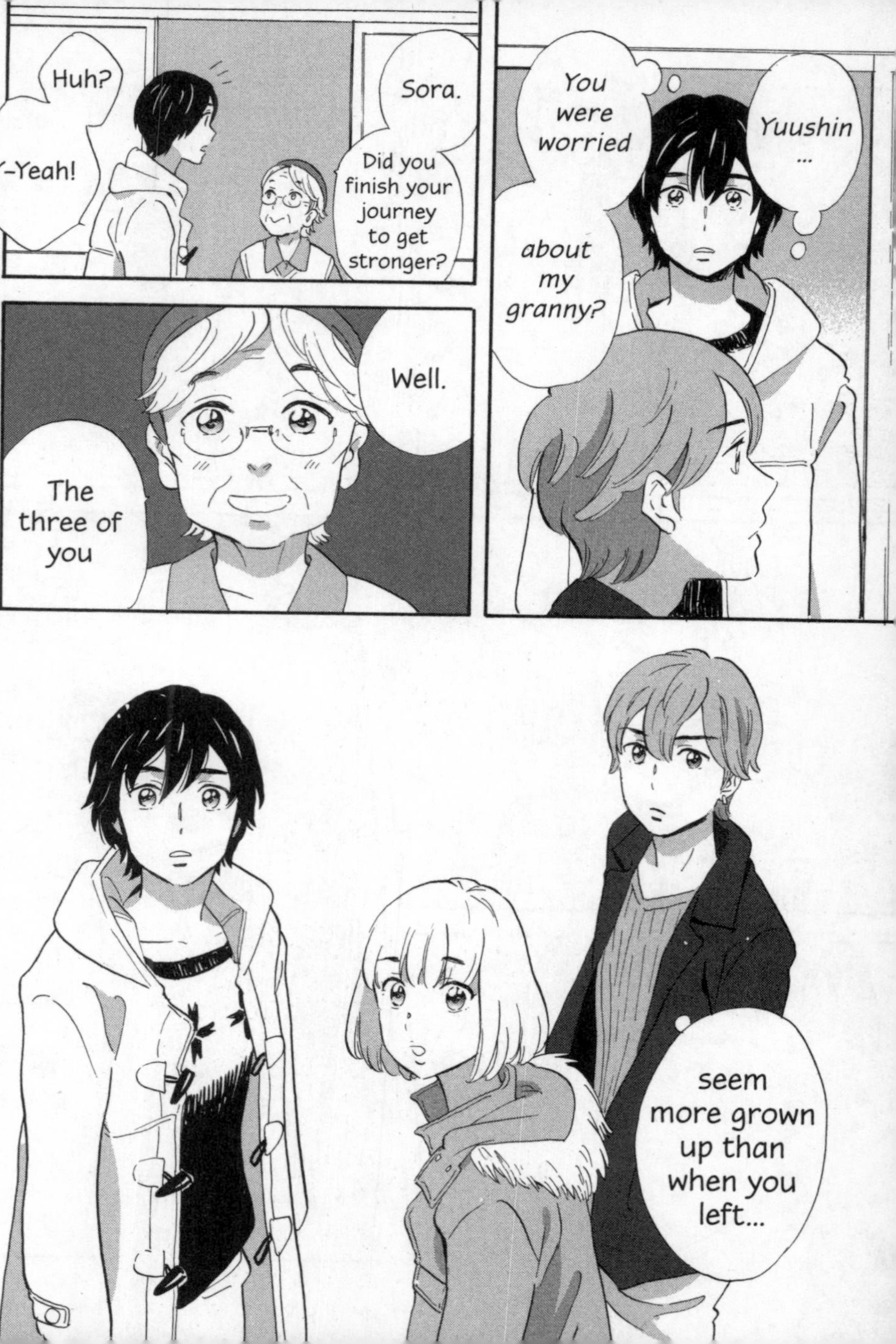
Yuushin ...
You were worried about my granny?
Sora.
Did you finish your journey to get stronger?
Huh?
Y-Yeah!
Well.
The three of you
seem more grown up than when you left...

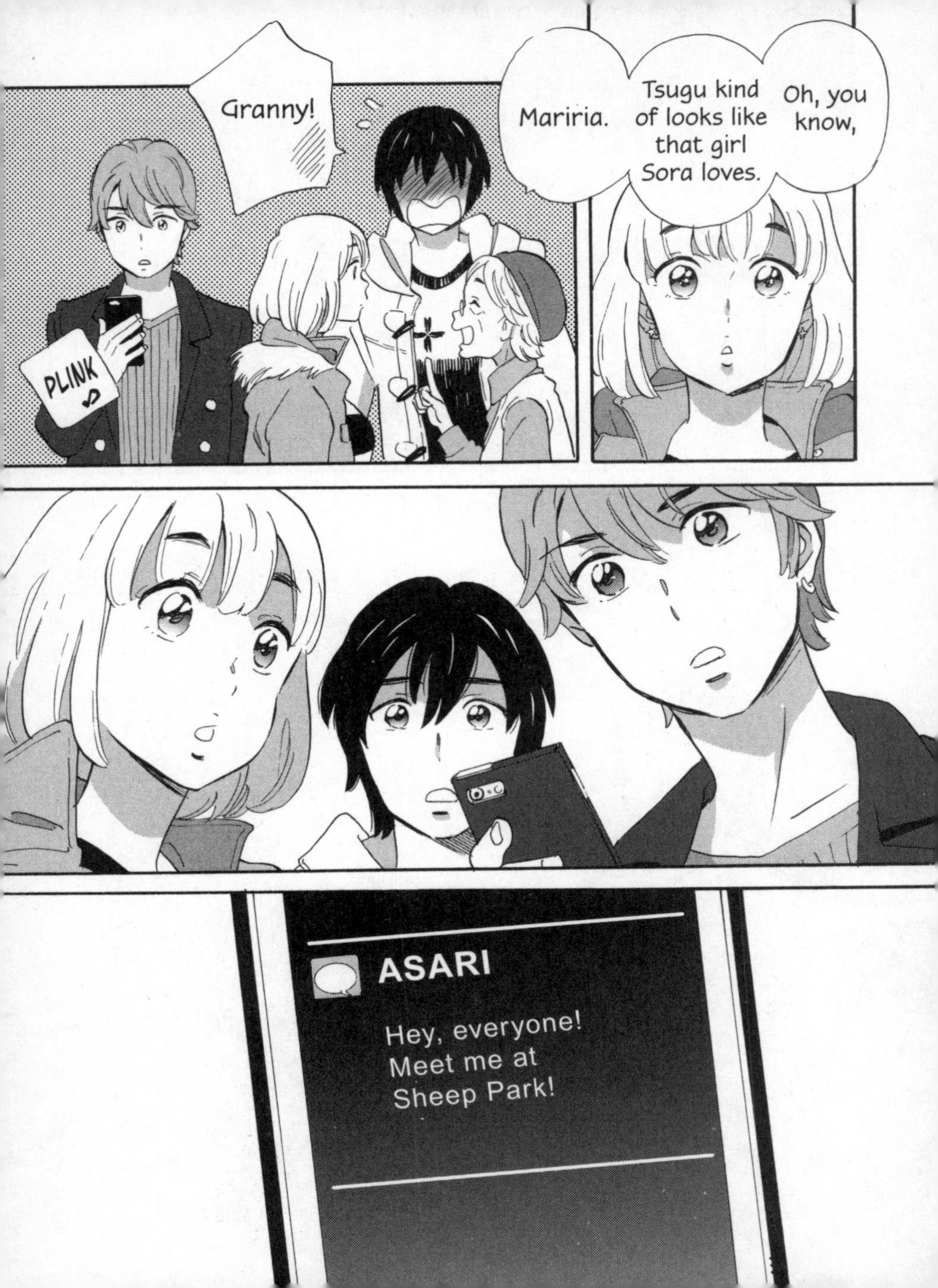
Oh, you know, Tsugu kind of looks like that girl Sora loves. Mariria.
Granny!
PLINK
ASARI
Hey, everyone! Meet me at Sheep Park!

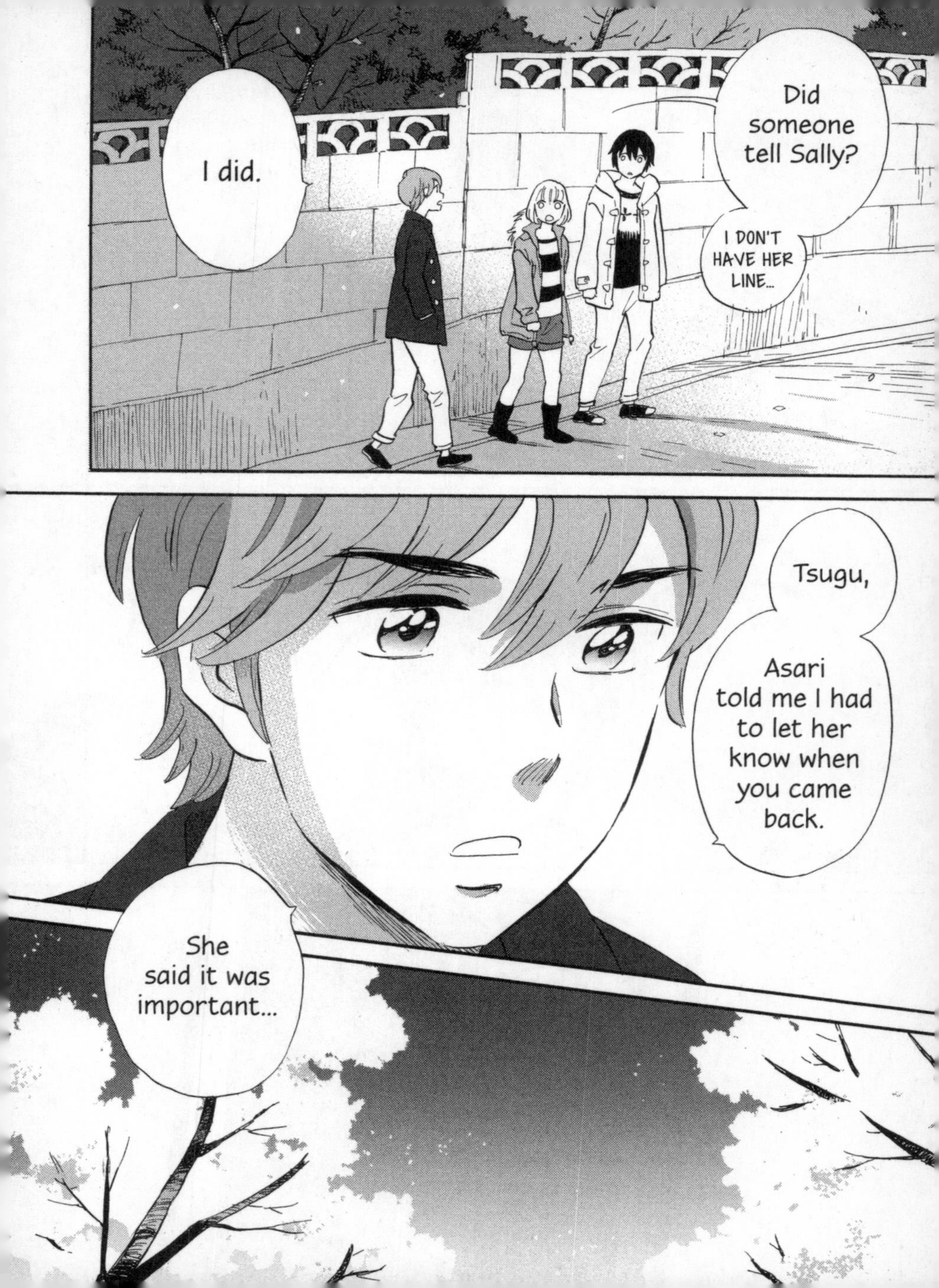
Did someone tell Sally?
I DON'T HAVE HER LINE...
I did.
Tsugu,
Asari told me I had to let her know when you came back.
She said it was important...

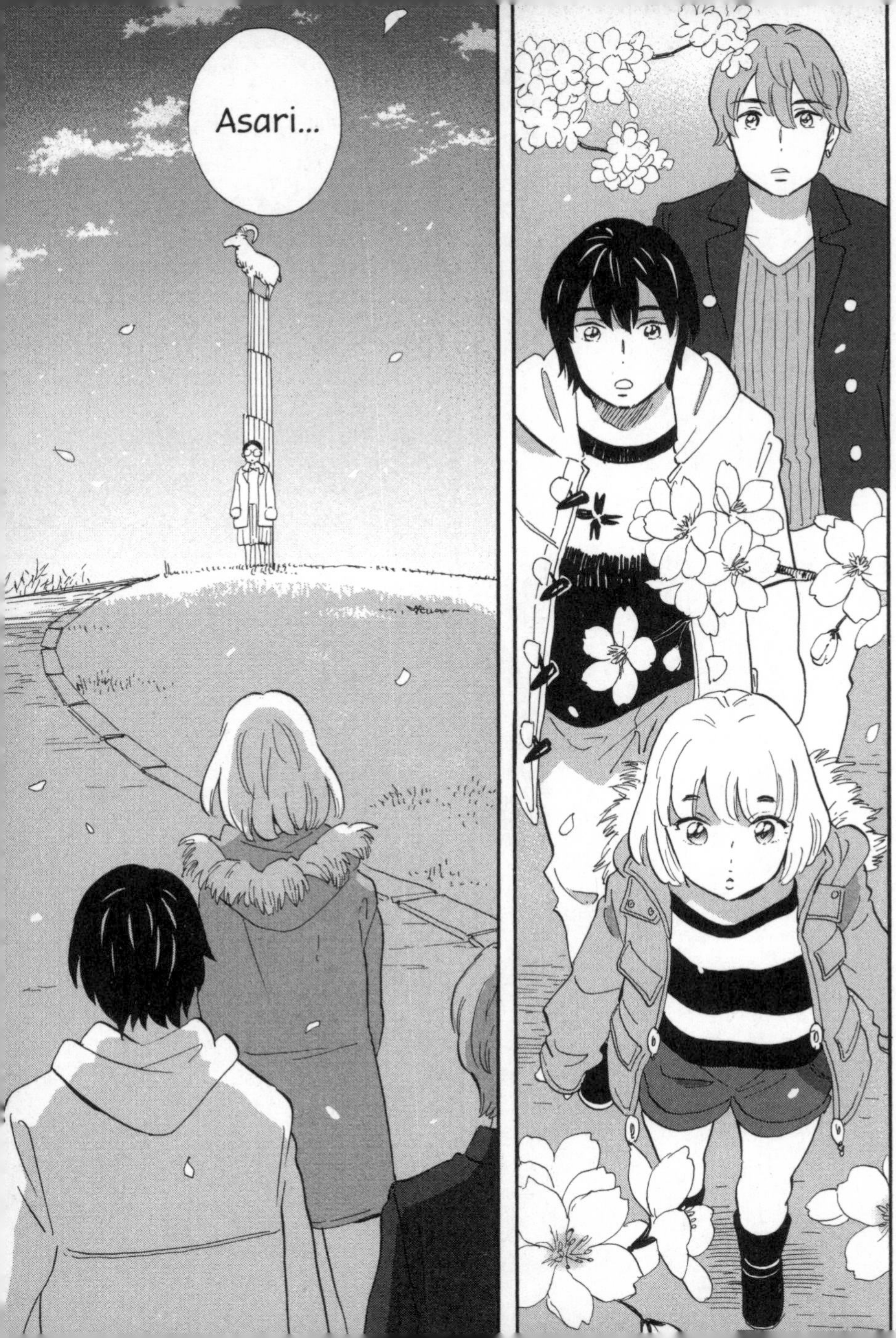
Asari...

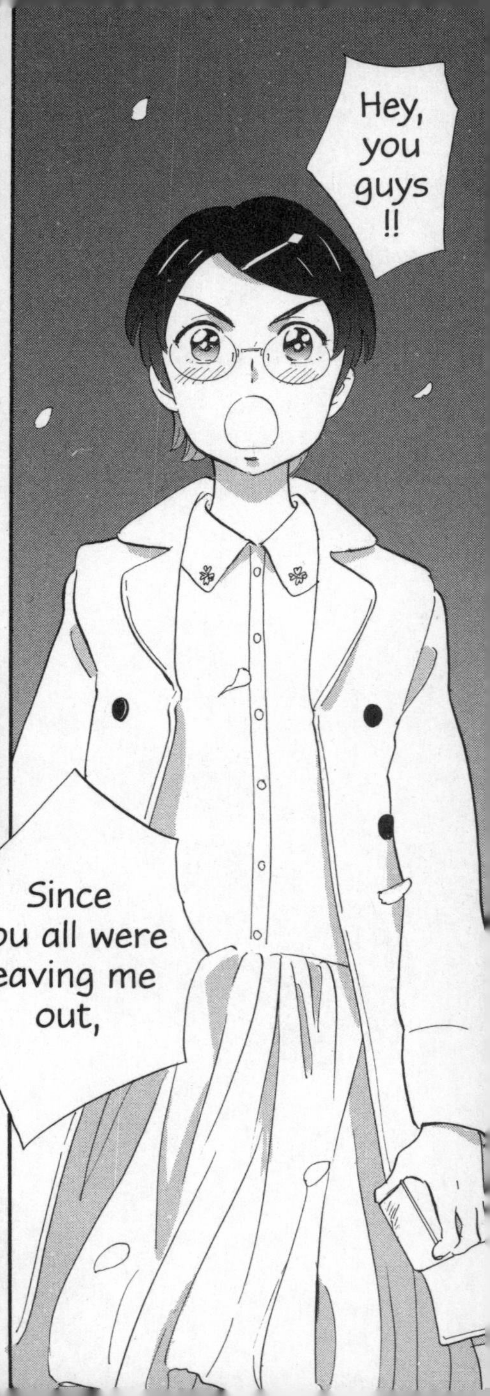
Hey, you guys !!
Since you all were leaving me out,
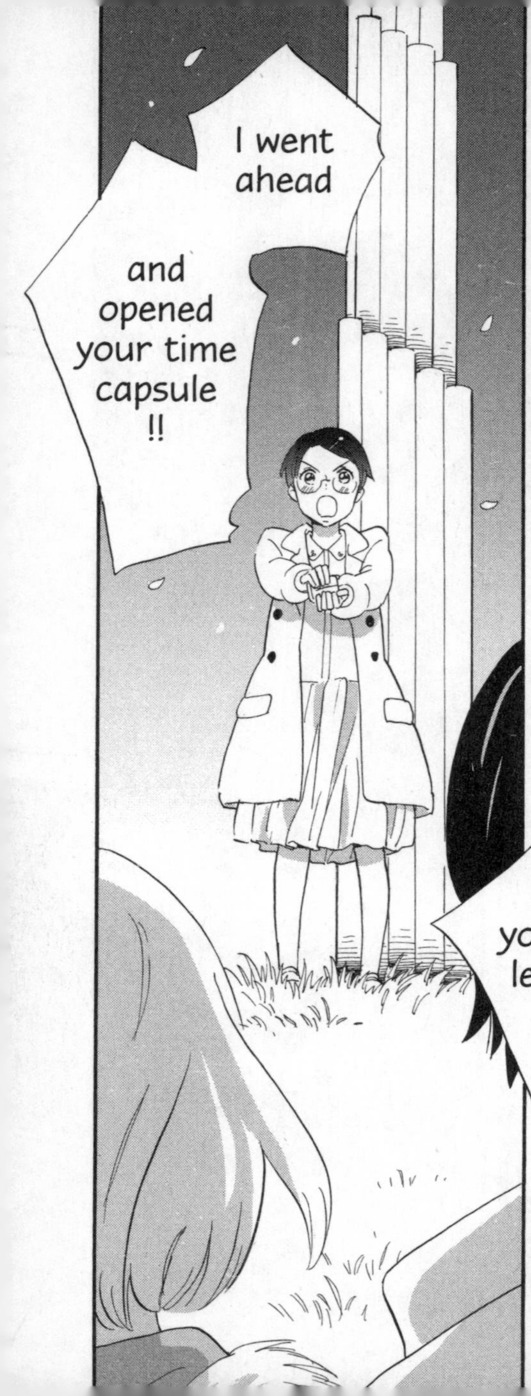
I went ahead
and opened your time capsule !!

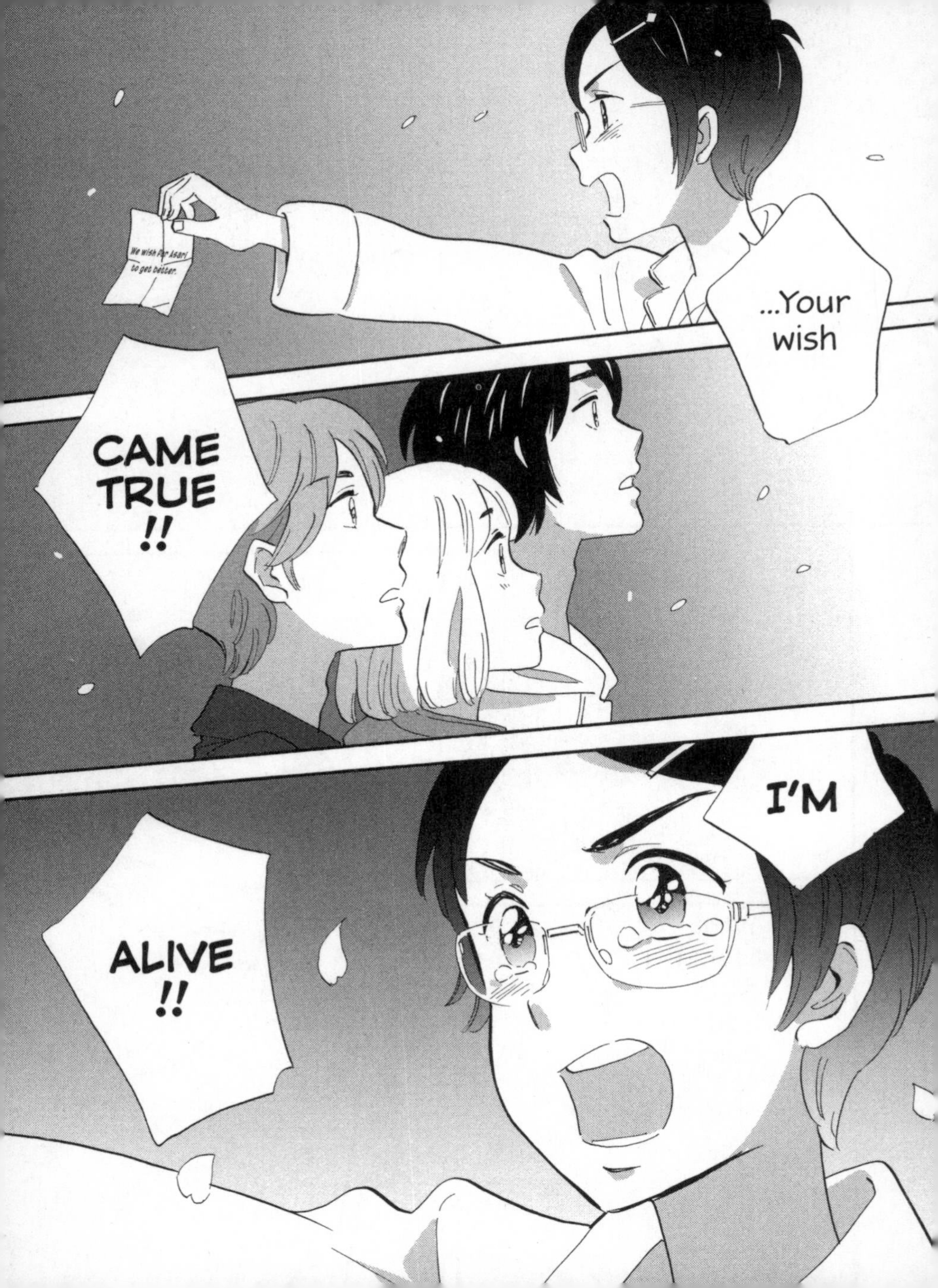
We wish for Asari to get better.
...Your wish
CAME TRUE !!
I'M
ALIVE !!

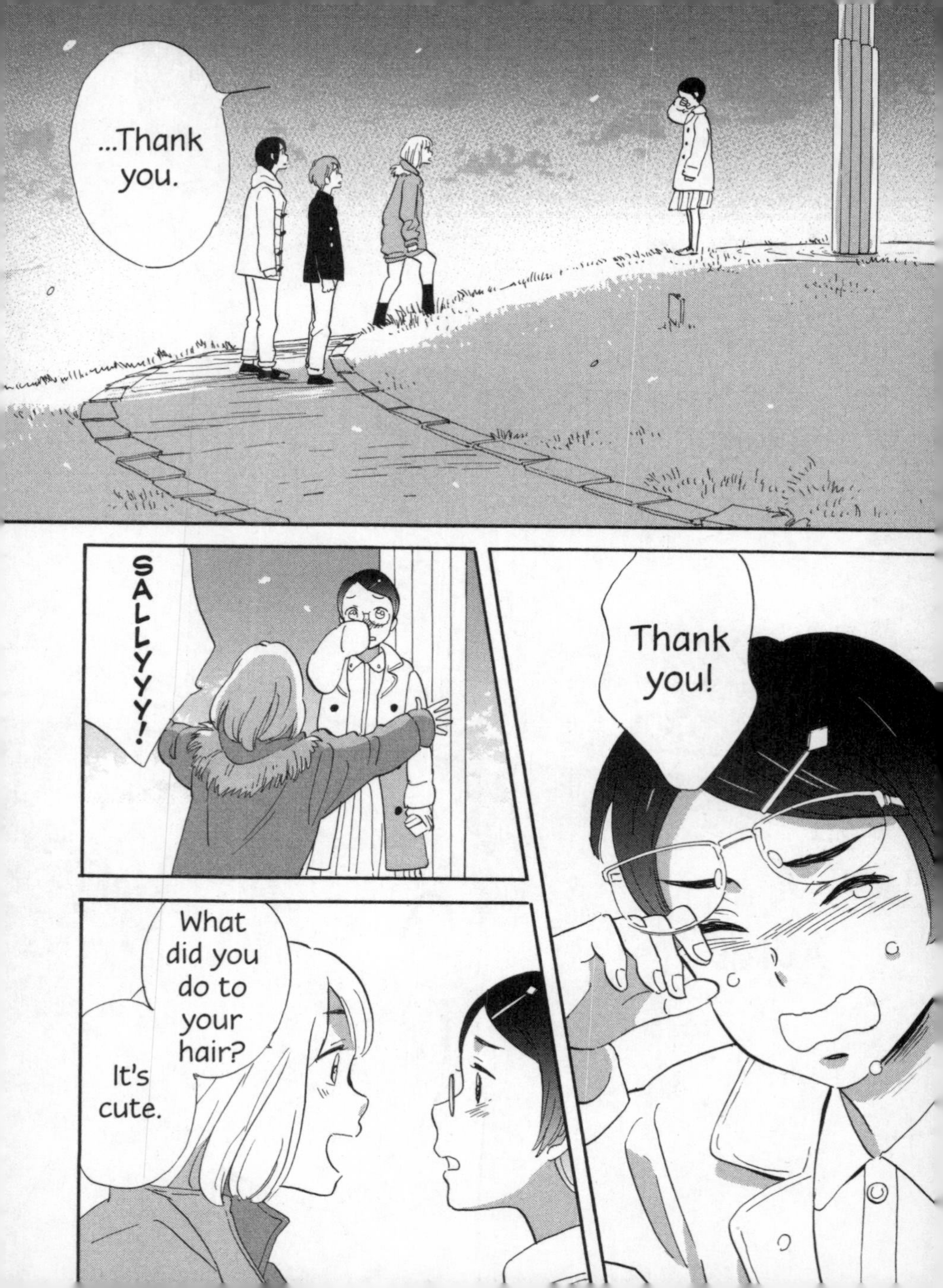
...Thank you.
Thank you!
SALLYYY!
What did you do to your hair?
It's cute.

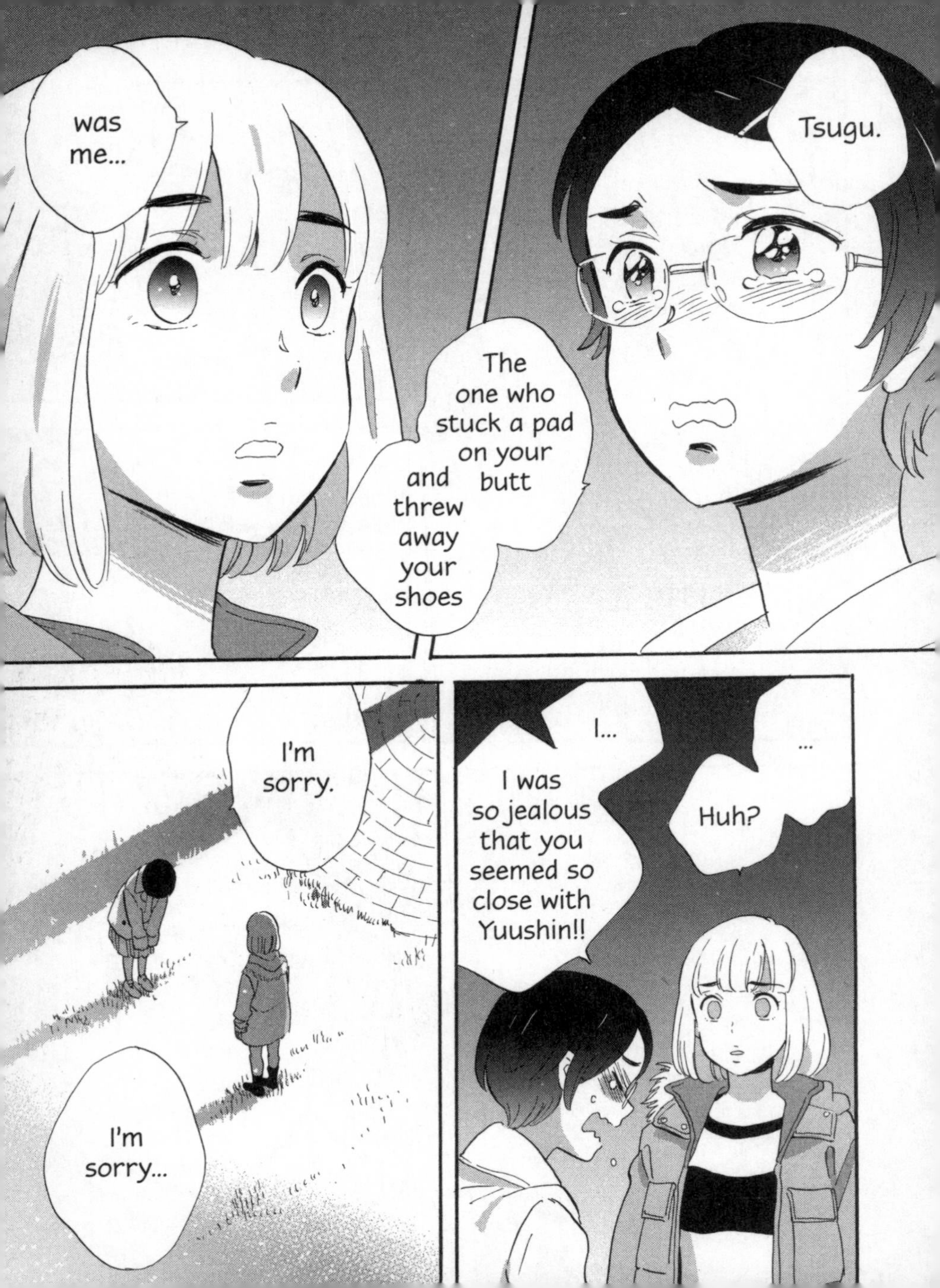

Tsugu.
The one who stuck a pad on your butt and threw away your shoes
was me...
I...
I was so jealous that you seemed so close with Yuushin!!
...
Huh?
I'm sorry.
I'm sorry...

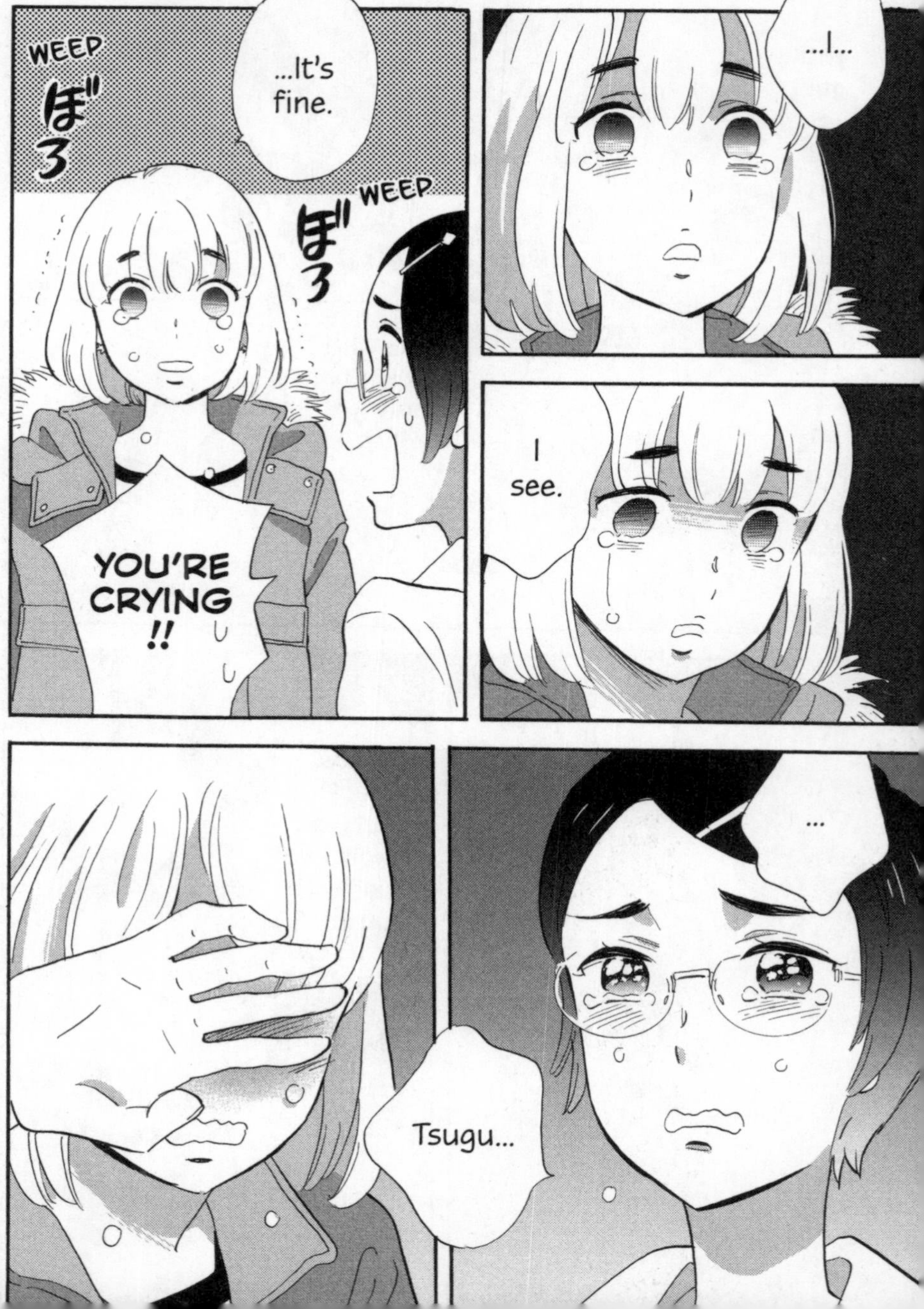
...I...
I see.
WEEP
ぼろ
...It's fine.
WEEP
ぼろ
YOU'RE CRYING !!
...
Tsugu...

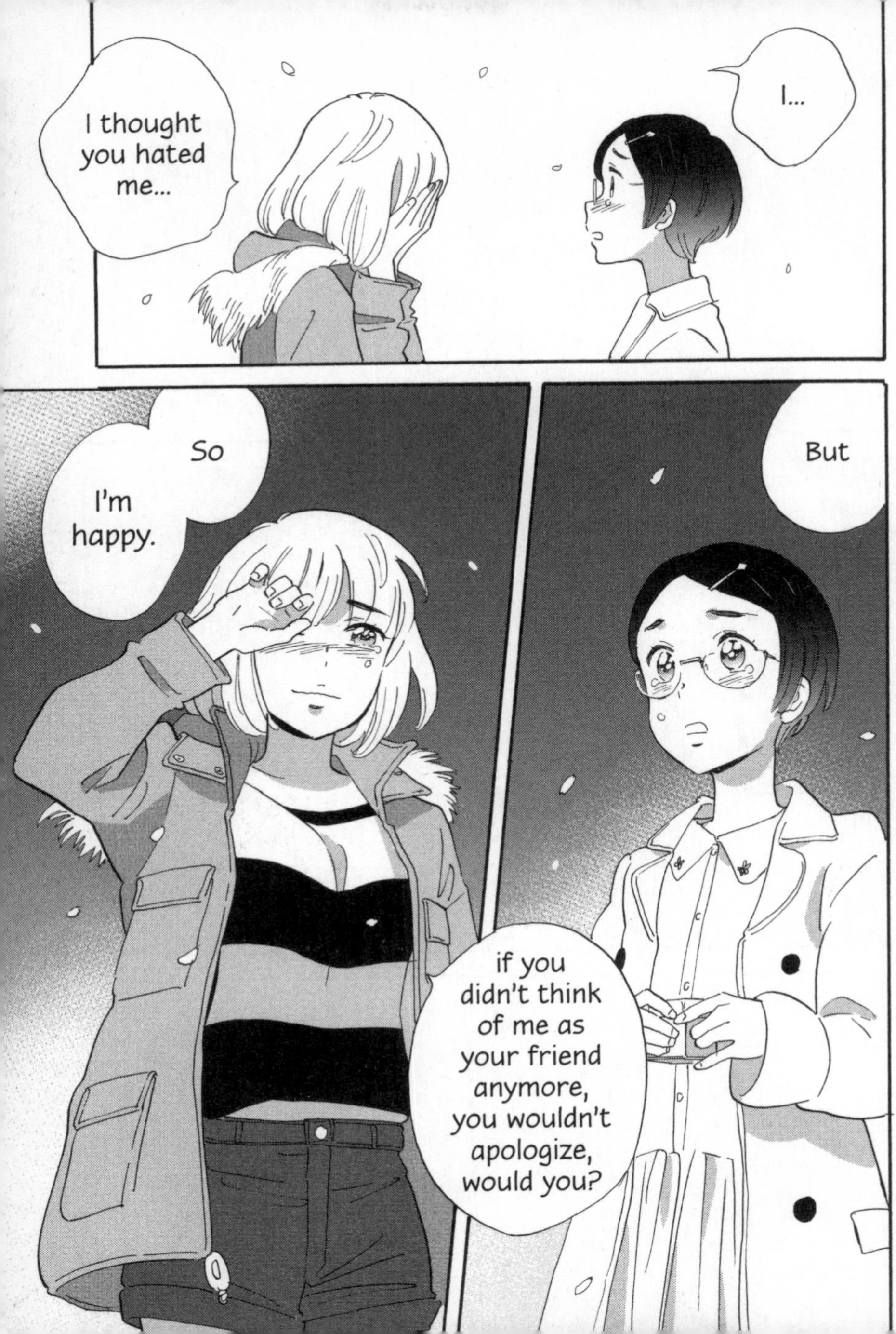
I...
I thought you hated me...
But
if you didn't think of me as your friend anymore, you wouldn't apologize, would you?
So I'm happy.

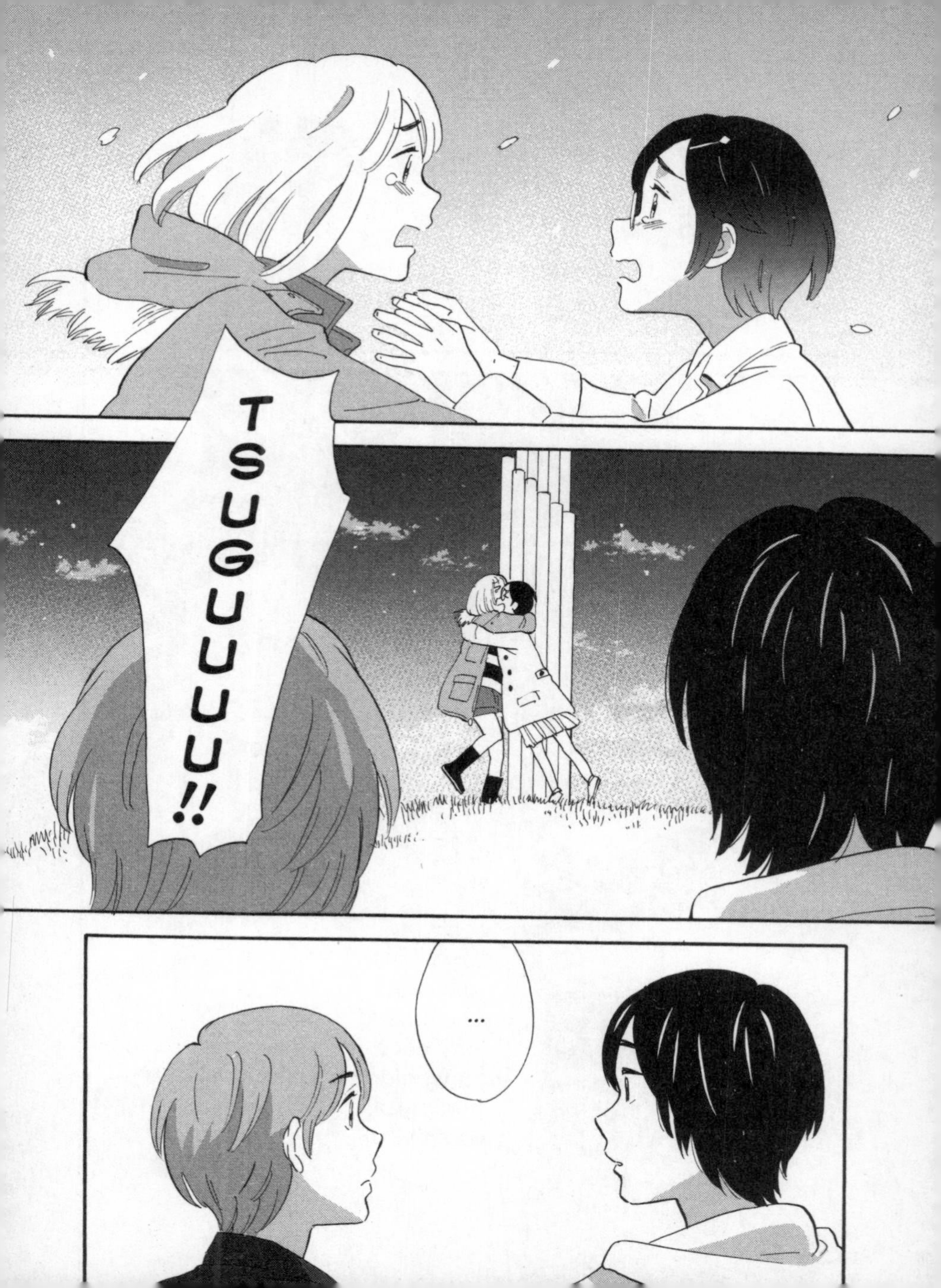
TSUGUUUUU!!
...

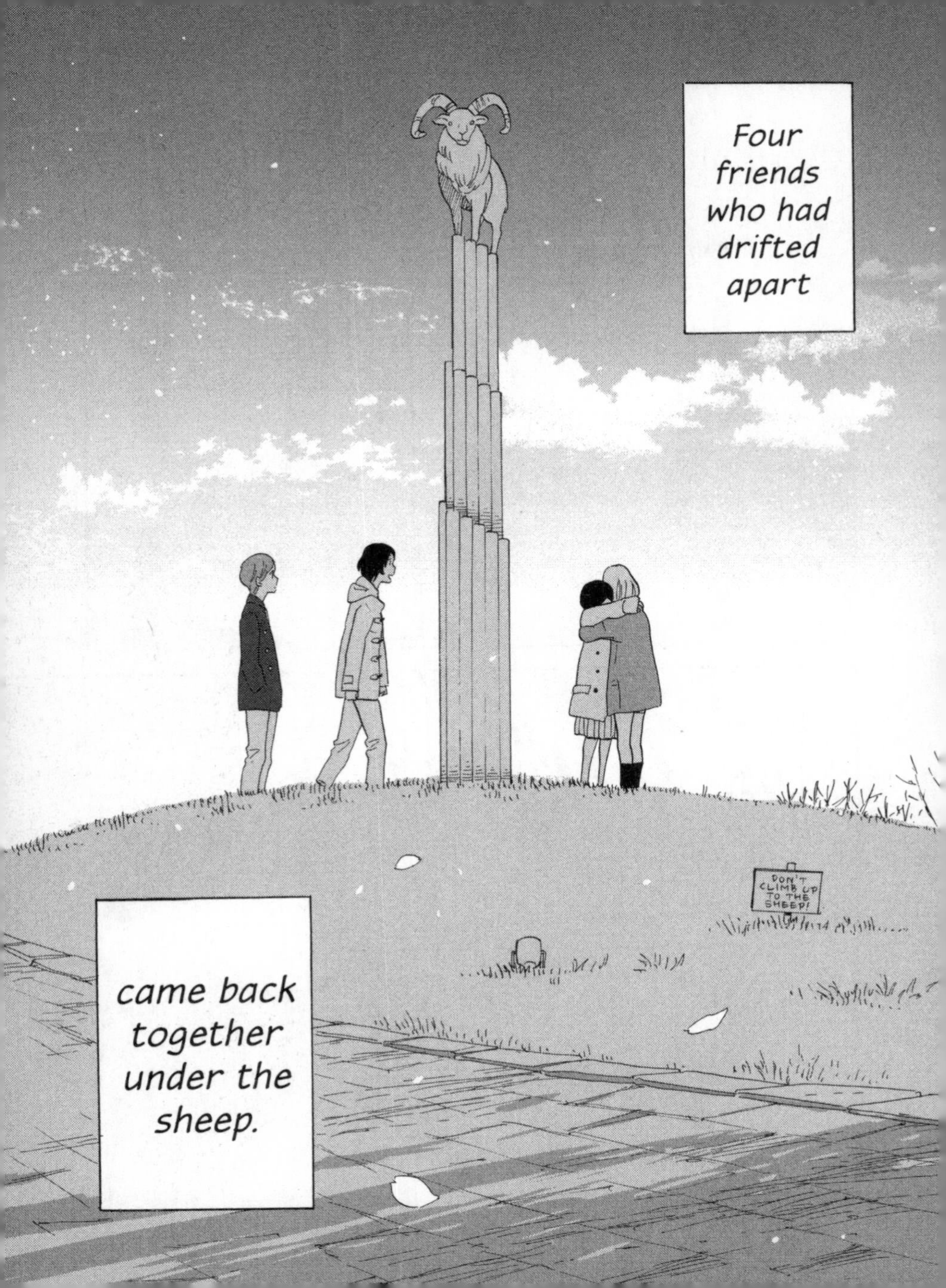
Four friends who had drifted apart
DON'T CLIMB UP TO THE SHEEP!
came back together under the sheep.

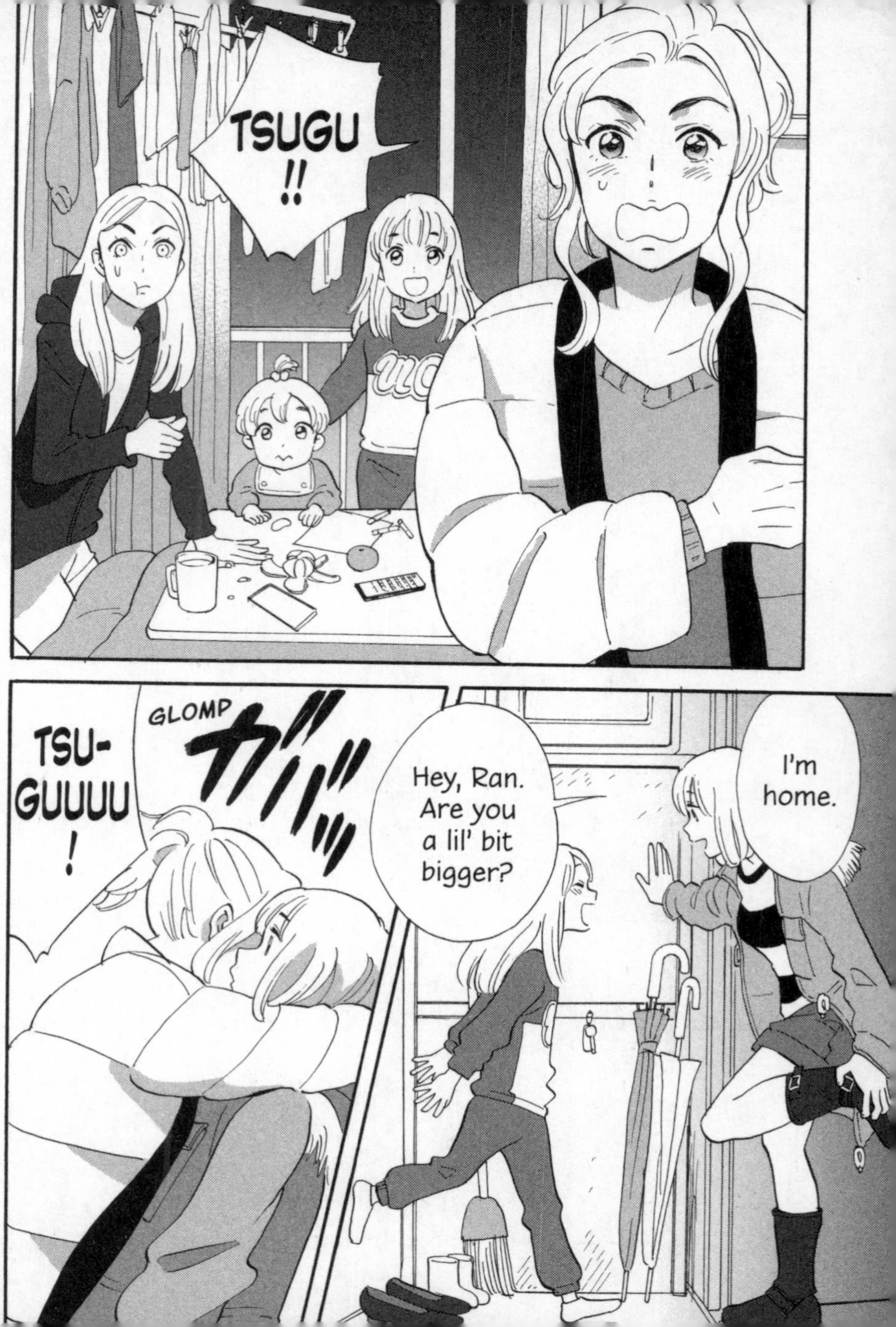
TSUGU !!
I'm home.
Hey, Ran. Are you a lil' bit bigger?
GLOMP
TSU-GUUUU !

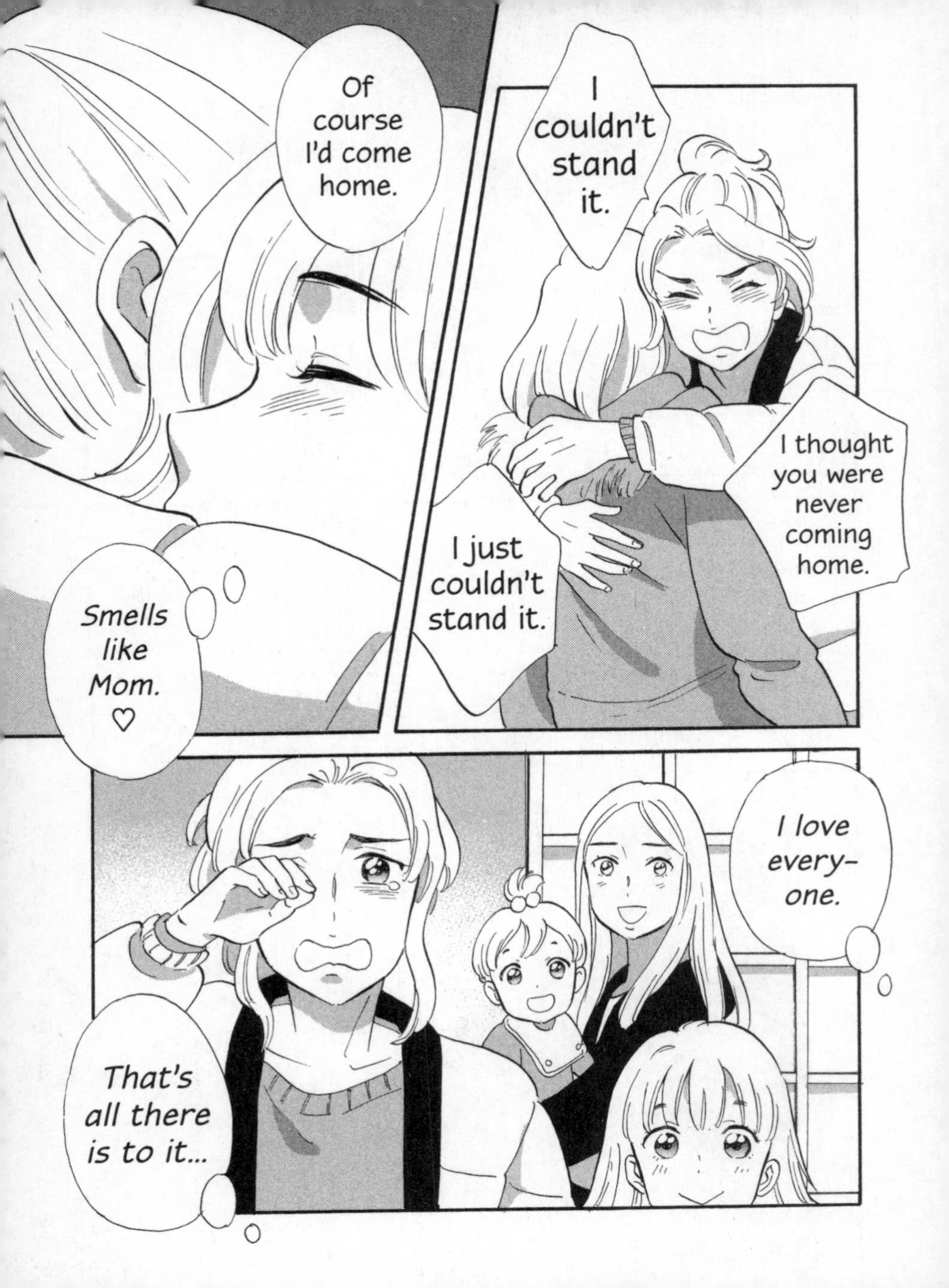
I couldn't stand it.
I thought you were never coming home.
I just couldn't stand it.
Of course I'd come home.
Smells like Mom. ♡
I love every-one.
That's all there is to it...

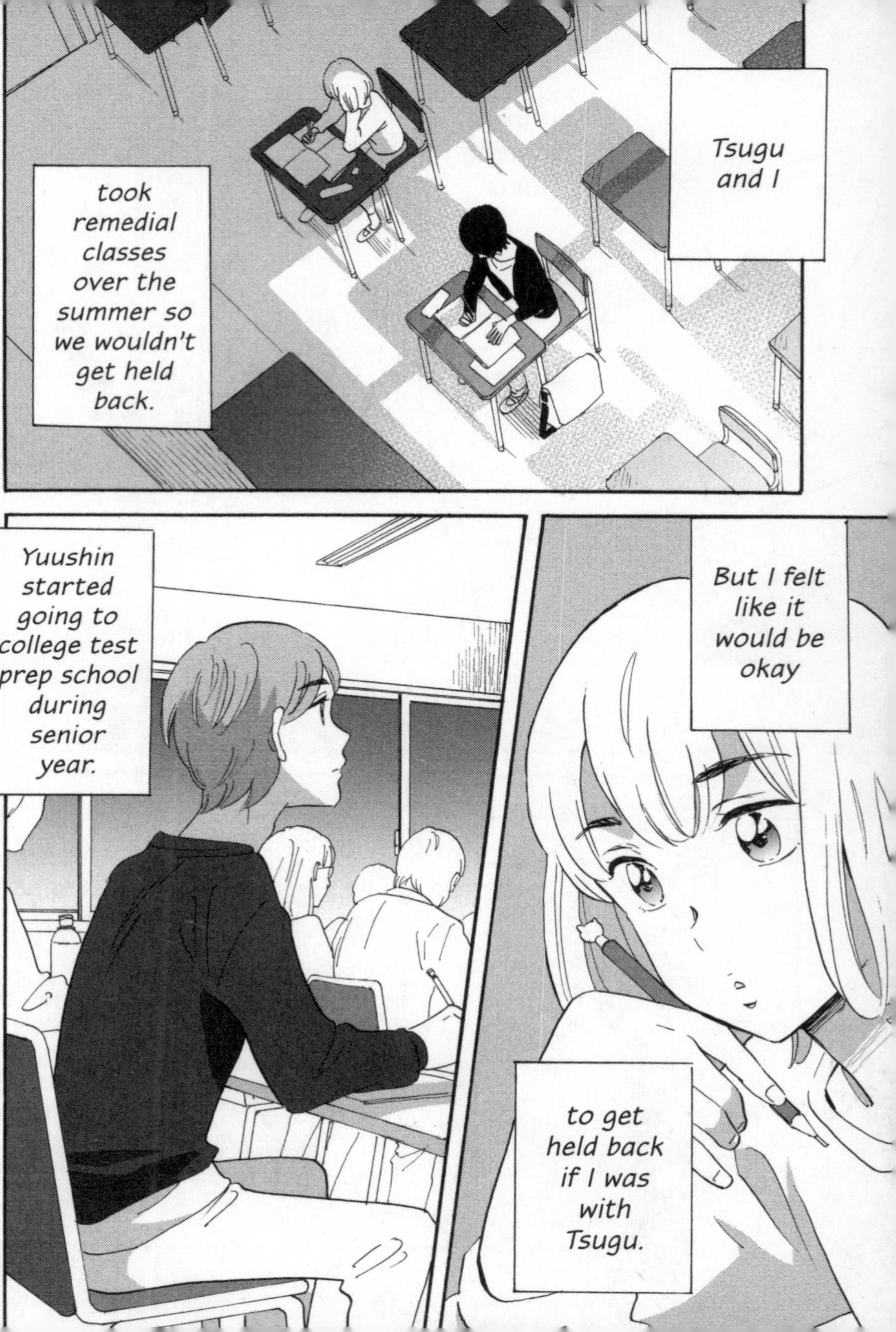
Tsugu and I
took remedial classes over the summer so we wouldn't get held back.
But I felt like it would be okay
to get held back if I was with Tsugu.
Yuushin started going to college test prep school during senior year.

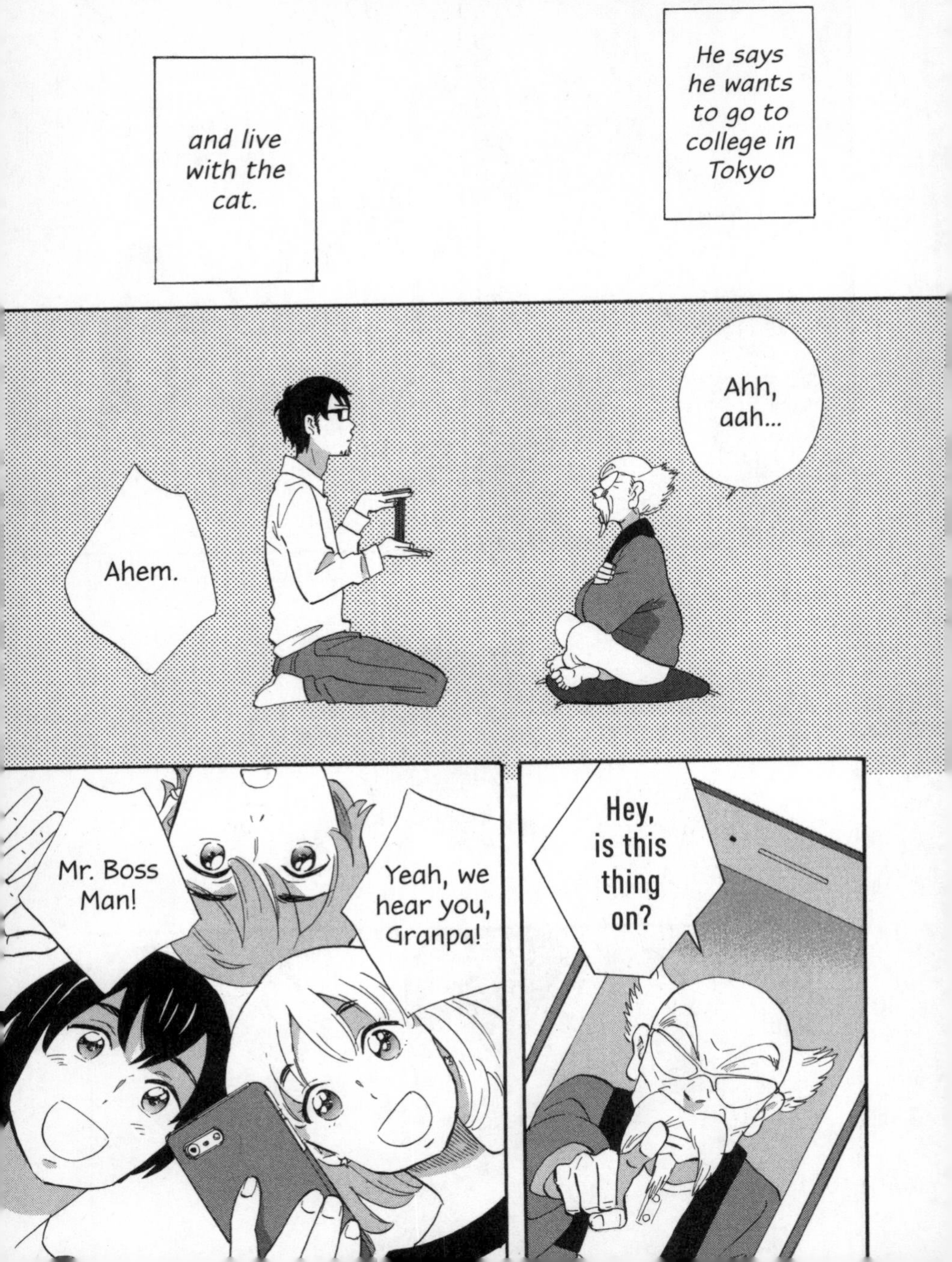
He says he wants to go to college in Tokyo
and live with the cat.
Ahh, aah...
Ahem.
Hey, is this thing on?
Yeah, we hear you, Granpa!
Mr. Boss Man!

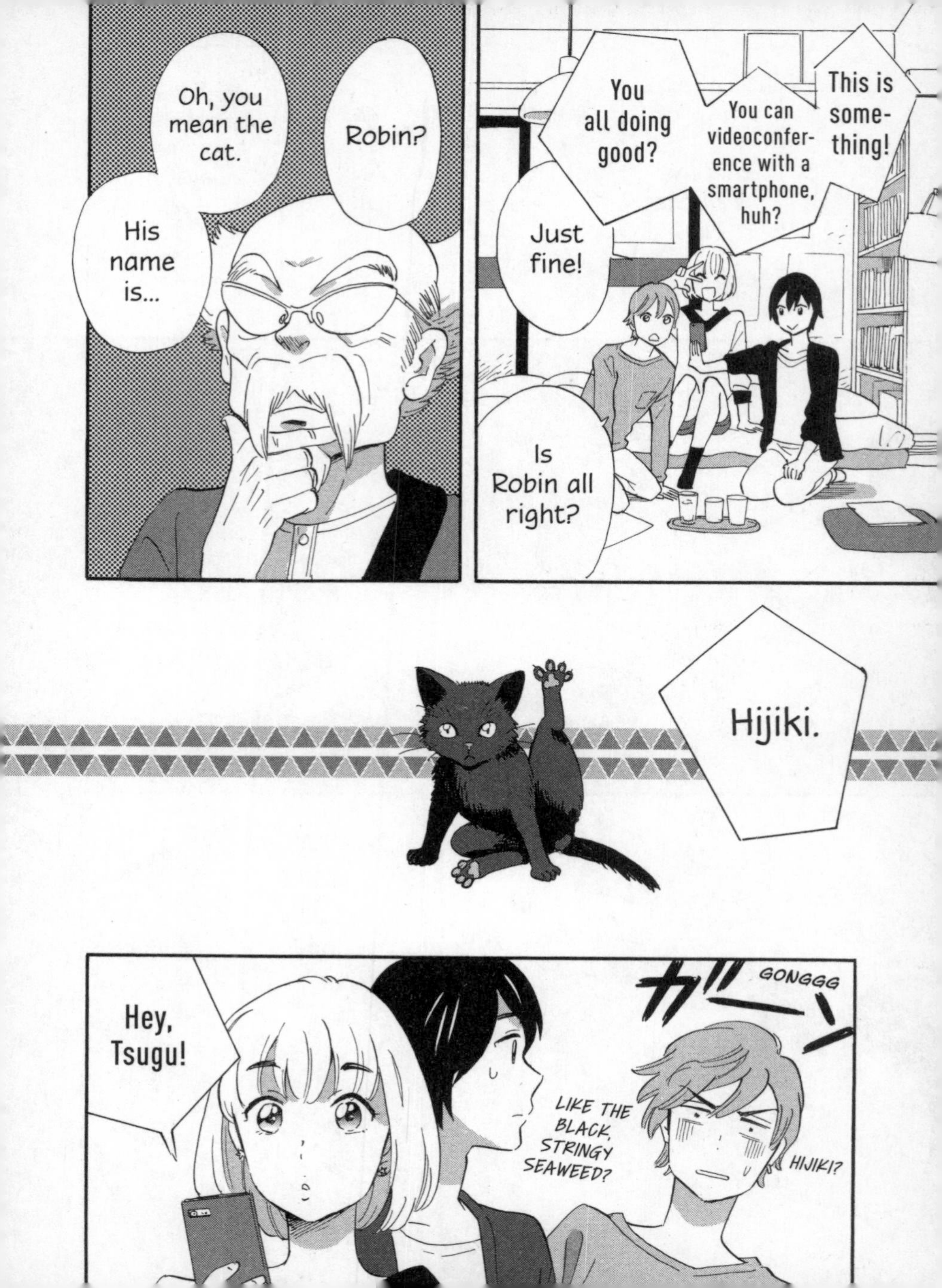
This is something!
You can videoconference with a smartphone, huh?
You all doing good?
Just fine!
Is Robin all right?
Robin?
Oh, you mean the cat.
His name is...
Hijiki.
GONGGG
HIJIKI?
LIKE THE BLACK, STRINGY SEAWEED?
Hey, Tsugu!

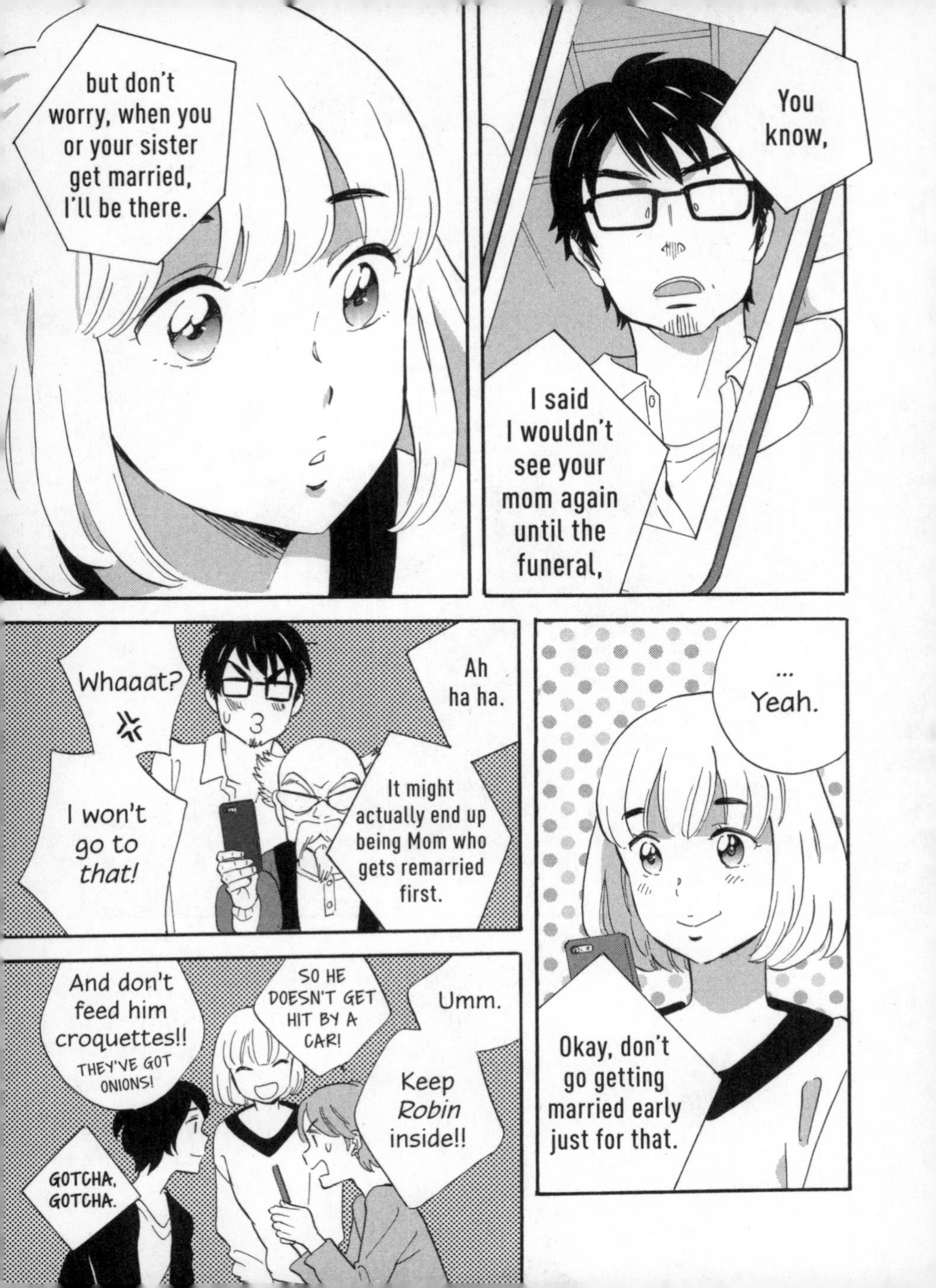
You know,
I said I wouldn't see your mom again until the funeral,
but don't worry, when you or your sister get married, I'll be there.
... Yeah.
Okay, don't go getting married early just for that.
Ah ha ha.
It might actually end up being Mom who gets remarried first.
Whaaat?
I won't go to *that!*
Umm.
Keep *Robin* inside!!
SO HE DOESN'T GET HIT BY A CAR!
And don't feed him croquettes!!
THEY'VE GOT ONIONS!
GOTCHA, GOTCHA.

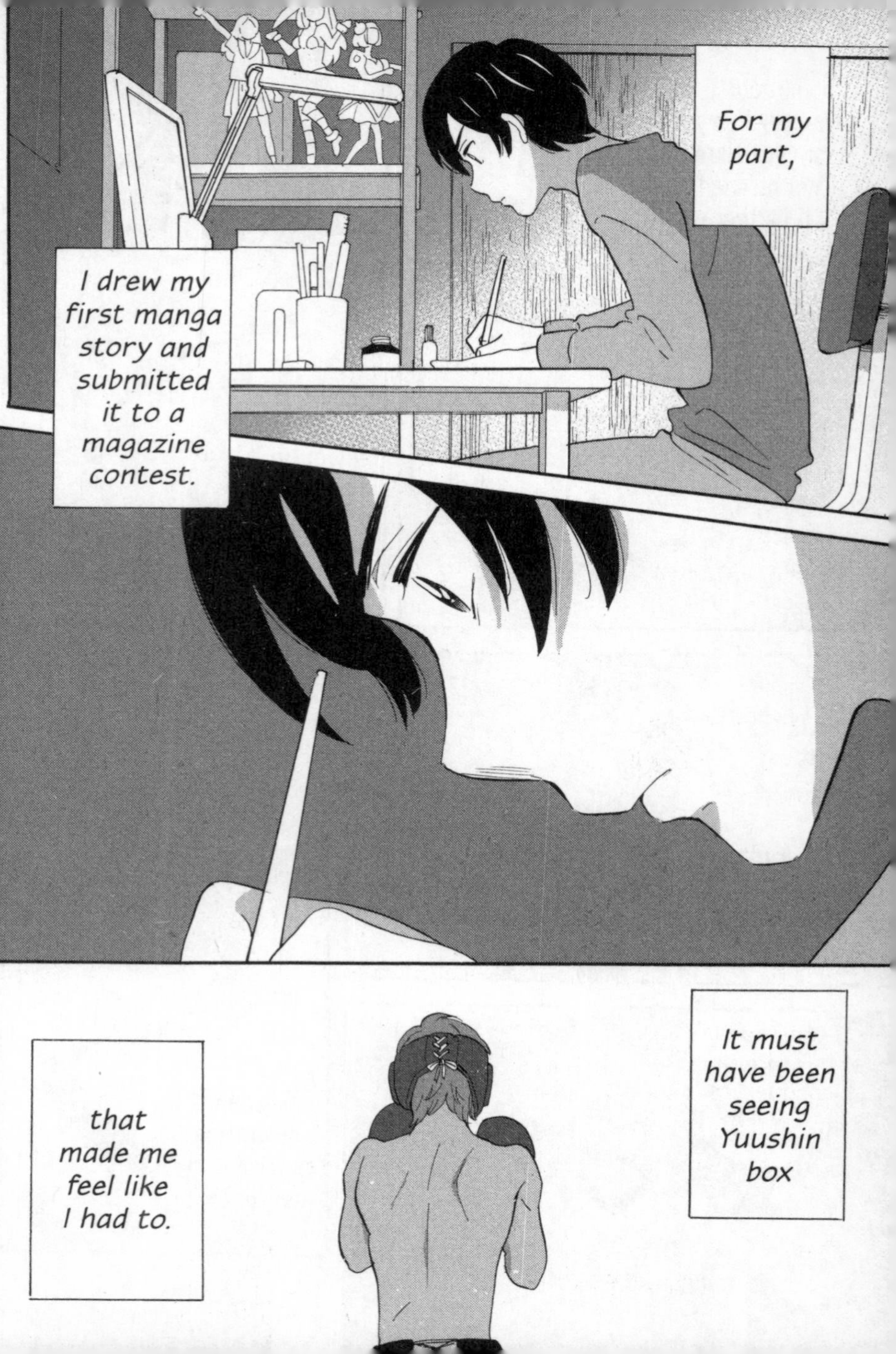
For my part,
I drew my first manga story and submitted it to a magazine contest.
It must have been seeing Yuushin box
that made me feel like I had to.

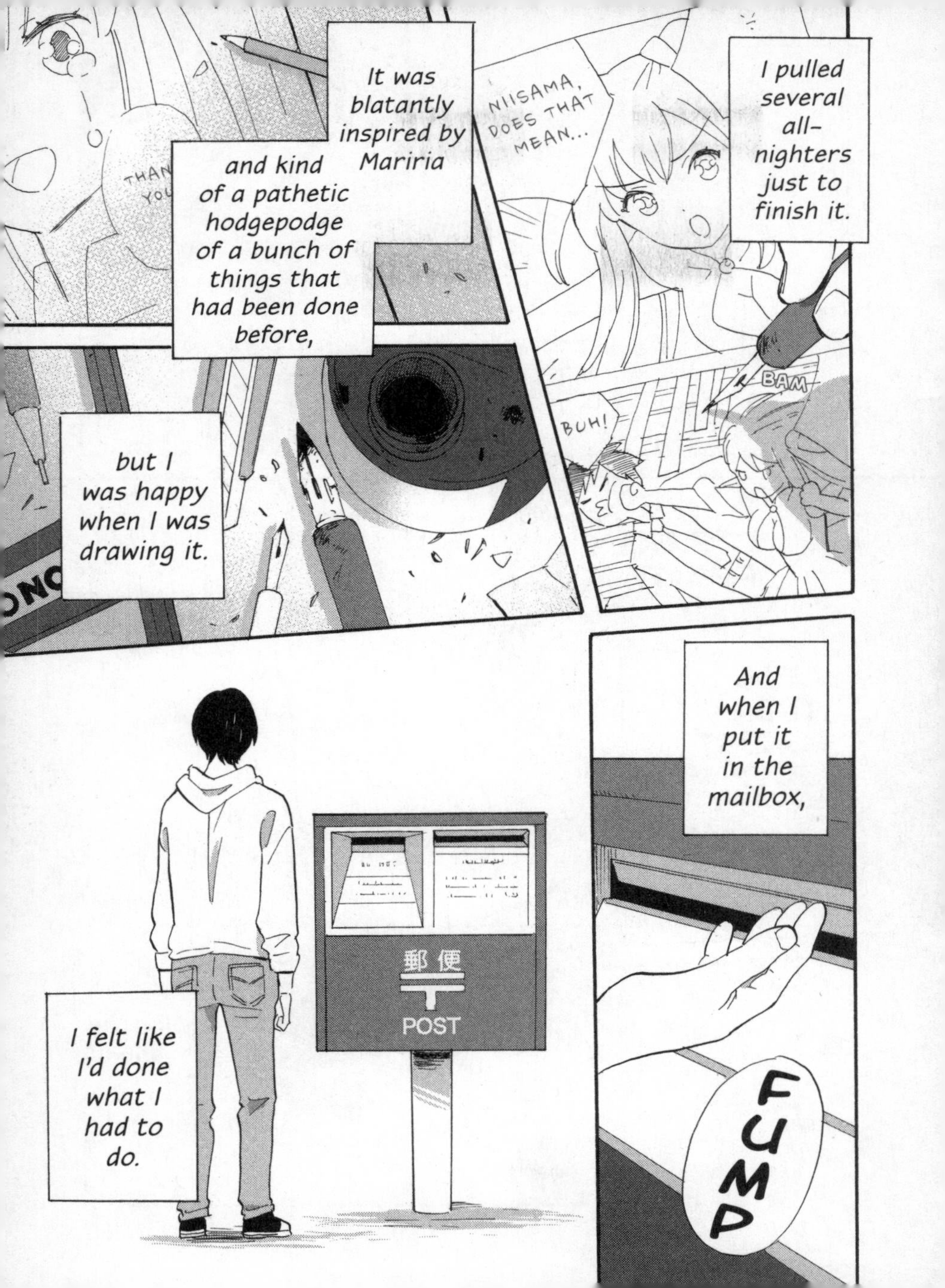
It was blatantly inspired by Mariria
and kind of a pathetic hodgepodge of a bunch of things that had been done before,
THANK YOU
but I was happy when I was drawing it.
I pulled several all-nighters just to finish it.
NIISAMA, DOES THAT MEAN...
BAM
BUH!
And when I put it in the mailbox,
FUMP
郵便
POST
I felt like I'd done what I had to do.

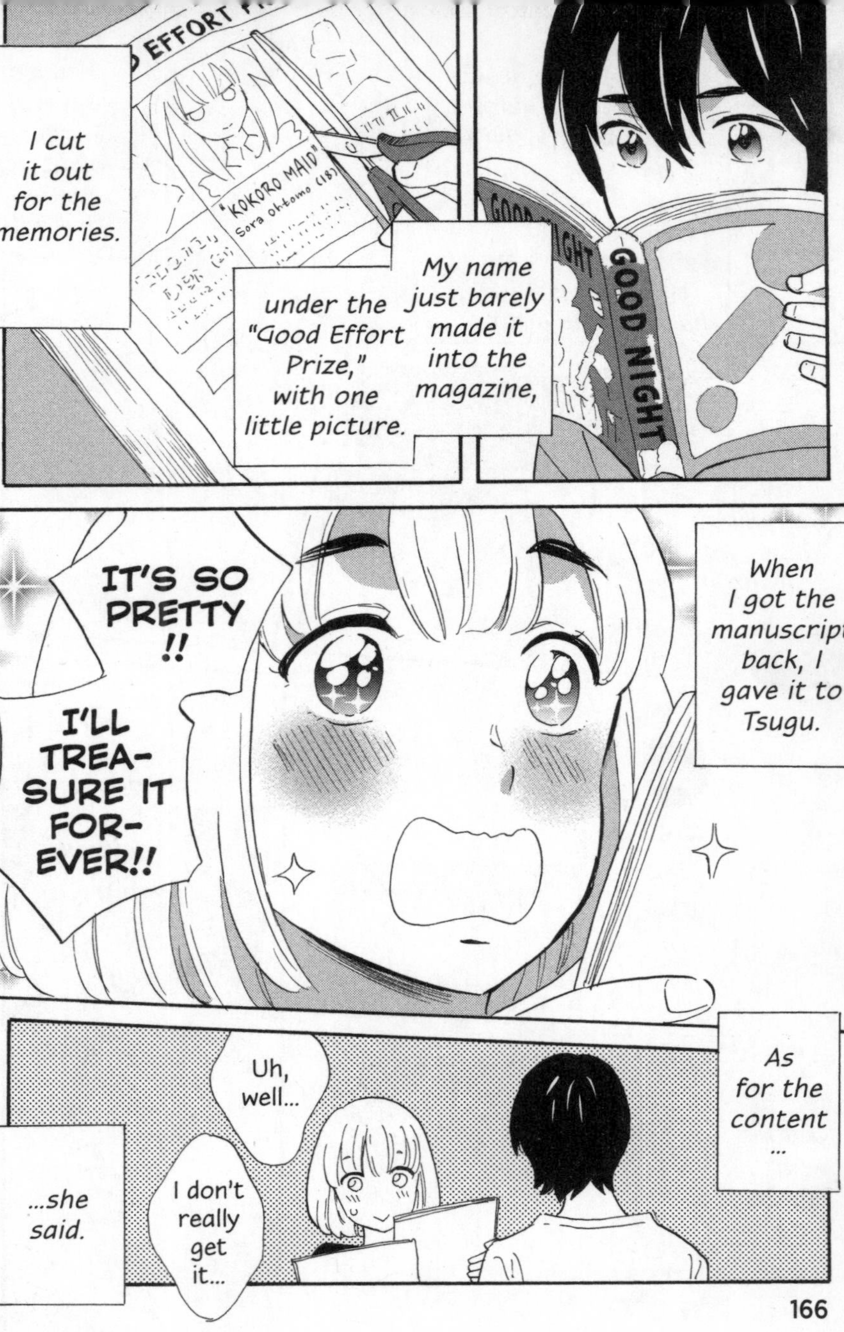
GOOD NIGHT
My name just barely made it into the magazine,
under the "Good Effort Prize," with one little picture.
"KOKORO MAID"
Sora Ohtomo (18)
I cut it out for the memories.
When I got the manuscript back, I gave it to Tsugu.
IT'S SO PRETTY!!
I'LL TREASURE IT FOREVER!!
As for the content...
Uh, well...
I don't really get it...
...she said.

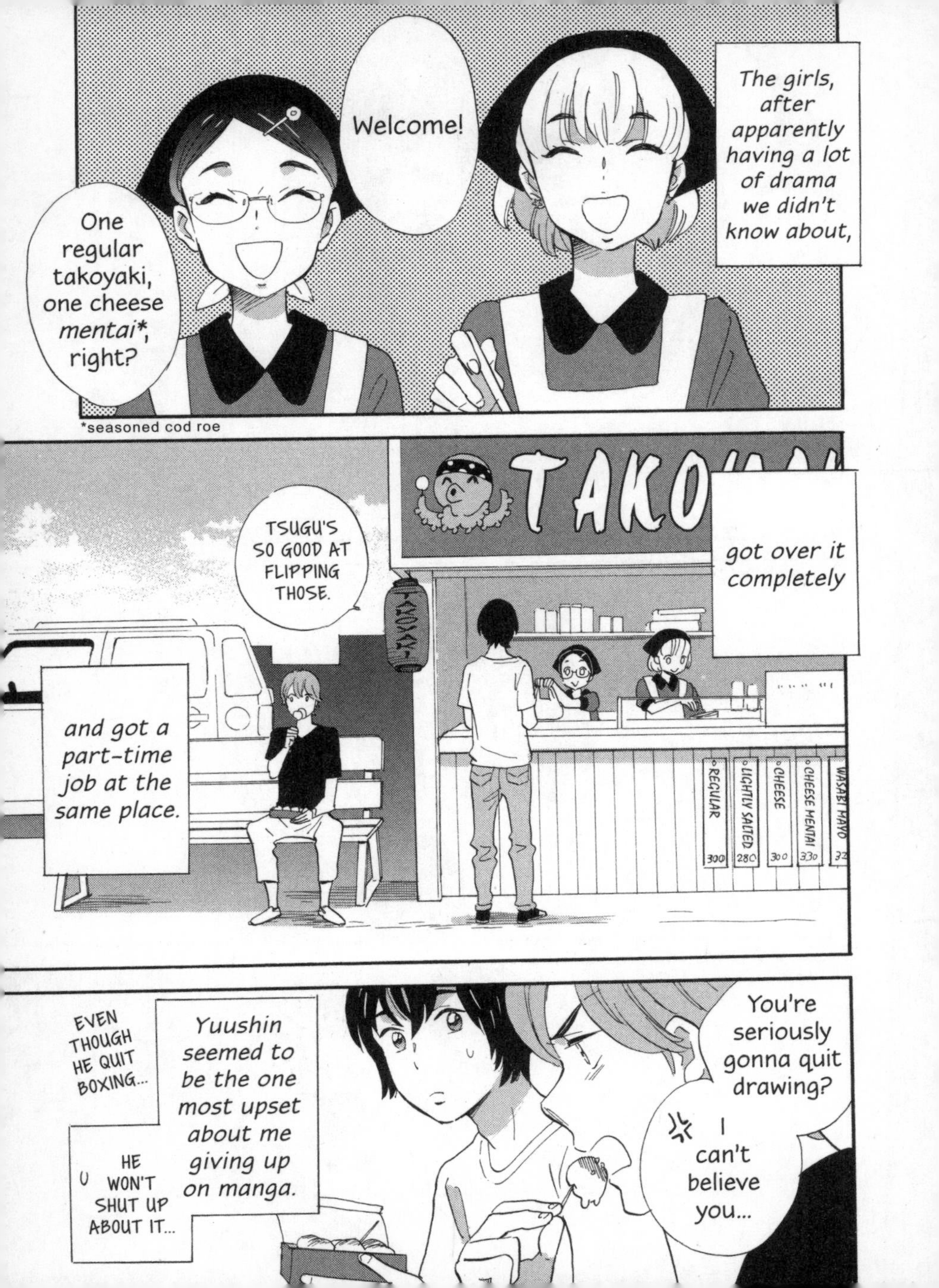
The girls, after apparently having a lot of drama we didn't know about,
Welcome!
One regular takoyaki, one cheese *mentai**, right?
*seasoned cod roe
got over it completely
TSUGU'S SO GOOD AT FLIPPING THOSE.
REGULAR 300
LIGHTLY SALTED 280
CHEESE 300
CHEESE MENTAI 330
WASABI MAYO
and got a part-time job at the same place.
You're seriously gonna quit drawing?
I can't believe you...
Yuushin seemed to be the one most upset about me giving up on manga.
EVEN THOUGH HE QUIT BOXING...
HE WON'T SHUT UP ABOUT IT...

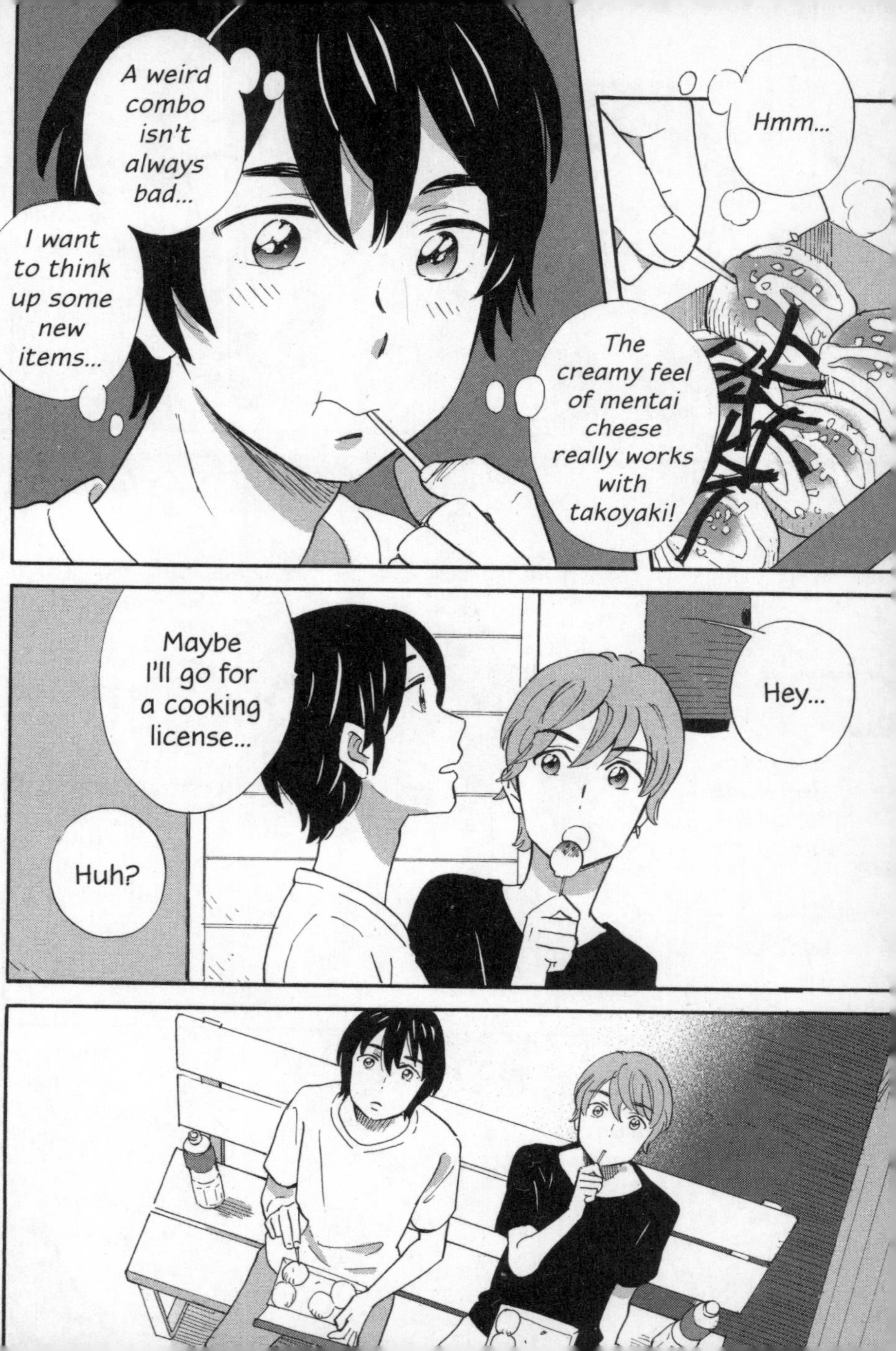
Hmm...
The creamy feel of mentai cheese really works with takoyaki!
A weird combo isn't always bad...
I want to think up some new items...
Hey...
Maybe I'll go for a cooking license...
Huh?

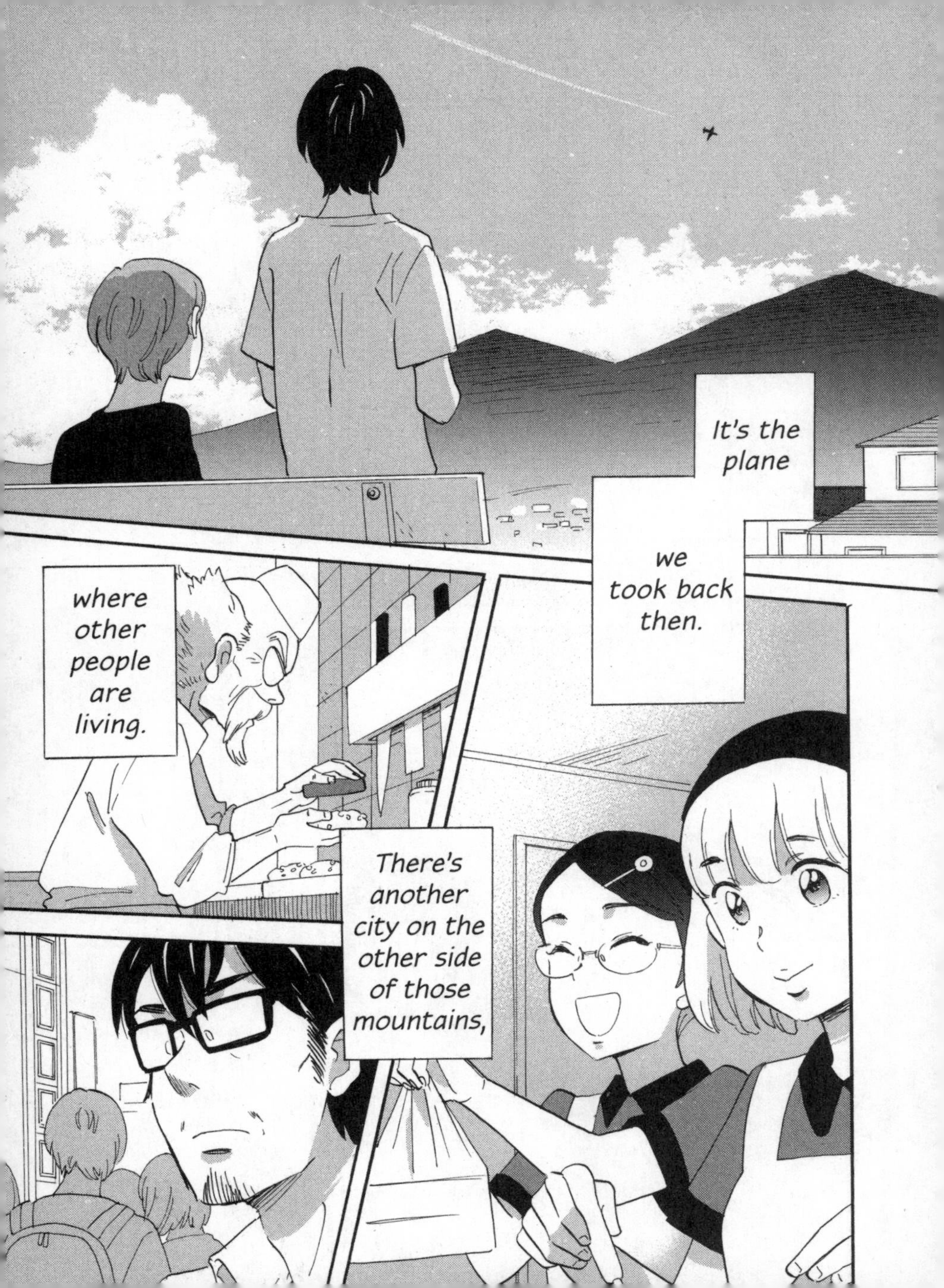
It's the plane
we took back then.
There's another city on the other side of those mountains,
where other people are living.

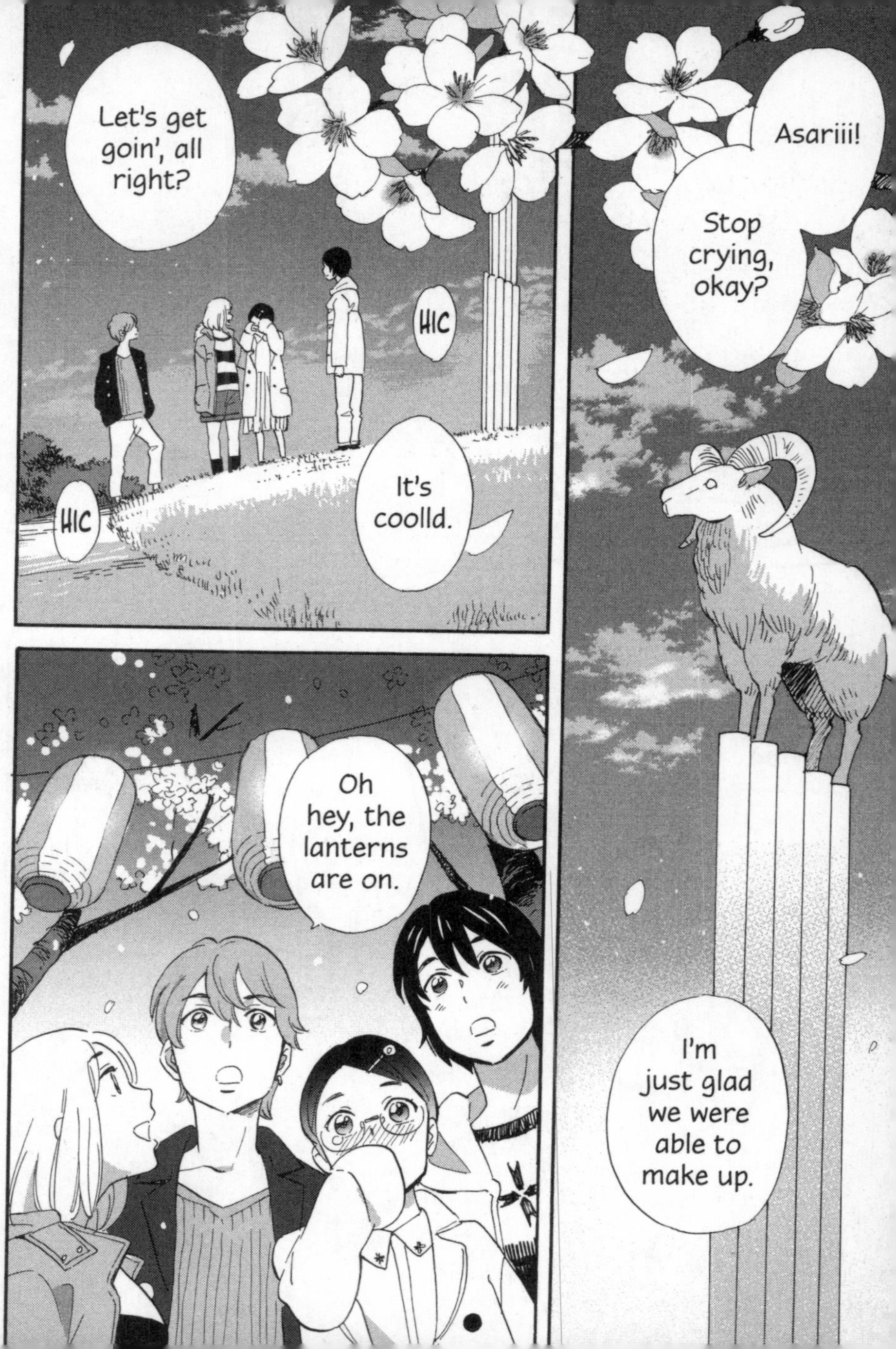
Asariii!
Stop crying, okay?
I'm just glad we were able to make up.
Let's get goin', all right?
HIC
It's coolld.
HIC
Oh hey, the lanterns are on.

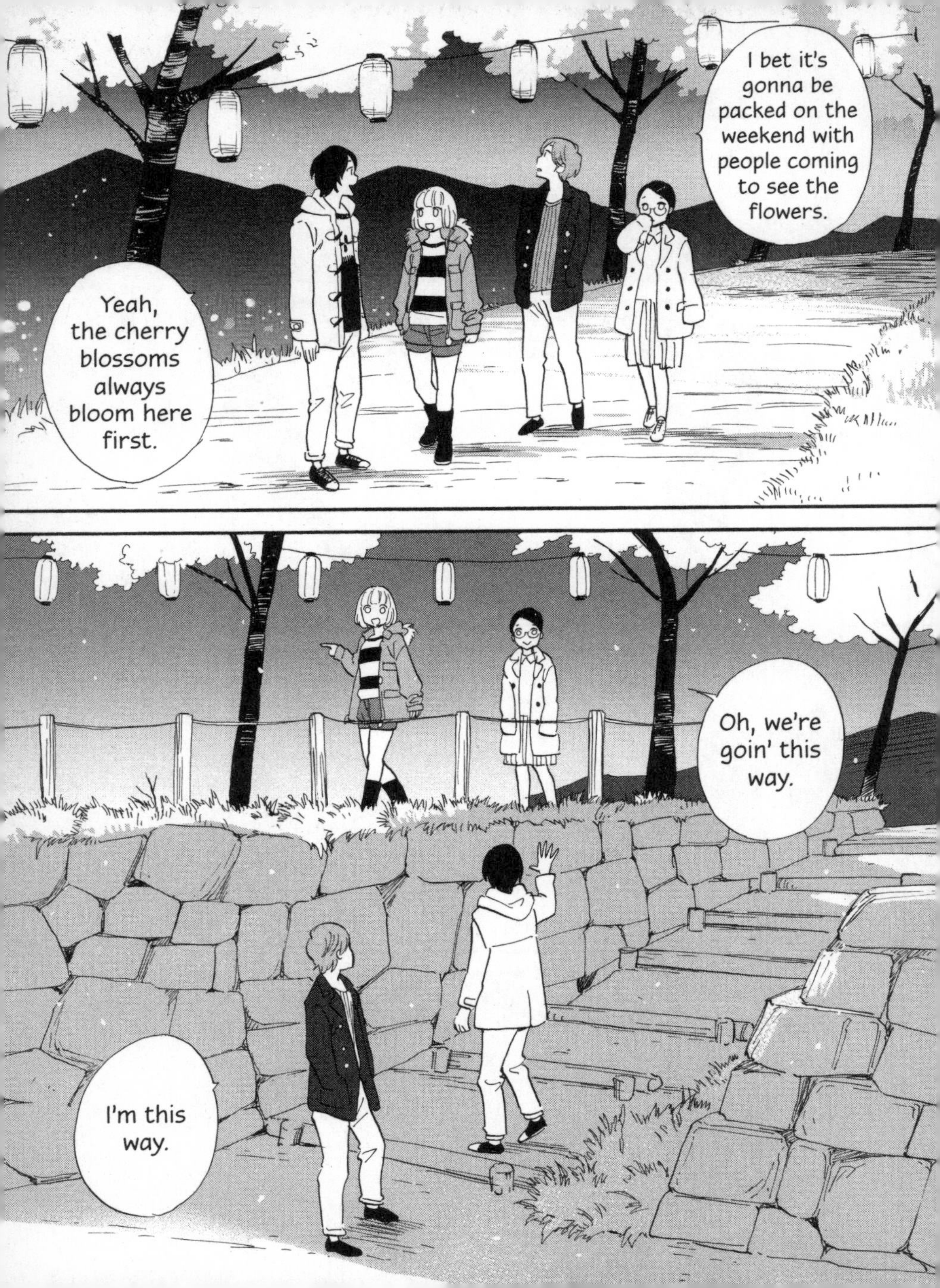
I bet it's gonna be packed on the weekend with people coming to see the flowers.
Yeah, the cherry blossoms always bloom here first.
Oh, we're goin' this way.
I'm this way.

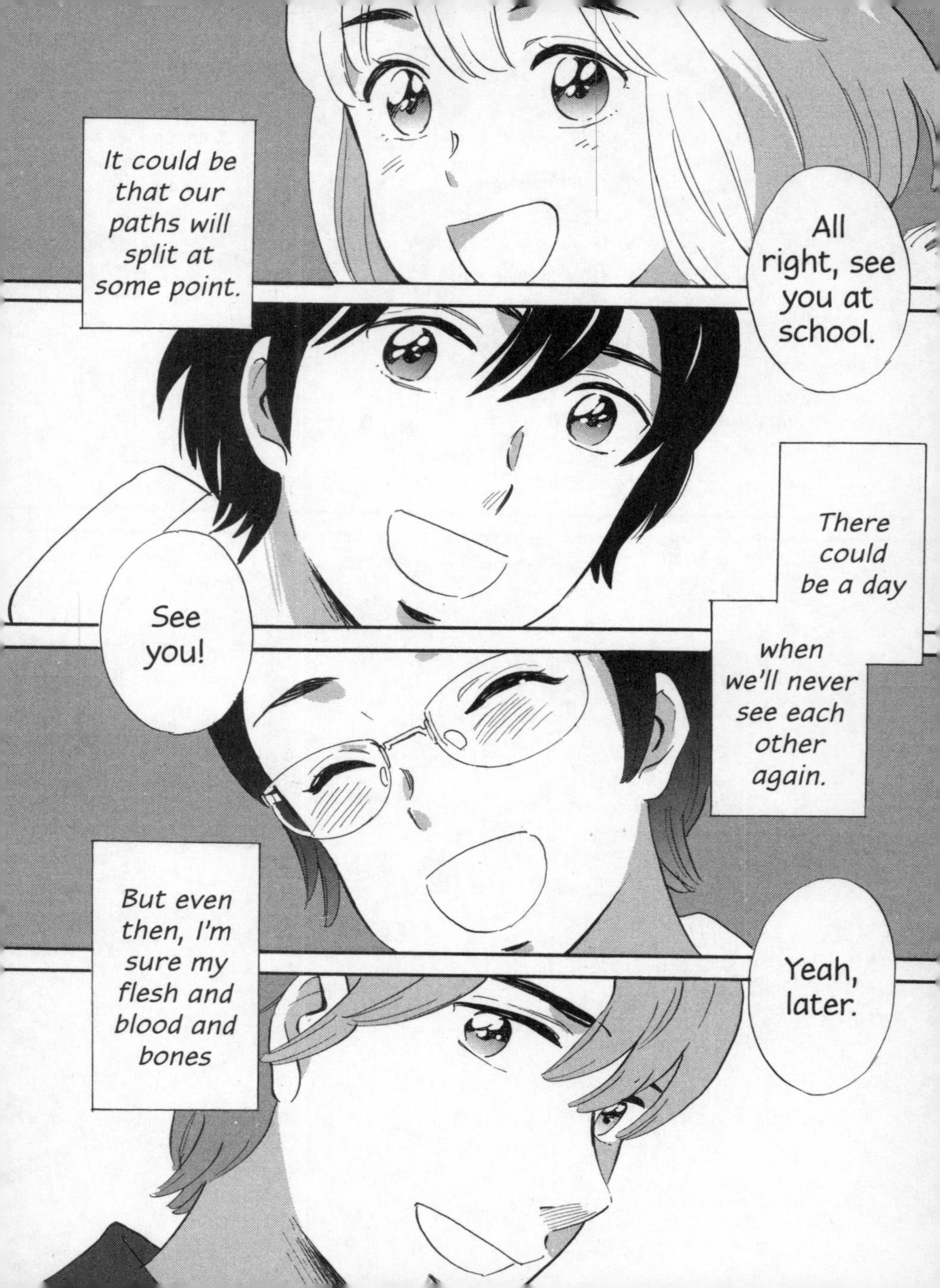
All right, see you at school.
It could be that our paths will split at some point.
There could be a day
See you!
when we'll never see each other again.
Yeah, later.
But even then, I'm sure my flesh and blood and bones

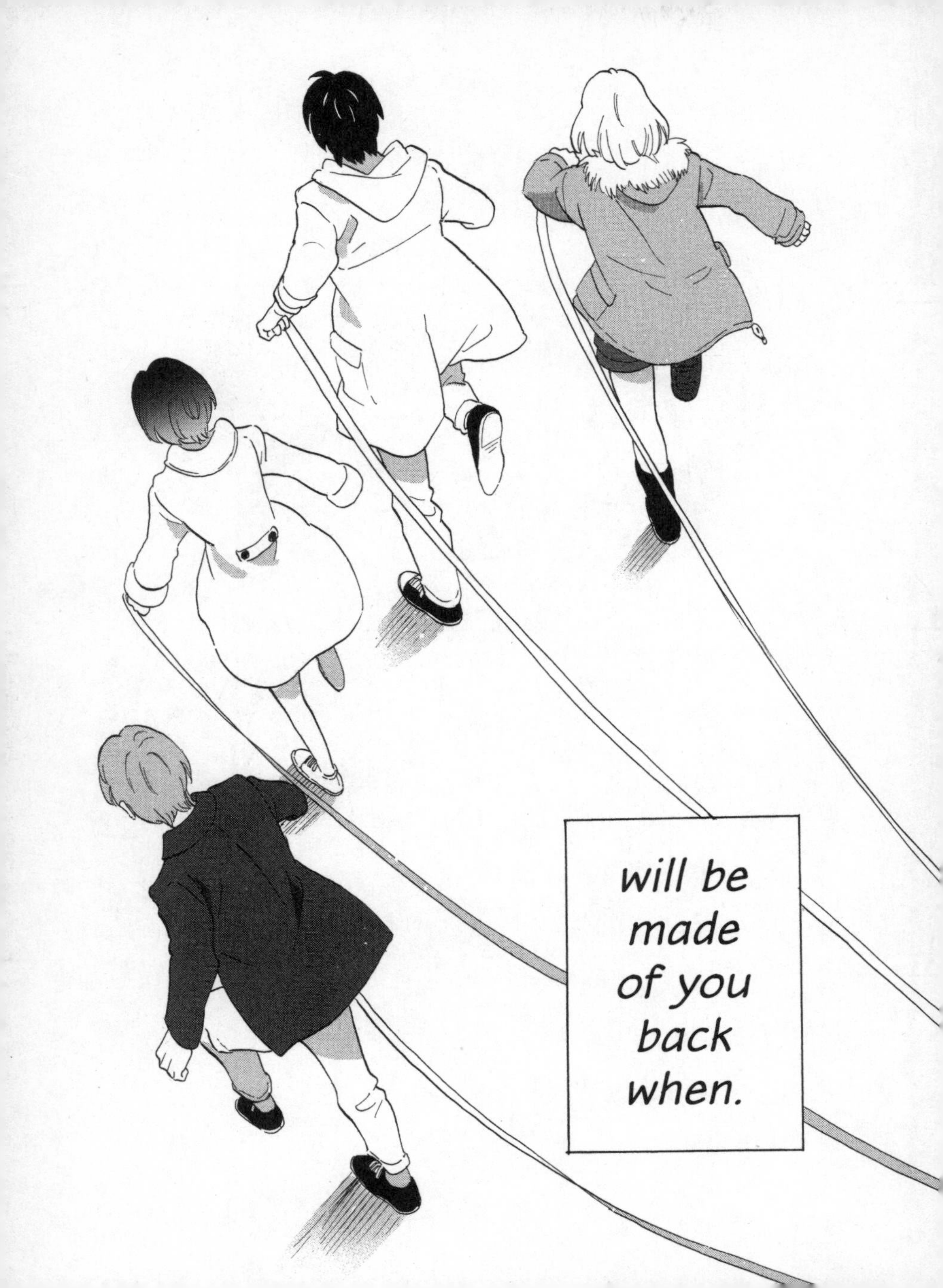
will be made of you back when.

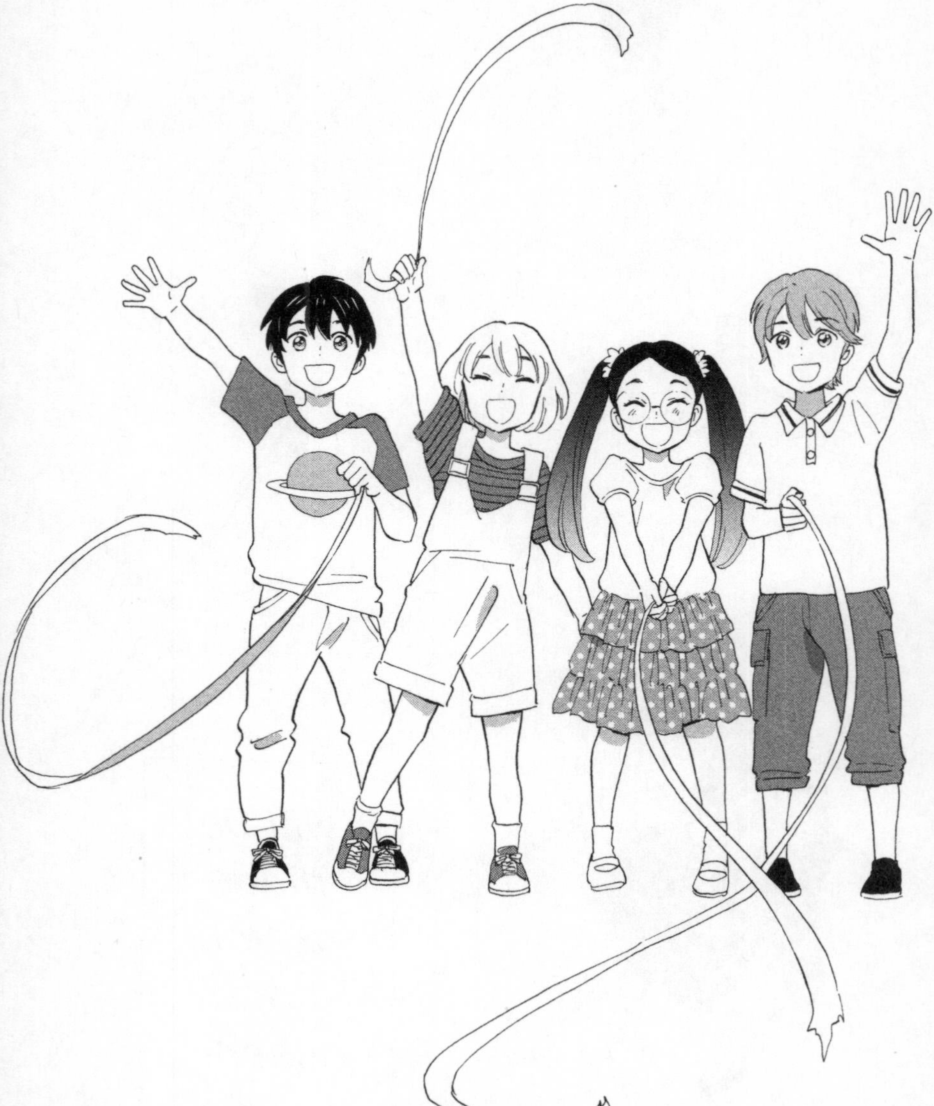

THE GOLDEN SHEEP | END |

THE GOLDEN SHEEP

@ RESEARCH ASSISTANCE

TSUTAYA O-CREST

THANK YOU!

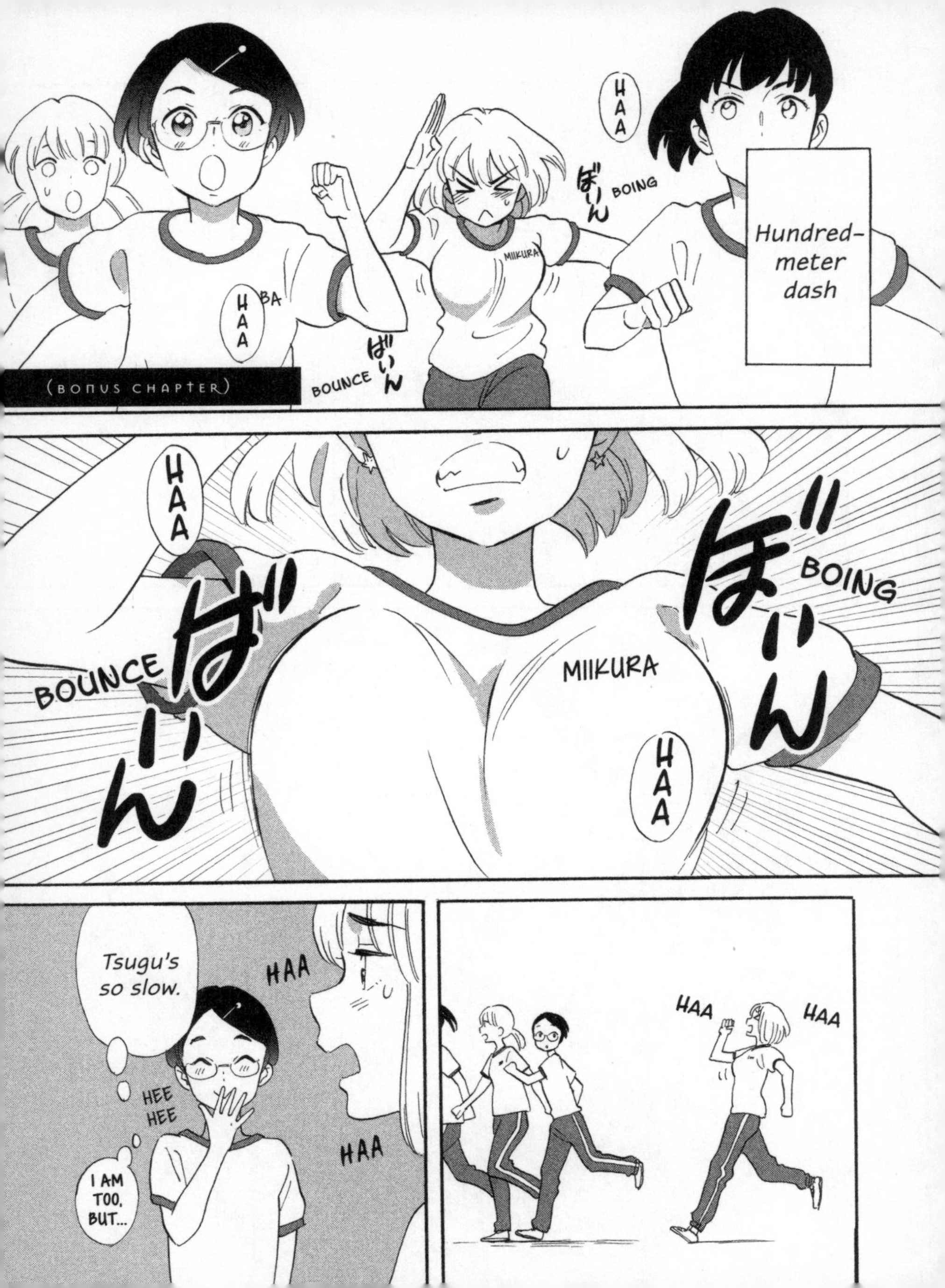
Hundred-meter dash
HAA
ばいん
BOING
MIIKURA
HAA
BA
ばいん
BOUNCE
(BONUS CHAPTER)
ばいん
BOING
HAA
HAA
ばいん
BOUNCE
MIIKURA
HAA
HAA
HAA
Tsugu's so slow.
HAA
HEE HEE
HAA
I AM TOO, BUT...

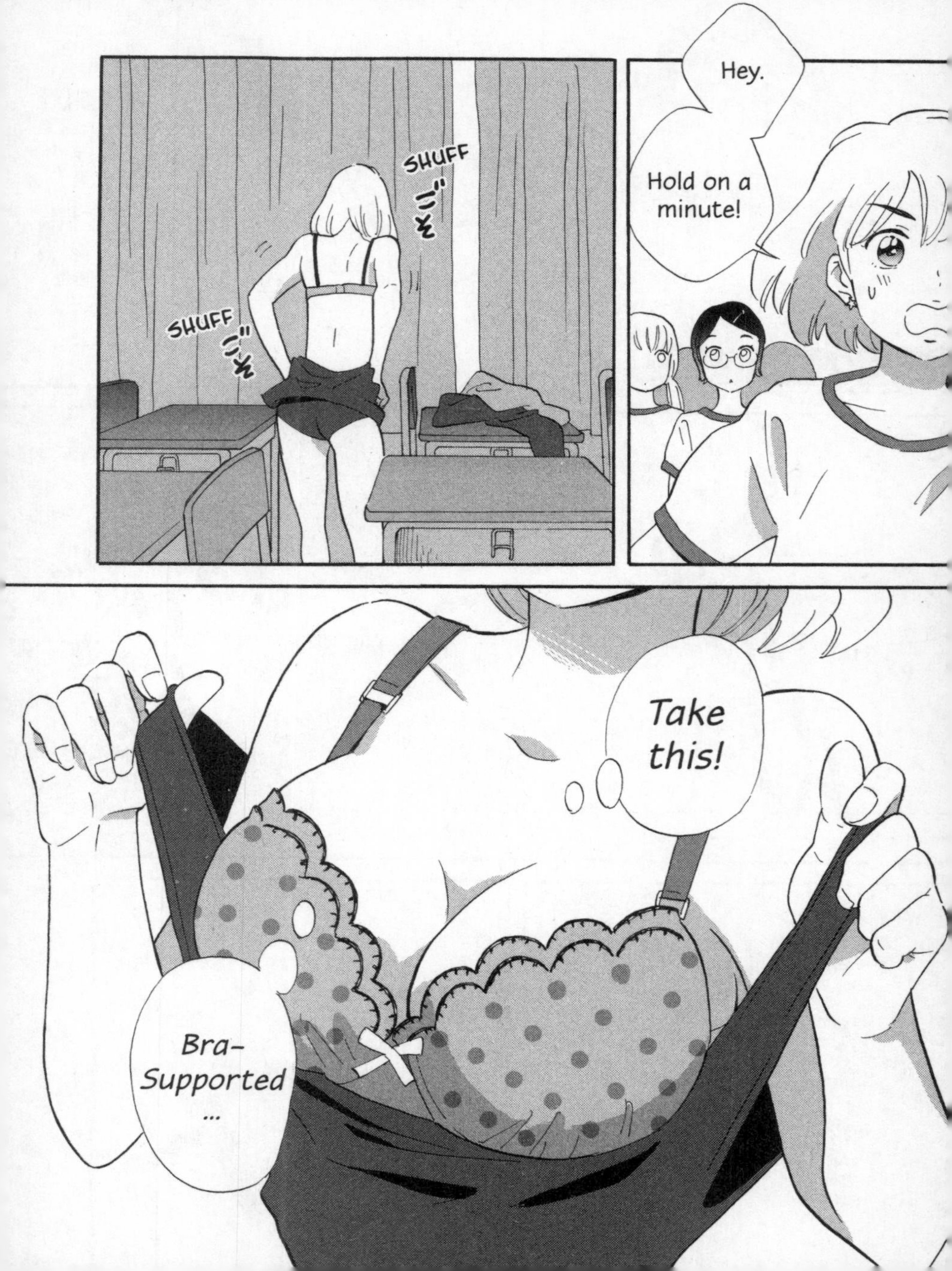
Hey.
Hold on a minute!
SHUFF ごそ
SHUFF ごそ
Take this!
Bra-Supported ...

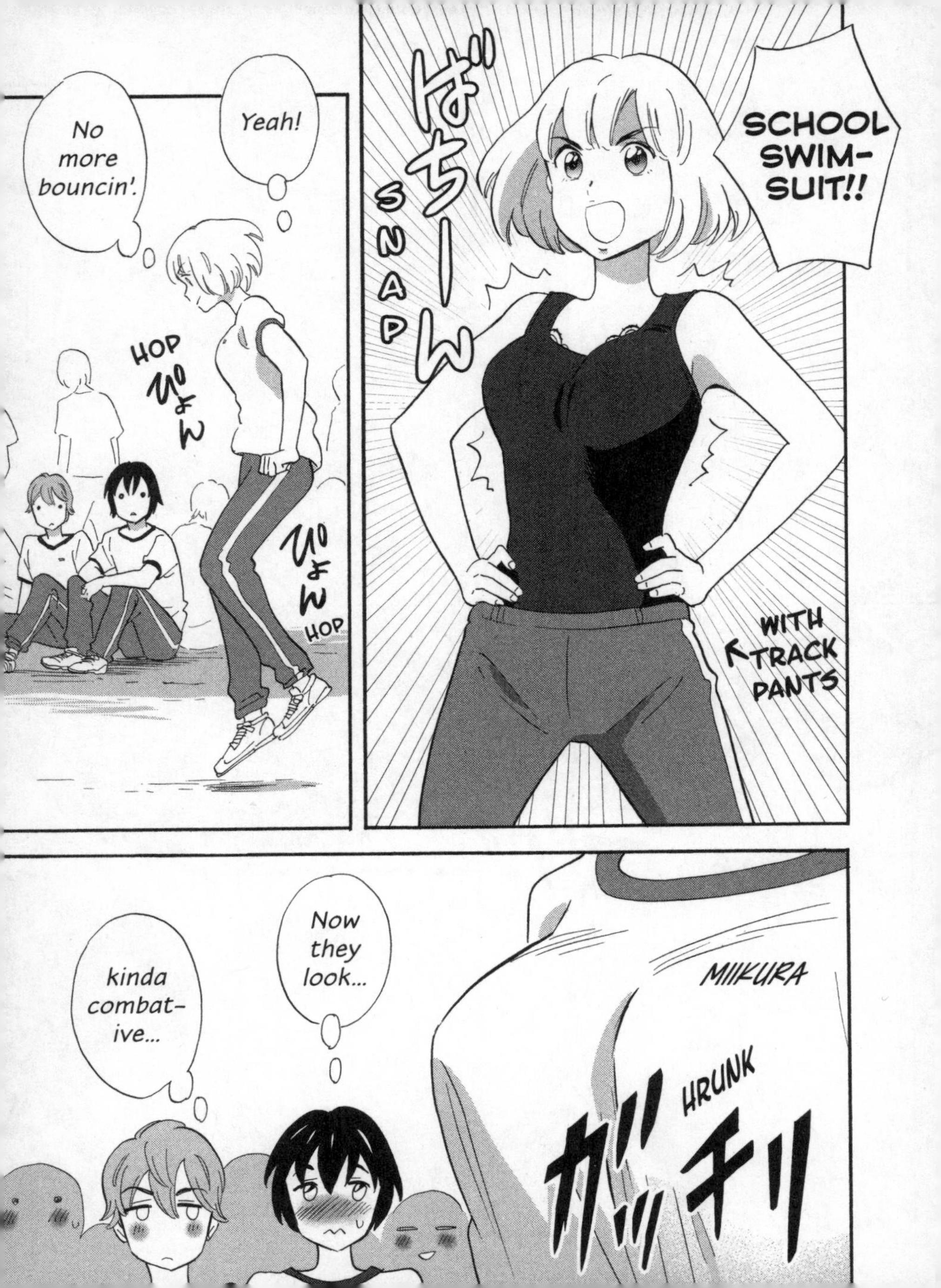
SCHOOL SWIM-SUIT!!
ばちーん
SNAP
WITH TRACK PANTS
Yeah!
No more bouncin'.
ぴょん
HOP
ぴょん
HOP
MIIKURA
ガッチリ
HRUNK
Now they look...
kinda combat-ive...

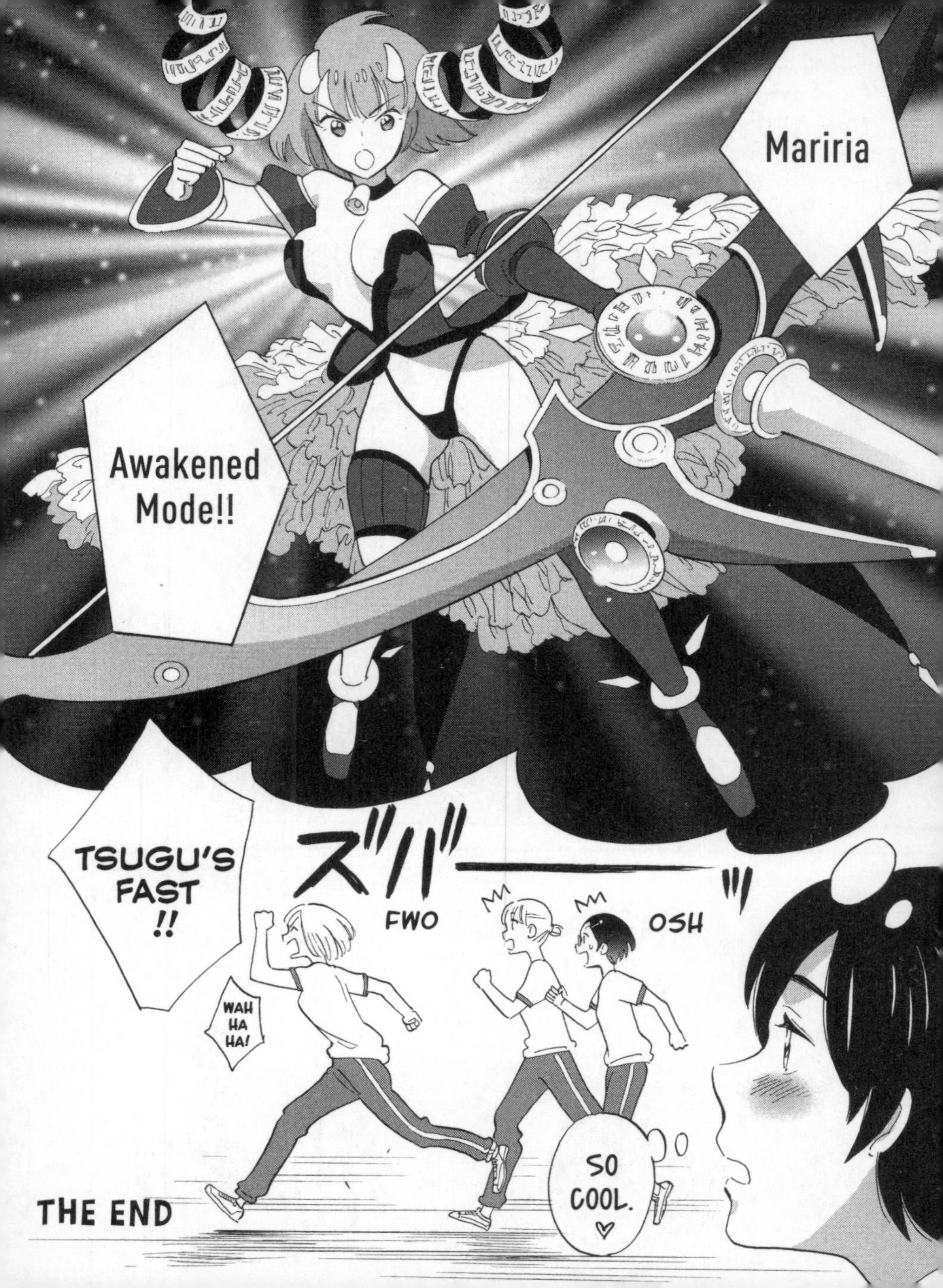

Mariria
Awakened Mode!!
ズバーーー
OSH
FWO
TSUGU'S FAST !!
WAH HA HA!
SO COOL. ♥
THE END

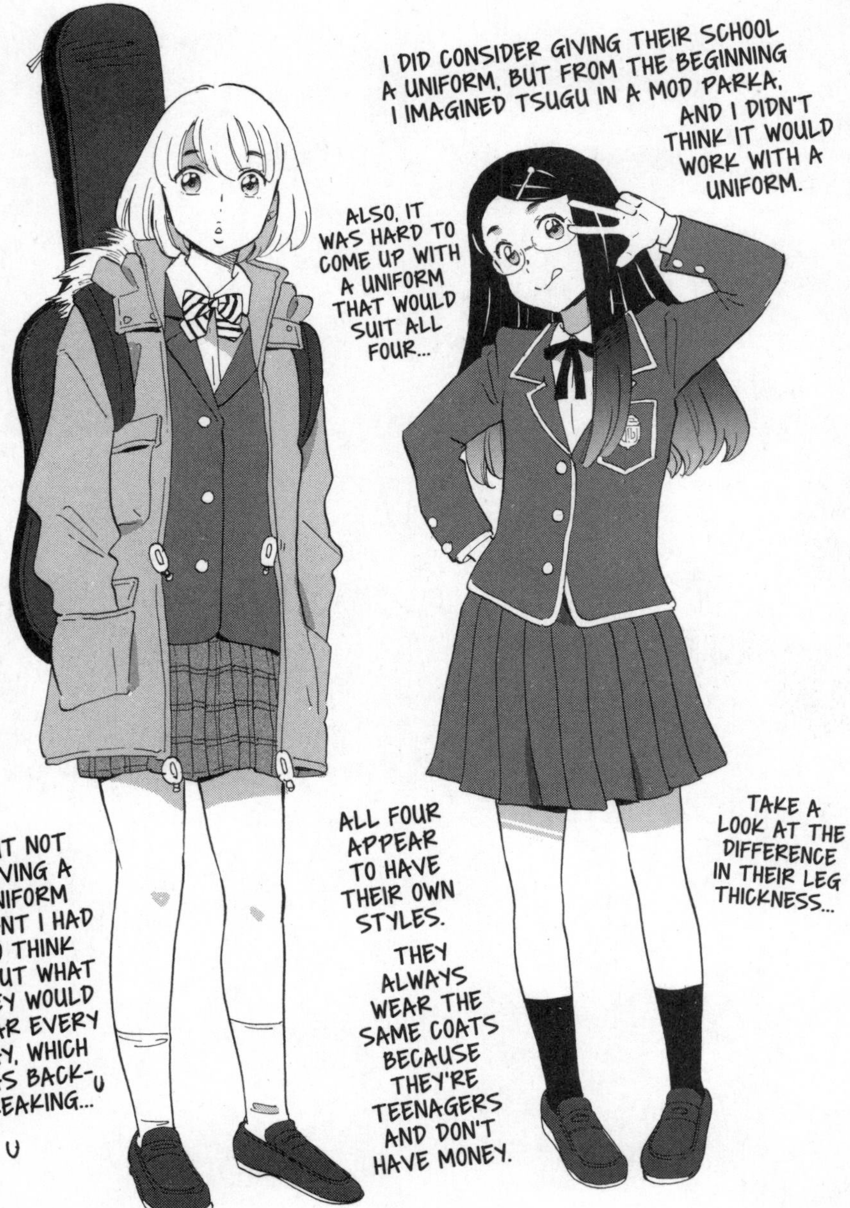
I DID CONSIDER GIVING THEIR SCHOOL A UNIFORM, BUT FROM THE BEGINNING I IMAGINED TSUGU IN A MOD PARKA,
AND I DIDN'T THINK IT WOULD WORK WITH A UNIFORM.
ALSO, IT WAS HARD TO COME UP WITH A UNIFORM THAT WOULD SUIT ALL FOUR...
TAKE A LOOK AT THE DIFFERENCE IN THEIR LEG THICKNESS...
ALL FOUR APPEAR TO HAVE THEIR OWN STYLES.
THEY ALWAYS WEAR THE SAME COATS BECAUSE THEY'RE TEENAGERS AND DON'T HAVE MONEY.
BUT NOT HAVING A UNIFORM MEANT I HAD TO THINK ABOUT WHAT THEY WOULD WEAR EVERY DAY, WHICH WAS BACK-BREAKING...

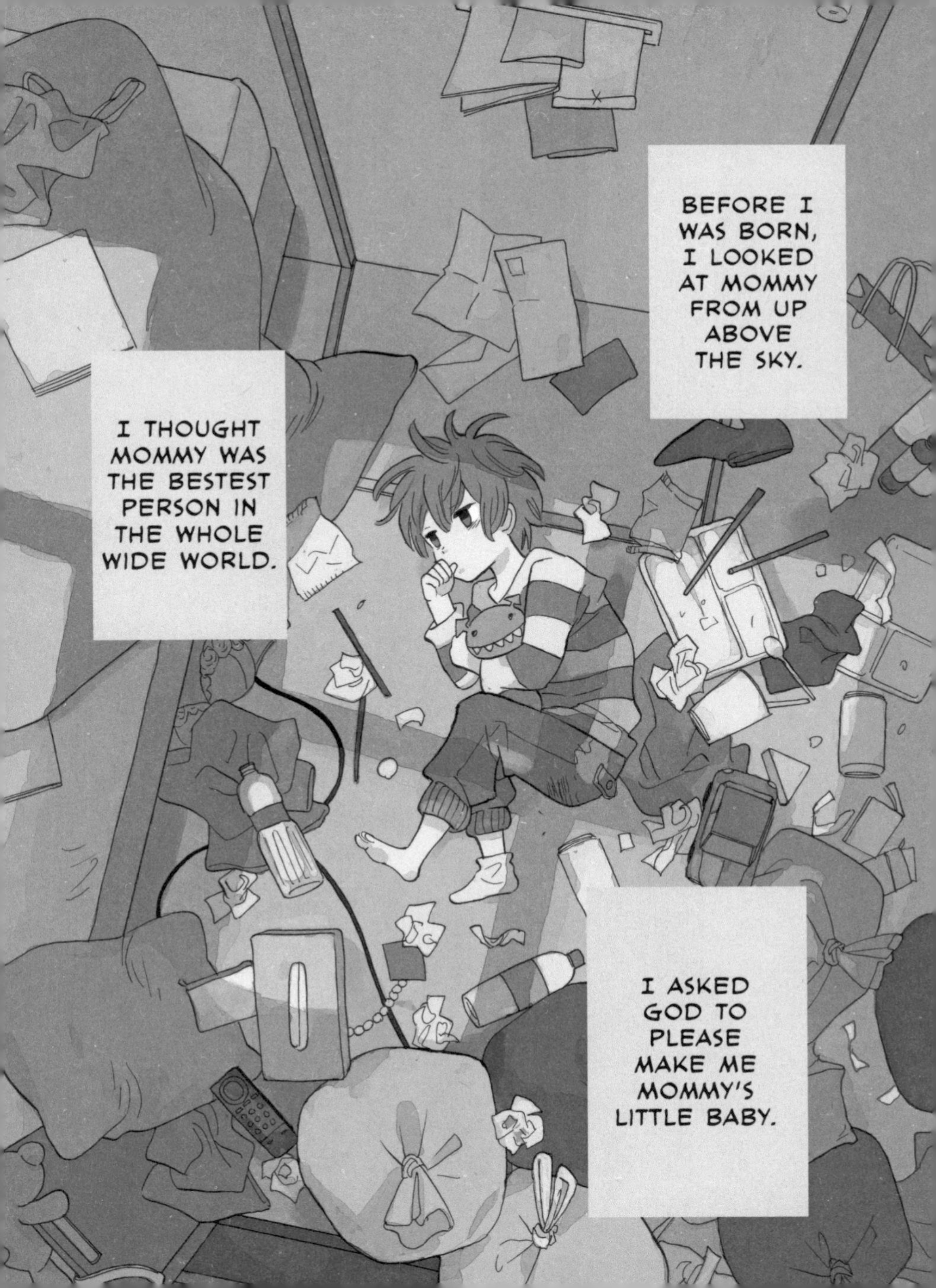
BEFORE I WAS BORN, I LOOKED AT MOMMY FROM UP ABOVE THE SKY.
I THOUGHT MOMMY WAS THE BESTEST PERSON IN THE WHOLE WIDE WORLD.
I ASKED GOD TO PLEASE MAKE ME MOMMY'S LITTLE BABY.

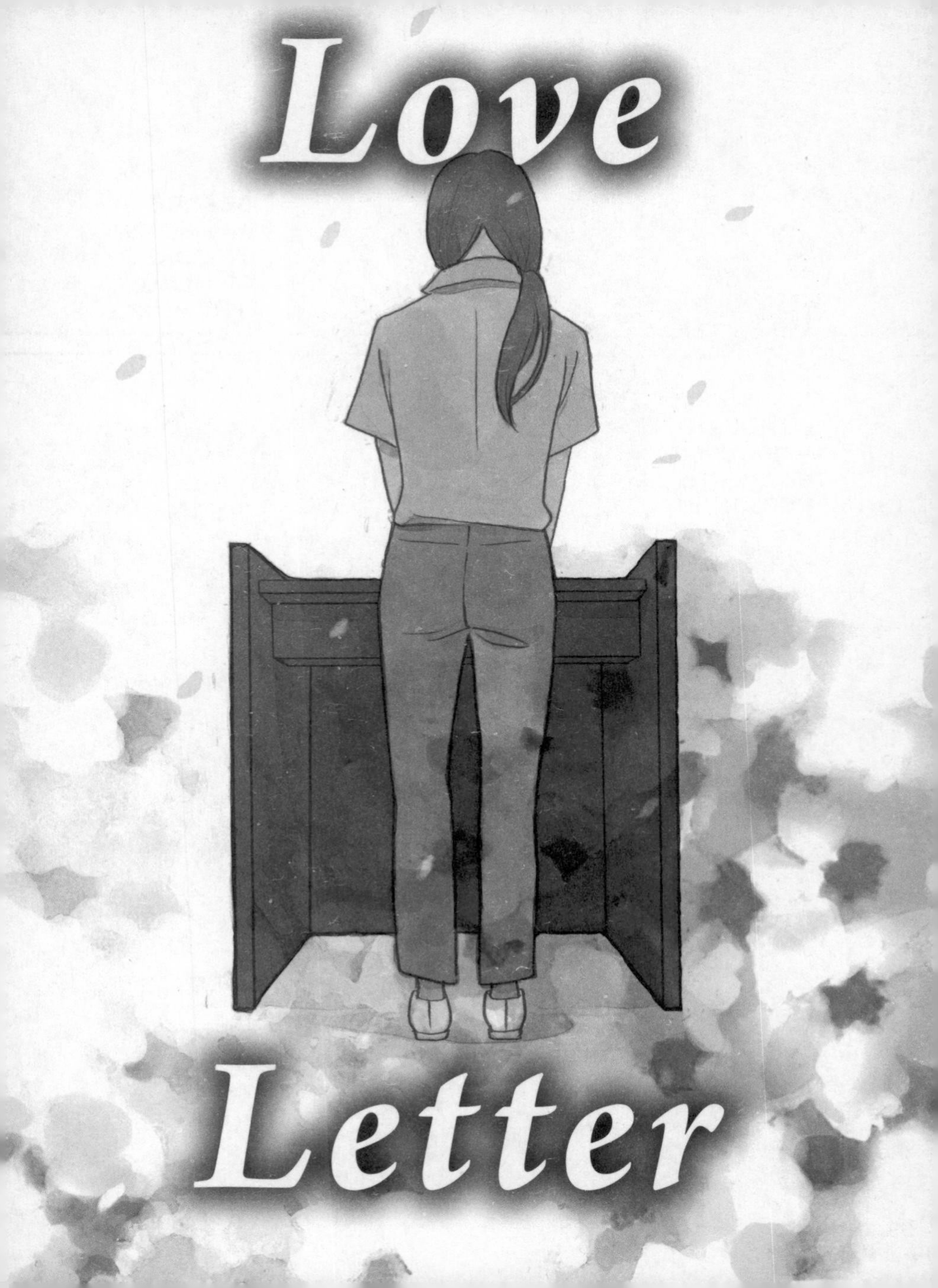
Love
Letter

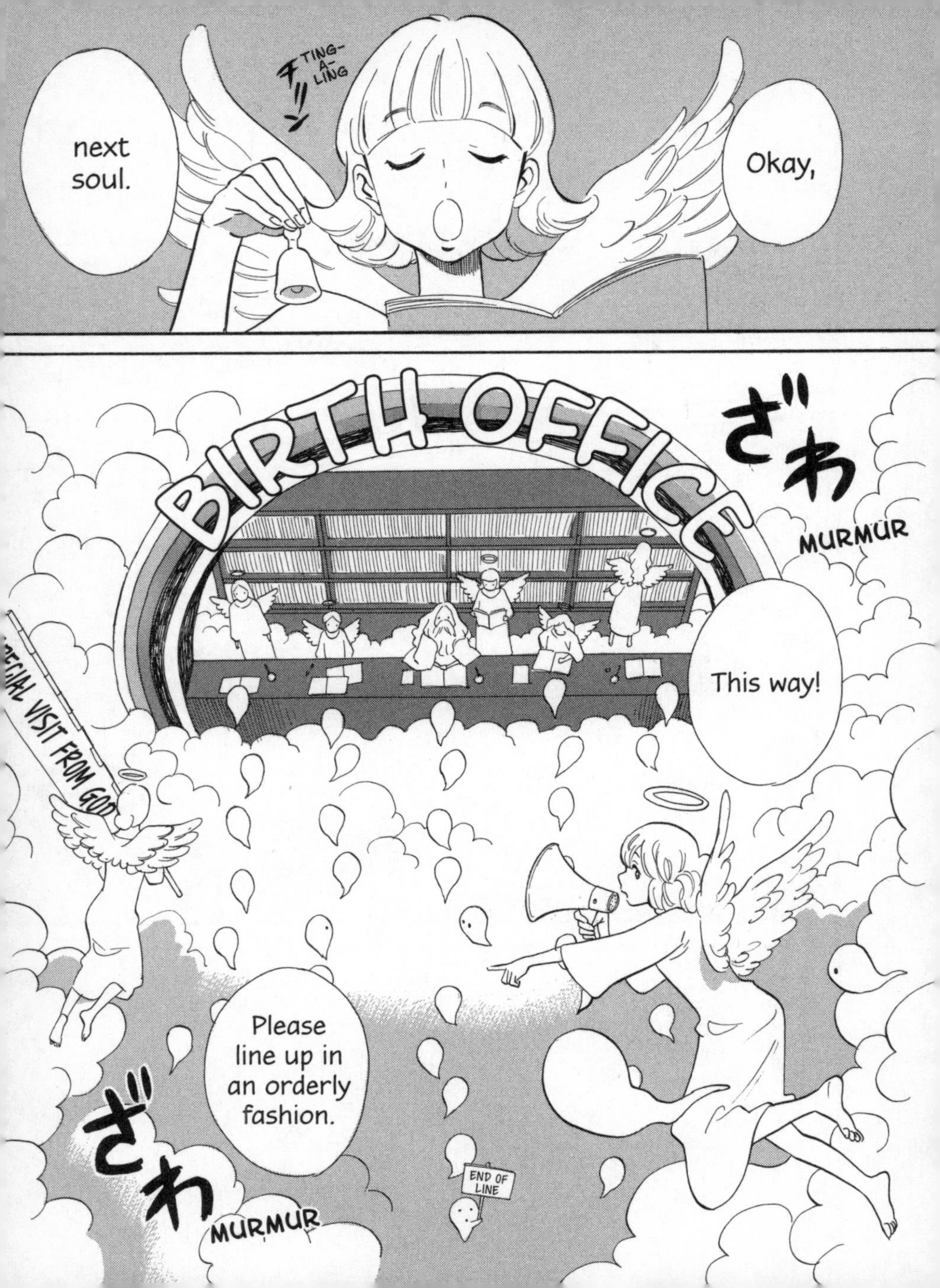
Okay,
チリン TING-A-LING
next soul.
BIRTH OFFICE
ざわ MURMUR
This way!
ECIAL VISIT FROM GOD
Please line up in an orderly fashion.
END OF LINE
ざわ MURMUR

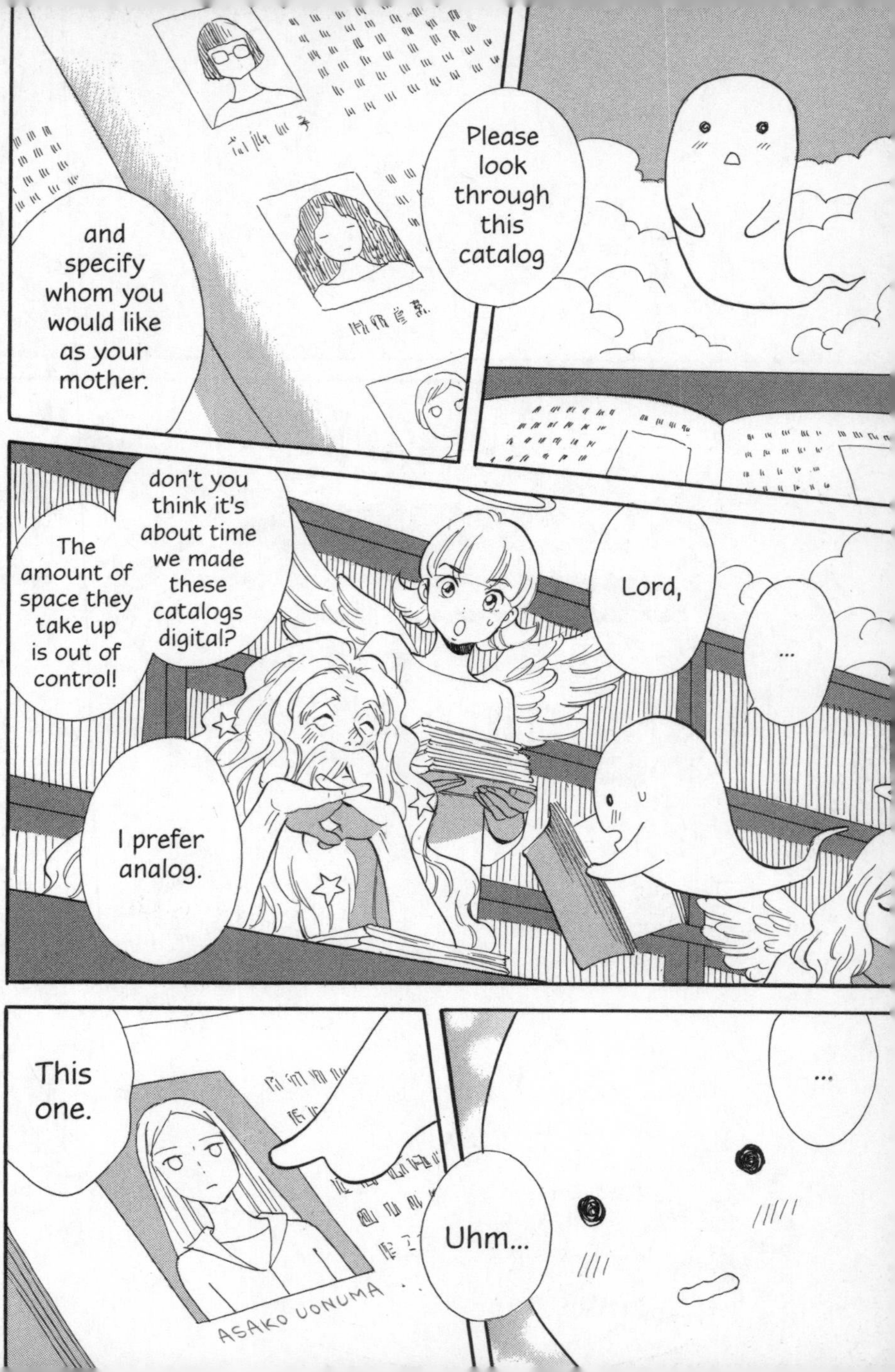

Please look through this catalog
and specify whom you would like as your mother.
Lord,
...
don't you think it's about time we made these catalogs digital?
The amount of space they take up is out of control!
I prefer analog.
...
Uhm...
This one.
ASAKO UONUMA

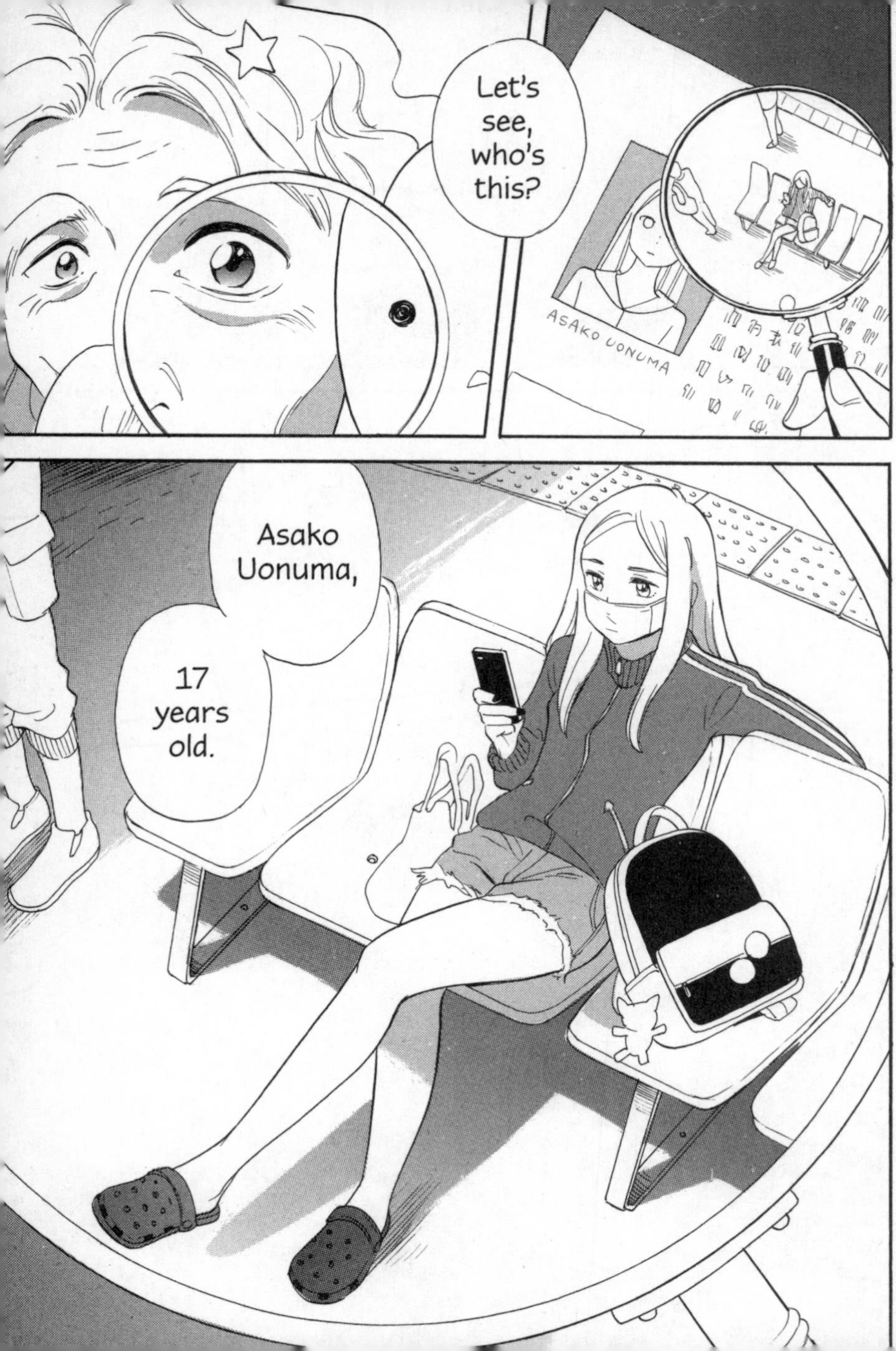
ASAKO UONUMA
Let's see, who's this?
Asako Uonuma,
17 years old.

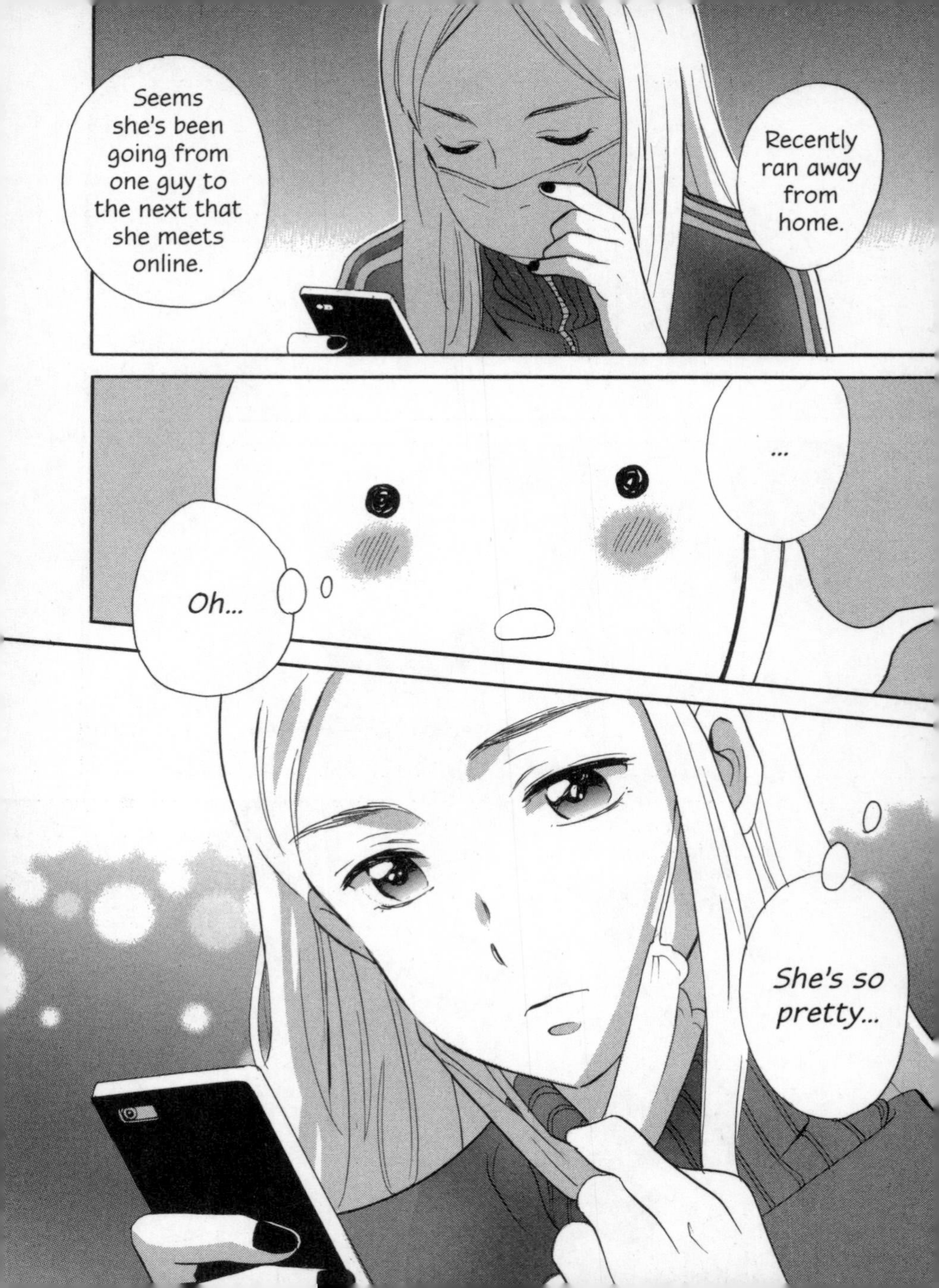
Recently ran away from home.
Seems she's been going from one guy to the next that she meets online.
...
Oh...
She's so pretty...

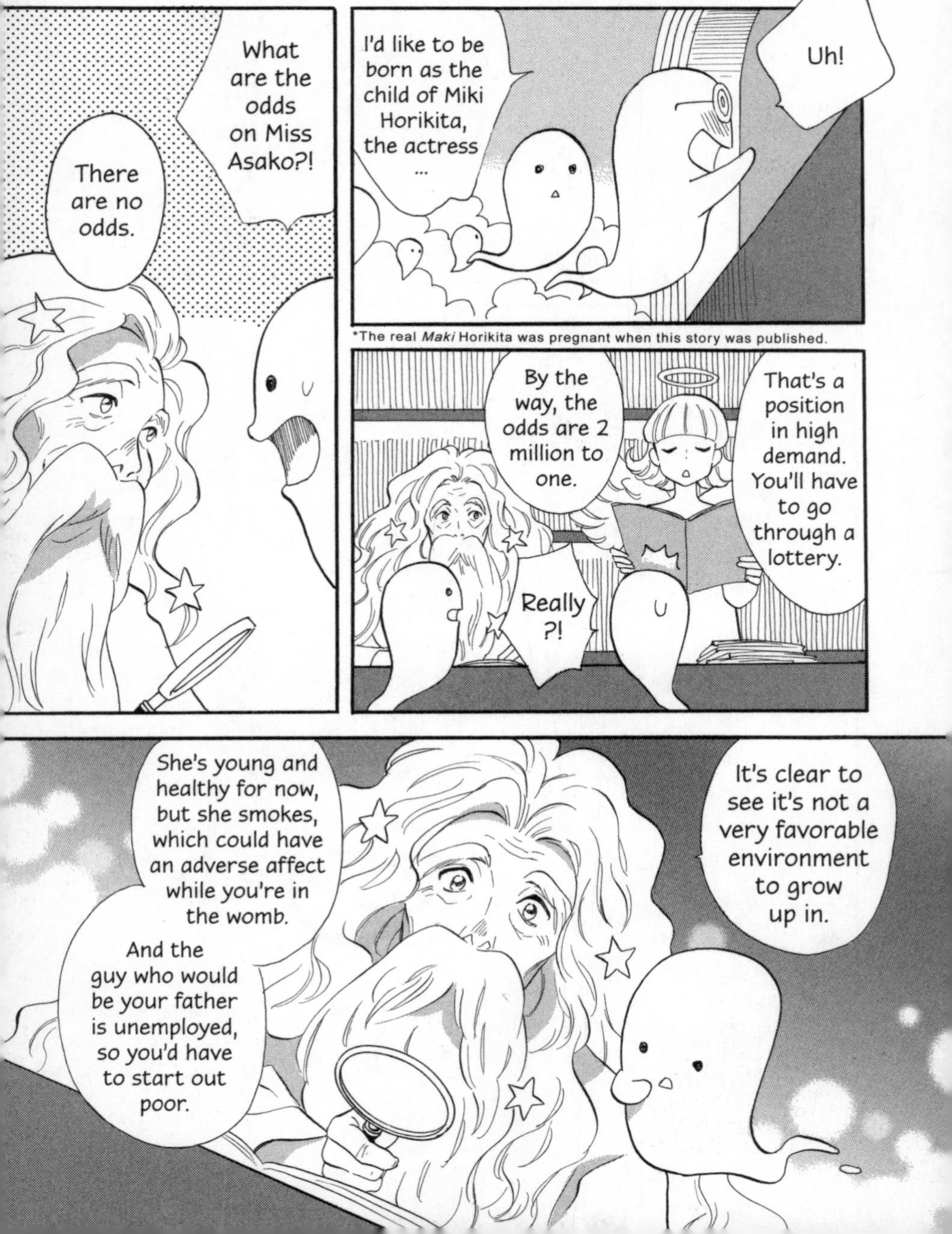

Uh!
I'd like to be born as the child of Miki Horikita, the actress ...
That's a position in high demand. You'll have to go through a lottery.
By the way, the odds are 2 million to one.
Really ?!
What are the odds on Miss Asako?!
There are no odds.
It's clear to see it's not a very favorable environment to grow up in.
She's young and healthy for now, but she smokes, which could have an adverse affect while you're in the womb.
And the guy who would be your father is unemployed, so you'd have to start out poor.

*The real *Maki* Horikita was pregnant when this story was published.

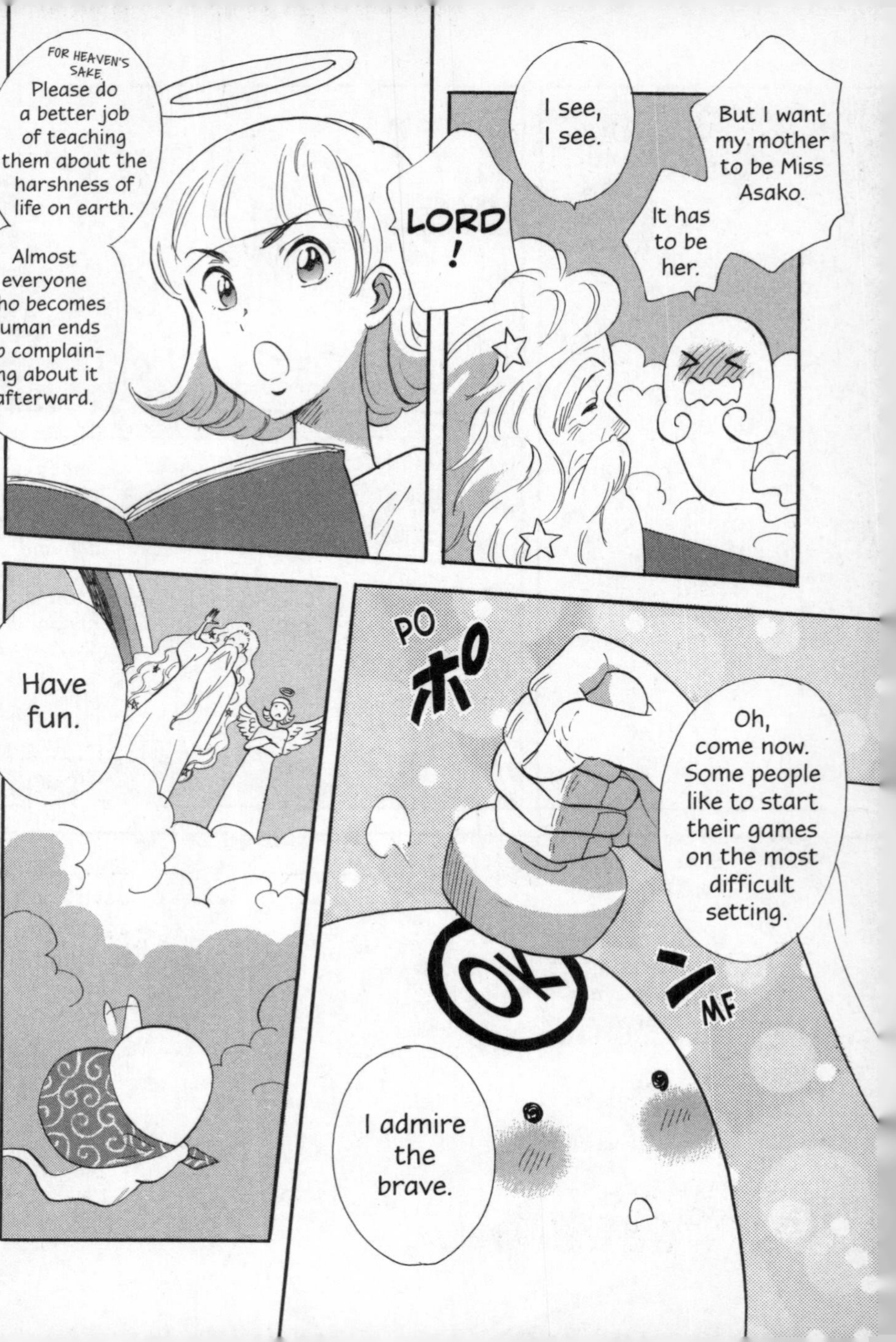
But I want my mother to be Miss Asako.
It has to be her.
I see, I see.
LORD!
FOR HEAVEN'S SAKE.
Please do a better job of teaching them about the harshness of life on earth.
Almost everyone who becomes human ends up complaining about it afterward.
PO
Oh, come now. Some people like to start their games on the most difficult setting.
OK
MF
I admire the brave.
Have fun.

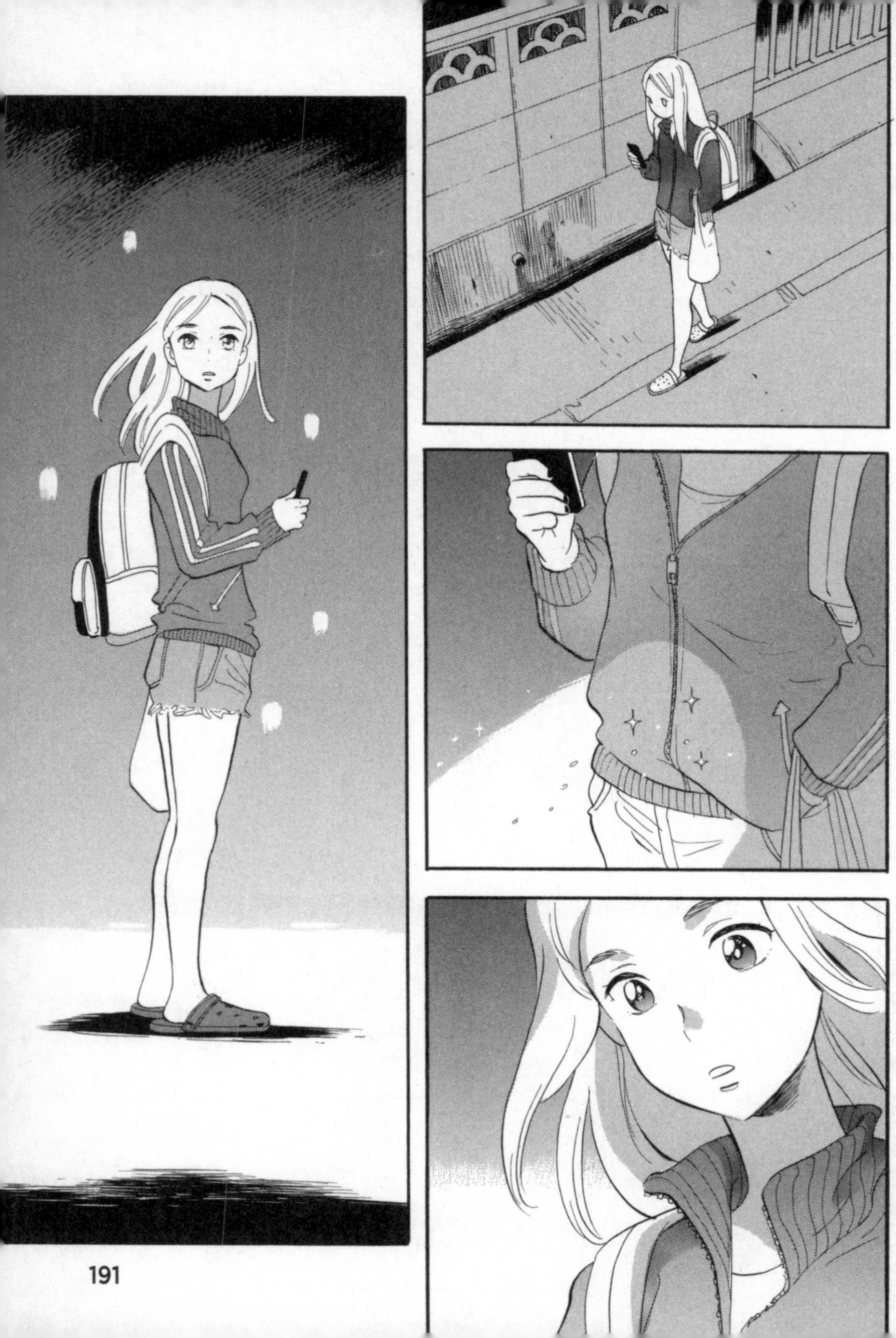

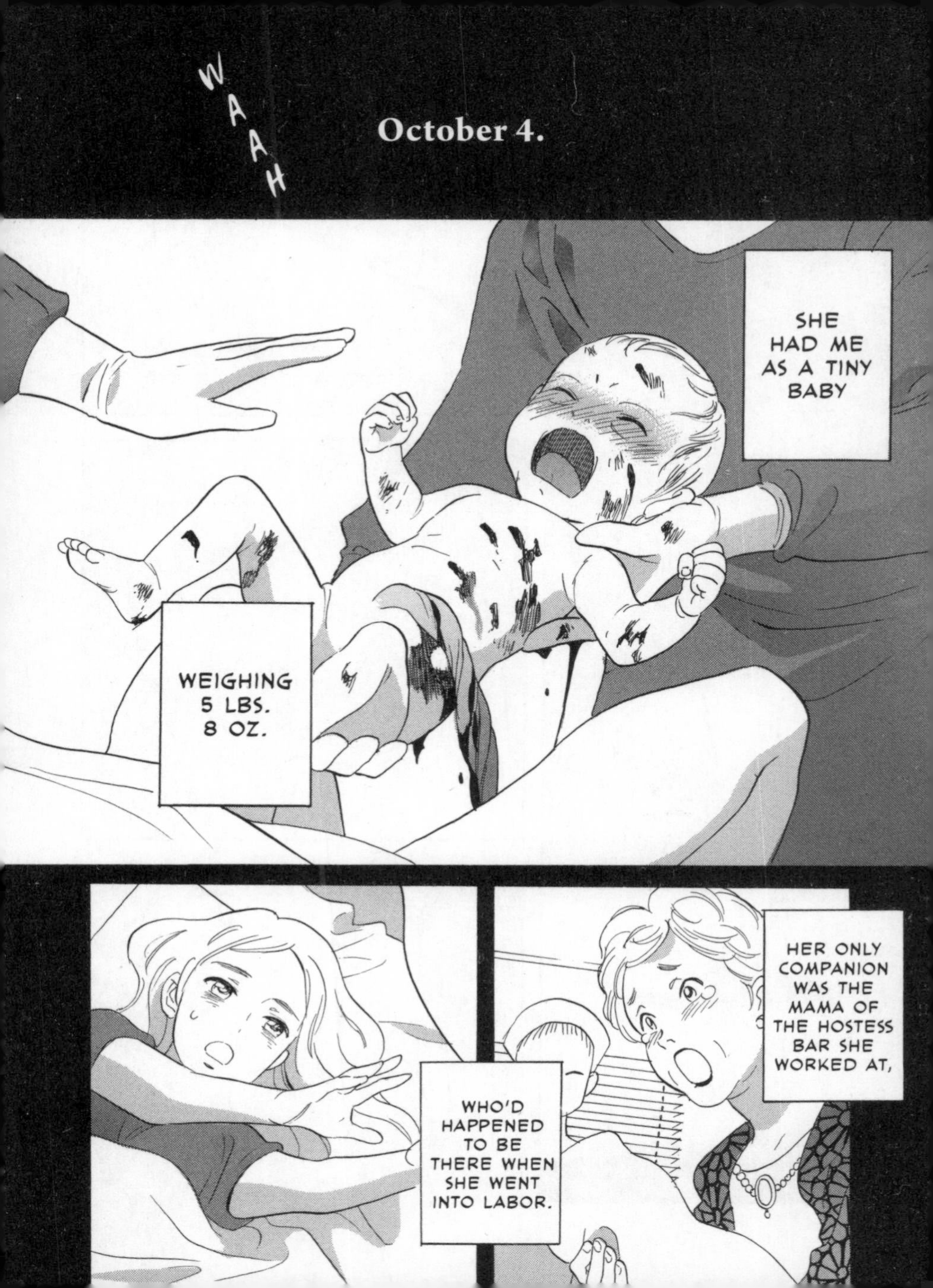
October 4.
WAAAH
SHE HAD ME AS A TINY BABY
WEIGHING 5 LBS. 8 OZ.
HER ONLY COMPANION WAS THE MAMA OF THE HOSTESS BAR SHE WORKED AT,
WHO'D HAPPENED TO BE THERE WHEN SHE WENT INTO LABOR.

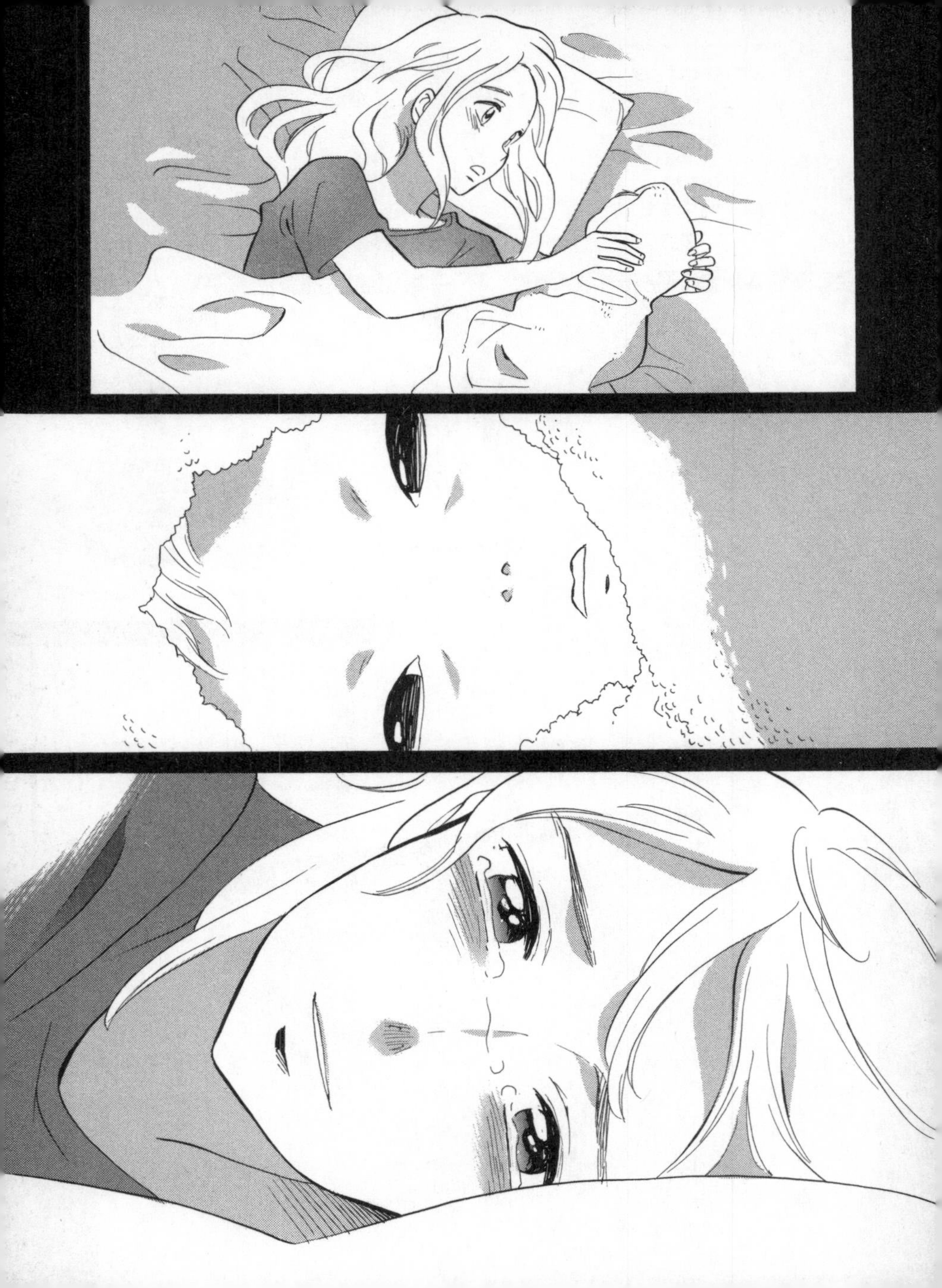

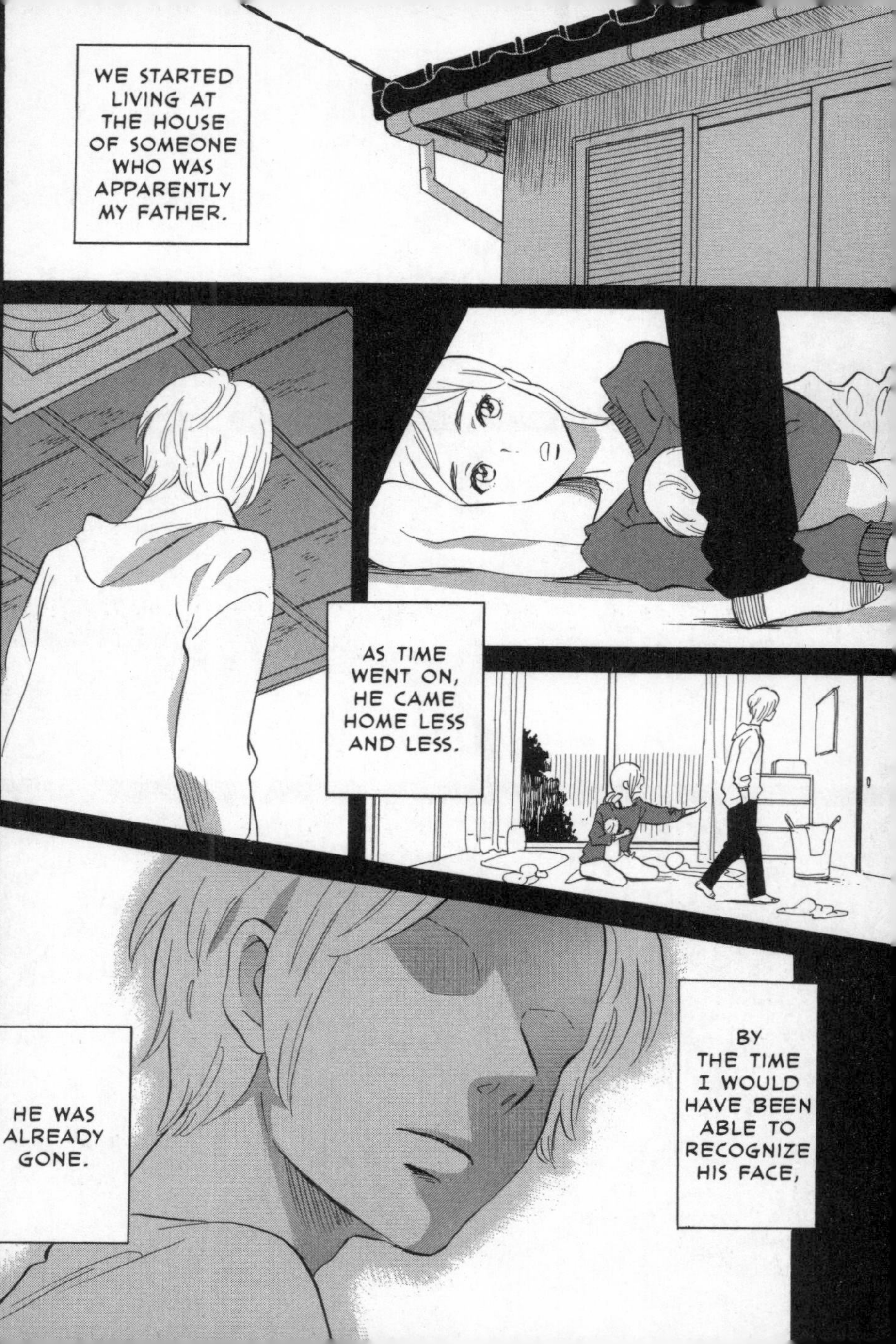
WE STARTED LIVING AT THE HOUSE OF SOMEONE WHO WAS APPARENTLY MY FATHER.
AS TIME WENT ON, HE CAME HOME LESS AND LESS.
BY THE TIME I WOULD HAVE BEEN ABLE TO RECOGNIZE HIS FACE,
HE WAS ALREADY GONE.

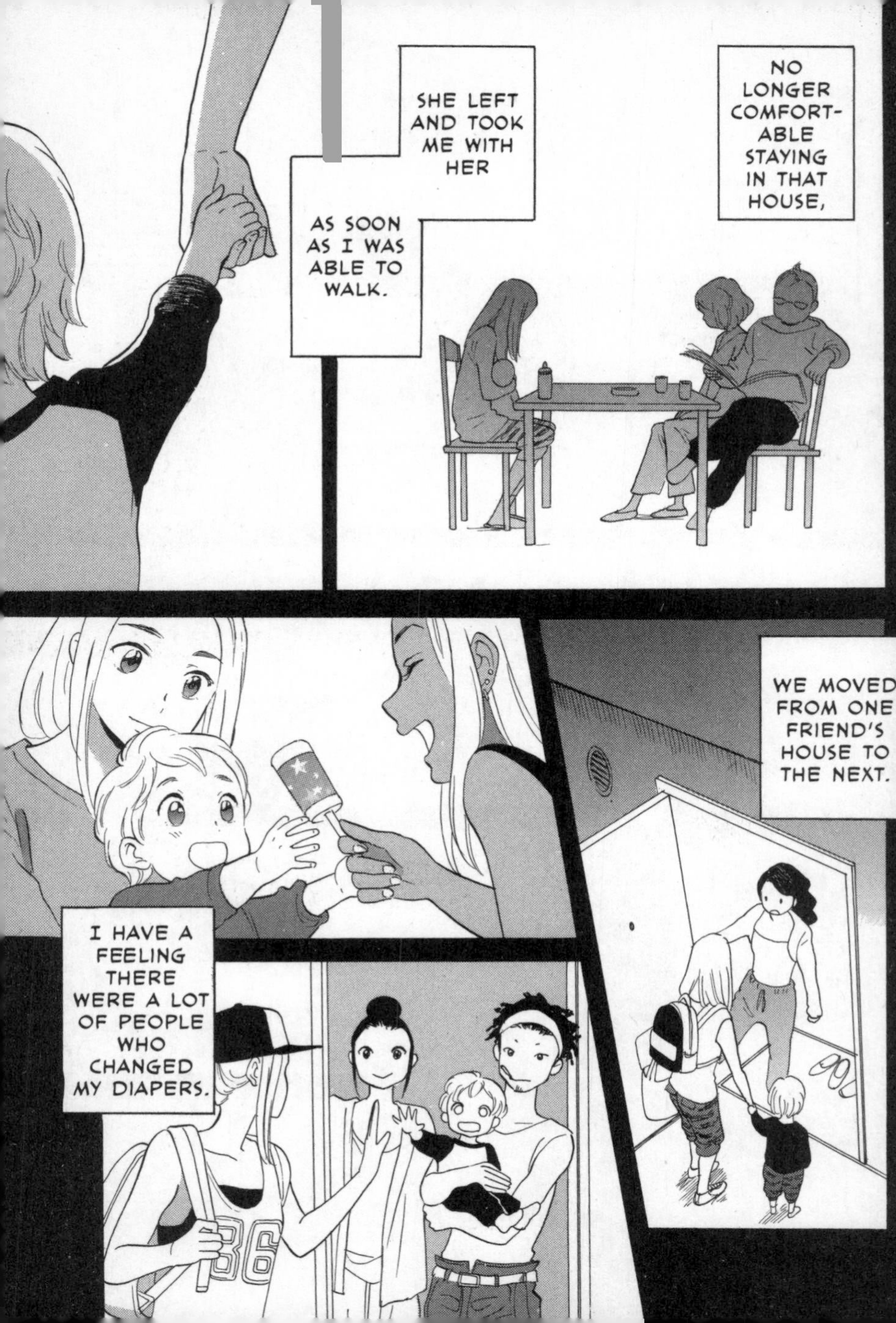
NO LONGER COMFORT-ABLE STAYING IN THAT HOUSE,
SHE LEFT AND TOOK ME WITH HER
AS SOON AS I WAS ABLE TO WALK.
WE MOVED FROM ONE FRIEND'S HOUSE TO THE NEXT.
I HAVE A FEELING THERE WERE A LOT OF PEOPLE WHO CHANGED MY DIAPERS.
36

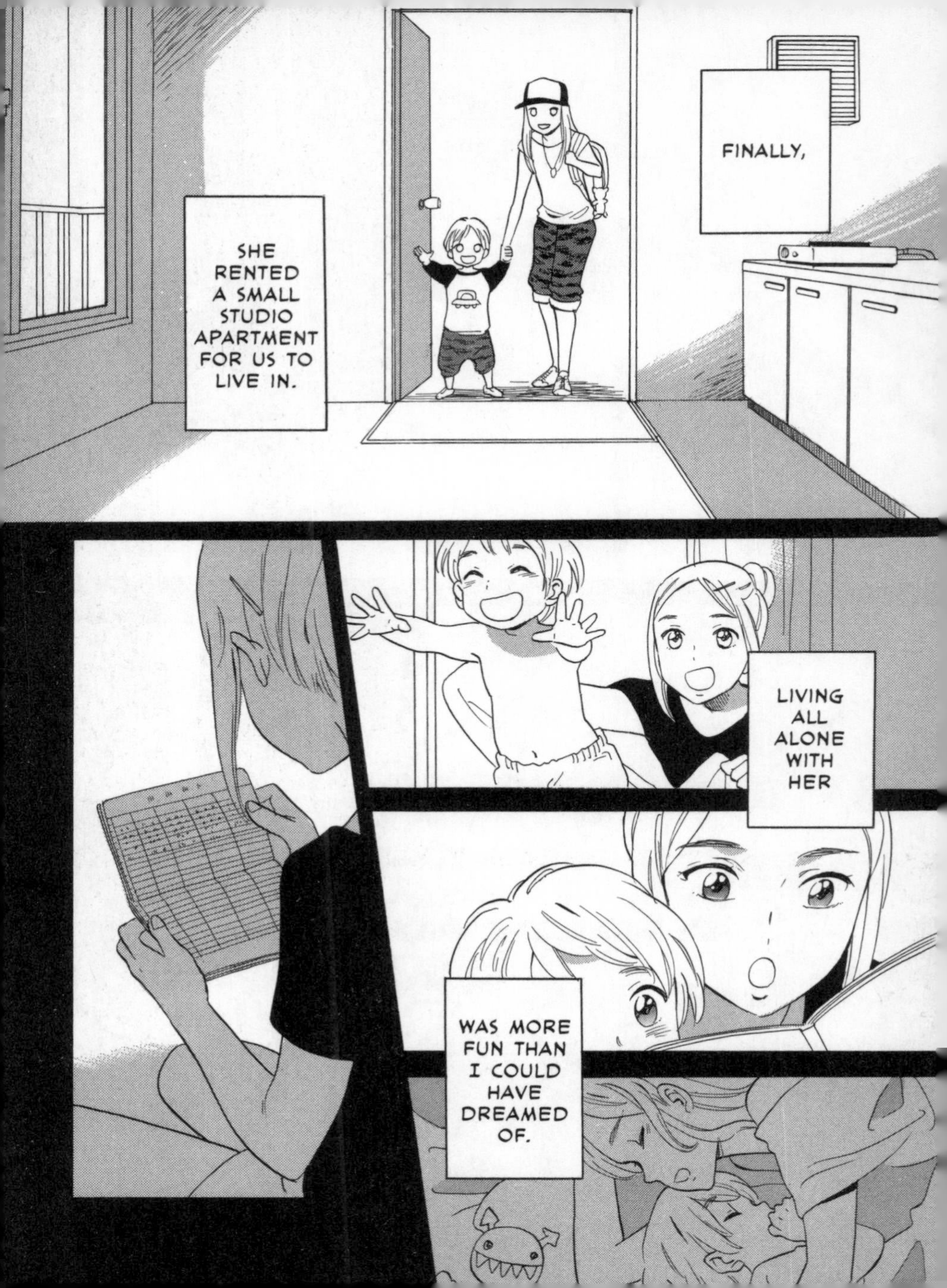
FINALLY,
SHE RENTED A SMALL STUDIO APARTMENT FOR US TO LIVE IN.
LIVING ALL ALONE WITH HER
WAS MORE FUN THAN I COULD HAVE DREAMED OF.

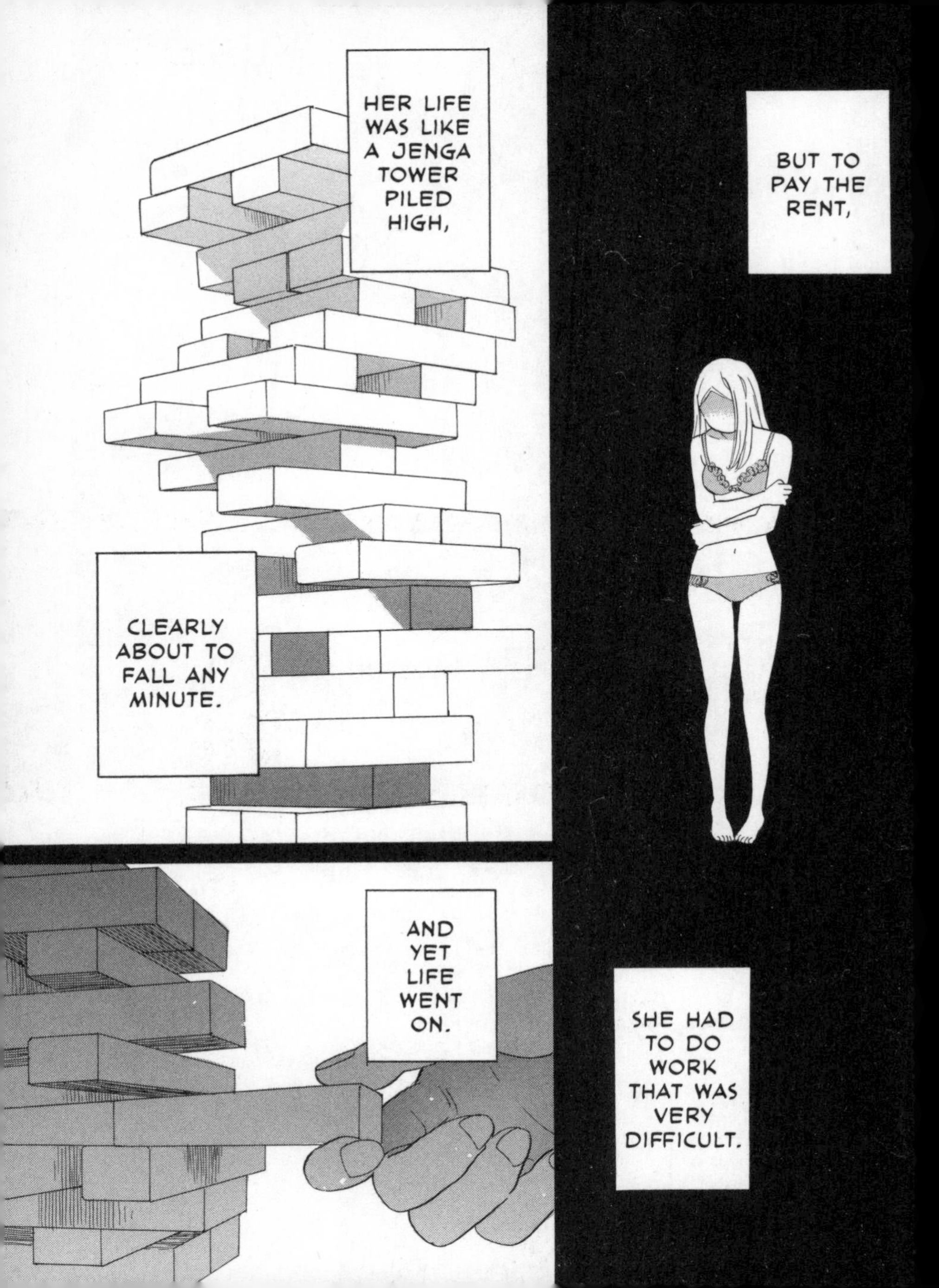
BUT TO PAY THE RENT,
SHE HAD TO DO WORK THAT WAS VERY DIFFICULT.
HER LIFE WAS LIKE A JENGA TOWER PILED HIGH,
CLEARLY ABOUT TO FALL ANY MINUTE.
AND YET LIFE WENT ON.

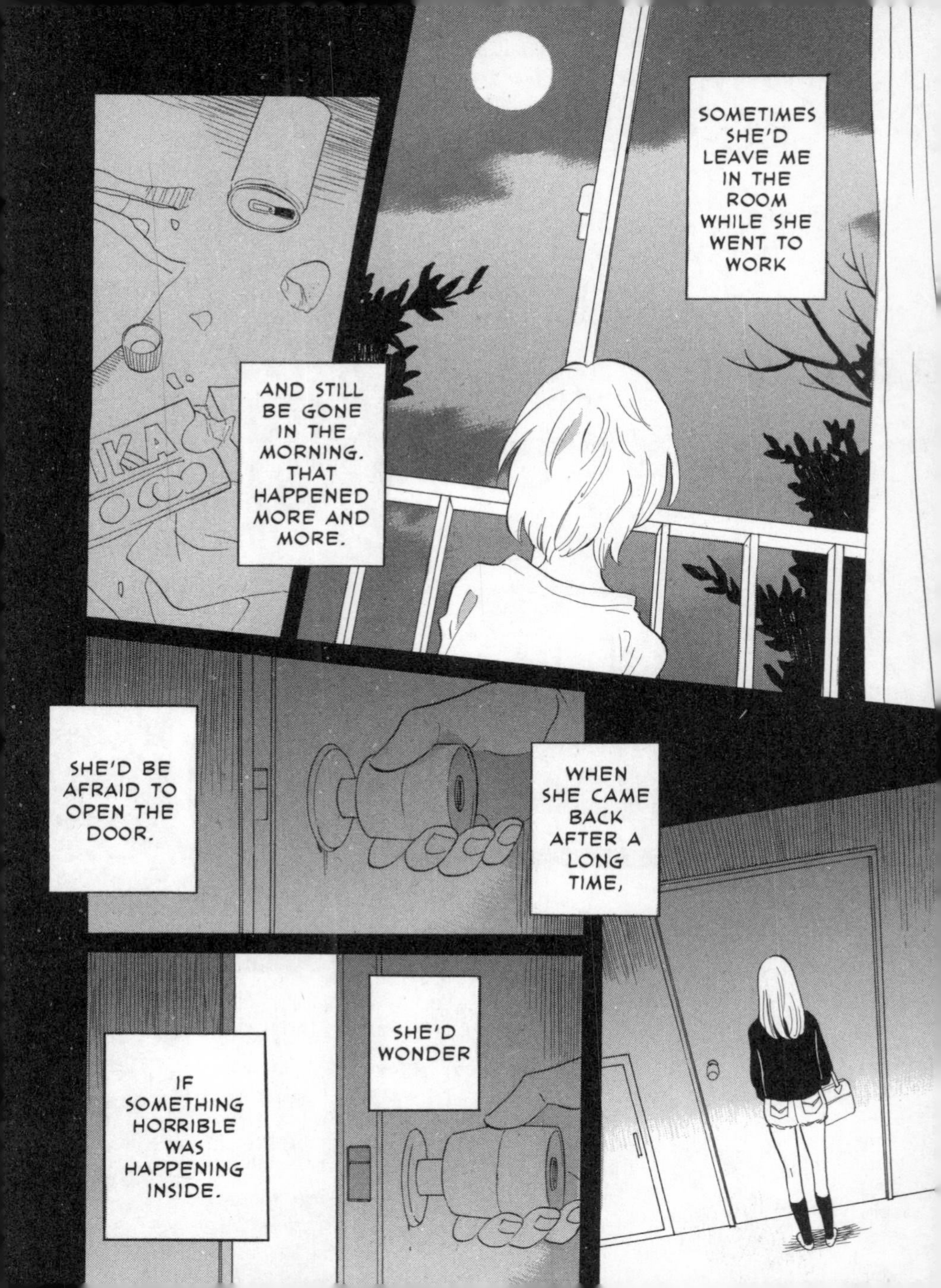
SOMETIMES SHE'D LEAVE ME IN THE ROOM WHILE SHE WENT TO WORK
AND STILL BE GONE IN THE MORNING. THAT HAPPENED MORE AND MORE.
WHEN SHE CAME BACK AFTER A LONG TIME,
SHE'D BE AFRAID TO OPEN THE DOOR.
SHE'D WONDER
IF SOMETHING HORRIBLE WAS HAPPENING INSIDE.

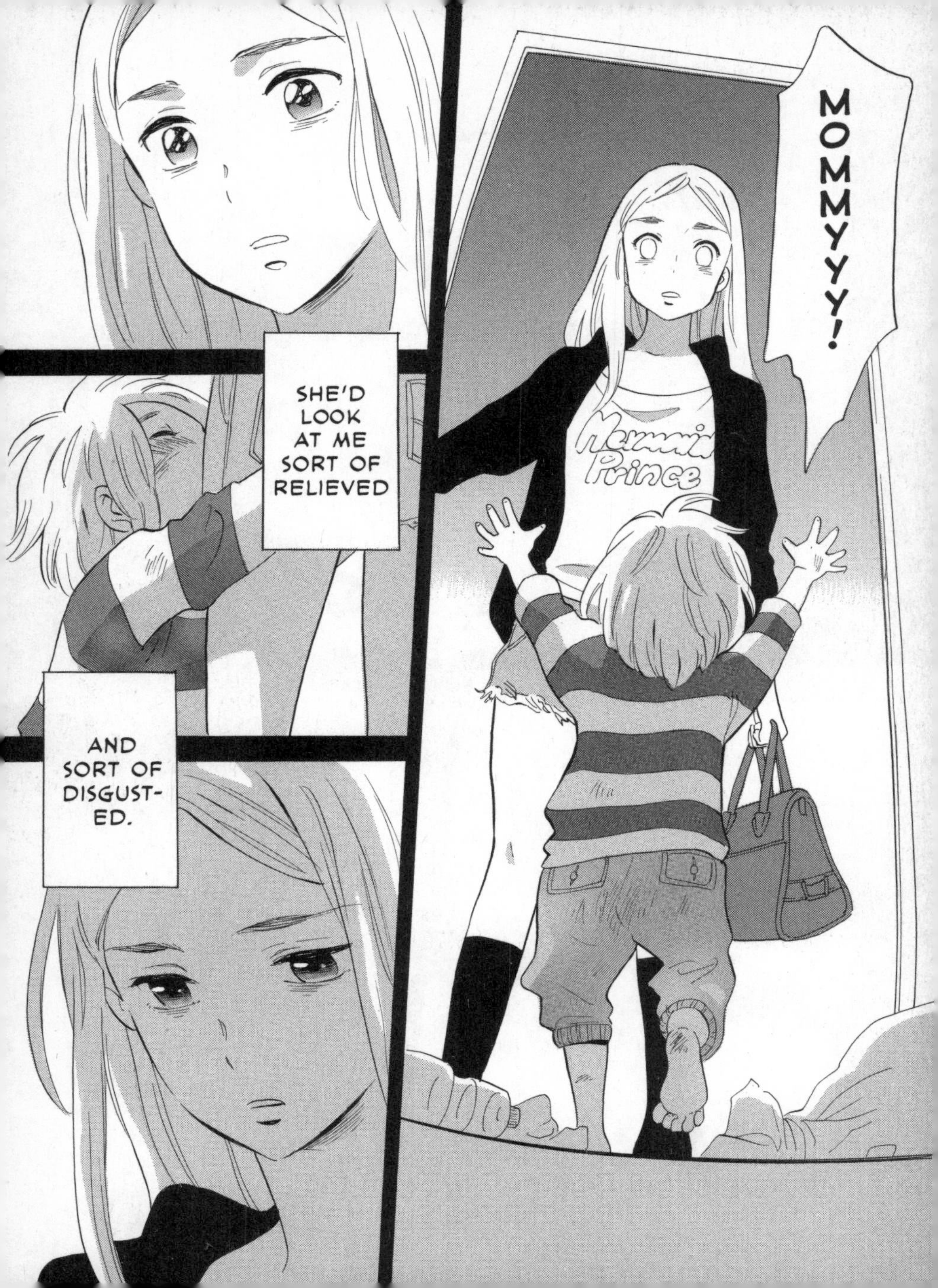
MOMMYYY!
SHE'D LOOK AT ME SORT OF RELIEVED
AND SORT OF DISGUST-ED.

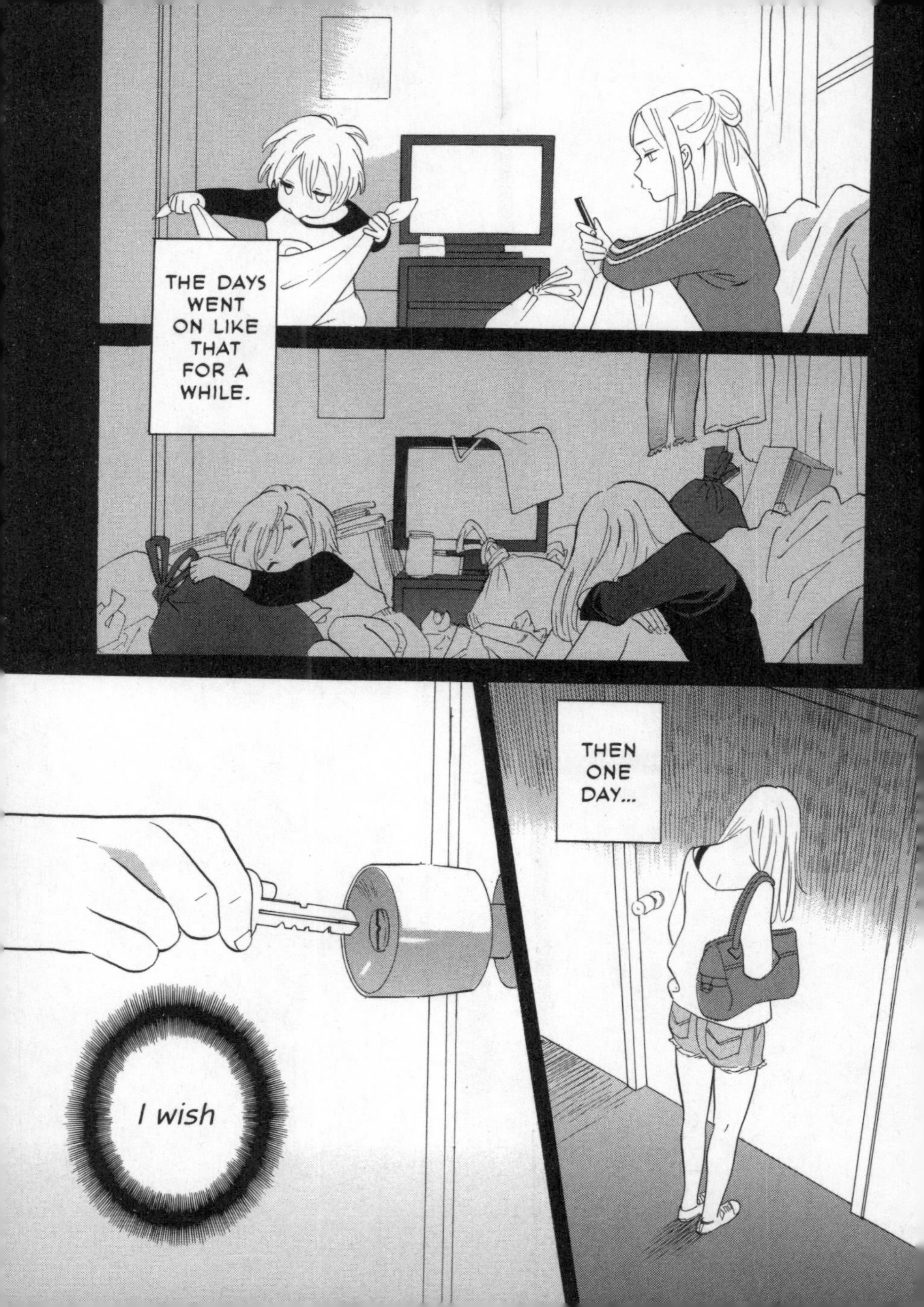
THE DAYS WENT ON LIKE THAT FOR A WHILE.
THEN ONE DAY...
I wish

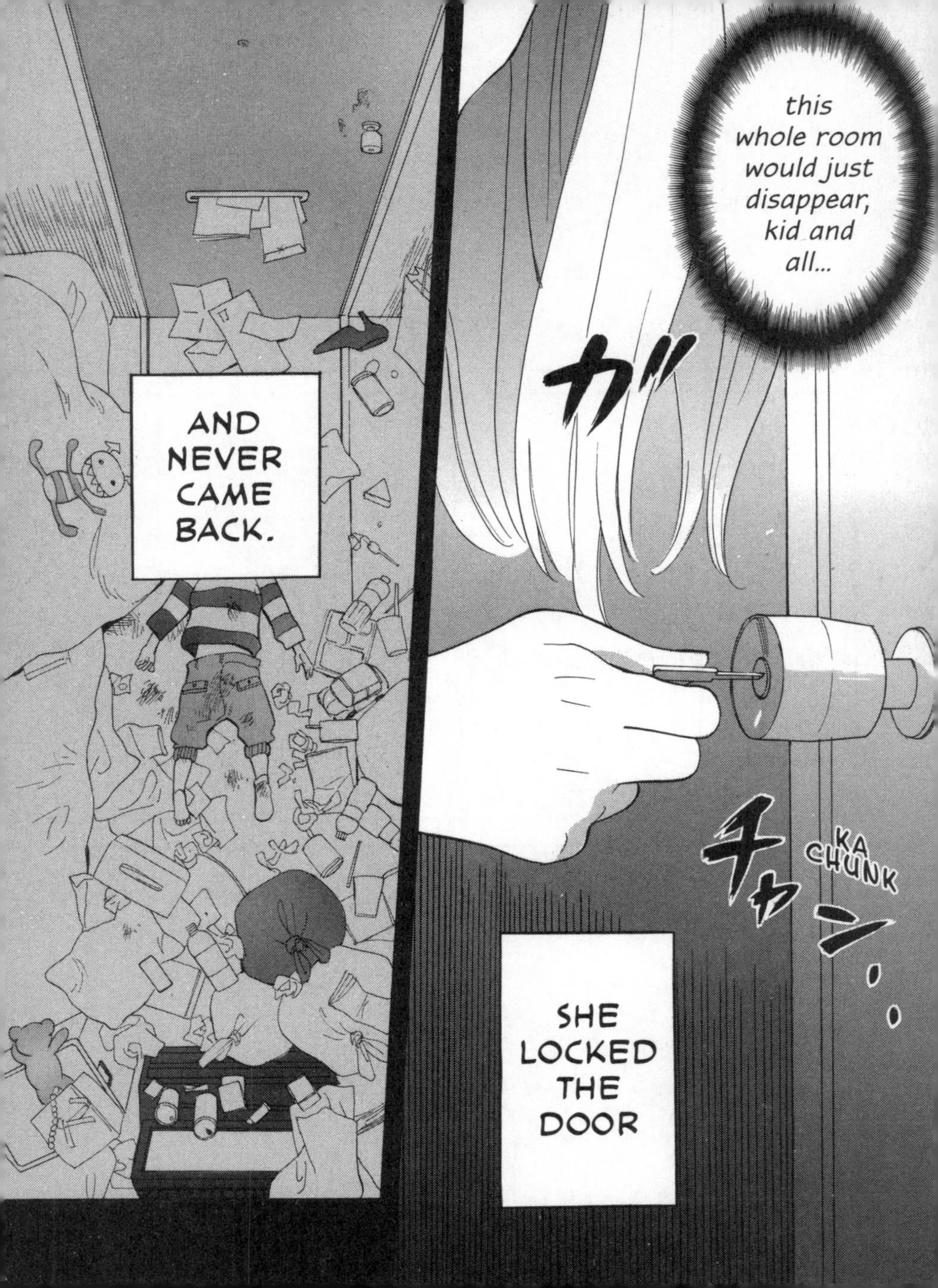
this whole room would just disappear, kid and all...
ガ
チャン
KA CHUNK
SHE LOCKED THE DOOR
AND NEVER CAME BACK.

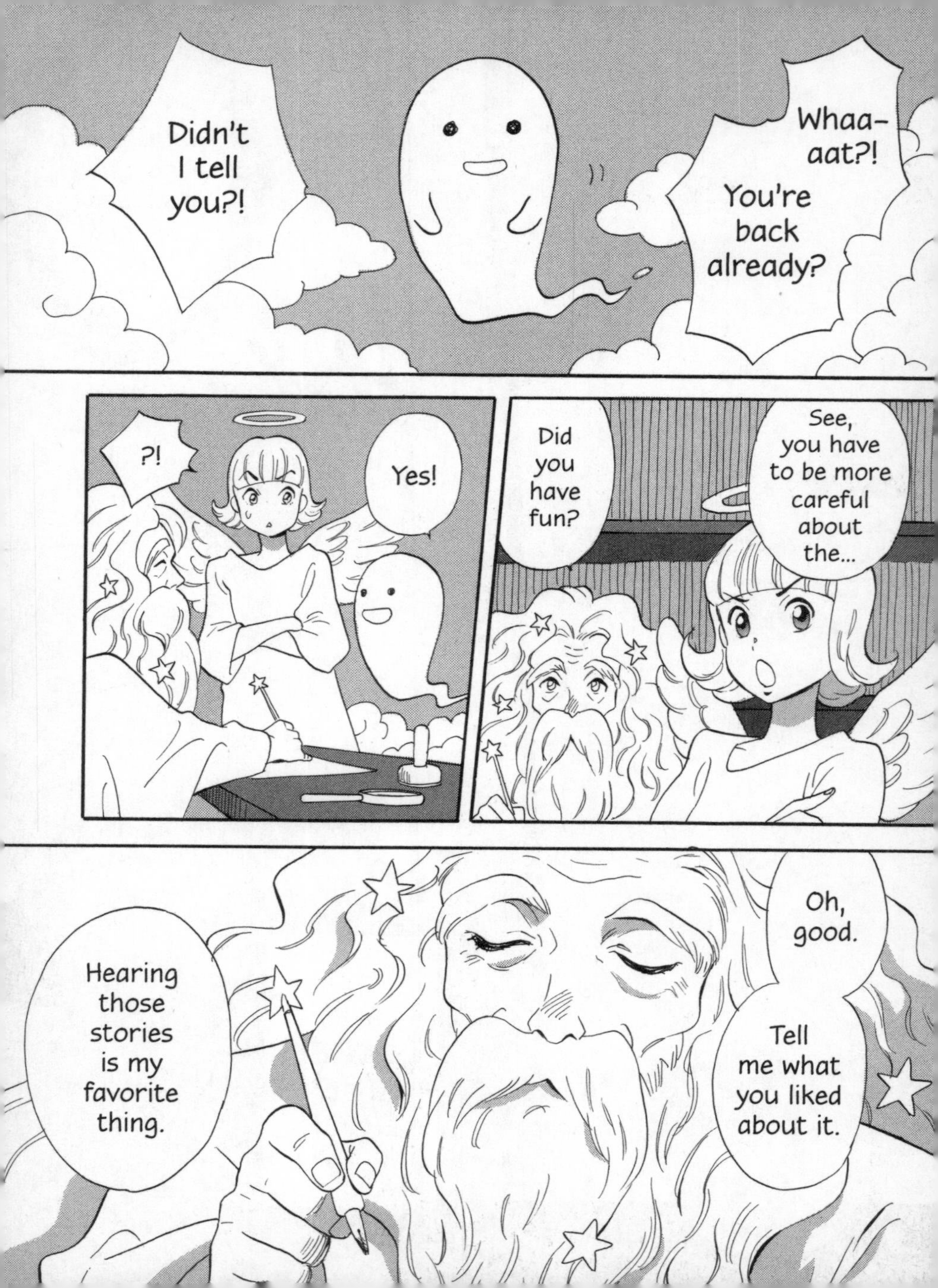
Whaa-aat?!
You're back already?
Didn't I tell you?!
See, you have to be more careful about the...
Did you have fun?
Yes!
?!
Oh, good.
Tell me what you liked about it.
Hearing those stories is my favorite thing.

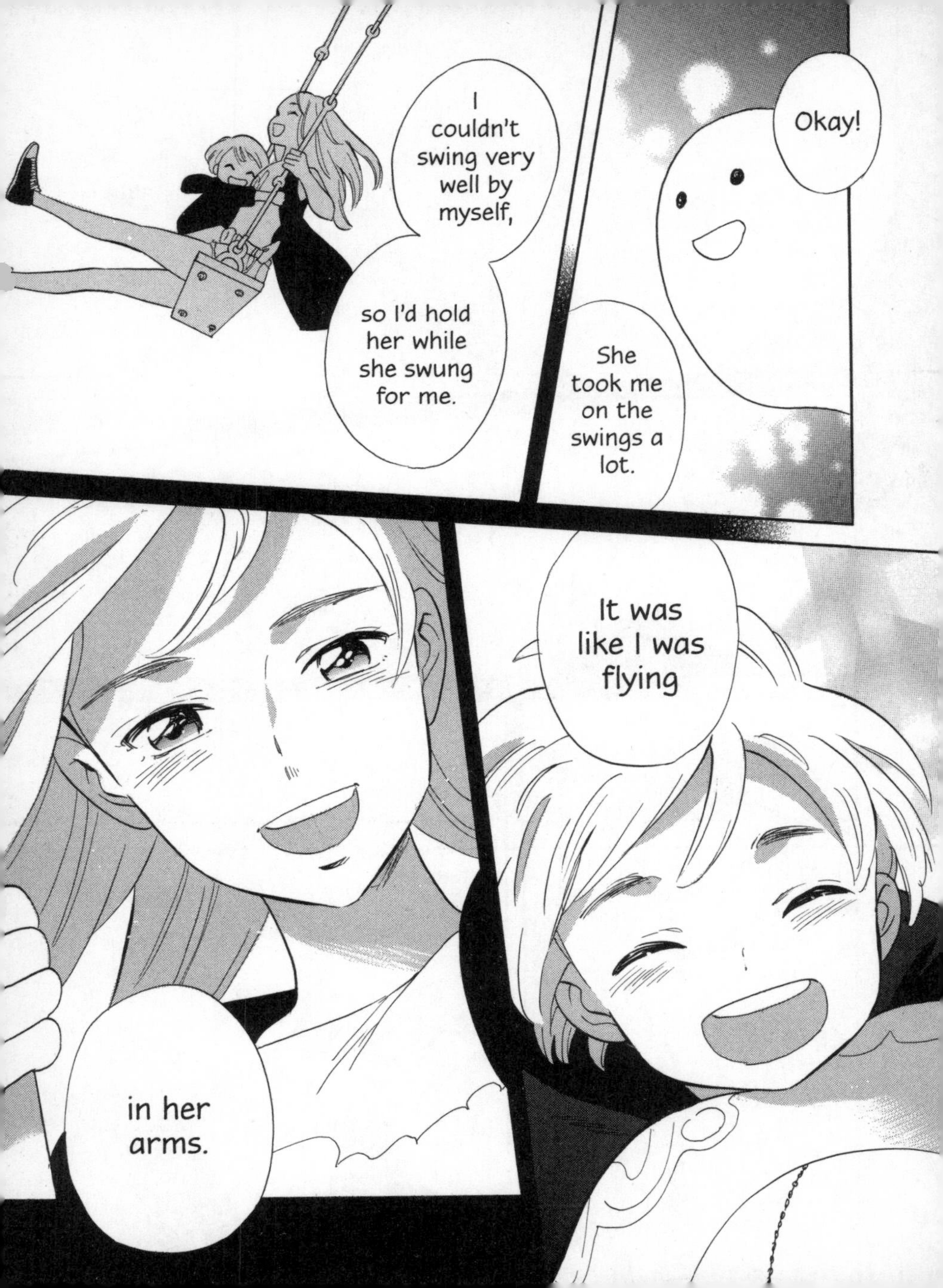
Okay!
She took me on the swings a lot.
I couldn't swing very well by myself,
so I'd hold her while she swung for me.
It was like I was flying
in her arms.

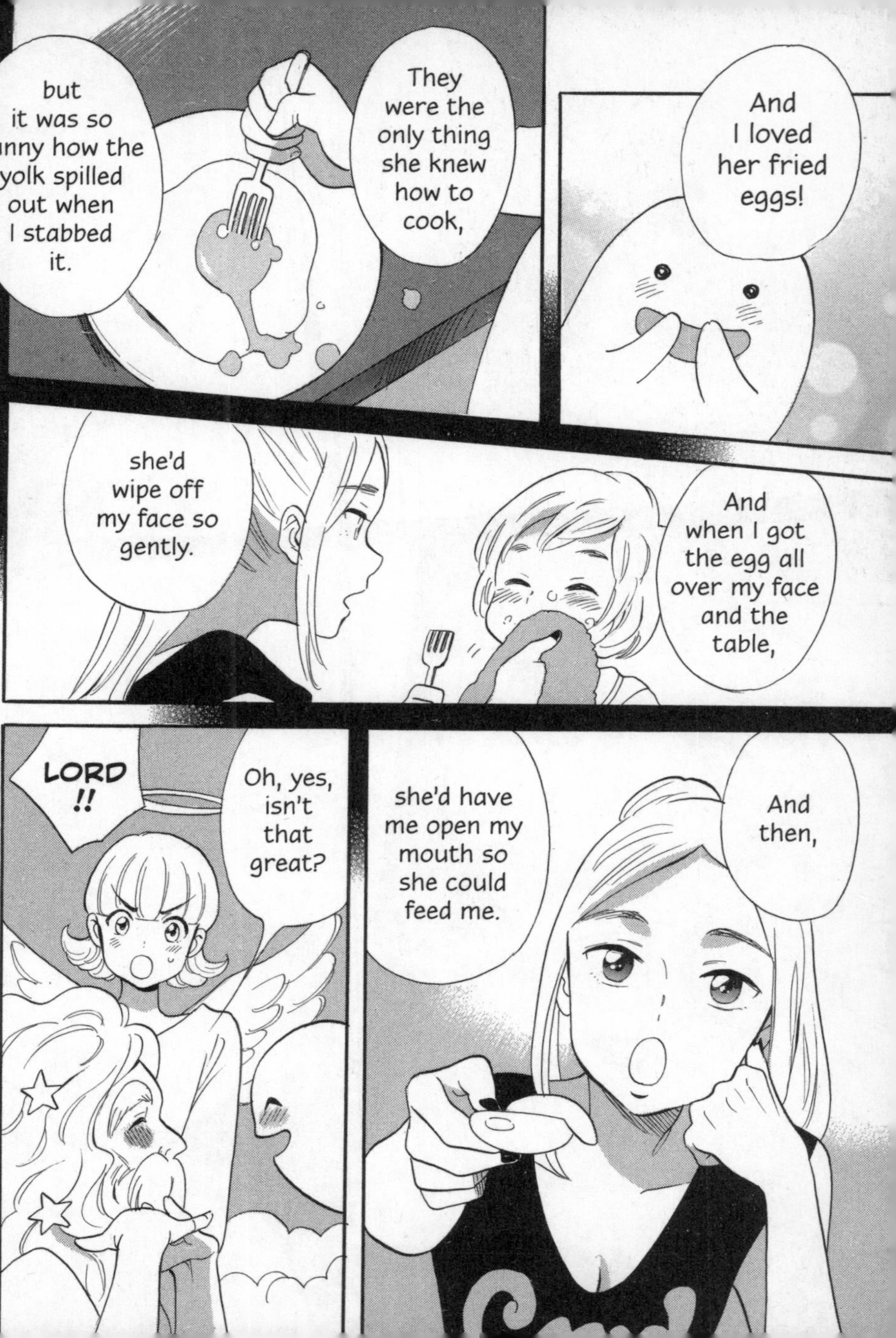
And I loved her fried eggs!
They were the only thing she knew how to cook,
but it was so funny how the yolk spilled out when I stabbed it.
And when I got the egg all over my face and the table,
she'd wipe off my face so gently.
And then,
she'd have me open my mouth so she could feed me.
Oh, yes, isn't that great?
LORD!!

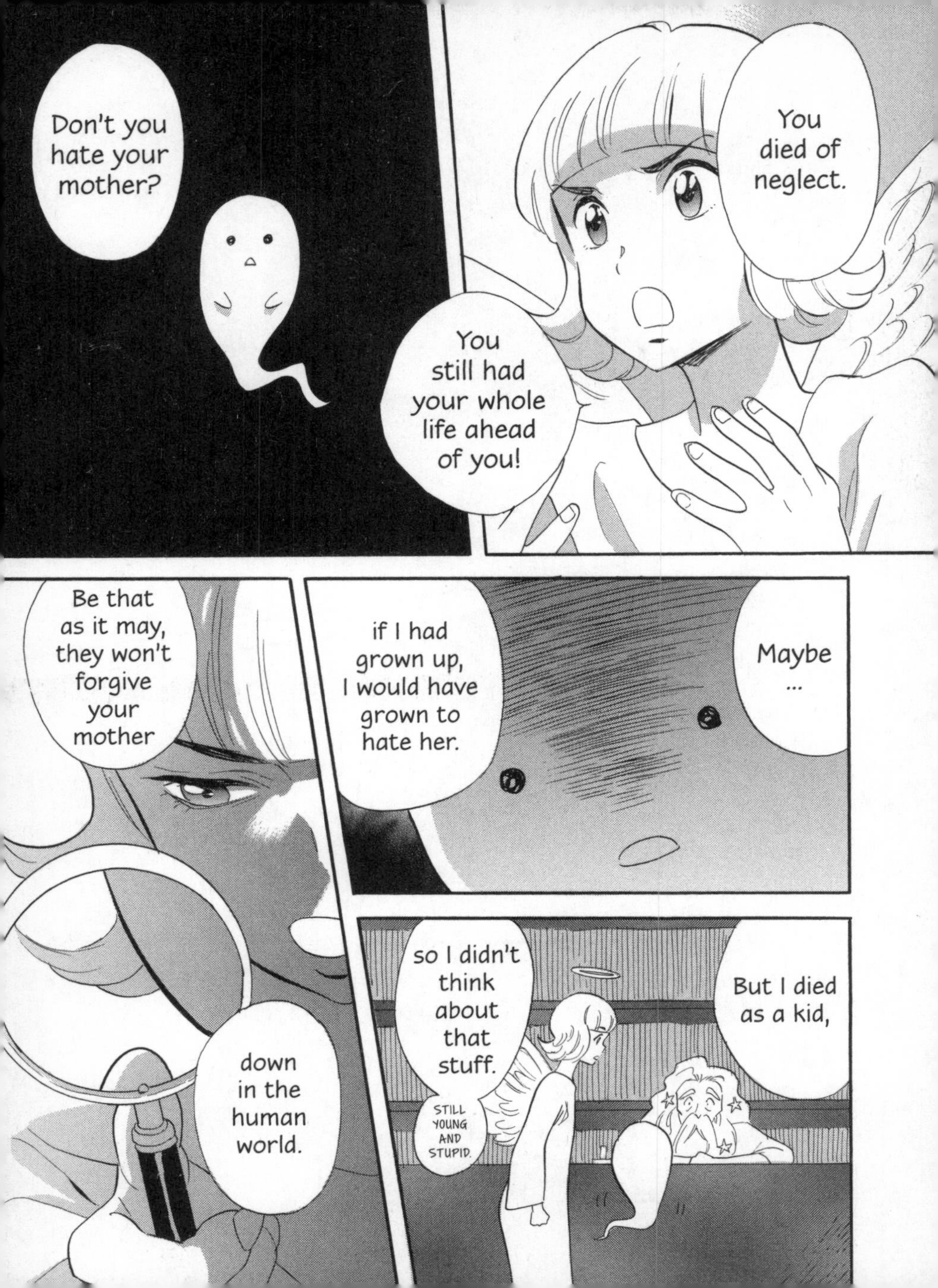
You died of neglect.
You still had your whole life ahead of you!
Don't you hate your mother?
Maybe ...
if I had grown up, I would have grown to hate her.
But I died as a kid,
so I didn't think about that stuff.
STILL YOUNG AND STUPID.
Be that as it may, they won't forgive your mother
down in the human world.

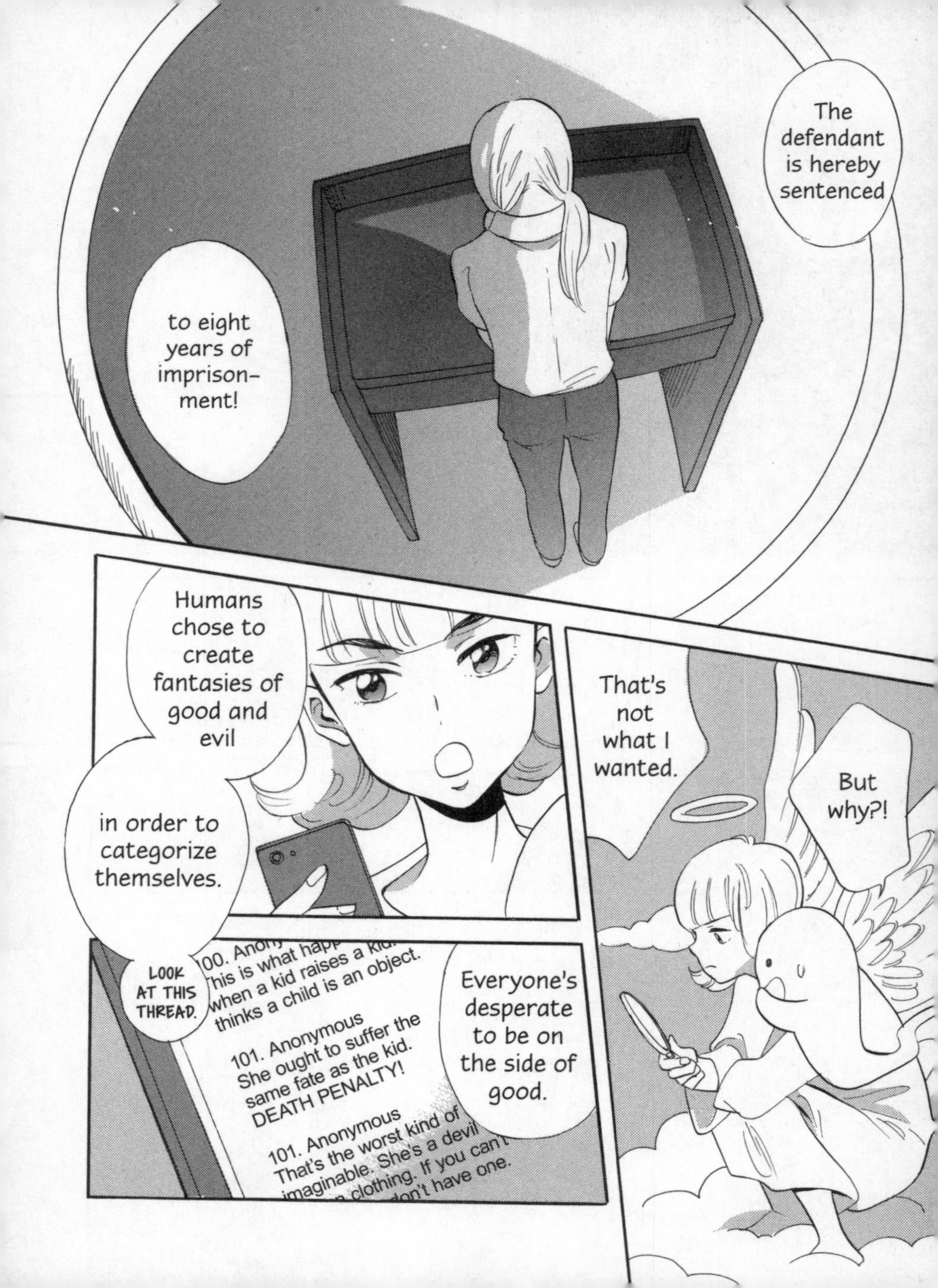
The defendant is hereby sentenced
to eight years of imprisonment!
That's not what I wanted.
But why?!
Humans chose to create fantasies of good and evil
in order to categorize themselves.
Everyone's desperate to be on the side of good.
LOOK AT THIS THREAD.
00. Anon
This is what happ
when a kid raises a kid.
thinks a child is an object.
101. Anonymous
She ought to suffer the same fate as the kid. DEATH PENALTY!
101. Anonymous
That's the worst kind of
imaginable. She's a devil
clothing. If you can't
don't have one.

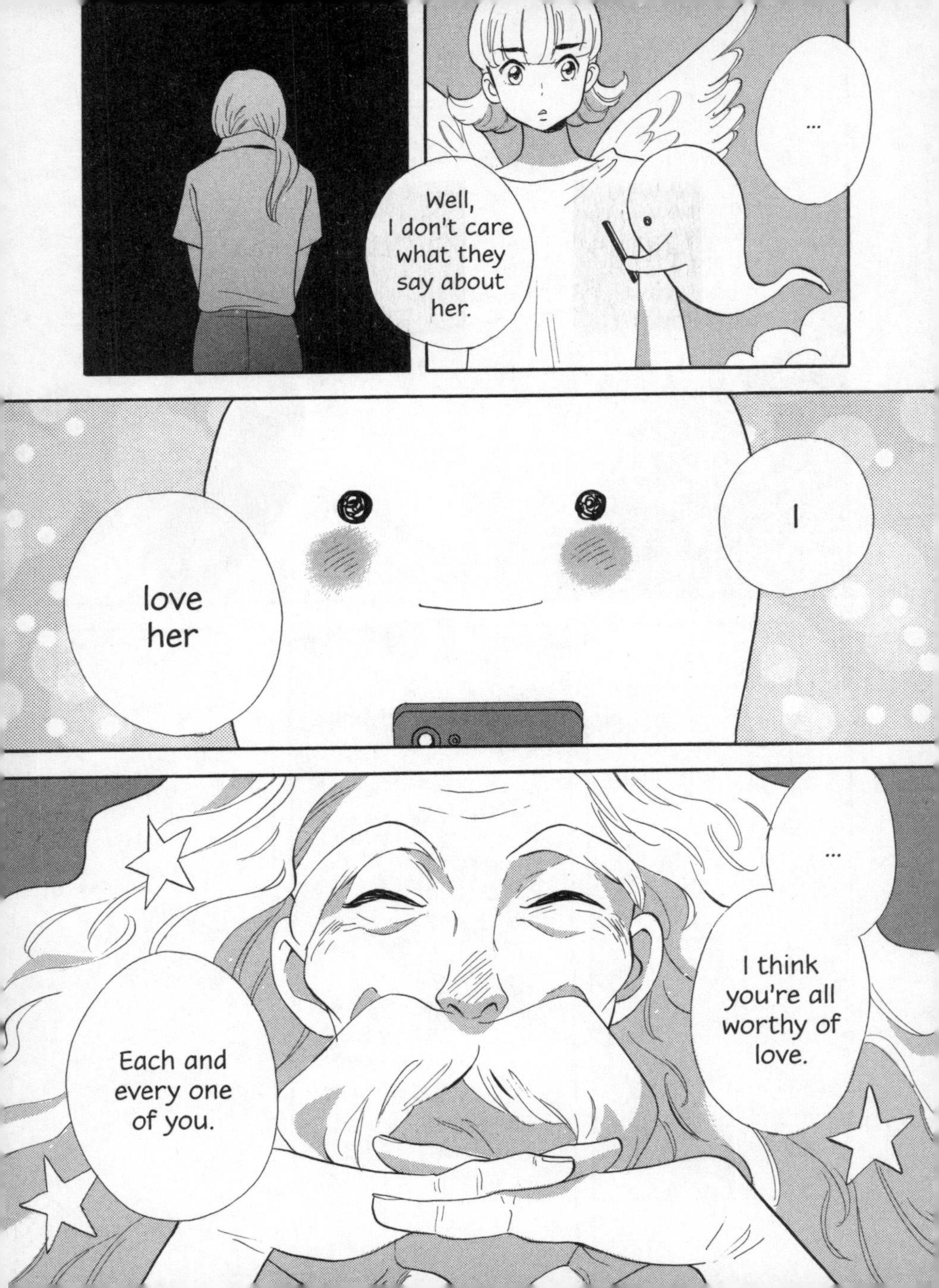
...
Well, I don't care what they say about her.
I
love her
...
I think you're all worthy of love.
Each and every one of you.

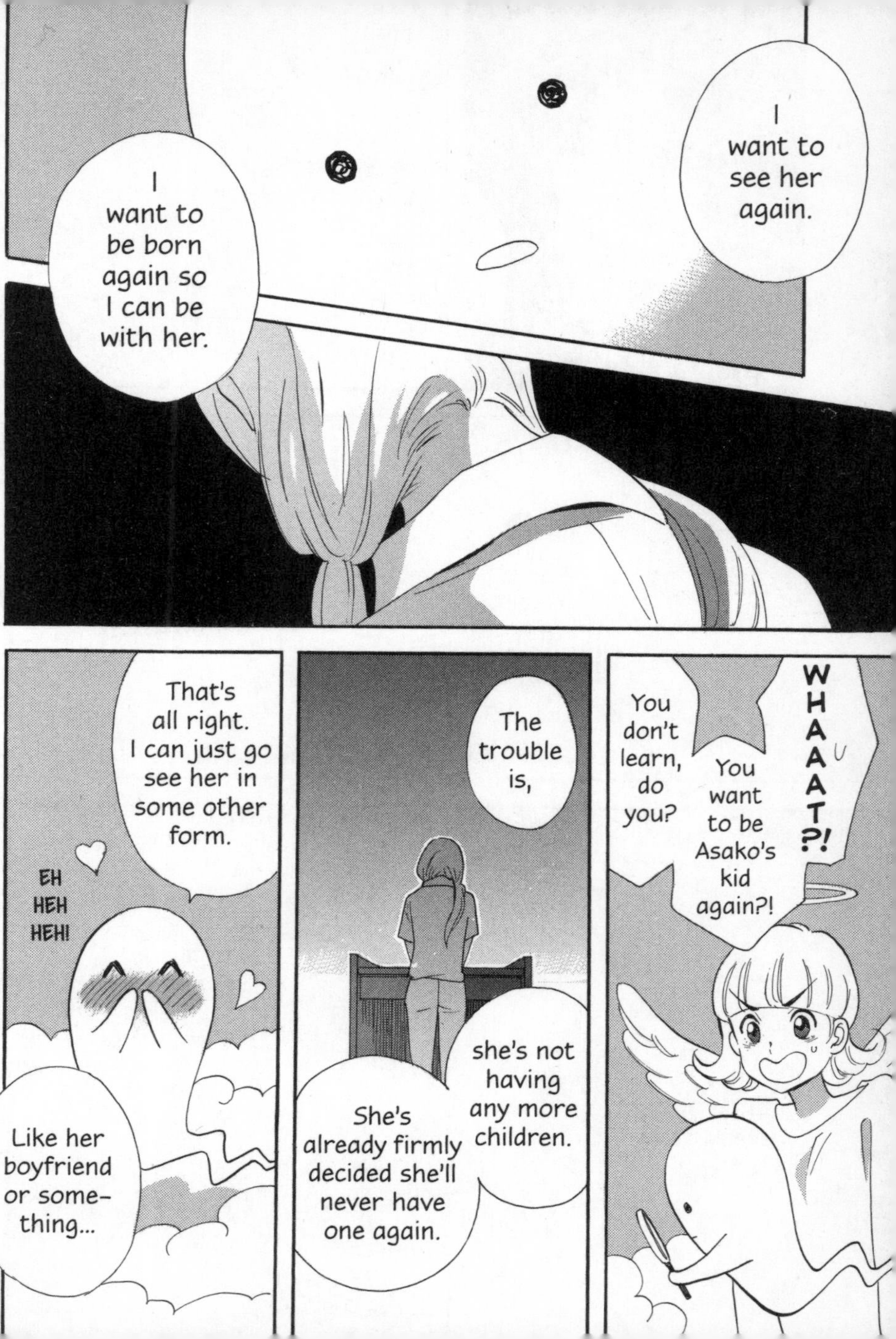
I want to see her again.
I want to be born again so I can be with her.
WHAAAAT?!
You want to be Asako's kid again?!
You don't learn, do you?
The trouble is,
she's not having any more children.
She's already firmly decided she'll never have one again.
That's all right. I can just go see her in some other form.
EH HEH HEH!
Like her boyfriend or some-thing...

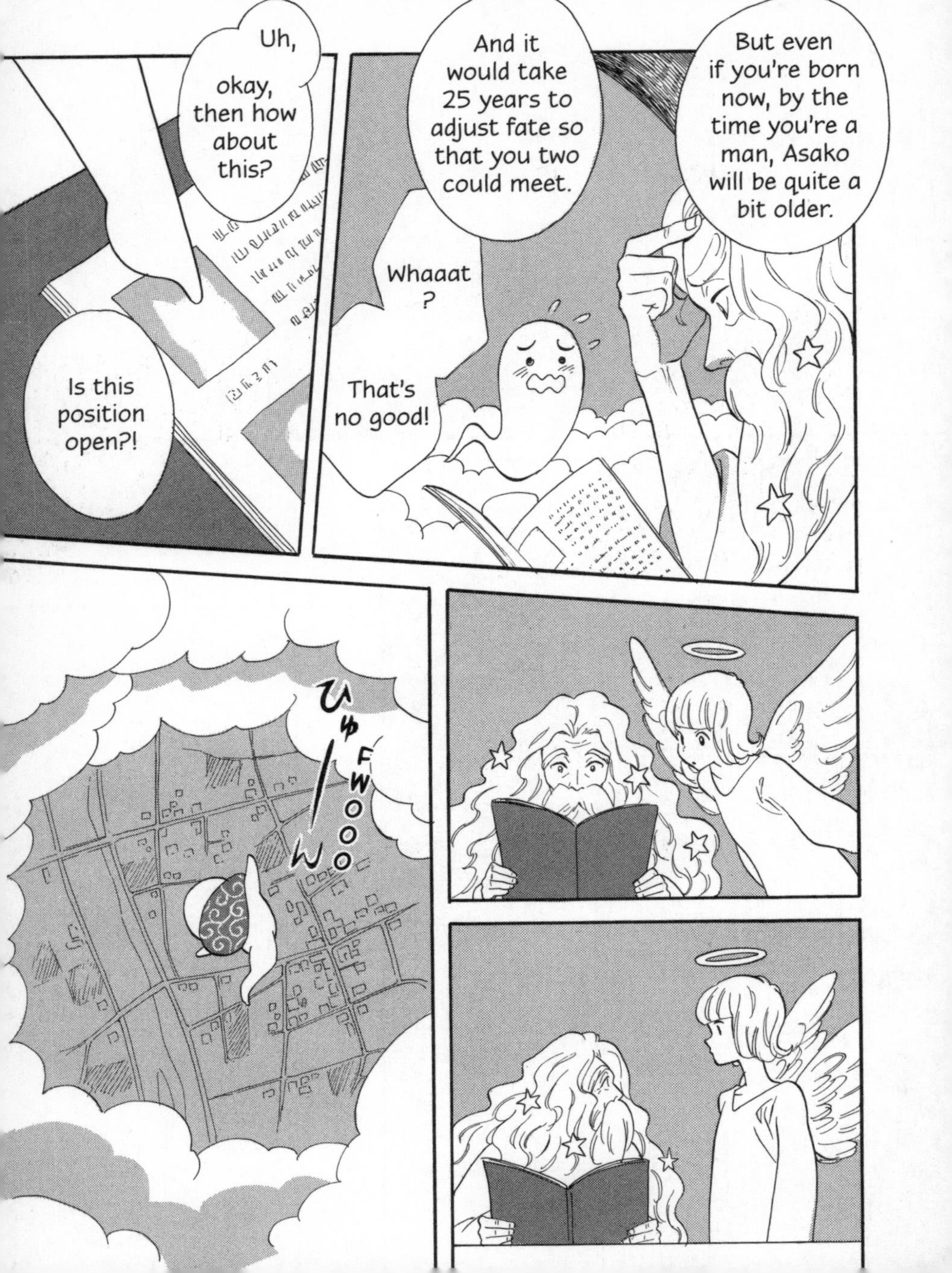
But even if you're born now, by the time you're a man, Asako will be quite a bit older.
And it would take 25 years to adjust fate so that you two could meet.
Whaaat?
That's no good!
Uh,
okay, then how about this?
Is this position open?!
ひゅー
FWOOOO

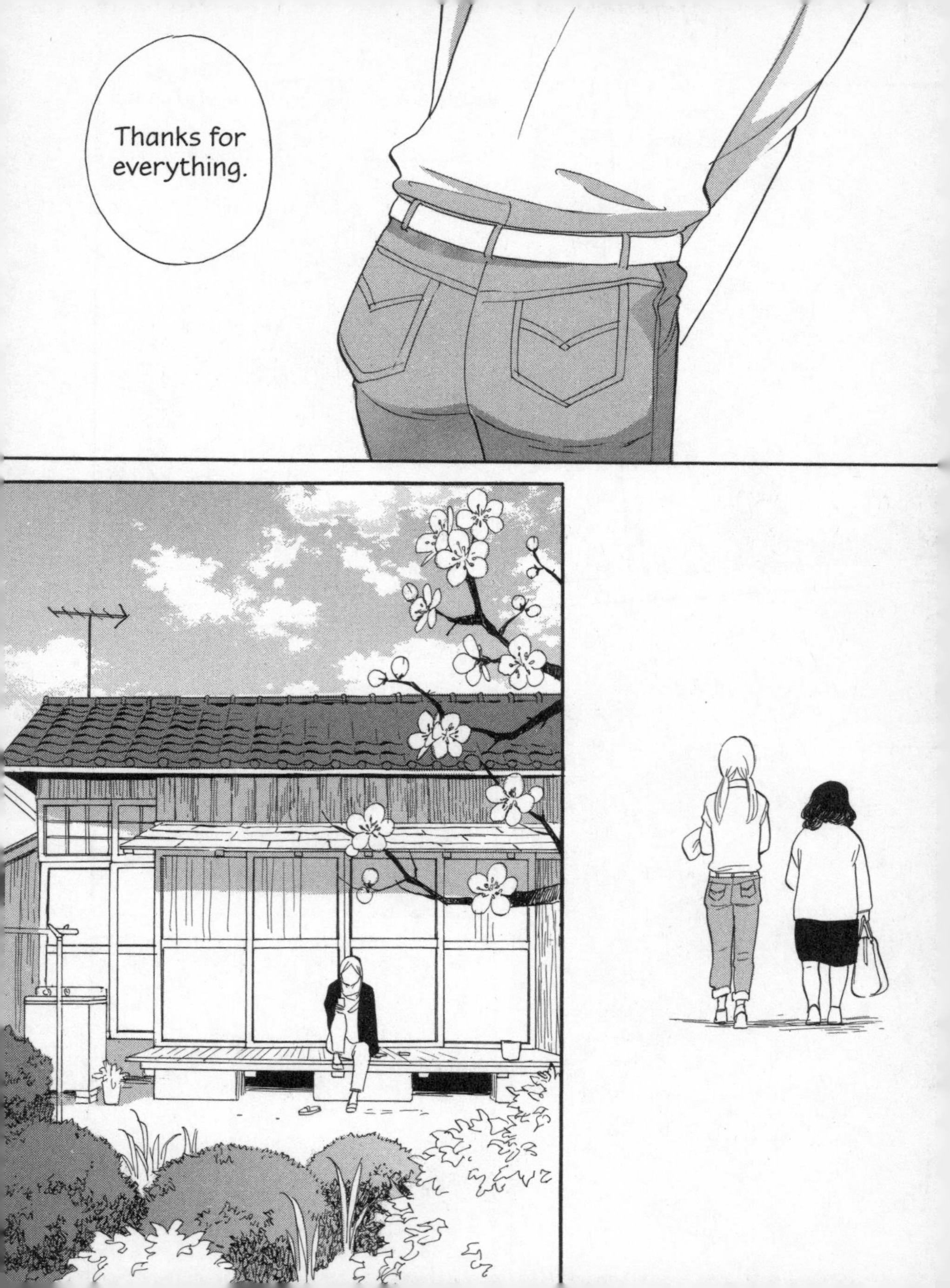
Thanks for everything.

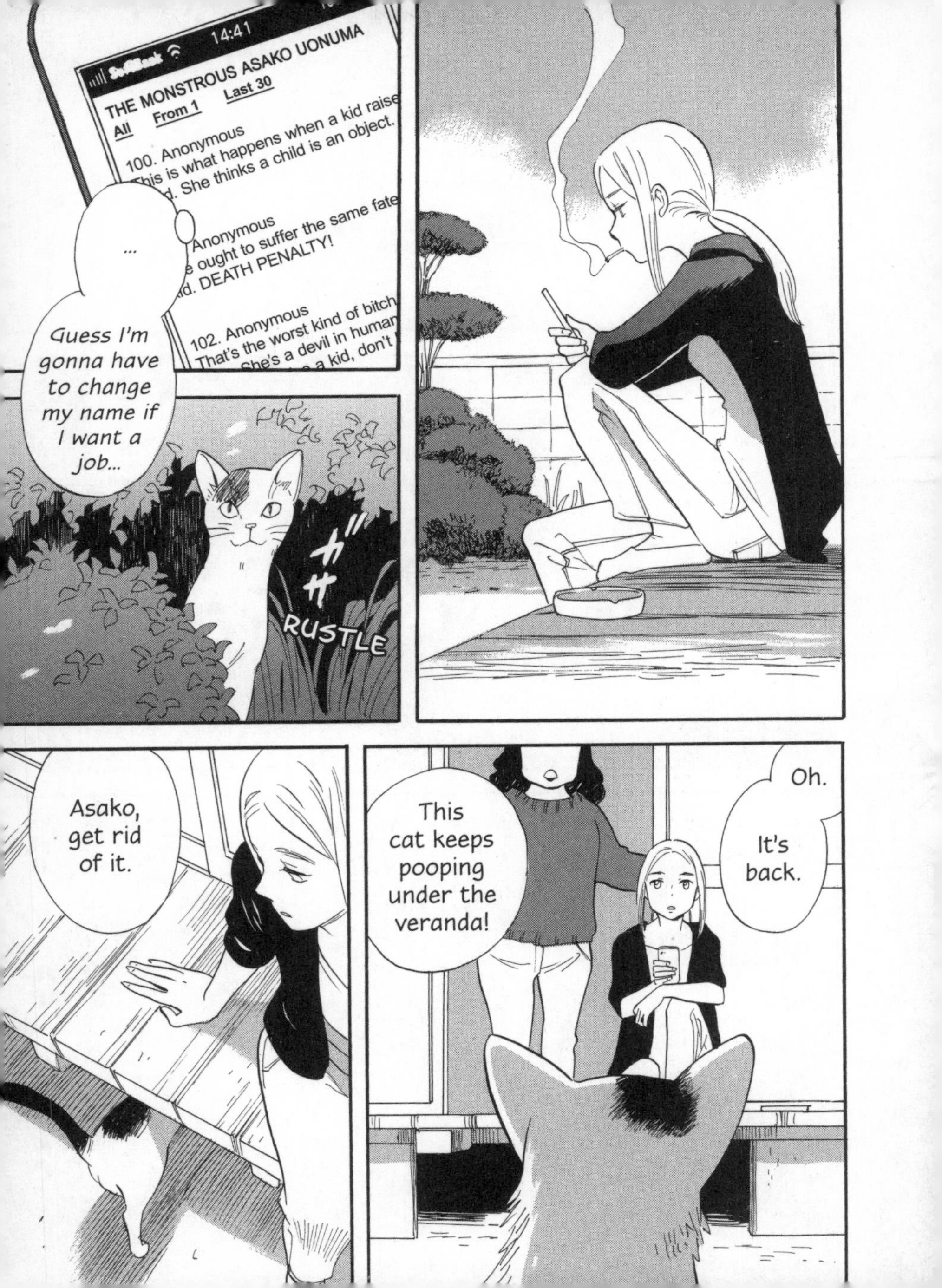
14:41
THE MONSTROUS ASAKO UONUMA
All From 1 Last 30
100. Anonymous
This is what happens when a kid raise
d. She thinks a child is an object.
Anonymous
e ought to suffer the same fate
kid. DEATH PENALTY!
102. Anonymous
That's the worst kind of bitch
She's a devil in human
...
Guess I'm gonna have to change my name if I want a job...
RUSTLE
Oh.
It's back.
This cat keeps pooping under the veranda!
Asako, get rid of it.

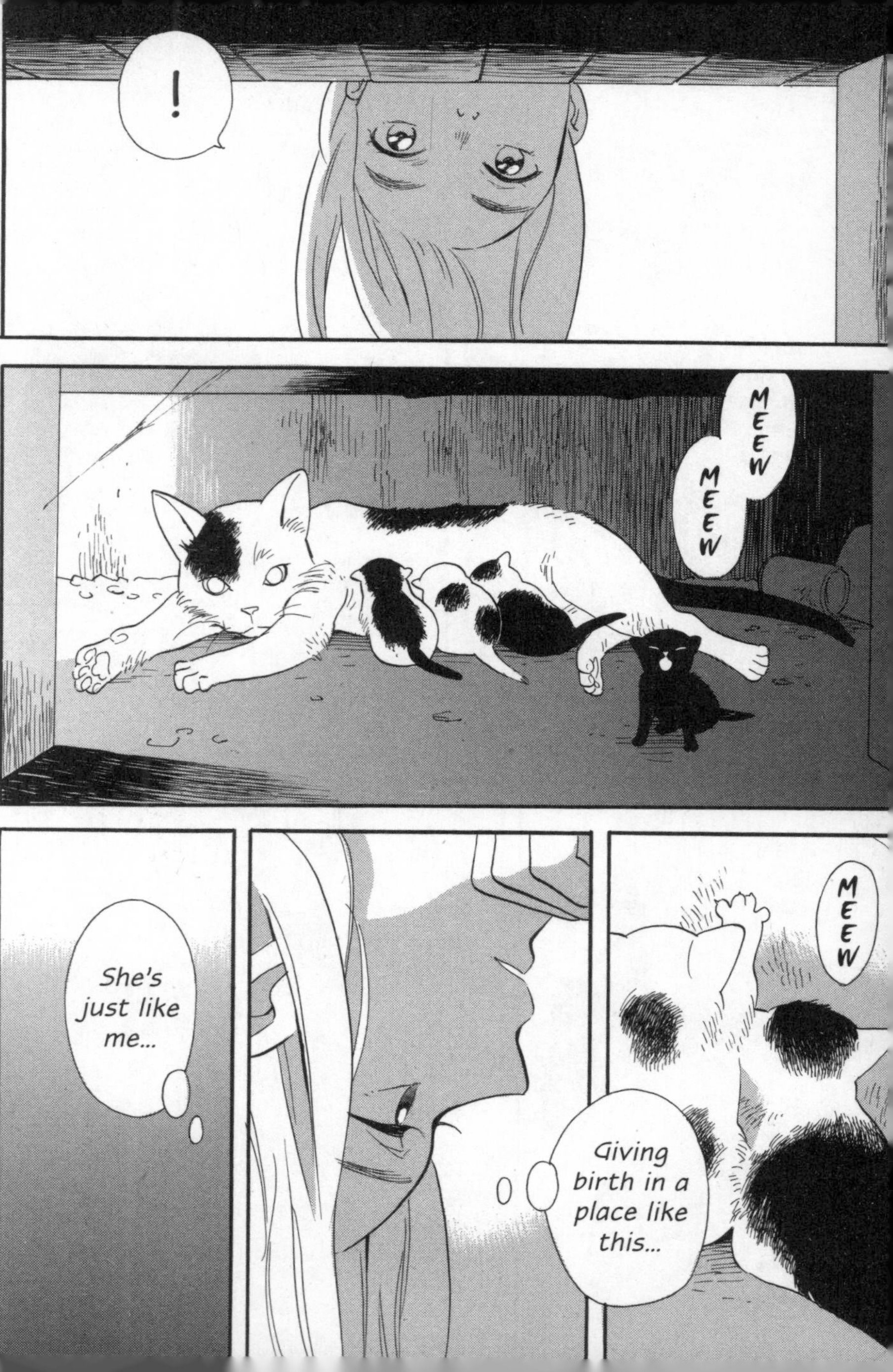
!
MEEW
MEEW
MEEW
Giving birth in a place like this...
She's just like me...

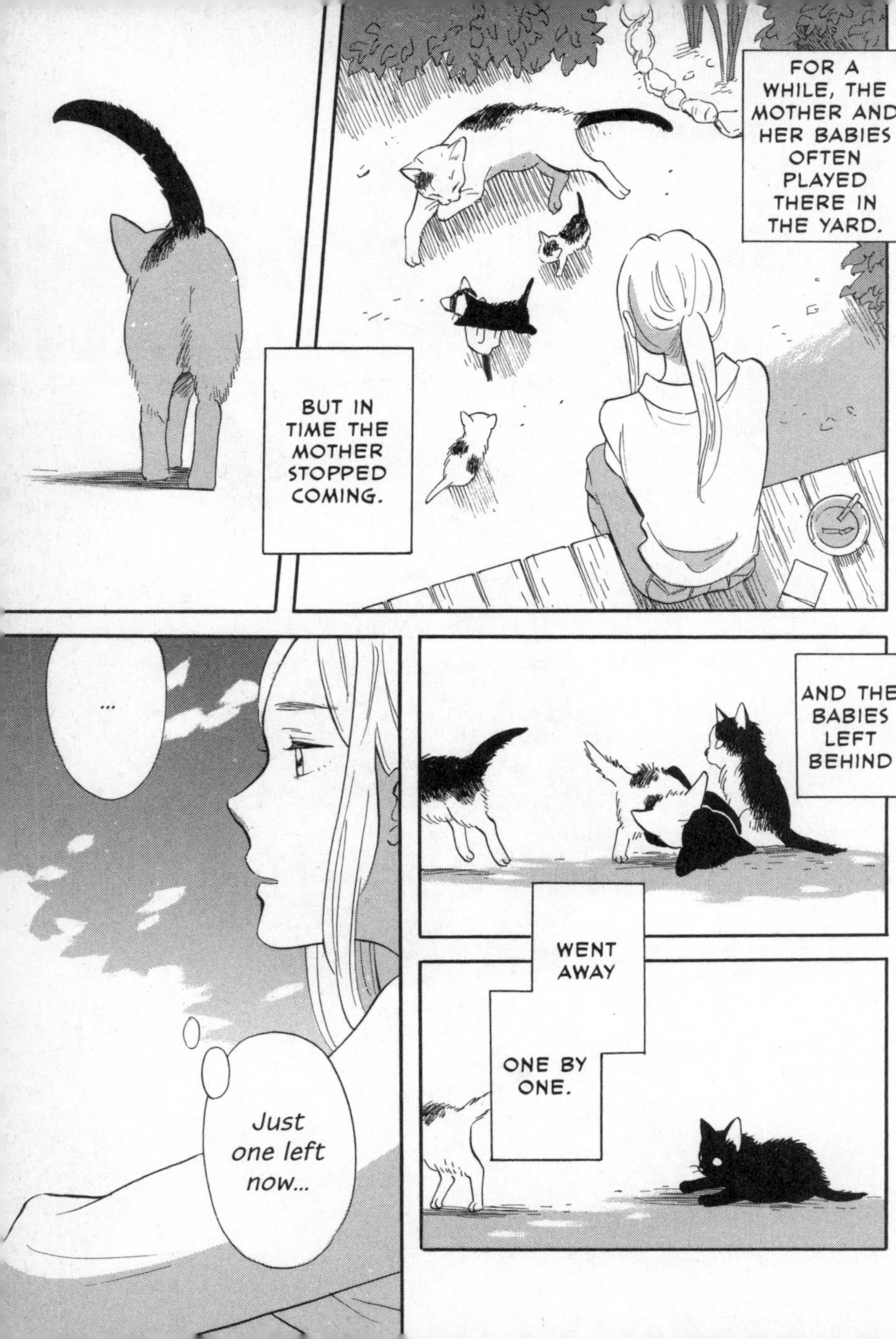
FOR A WHILE, THE MOTHER AND HER BABIES OFTEN PLAYED THERE IN THE YARD.
BUT IN TIME THE MOTHER STOPPED COMING.
AND THE BABIES LEFT BEHIND
WENT AWAY
ONE BY ONE.
...
Just one left now...

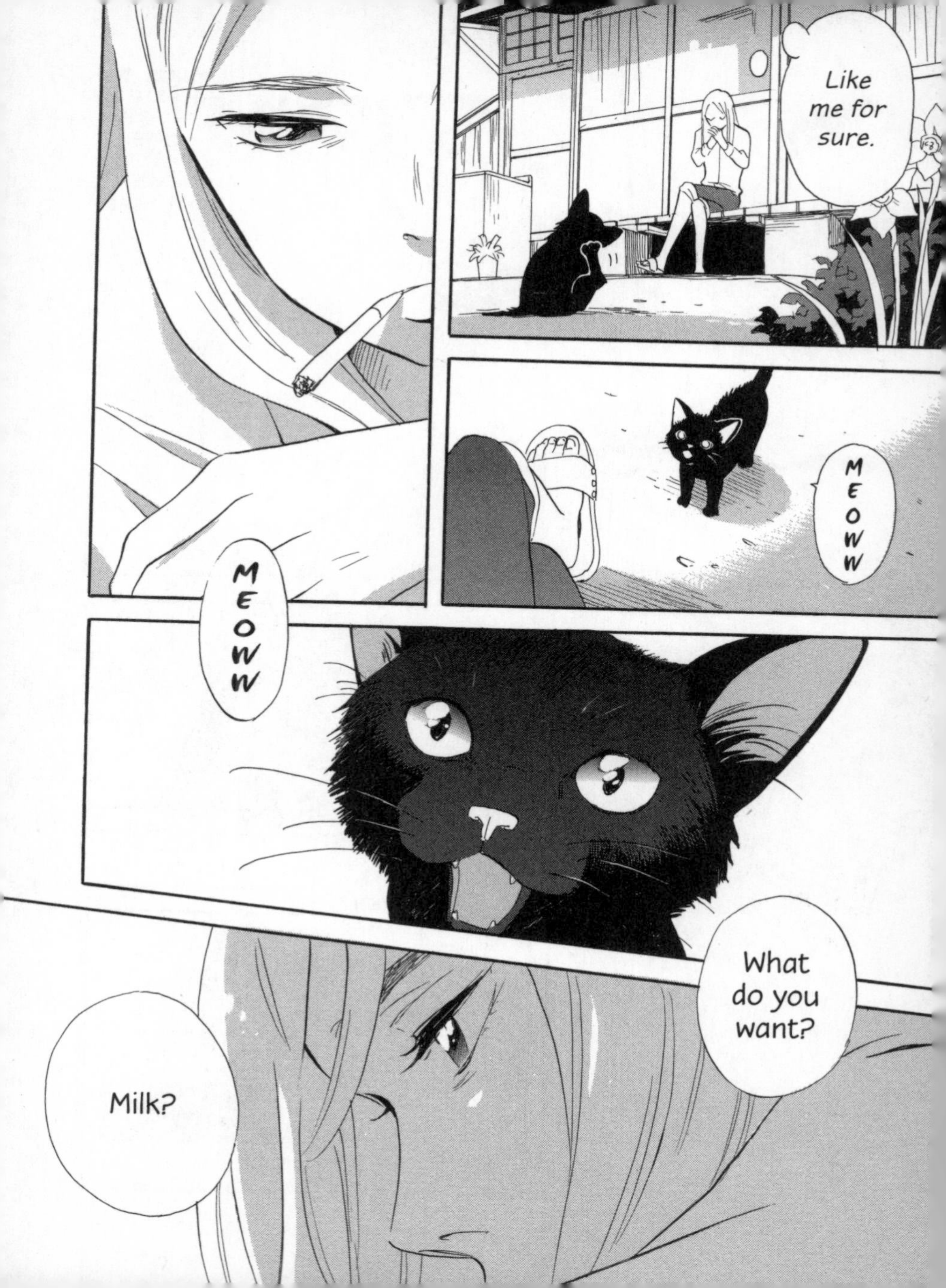

Like me for sure.
MEOWW
MEOWW
What do you want?
Milk?

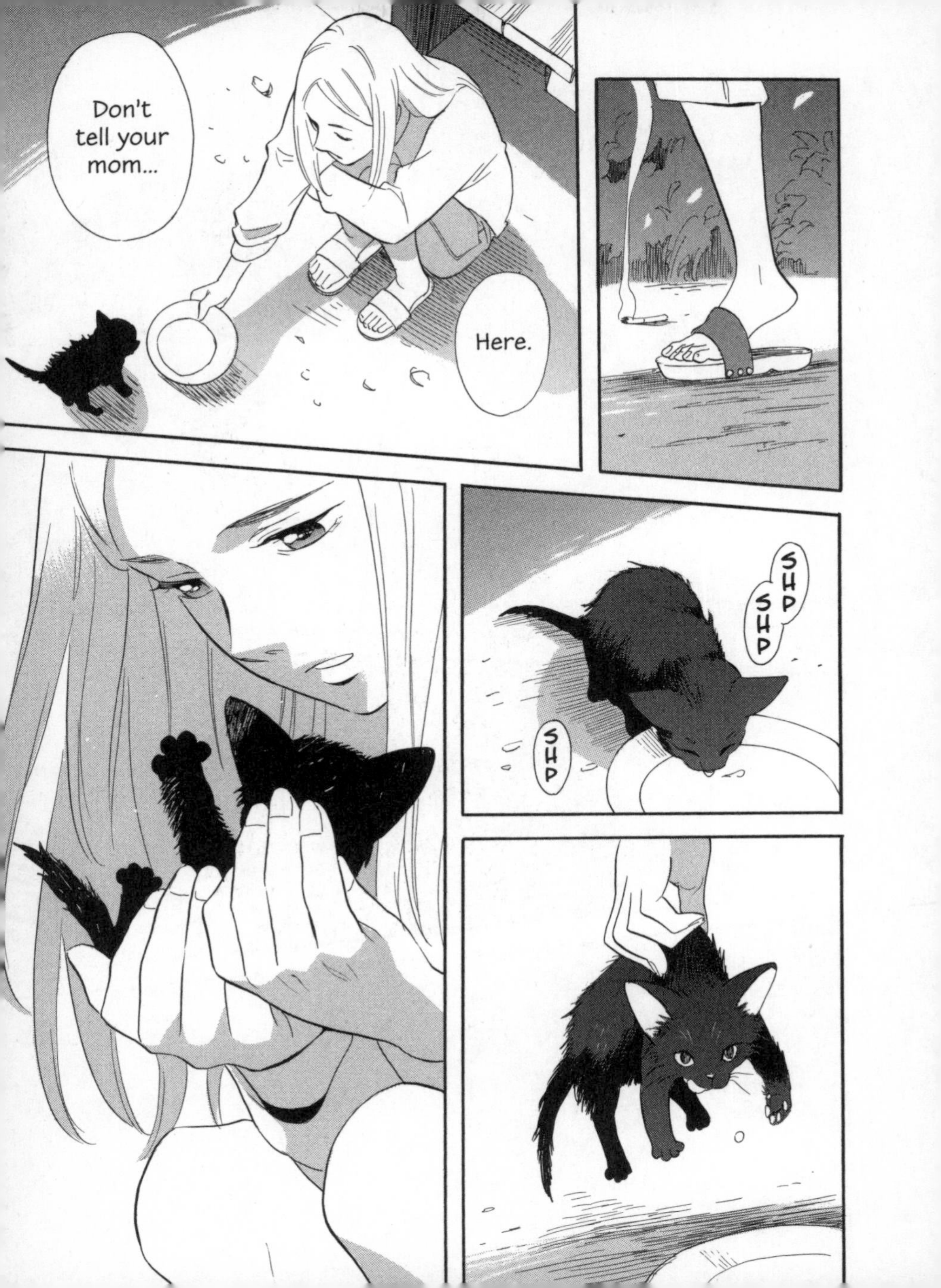
Here.
Don't tell your mom...
SHP SHP
SHP

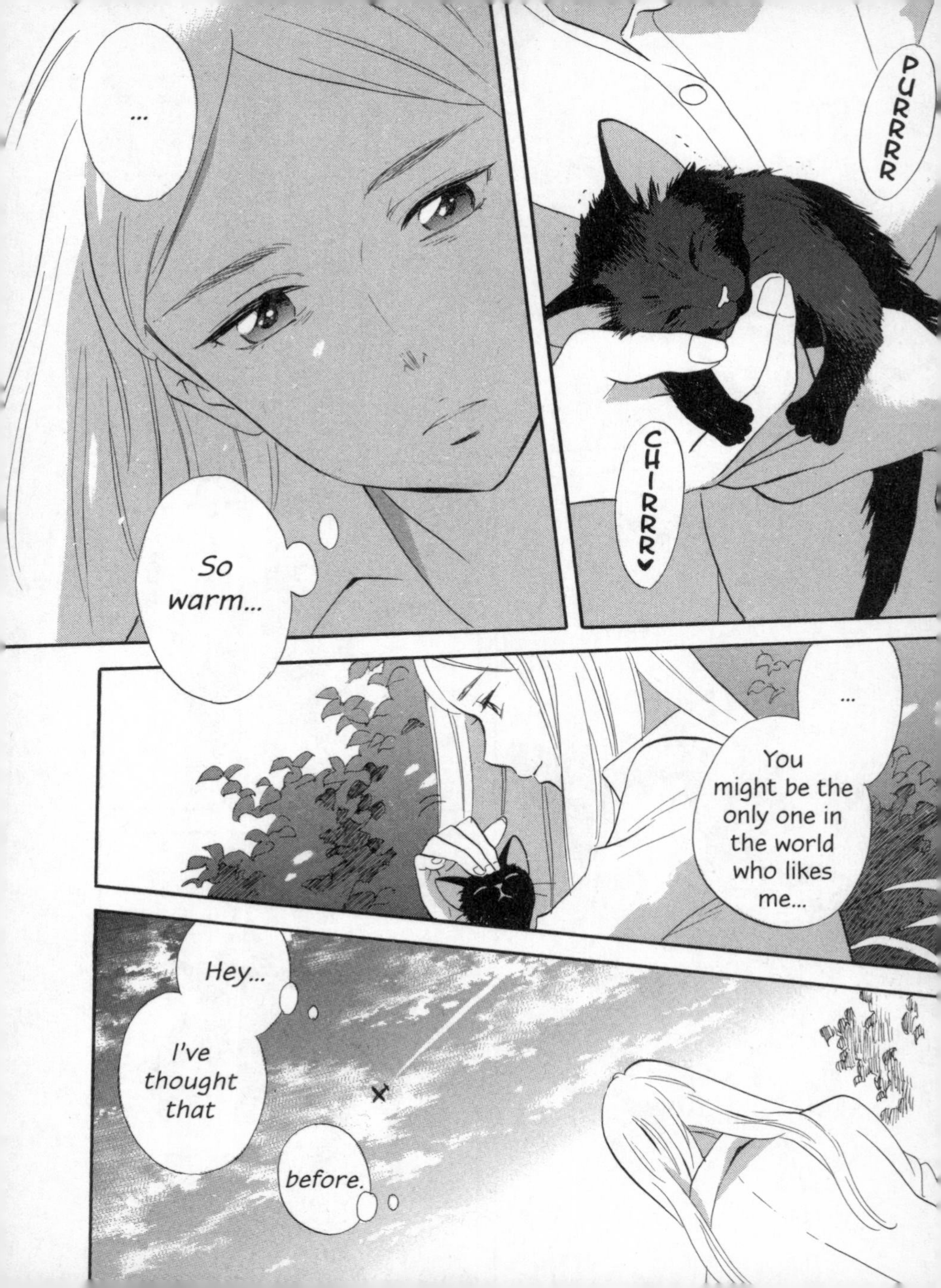
PURRRR
CHIRRR♥
...
So warm...
...
You might be the only one in the world who likes me...
Hey...
I've thought that
before.

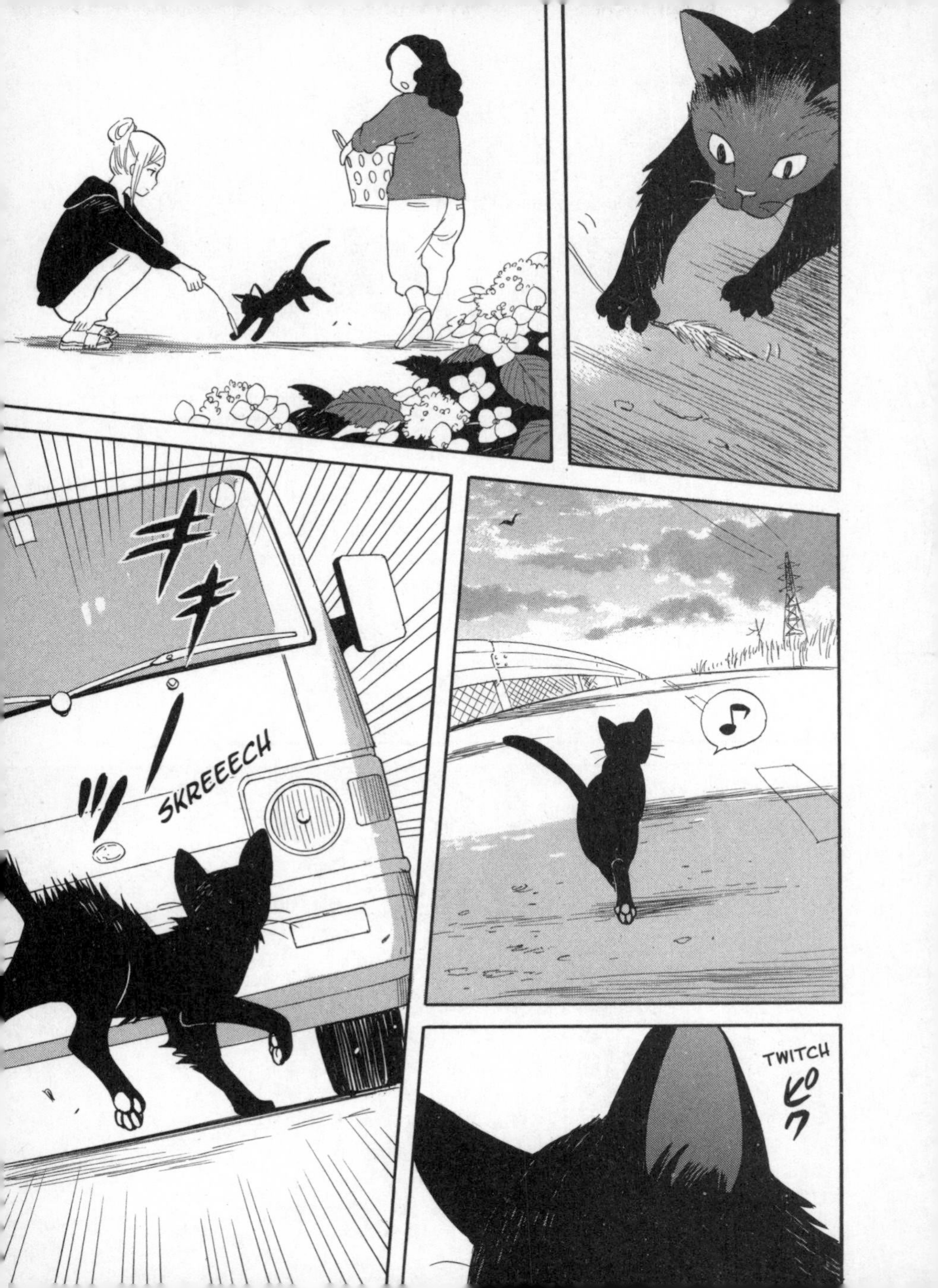
♪
TWITCH
ピク
キキーッ!!
SKREEECH

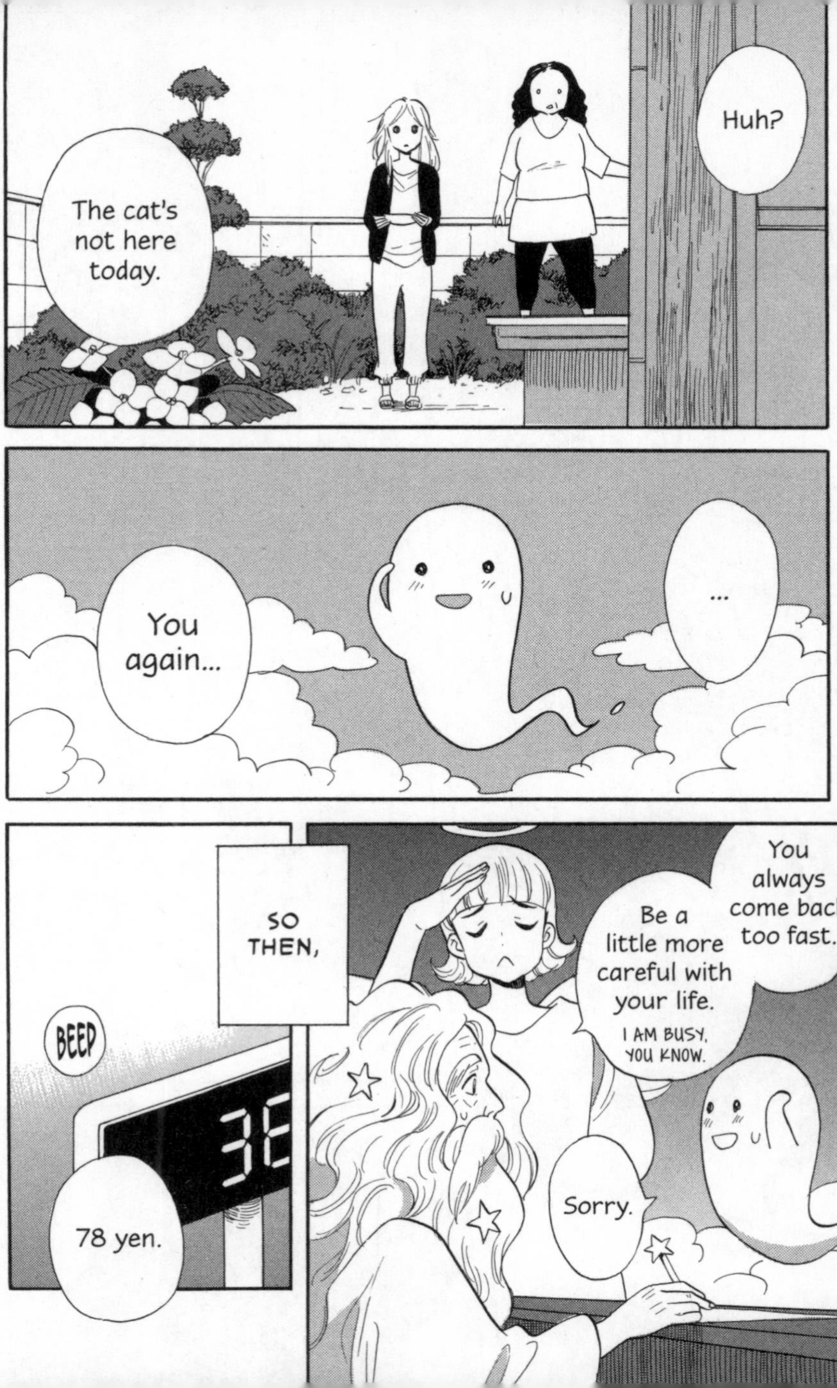
Huh?
The cat's not here today.
...
You again...
You always come back too fast.
Be a little more careful with your life.
I AM BUSY, YOU KNOW.
Sorry.
SO THEN,
BEEP
78 yen.

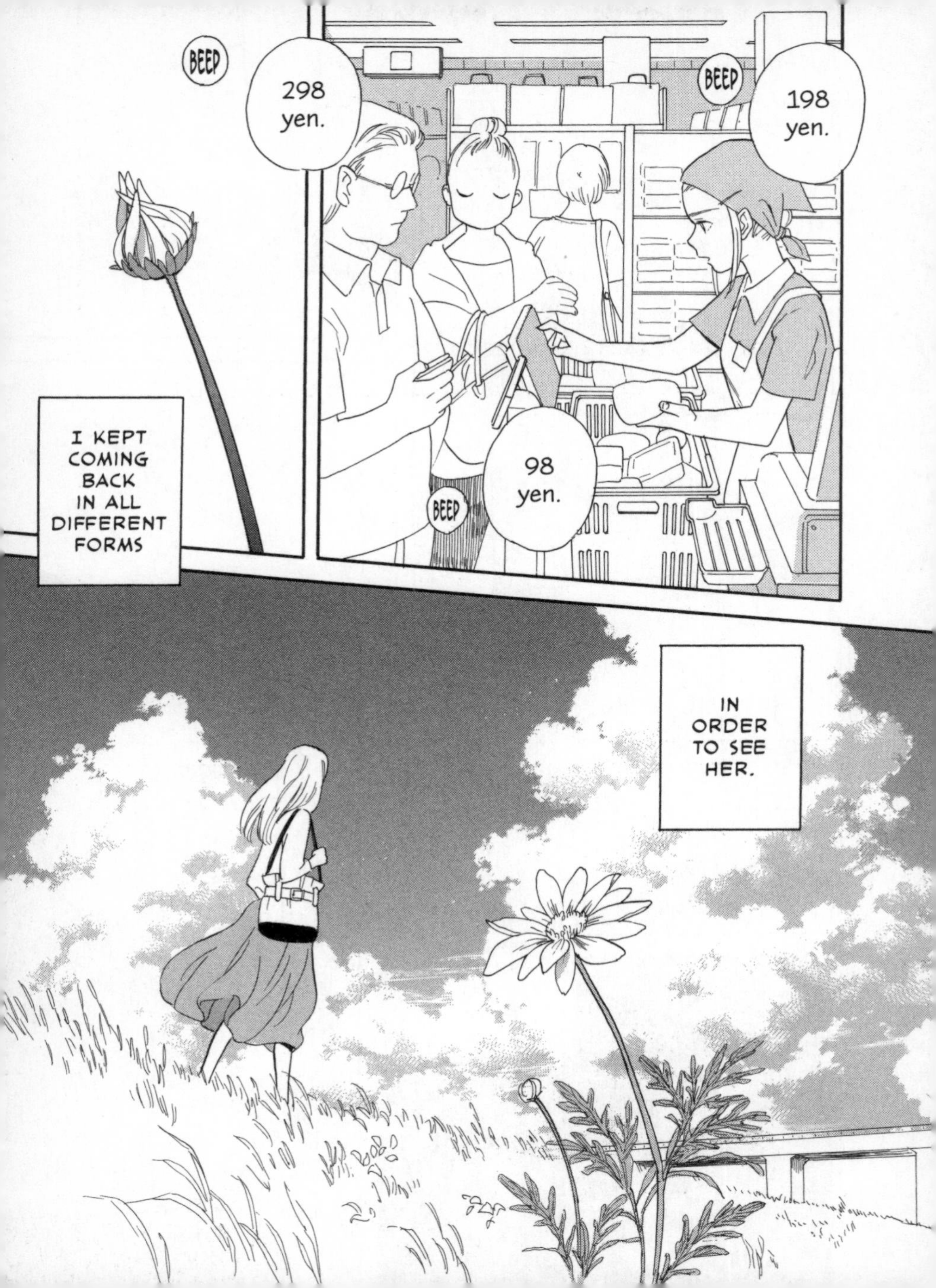
BEEP
198 yen.
298 yen.
98 yen.
BEEP
BEEP
I KEPT COMING BACK IN ALL DIFFERENT FORMS
IN ORDER TO SEE HER.

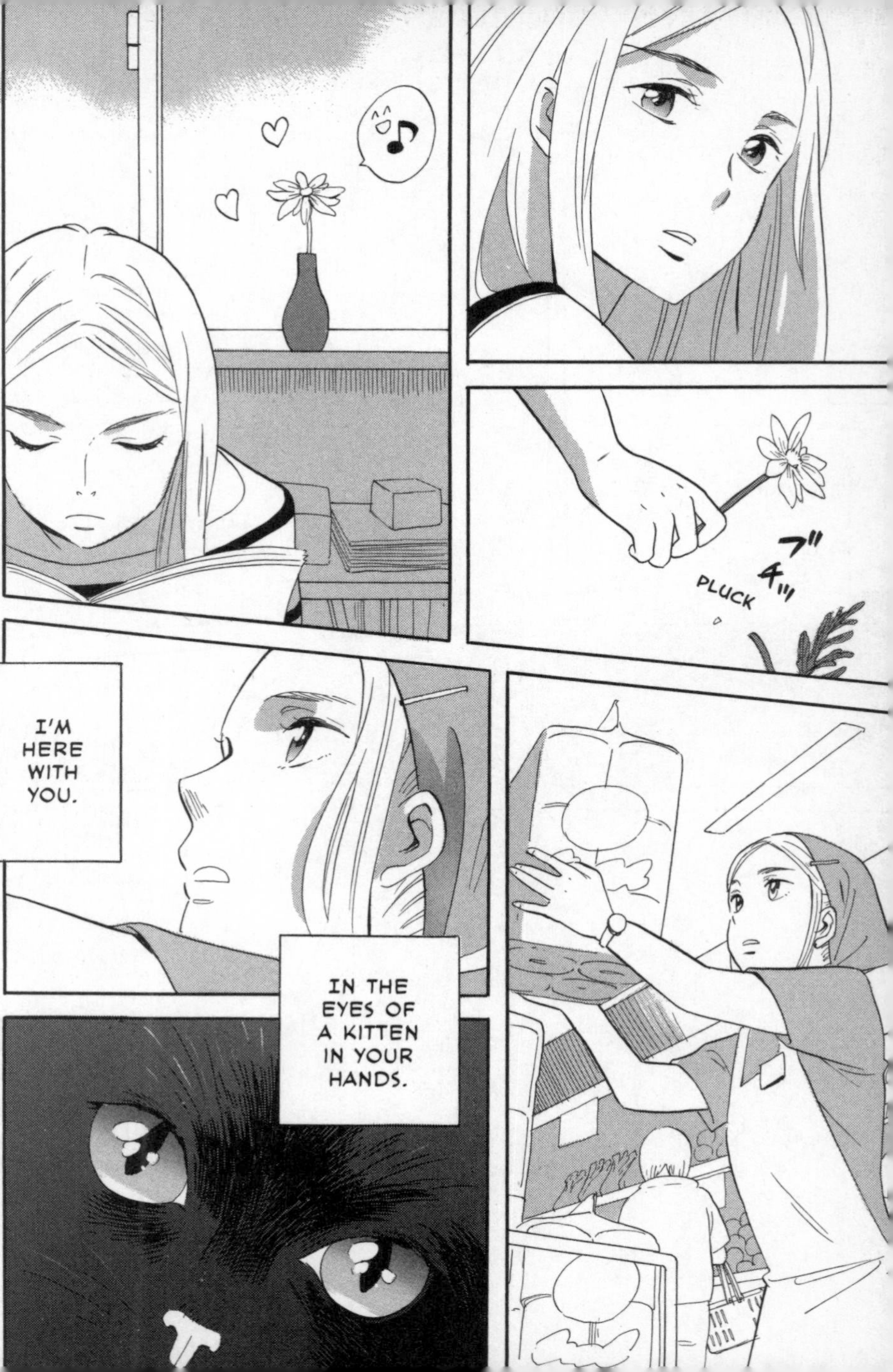

ブチッ
PLUCK
I'M HERE WITH YOU.
IN THE EYES OF A KITTEN IN YOUR HANDS.

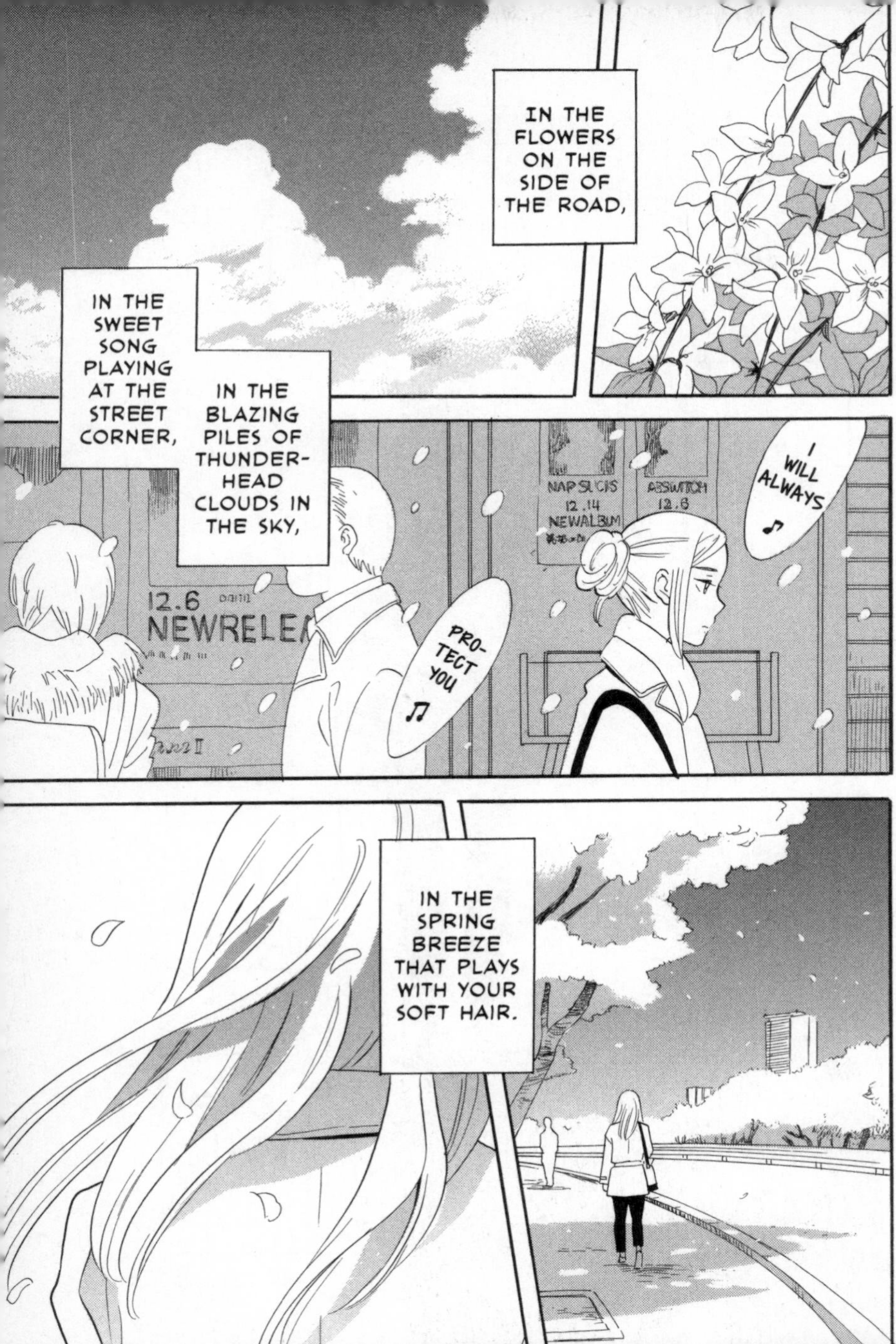
IN THE FLOWERS ON THE SIDE OF THE ROAD,
IN THE SWEET SONG PLAYING AT THE STREET CORNER,
IN THE BLAZING PILES OF THUNDER-HEAD CLOUDS IN THE SKY,
I WILL ALWAYS ♪
PROTECT YOU ♫
IN THE SPRING BREEZE THAT PLAYS WITH YOUR SOFT HAIR.

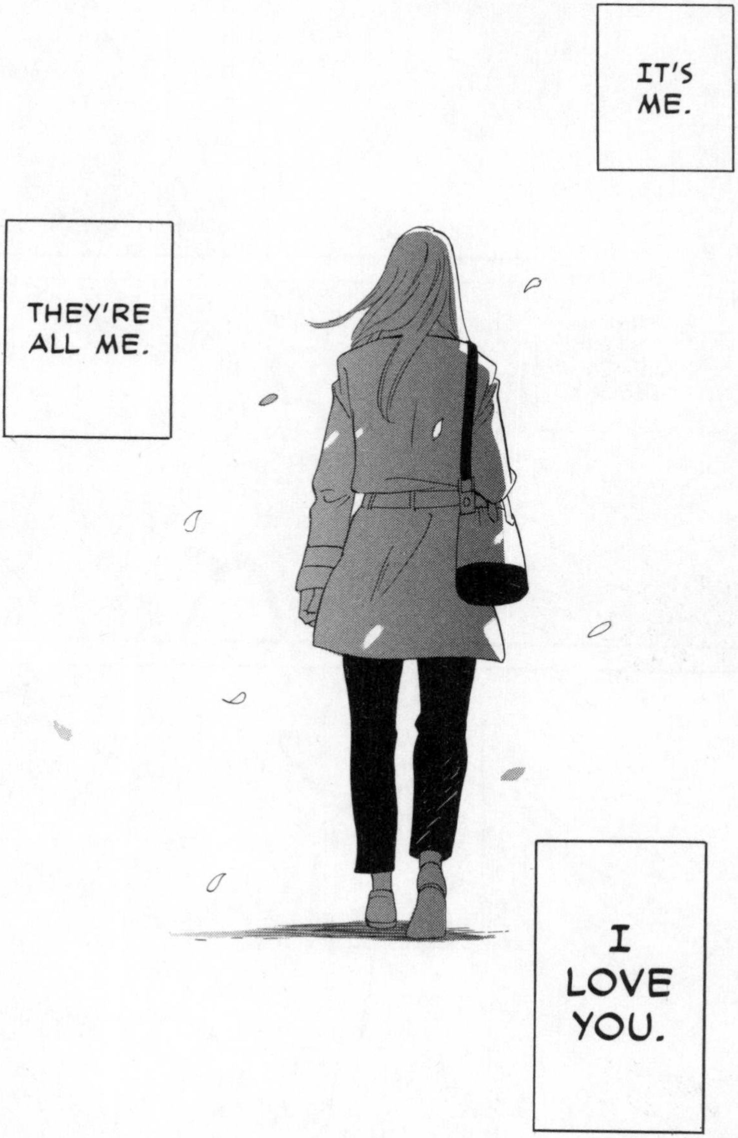
IT'S ME.
THEY'RE ALL ME.
I LOVE YOU.

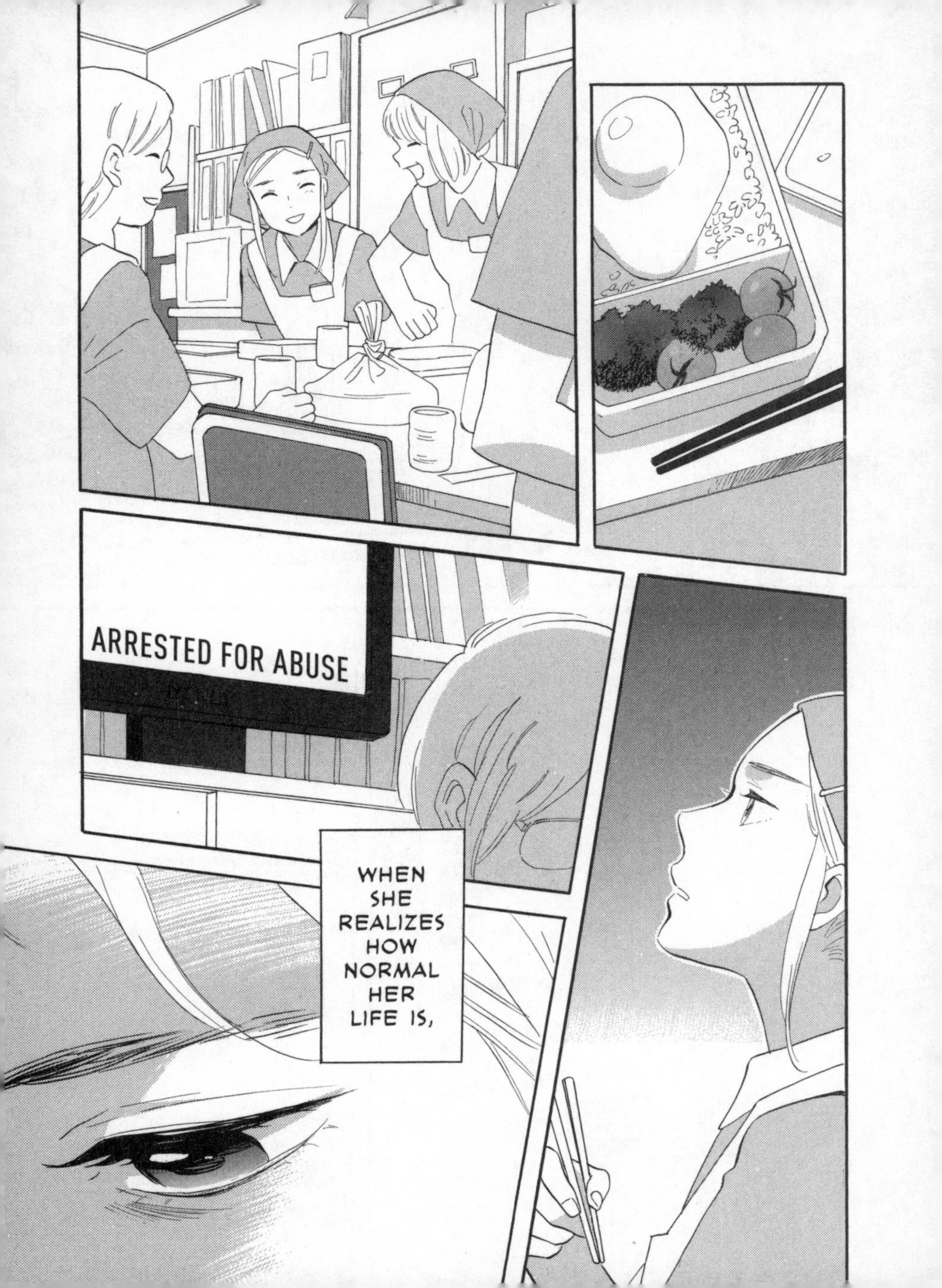
ARRESTED FOR ABUSE
WHEN SHE REALIZES HOW NORMAL HER LIFE IS,

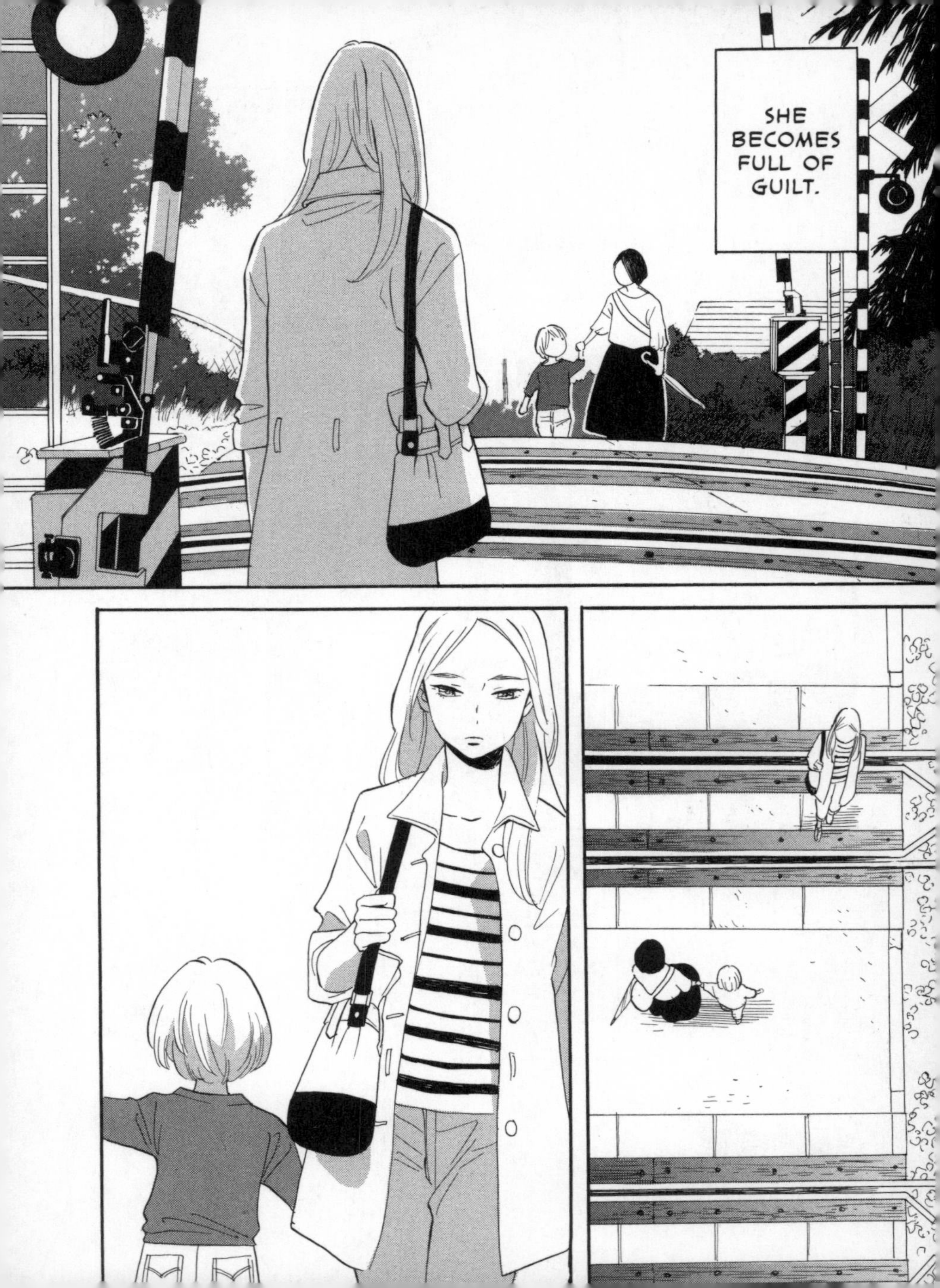
SHE BECOMES FULL OF GUILT.

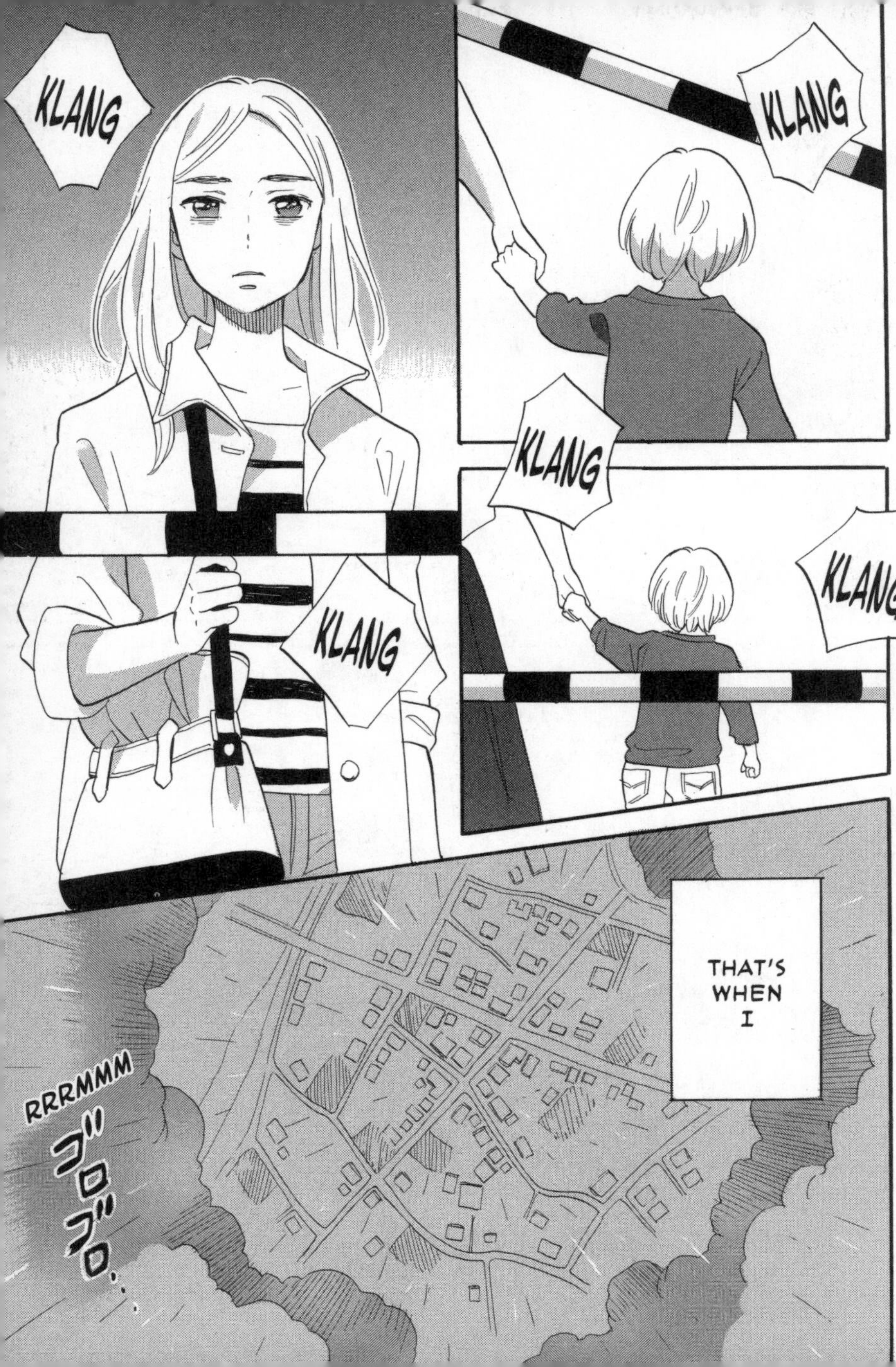
KLANG
KLANG
KLANG
KLANG
KLANG
THAT'S WHEN I
RRRMMM
ゴロゴロ…

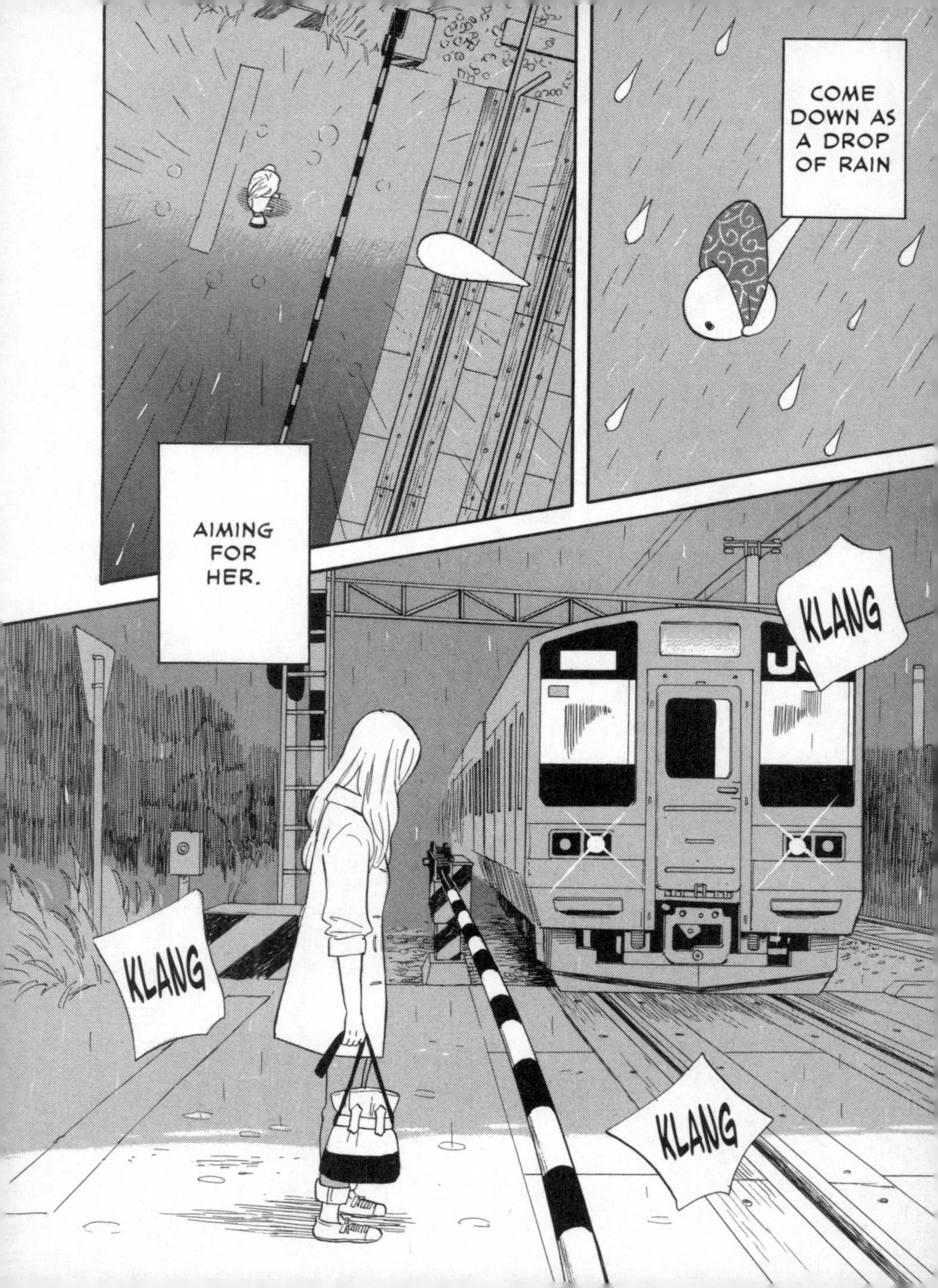
COME DOWN AS A DROP OF RAIN
AIMING FOR HER.
KLANG
KLANG
KLANG

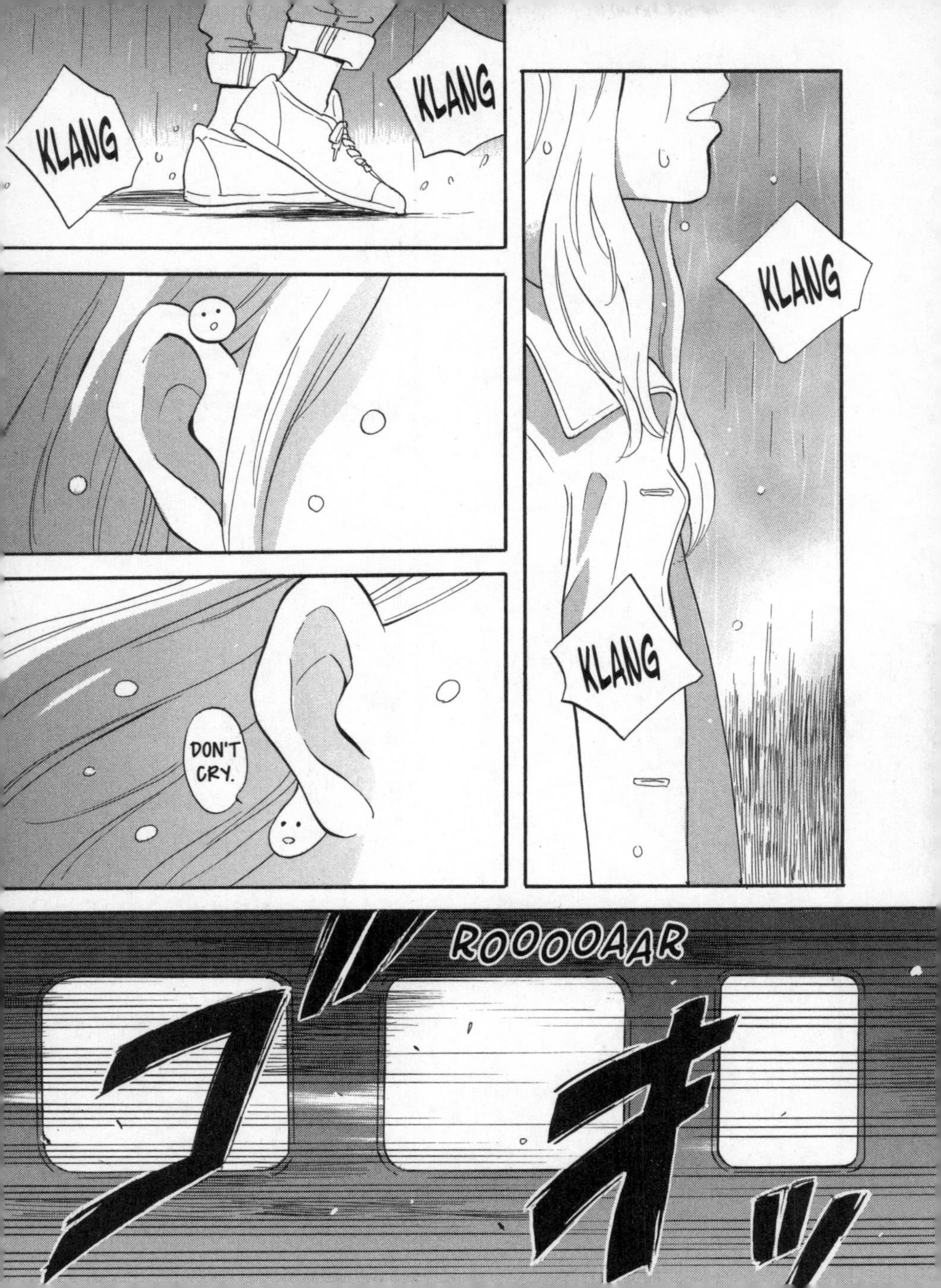
KLANG
KLANG
KLANG
KLANG
DON'T CRY.
ROOOOAAR
ゴオッ

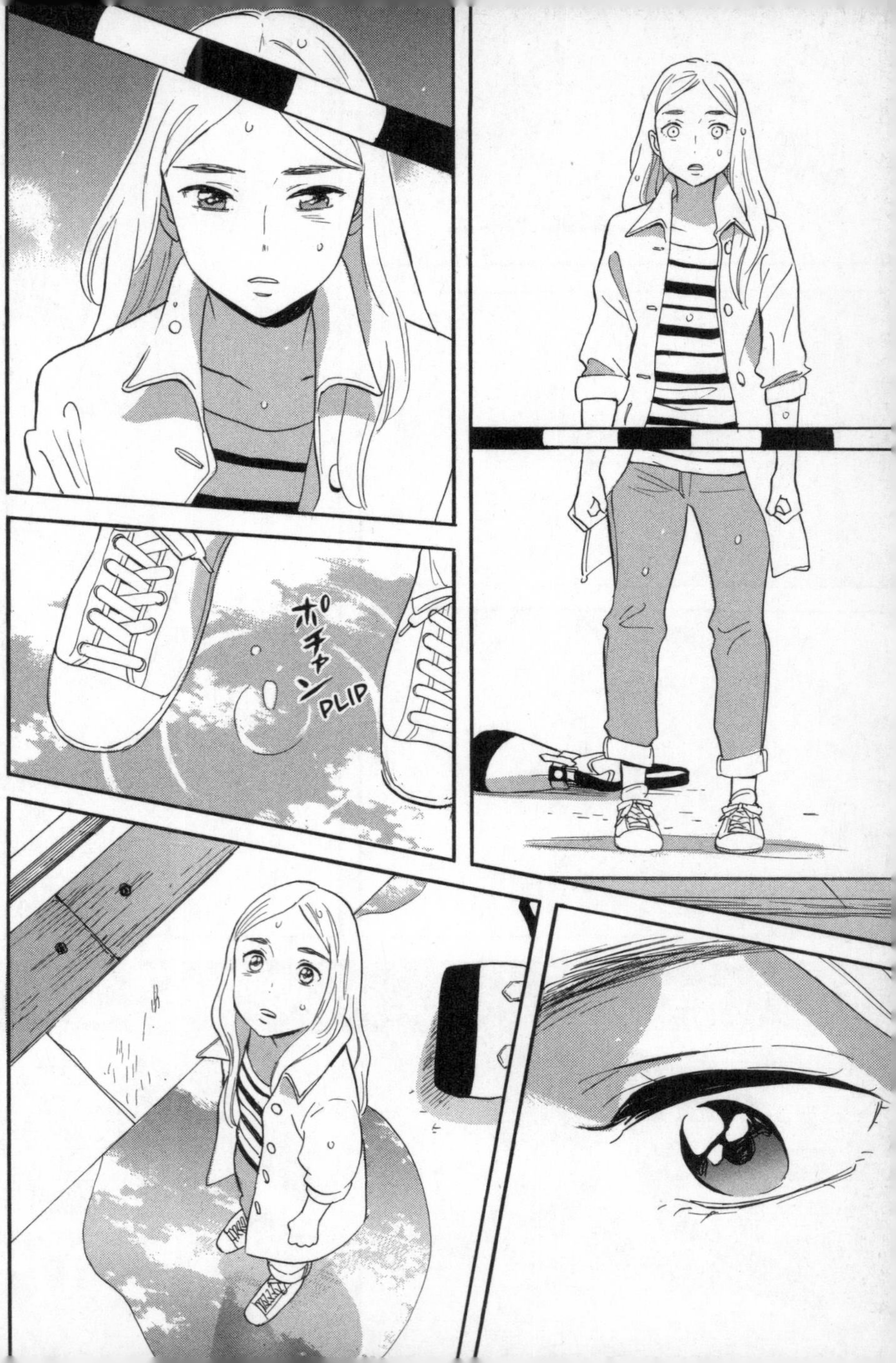
ポチャン
PLIP

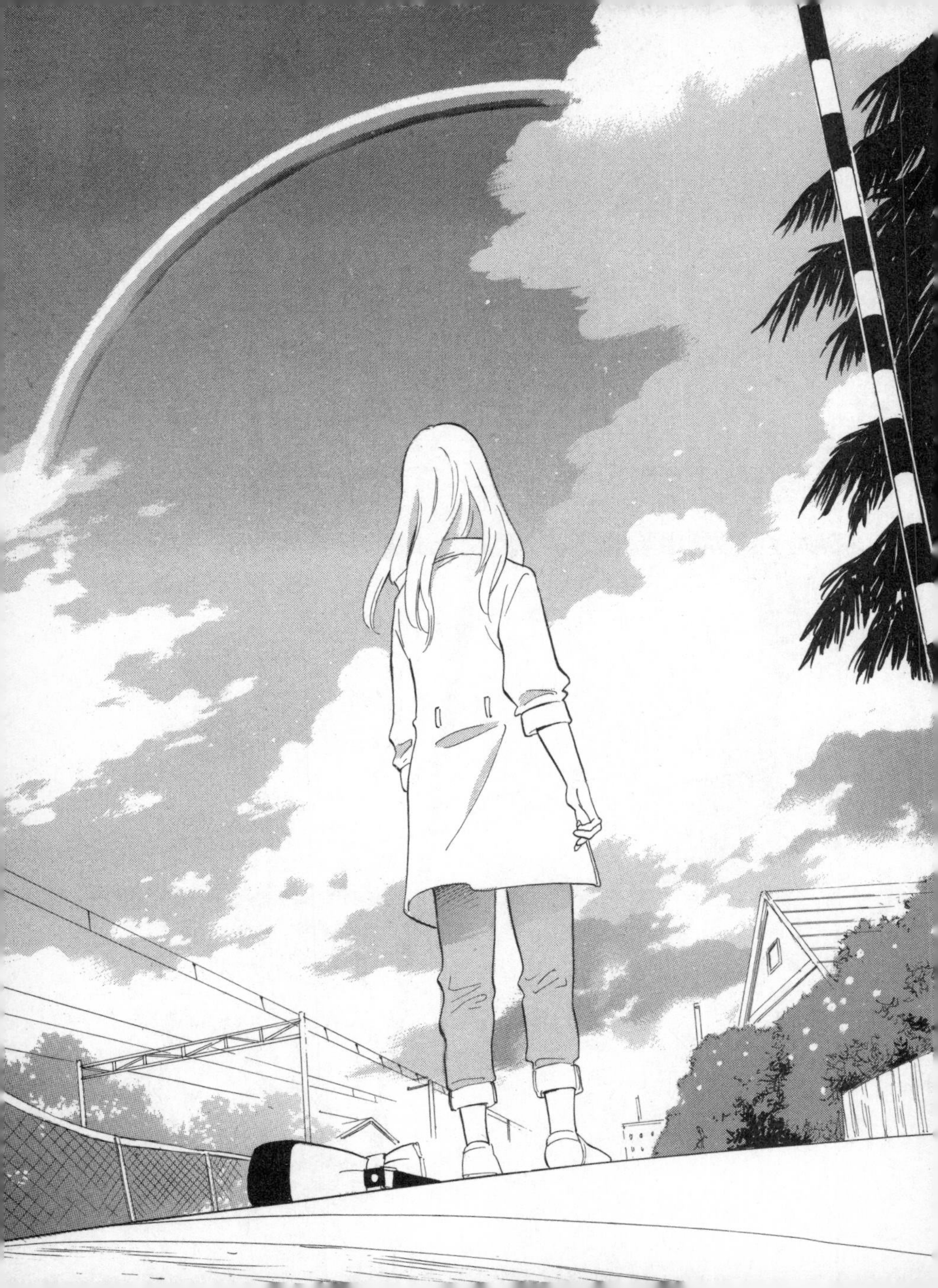

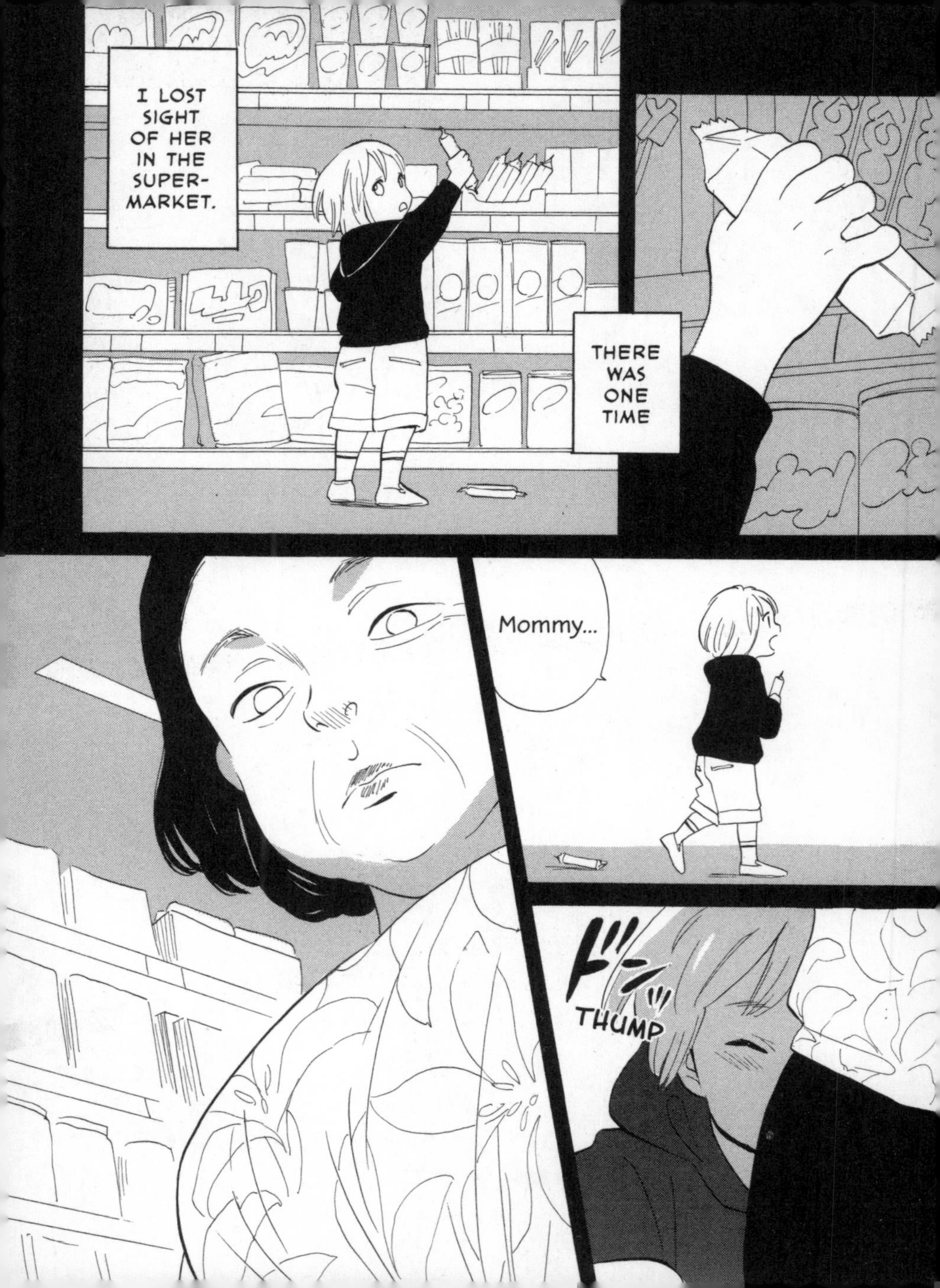
THERE WAS ONE TIME
I LOST SIGHT OF HER IN THE SUPER-MARKET.
Mommy...
THUMP

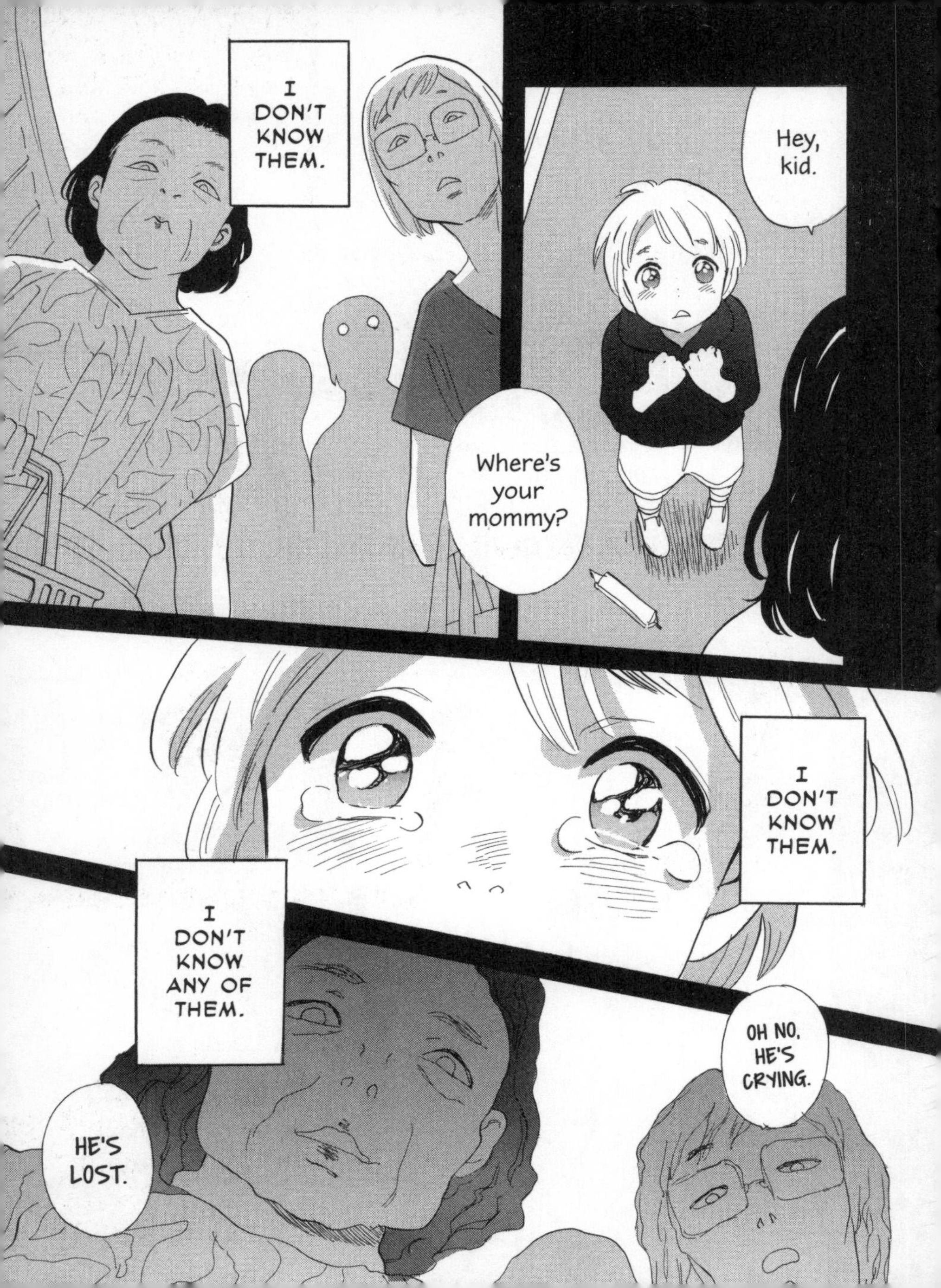

Hey, kid.
Where's your mommy?
I DON'T KNOW THEM.
I DON'T KNOW THEM.
I DON'T KNOW ANY OF THEM.
OH NO, HE'S CRYING.
HE'S LOST.

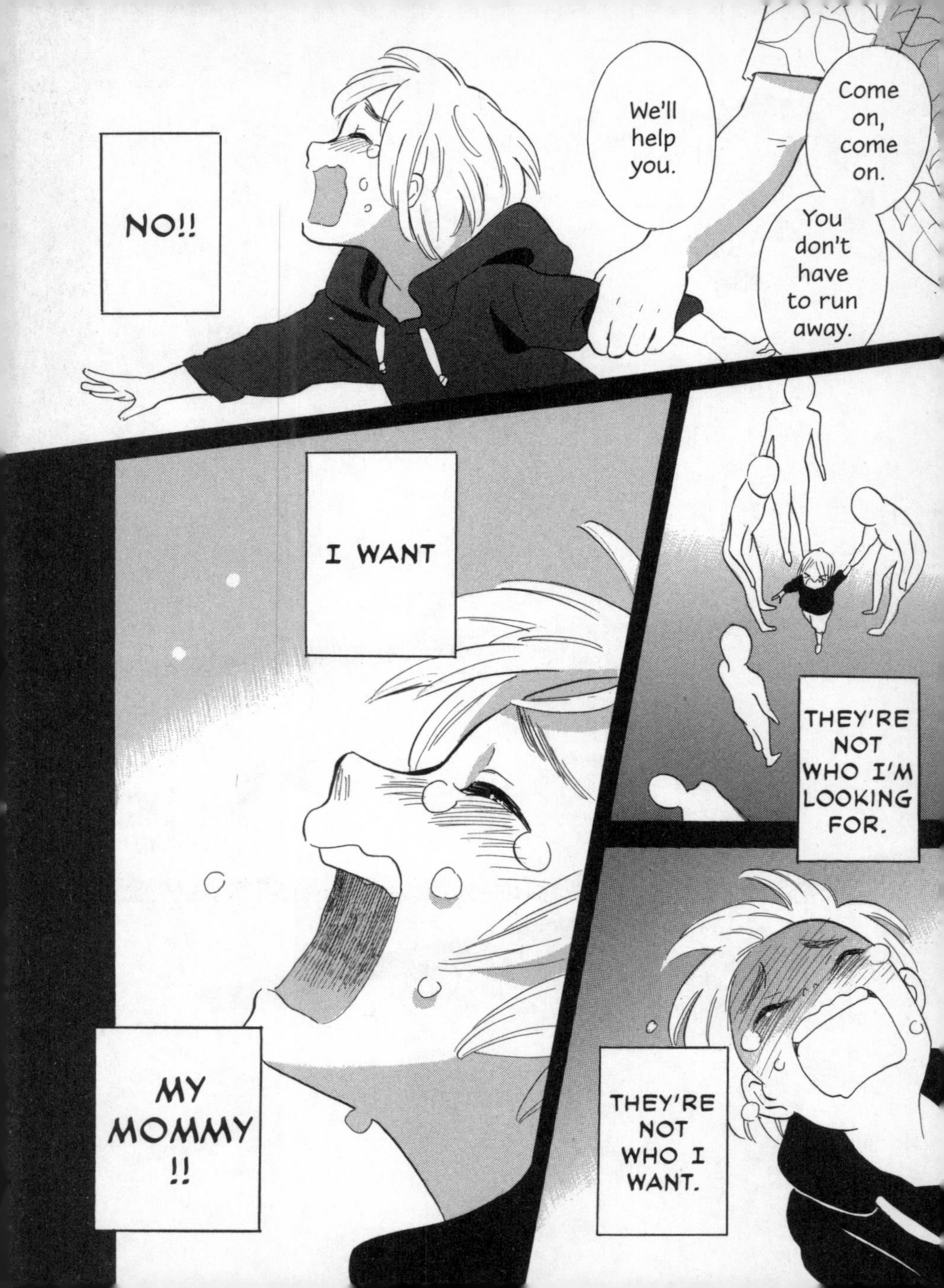
Come on, come on.
You don't have to run away.
We'll help you.
NO!!
THEY'RE NOT WHO I'M LOOKING FOR.
THEY'RE NOT WHO I WANT.
I WANT
MY MOMMY !!

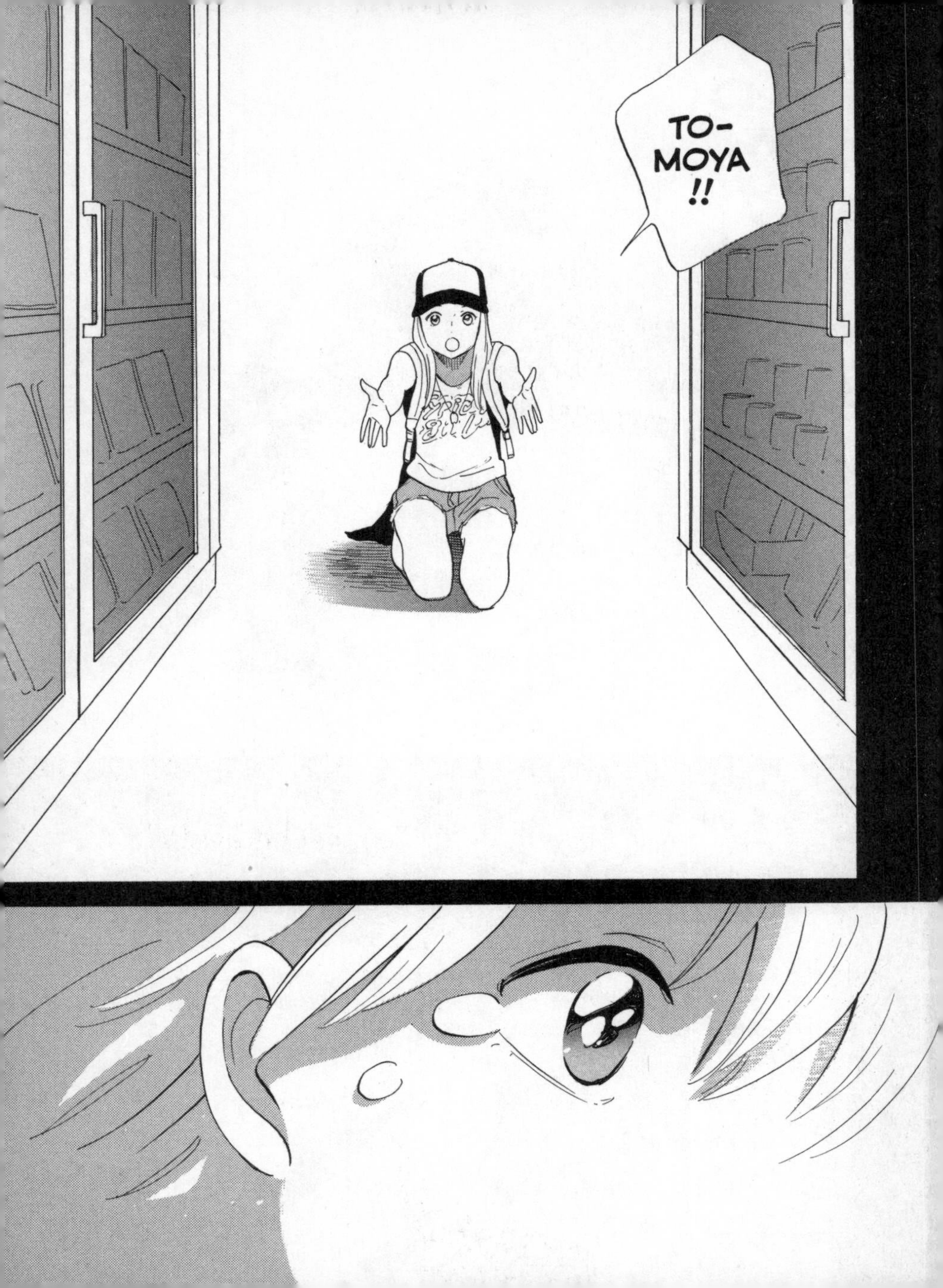
TO-MOYA !!

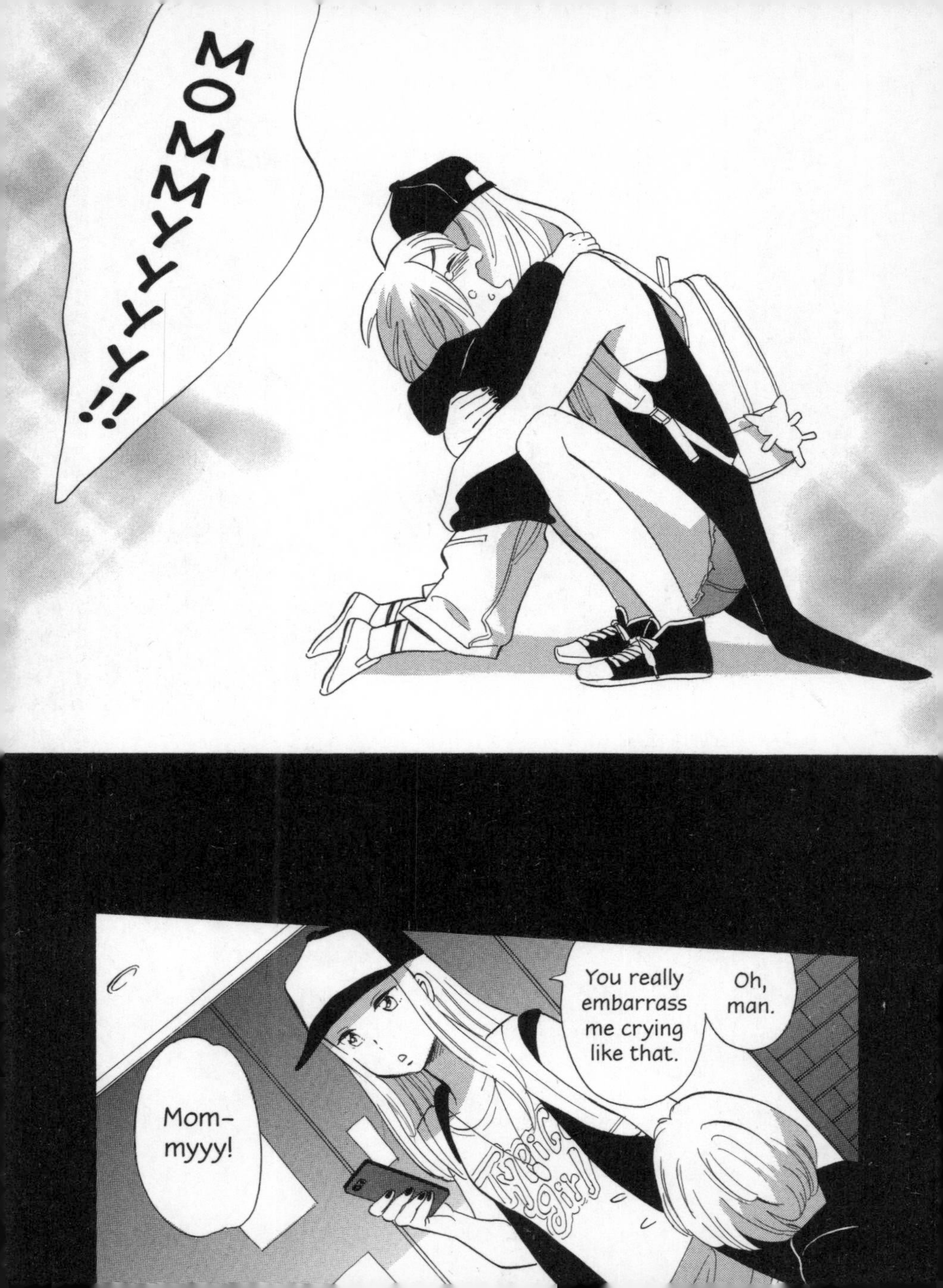
MOMMYYYYY!!
Oh, man.
You really embarrass me crying like that.
Mom-myyy!

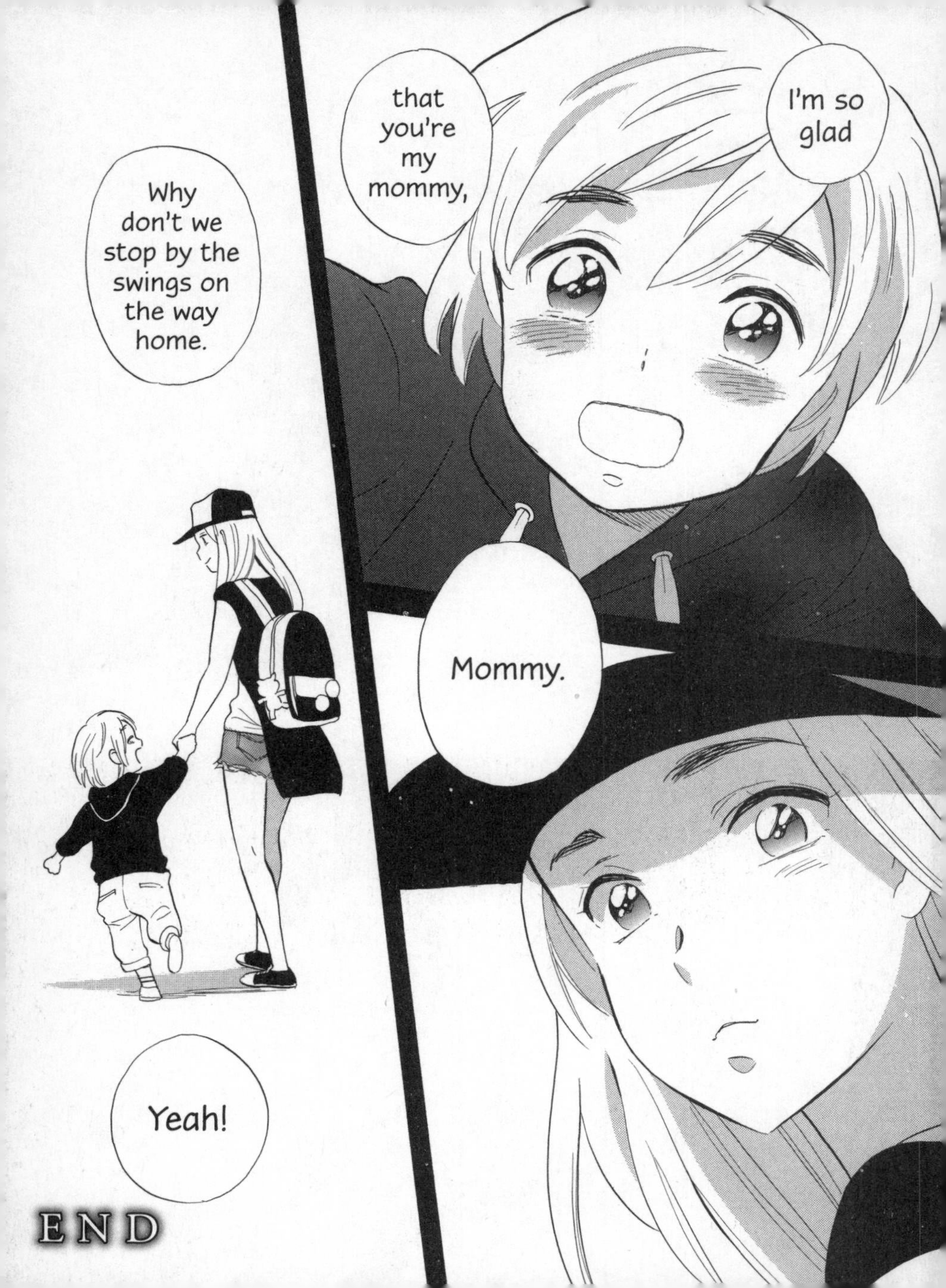
I'm so glad
that you're my mommy,
Mommy.
Why don't we stop by the swings on the way home.
Yeah!
END

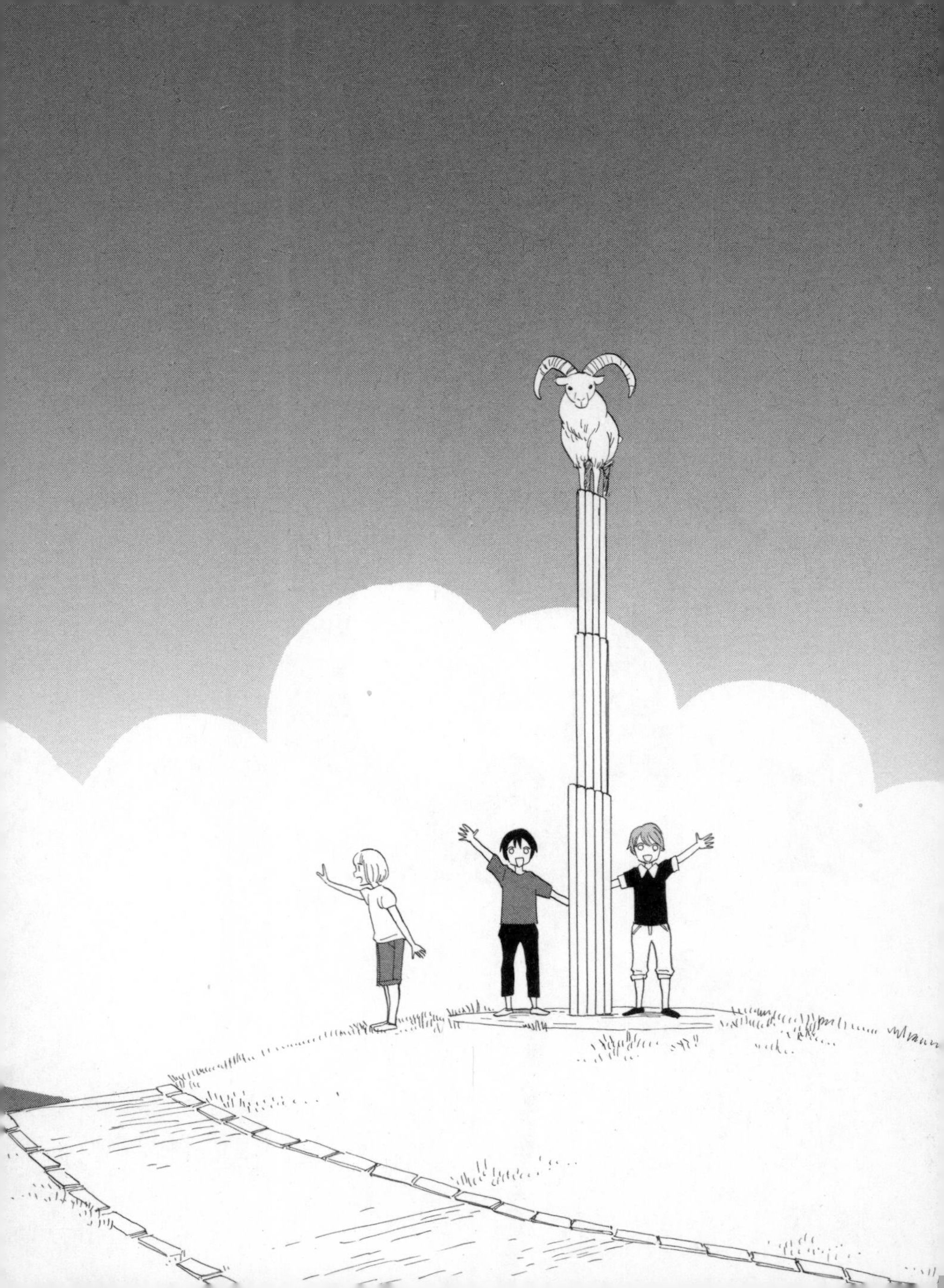

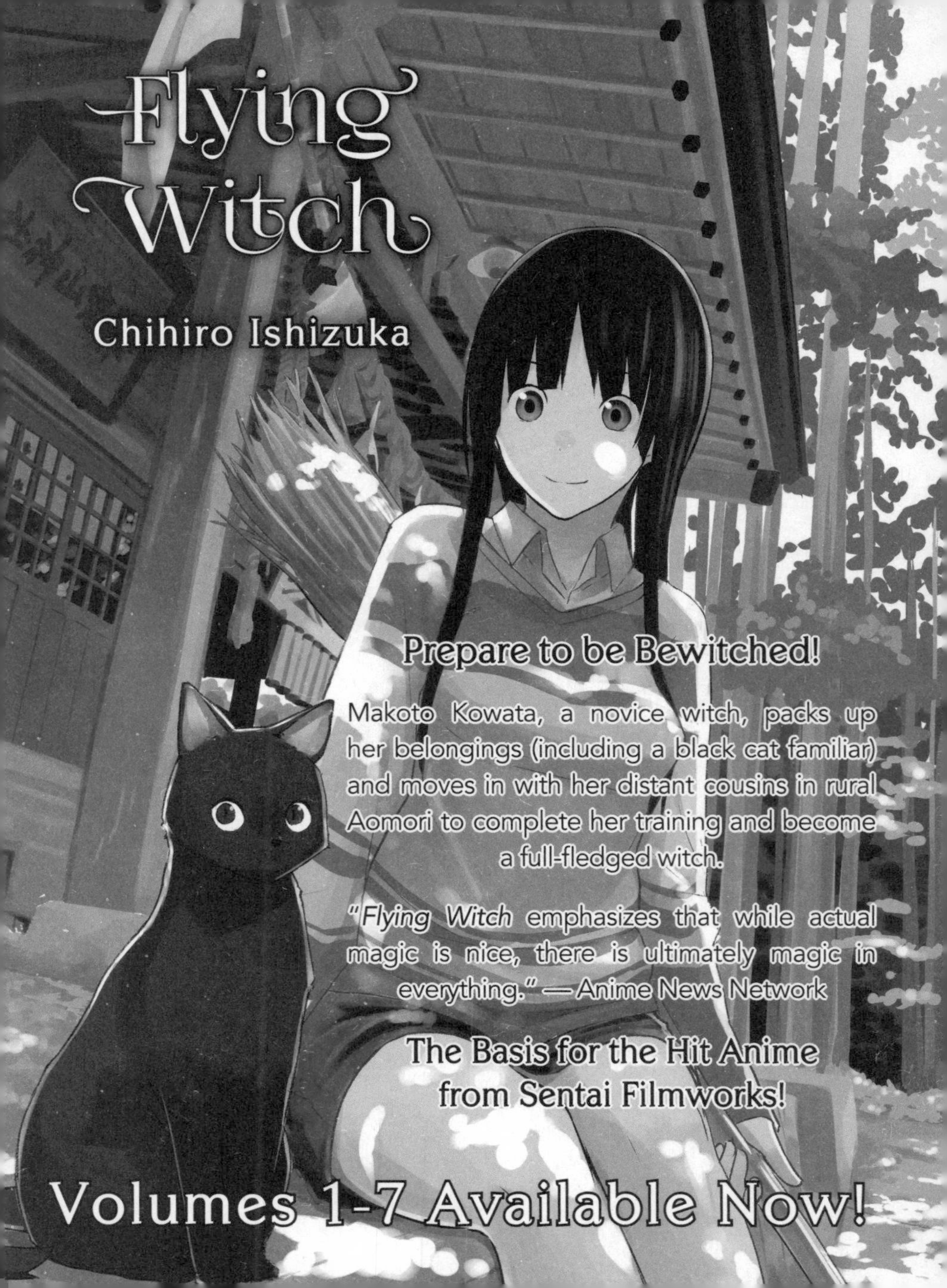
Flying Witch
Chihiro Ishizuka
Prepare to be Bewitched!
Makoto Kowata, a novice witch, packs up her belongings (including a black cat familiar) and moves in with her distant cousins in rural Aomori to complete her training and become a full-fledged witch.
"Flying Witch emphasizes that while actual magic is nice, there is ultimately magic in everything." — Anime News Network
The Basis for the Hit Anime from Sentai Filmworks!
Volumes 1-7 Available Now!